Total-E-Bound Publishing books by Aliyah Burke:

Code of Honour
A Marriage of Convenience
The Lieutenant's Ex-Wife
A Man Like No Other
When Stars Collide

Through the Fire
Seducing Damian

I0691658

In Aeternum

CASANOVA IN TRAINING

ALIYAH BURKE

Casanova in Training
ISBN # 978-1-78184-525-7
©Copyright Aliyah Burke 2012
Cover Art by Posh Gosh ©Copyright July 2012
Interior text design by Claire Siemaszkiewicz
Total-E-Bound Publishing

CASANOVA IN TRAINING

Dedication

To all those who are told you can't and you not only
do but you excel. To my Dad who gave me the idea
for this story. I love you! Thanks for the endless
support you've given me over the years. To my
husband who has always believed in me even when I
didn't. Finally, but never last, to the men and women
who protect this country.
Thank you for your sacrifices.

Chapter One

Rain ran in rivulets from both his black coat and the brim of his cover. Lieutenant Commander Giovanni Cassano barely moved, even with the loud and angry retorts of gunfire. The noise sounded ominous. Three sets of shots fired by the seven impassive men. He flexed one hand into a fist before relaxing and allowing the smooth glove to straighten.

Through the dreariness, the beginning notes of Taps started to play, weaving in and out of the raindrops with haunting precision. His right hand snapped up in a sharp salute as his shoulders automatically squared even more.

With a deep breath, he fixated on the casket and the two stoic men who had the honour and privilege of folding the flag. Their movements precise and perfected. Each of the thirteen folds corresponded to an important meaning and allowed him to see the wet gloves the men wore. White cotton to his black leather.

First fold was representative of life. He swallowed hard and blinked. Two, three and four took place. The fifth fold, a tribute to the country. Tears burned the corners of his eyes. Six, seven, eight and nine. The tenth fold was a tribute to fathers, for they, too, had given both sons and daughters for the protection of the country since they were first born.

Stiffening his spine, Giovanni clenched his jaw as he watched the remaining three folds to complete the thirteen, so the flag looked like a cocked hat. A reminder of the soldiers who served under George Washington, the sailors and marines who served under Captain John Paul Jones, and all those men and women who followed them in the United States Armed Forces, preserving the rights, privileges and freedoms enjoyed today. As the two men finished folding, the final poignant note faded from the air. And the salutes ended.

He stood ramrod straight. Only his gaze moved as he tracked the presenter who paused before the slender auburn-haired woman clad in black. Michelle Walker. She sat there under a canopy beside her father to accept the flag.

None of the military members there seemed affected by the steady downpour.

"On behalf of a grateful nation," the presenter said, offering the folded flag.

Giovanni saw Michelle hesitate. The man with the flag waited, unmoving, until she finally took it. His hand rose into a salute and, when she gave him a nod, he completed it. The rain increased but Giovanni watched Michelle hold the flag to her chest.

Over the pounding of the rain came the unmistakable sound of fighter jets. He lifted his gaze to see the four planes scream overhead, his heart clenched with a mixture of pain and regrets that he wasn't even close to being ready to face. A lone jet peeled off and his heart did that same thing again. It should have been him up in the one that honoured the fallen man. But no... He had yet to be cleared for flight status.

He ground his jaw and ignored the threatening tears. One by one people filed away, the rain not allowing the mourners any respite. Finally it was him and the two family members. His legs wouldn't cooperate and he had to force them to move him closer.

Stopping at the middle of the closed casket, he took a deep breath, and snapped a salute. "Goodbye, my friend," he murmured before lowering his hand and walking off.

Anger ate at his gut. It was never easy to lose a member of the military. However, when it was a fellow pilot and best friend, it became that much harder.

"Giovanni?" a rattled yet distinctly feminine voice reached him. And halted him.

He swallowed before pivoting around to face her. *Damn it!* For a brief second he was seeing him again. Alive and well. Michael Walker. Sidewinder. Best friend.

She moved closer, the folded flag still clasped tightly to her chest. It hurt looking at her. Mike's twin. A softer, feminine version of Michael, but he was still there in her delicate features.

"Michelle." He hated how gravelled his voice sounded.

Green eyes watched him steadily. "You were going to leave without a word?"

He put his gaze on their...her father. Martin Walker showed his age. He seemed so tired and worn out. However, in his eyes, there was anger. The siblings had taken after their mother. Giovanni had always teased Mike about being so pretty. Now his body had been so badly burnt and mangled it had had to be a closed-casket ceremony.

"No," he managed to say as he glanced from father to daughter. "I was going to wait by the car. Allow you final moments."

Martin shook his hand briefly then nudged Michelle. She lifted one gloved hand to wipe the tears from her eyes. "Take this." She held the flag out to him.

His heart seized as he glanced at the flag. *Stars uppermost to remind us of our nation's motto.*

"No. I can't. That is for you."

Her smile was shaky at best. "Mike would want you to have it."

Giovanni glanced to Martin, ready to plead his case, only to pause. The look Martin bore told him the flag wouldn't be going back with them. Martin was in a rage from having just buried his only son. He focused on Michelle and saw the opposite. She loathed to give it up and was only doing so for her father.

Almost as if he hovered outside his body, he saw himself reaching for the flag. Michelle relinquished it to him but didn't step back. Instead, she lifted his hand, pressed the flag against his chest, and hugged him.

"Keep him safe," she whispered in his ear.

More of those damn tears threatened. "When you're ready to take it…" He trailed off.

"Thank you, Giovanni."

"Michelle!" Martin barked.

She flinched at the tone but squeezed him one more time. A quick peck on the lips and she was gone. They were gone. Moreover, he stood in the raining cemetery, holding the flag given for the loss of his best friend's life. The thunder rolled, ominous, and the rain picked up even more.

He needed a drink. Badly. And, after he returned to his hotel room and changed from his uniform, he set off to do just that.

* * * *

The bar was crowded and noisy. Just what he wanted — a place to become invisible. He claimed a corner booth and sat there, bottle of Jack on the table beside him. He poured a drink for his fallen friend and drank it.

"Here's to you, Sidewinder."

Then he did his best to forget the pain inside him. He knew what Mike would have said. "Find a woman and enjoy life. Don't cry for me."

Easier to think than to do. With dispassionate eyes, he watched the activity around him. Many women sauntered up to him, only to leave again when he ignored them.

He poured another drink, craving the blur it made of his memory. He paused with his glass halfway to his lips. An unfamiliar tingle skated along the back of his neck. Glancing around the establishment, he found himself focusing on a woman he didn't recognise or recall entering. She sat with another but he couldn't look away from her.

She had skin that reminded him of hot chocolate, with some whipped cream blended in. Lickable. Black hair drawn up and away from her face in a ponytail, it fell down to almost her shoulder blades. A low, purely animalistic reaction hit him square in the gut. His cock sprang to attention and he was halfway out of the booth before he realised it.

He sat back down, continuing to stare unabashedly at her. He could see she wore an ice blue crossover top. All he longed to do was trail the straps with his tongue and see where they would lead. Discover her taste, her smell.

Her head fell back and her laughter—he assumed it was laughter by the smile on her and the other woman's faces—seemed to add to the glow about her. He scowled when two rather large men blocked his view.

Draining his drink, he pushed to his feet then headed over there. It made absolutely no sense, especially for not having even been introduced to her, how possessive he felt towards this mystery woman. He came up around them and immediately his gaze honed in on her.

Yes, definitely lickable. And biteable.

She had full lips he wanted to kiss, a small, cute nose, and large eyes that were framed by thick, curved lashes. A punch to his solar plexus had him sucking for air when she pinned her gaze on him. Those eyes were killers, multi-hued like a tortoiseshell, and he felt himself willingly falling in.

He glanced at the other two men, moved his gaze on to the second woman before settling once more on his woman. "Dance with me." It wasn't a question or a request, but that was his way.

She stared at him, her unique eyes assessing, and he fought the urge to shift when he believed she'd seen past the outer shell. A slight grin lifted the corners of her lush mouth.

"Sure." Her voice fell smooth, thick, and rich like honey.

She slid from the booth and he held his ground so she would have to brush against him. A plan that didn't work as he'd intended. His cock was ready to punch free at the tantalising sweep of her full breasts across his chest.

"Let's go," she said with a smile that made him think about thrusting his shaft in and out of her mouth.

Gesturing for her to lead the way, he followed the seductive sway of her hips, which were draped in a tight, white leather skirt. He groaned and dragged his gaze down and over her long, lean legs and her fuck-me heels the same colour as her shirt.

Fuck!

He almost lost it right then and there. So he lengthened his stride to catch up to her. With those sexy heels, she would fit just right against him. He guessed her height without heels to be about five-seven.

She tossed her head and rotated back to him. Her gaze took another trip along his body and he bit back his responding groan. The music changed to a slow, sultry ballad. Her eyes showed her hesitation and he reached out to draw her close before she left him standing there.

A flirtatious smile lifted her lips as she willingly came closer to him. Her bare arms slipped around his neck and he took a shuddering breath when she pressed tight against him. Ignoring the fire in his blood, he placed his hands at her waist, fingers grazing the small of her back.

"What's with guys and issuing demands? You could have asked me to dance, you know."

He slid his hands around to cup her ass, bringing her flush to his blatant erection. "You could have said no."

"I get the feeling that isn't a word you hear very often."

It was true. His call sign wasn't Casanova without good reason. "Not too much."

Her fingers stroked along the back of his neck. He felt on fire, both inside and out. Each step took them closer to the edge of the dance floor. By the time the song ended, the two of them were in a darker hallway.

He lowered his head, giving her half a second to stop him. She didn't. Her mouth met his. She played the aggressor, sliding her tongue in and around his. Lust blazed to life in him and he ground into her, making his desire very clear. She moaned, a sexy sound—it came from the back of her throat and moved through him like electricity.

His grip on her grew possessive as he took control of the kiss. She tasted like mint. Not peppermint or spearmint. Raw mint. Pure mint. It was addictive as hell and he couldn't get enough. The feel of her against him, the taste of her—together they lessened the pain that had consumed him since the accident.

He tore his mouth from hers and nibbled his way down her neck. Her gasp of pleasure coinciding with how she tilted her head to give him better access spurred him on. It didn't matter that they were in a busy bar hallway. All that mattered was her. And sinking his hard length fully within her molten heat.

His hands began moving beneath her short skirt, seeking his prize. She pushed on him and he drew back to glance down at her. Flushed. Passionate. Delectable.

"Hold on there, handsome. I'm not into exhibitionism."

He gazed to his right and saw two men loitering there. Voyeuristic pleasure on their faces. "Go!" he said in a growl so low the word was hard to decipher.

The meaning not. They left after only a few more leers at the woman in his arms. Again alone, he placed his gaze back on her. He held her stare before slanting his mouth back over hers.

"We need to stop," she said, a bit breathlessly, when he broke the kiss.

"Why?"

She took some deep breaths. "I came for a dance with you. Not to get fucked against a wall." She gave him a small grin. "Besides, I'm the DD and I have to get them home."

Fury licked at his veins. "Don't go with them. Those guys aren't right for you." What'd she need two of them for? He was more than enough for her.

She tipped her head back and laughed. A vibrant sound that made his knees shake.

"That's cute, really. You think you know what's best for me based on one dance and having your tongue down my throat." It wasn't a question. "Those two are like brothers to me, not that it's any of your biz. Now I have to go. Early flight."

She gently removed his touch from her then stepped around him. Unwilling to let her go, he captured her wrist and tugged. "Come with me."

"You're good," she said with a small sigh. "Too good. That's another thing I don't do. You've got to me enough to get this far."

She captured her lower lip in her teeth before moving nearer. With her free hand, she cupped the back of his head and pulled him close. Her eyes darkened and she kissed him. Her nails scored the back of his head as her tongue invaded. He went from controlled to locked and loaded in a flash.

The kiss ended and she pulled back. "Goodbye."

Then she walked away. Her friends met her and he moved towards them to hear her voice. Her laughter. She expertly herded her group to the door where she paused and glanced back at him. Her eyes flared with heat and it took every last ounce of his control to remain where he was. In a flash of blue and white, she was gone and his world got considerably darker.

"I'm available."

At the statement, he looked to see a woman dressed in too-tight clothing. "Of that I have no doubt."

He strode off, ignoring her gasp of outrage. Barely slowing, he grabbed his jacket and made his way to the door. The night hadn't gone exactly according to plan. With a snarl of frustration, he waved for a taxi. Slumping in the back seat, he gave the hotel before closing his eyes and using his memory to recreate the vixen from tonight.

He half stumbled from the taxi to his room, only to fall face first across his king-sized bed. Yep. He was close to wasted. Real close. Granted, touching his mystery woman had made the drinks' effects slip away. All his focus had been on her, her minty flavour and that skin, that delectable, tempting, hot-chocolate skin.

All he'd wanted to do was bite, lick, and suck. Christ, even now—just thinking of her—his cock stiffened in his pants. He wanted her bad. Yes, he'd loved women before, but this was different. This woman got to him on a molecular level.

"Fuck it!" he uttered, flopping on to his back. Eyes closed he tried to forget he'd just buried his best friend.

He slept through all of the next day and was back at the bar the following night. Sat in the same booth and watched the door. He only nursed his drink this time. Hours passed, and he was ready to get up and leave when someone slid in across from him. He snapped his head over to growl, only to find himself staring into sparkling tortoiseshell eyes.

It took him a few moments to remember to breathe. She put his visual recollection of her to shame. Unlike last night, her hair fell loose around her face. Her large eyes peered at him unblinkingly. *How did she get here without me knowing?*

She reached out and took his drink from him, moving it to the side. He reacted swiftly, capturing her hand in his. Hers was almost delicate, but he could feel both strength and calluses. He threaded their fingers, pleased to be touching her again, and returned his gaze to her face.

"Thought you had an early flight." He stroked the inside of her wrist with his thumb.

"I missed it."

"Babysitting tonight?"

"Nope."

He swallowed. "Come with me."

Her response was to get to her feet and tug him up. He went willingly and drew her in close. Damn but he wanted to kiss her. Her confusion when he didn't was obvious.

"I kiss you now, sweets, and we will be fucking right here on this table." He watched heat flare in her eyes, making them almost molten gold. "Let's go."

He slid his arm around her waist and headed for the door. He moved the tips of his fingers in small circles on her hip. Outside he waved for a cab then looked at her.

She wore another amazing outfit. A tight ribbed coral tank top and another short leather skirt, black this time. More fuck-me heels, the colour of which matched her shirt.

"Why'd you come back?" he asked as the cab took them to his hotel.

"I don't know. I tried to get on the plane but I couldn't."

He leaned close and nuzzled the side of her neck. She smelt as delicious as she had yesterday. He licked along her pulse and his cock throbbed at her answering moan.

"You okay with this?" He had to be sure.

She moved her head to the side, giving him better access. "Yes," she said on a breathy sigh.

He shifted and placed his hand on her thigh, stroking just above her knee on the inside. He kissed her. Sucked on her tongue and searched for all the corners he could find. She leaned into him, one hand settling on his chest. Her response was explosive and he wanted to be away from public eyes.

The cab stopped and he barely looked at the man before tossing him some bills to cover the fare. Her hand in his, he led the way to his room. He was on her the second the door closed behind them.

Control gone, he dominated her mouth as he gripped her ass and pulled her flush to his rampant erection, ensuring she felt it. Her fingers threaded in his hair, pulling lightly, and he growled, a warning, or a promise, he wasn't sure.

"Bed," he rasped, tearing his mouth from hers. God, he was burning up. From the inside out.

"No. Here. Now."

He fished a condom out of his pocket, freed himself, then sheathed his stiff cock. Pushing up her skirt, he found a fire-engine-red lace thong. "Shit, you're killing me here."

He yanked on it, relishing how it snapped beneath his tug. There was no foreplay and no gentle words of love. He gripped the base of his cock and moved it along her wet slit then slammed home hard. Her scream of pleasure raced up his spine.

Fuck me! He began to move within her hot, tight pussy as the velvet walls held him.

Fuck me!

Jaydee Amos moaned again and again, as the man pinning her against the wall drilled his cock into her over and over. He stretched her, filled her, and blew her mind. It was rough, and not at all sweet or tender. It was perfect.

His mouth latched on to her neck as he thrust into her. She scraped her nails along the back of his neck and shoulder. Lifting a leg, she hooked it around his waist. He grunted, palmed a breast, and moved faster. She came hard when he tweaked her nipple and grazed his teeth along her neck. He erupted soon after that, his powerful body shuddering before seeming to sink into her.

He drew back and she smiled at him, a languid smile. A well-pleasured smile. His tanned skin was covered in sweat. He had hazel eyes that burned with hunger. One hand brushed some of her sweaty hair back.

"Bed now," he demanded, whipping off his shirt.

Her mouth went dry at the sight of his chiselled torso. He was all ridges and rippling muscles. She reached out to touch him, felt the sweat and dragged her fingers over one pectoral. Inside her, his cock hardened.

When he withdrew, she bit back a whimper of disappointment. One that changed to a moan of approval as he shucked the rest of his clothes. Not an ounce of fat on him. His cock, again hard, stood out proudly from a nest of black hair. It was bare and the evidence of his cum was smeared along the head. He'd disposed of the condom. She stretched out to touch him, only to stop at his gravelled command.

"Undress."

She removed her shirt and followed with her bra. His eyes darkened and she moved to her skirt. His cock bobbed and it sidetracked her for a moment.

"Leave the shoes," he said, dragging a finger around one puckered nipple.

So she did.

He laid her back on the bed and settled himself between her legs. She stared at him, lost in the intensity of his eyes. His fingers skimmed over her pussy and she widened her legs in silent invitation. He ripped open another condom and covered himself. She didn't even recall him grabbing more foil packets. Then he slid the broad head of his shaft into her and nothing else mattered. Over and over again, he escorted her to the pinnacle of pleasure only to back off and start over. The first time had taken the edge off his need and now he seemed content to go slow. She burned all over as he flexed in her with nice, easy strokes.

"Harder." She worked her internal muscles.

He shuddered. "Slow and gentle."

Her protest was stopped when he drew a nipple into the warmth of his mouth.

"Ahh!" she cried, arching into him. "Oh…yes…sweet…" She continued to babble as he thrust in tandem with the sucks on her breast. So many sensations bombarded her.

His rumble vibrated against her nipple as he powered deep and she exploded around him. She gripped him as he released the control and pistoned his hips into her. Over and over. Unrelenting. Like a machine. Willingly, she met each thrust, hungry for more, her heels grinding into his ass. He came with a roar and collapsed on her. The room smelt of sex and sweat.

Exhausted, she barely moved when he withdrew and left the bed. She cracked her eyes open when his touch was on her feet. *How sweet, he's removing my shoes.*

Boneless, Jaydee sank against him after he turned off the light, climbed back into bed, and covered them with the blankets. Thoughts of leaving were the furthest thing from her mind as he draped a corded, muscular arm over her waist and tucked her in close. She fell asleep with his deep breathing in her ear and his scent in her nose. There was also the warmth and security of his touch.

* * * *

She woke and lay still as her mind worked out where she was. This wasn't her bed. Strong arms curled around her body, keeping her near…and warm. A head nestled into her breasts, stubble abrading her skin with each breath she took. She sought the clock and sighed. *Time to get going.*

21

How to untangle herself? She shifted to the side only to freeze when warm lips settled over one nipple, drawing tight. Desire unfurled within her and she moaned, arching, before she realised it.

A moan that turned to a cry of pleasure as he sank two fingers into her pussy. Her last coherent thought was, *I can leave later.* He brought her to another explosive orgasm, draining what little energy she actually had left. So, again, sated and fatigued, she drifted back off to sleep.

Twice more she woke and attempted to sneak away. Twice more he fucked her back into exhaustion. The third time she opened her eyes and just lay there. She was so sore. In a good way, but so sore.

"Close your eyes," a deep voice said.

Turning her head, she found him staring down at her. Him. *I don't even know his name.* His hazel eyes still smouldered and, despite everything, she felt herself respond.

"I need to get up."

"I am up," he said with a languid wink. One large hand skimmed over her belly before settling with familiarity on her pussy. He used a lone finger to stroke her and she bit back her purr of contentment as she widened her legs.

"Good girl." In and out he moved the single digit. "I think I could get used to this in the morning," he muttered in her ear as he slid inside her willing body with one smooth thrust.

Me too.

Accepting she'd not be leaving the bed anytime soon, she gave herself over to her stranger's masterful touch. They spent all day in bed. One time when she woke, he'd brought some food to the room. After which they went back to bed. She didn't understand, she was supposed to get him out of her blood yet the longer she was there it felt like he was deeper in it.

She urged her aching body out of bed and dressed while he was in the shower. Sure, it was the coward's way out but she knew all it would take was one touch from him and leaving would fall by the wayside. One ear tuned to the shower, she shoved her feet into her shoes and made a call.

With one last, longing look to the closed bathroom door, she bit her lower lip and slipped from the hotel room, totally not understanding why leaving this man—whose name she still didn't know—was so difficult. Forcing herself to leave, she closed the door behind her. She took a deep breath and strode from the hotel, clad in her club wear with her head held high. Not much later, a black Mitsubishi Spyder roared up to the entrance and she climbed in.

"Almost a day," the woman behind the wheel said.

"Stuff it, Lexy." There was no malice in her tone.

"Same guy as the previous night?"

She hung her head. "I couldn't help it. There is...was...something about him."

Lexy laughed. "I'm sure. I saw the two of you in the hall at the bar." A sideways glance. "Are you hungry? Bet y'all didn't come up for air much."

She ground her teeth at Lexy's over-syrupy Southern drawl. "Bitch."

Another laugh as Lexy tore around a truck going too slow in her estimation. "You know it. Besides, I would assume you'd want to go change and hide that big-ass hickey on your neck. I bet you have them other places, too. Don't you? Thighs? Ass?"

"Drive, you foul-mouthed bitch."

Jaydee leaned her head against the window and closed her eyes. Even now, she could feel the caress of his callused hands on her skin. Moisture began to flow and she shifted on the seat.

Lexy whipped into her drive and pulled into the garage. "Come on, you go shower and change while I make you some food."

It was already dark, had been when she left the hotel, and Jaydee's stomach growled. "Thanks, Lexy." She trudged, sore and tired, into the house then to the guest room. After showering and dressing in something a bit more conservative — a bit more her — Jaydee made more flight plans. She had to get to her destination — staying longer had cut into her time of learning the area.

After a filling meal, Lexy drove her to the airport and dropped her off. They shared a hug.

"I want to know about this guy."

"I told you everything over dinner, Lexy." She grabbed her bags and headed for the door. "I'll call you when I land. Thanks for everything."

"Name!" Lexy yelled. "What's his name?"

Glancing back, she shrugged and placed her bags down. "I don't know, we never exchanged them."

Lexy's grey eyes grew wide as an ear-to-ear grin split her face. With a fist pump, she gave a wolf whistle. "I always knew you had it in you. Love you!"

Jaydee rolled her eyes and ignored the stares. With a wave over her shoulder, she grabbed her luggage again and continued. Once on board the plane, she settled in her seat and sobered. There was a lot of work to be done at her new duty station. Best to be met with a clear head. She covered up with a blanket and closed her eyes, settling in for the flight. Jaydee fell asleep even before they reached cruising altitude.

* * * *

Two weeks later, Jaydee's boots made very little noise as she headed to the briefing room. Her belly was full of knots, although she ensured none of her distress or unease displayed on her face. It was always difficult coming in to a new squadron. Even a test pilot one. And even more so when she was replacing a fallen pilot and friend.

Voices, loud and male, drifted out into the hall and to her ears.

"Who's taking his place?" A slight pause. "I mean who's filling his spot? Sorry, Casanova, I know no one can take Sidewinder's place."

Casanova? Well, guess it isn't hard to figure out what he's done to get that nickname.

The response was too low for her to make out. Then another man spoke. "Lieutenant Commander Jaydee Amos, call sign Dusti."

She paused right before entering. They were talking about her and she bet anything they were assuming her first name was initials. It normally happened. The next speaker's voice made her pause it was filled with so much anger. "Jaydee, never heard of him."

She was right—they assumed she was a male.

"Comes highly praised. Apparently some sort of hotshot pilot."

"We'll see." The angry one spoke again.

Jaydee forced her legs to carry her into the room. Silence descended as numerous gazes fell upon her. A low whistle filled the air and several men eyed her up and down as if she was their next meal.

"You seen the new chick, Casanova?" a blond asked.

"Who are you?" a different blond questioned.

She opened her mouth to answer only to see another man step into her line of sight. Her body reacted violently and expediently. Staring back at her was tall, dark and handsome from her wild and impetuous twenty-four-hour dalliance.

Male laughter erupted. "Looks like she's already smitten with Casanova."

He's Casanova? Hell, he's a pilot? And why is he here? She rallied and drew on the ice that flowed through her veins. Unbidden, her gaze drifted back to Casanova. His beautiful hazel eyes had narrowed suspiciously as he stared at her. She'd been doubted because of her gender before, it wasn't anything new.

"Who are you?" The question was repeated.

She answered simply, "I'm Lieutenant Commander Amos."

You could have heard a pin drop. Casanova's features hardened.

"Hell no!" he snapped, fire blazing from his eyes. "You're the pilot? Jaydee?"

She couldn't believe this was the same man who'd loved her so thoroughly and completely that night two weeks ago. A gaze that had smouldered and stared at her with relentless hunger were now furious.

"That's me. Many people assume I'm a man from my name." She shrugged. "I'm not."

"You're a girl."

Derision dripped from his words. He prowled towards her, looking all kinds of hot in his flight suit. Around them, the room fell silent. She held his stare, her expression blank. He stalked around her, teasing her senses. Again, face to face, he scowled at her.

"Have you even flown a B-2?"

All remaining gentle feelings towards him about their shared night vanished in a puff of smoke. "Obviously, or they wouldn't have sent me. Don't try to measure your dick to mine, Commander. You're sure to come up short."

Laughter erupted around them yet she ignored everything but the man going toe to toe with her. He crossed his arms, his glower deepening. It took a bit of time for her to ignore the power she knew rippled beneath the flight suit.

"Can it, Cassano!" a new voice intruded. "Leave her alone. Listen up, everyone. We've been a man down with the loss of Walker, and Amos here is filling in. Until we get a permanent pilot assigned."

"Better not be too long," Casanova muttered beside her.

"Listen up, Cassano," the CO demanded. "Nothing fancy today. We'll brief in the air. Make sure you introduce yourself to Amos." He slammed his book shut and left. Leaving her to fend for herself.

A blond man—the one who'd previously called her 'chick'—approached her, his blue eyes sharp and assessing. "I'm Keel. You're my pilot."

She nodded, understanding that, if they were called up, he'd be the mission commander. "Dusti." Keel didn't offer his hand, just sized her up. There were two other women there in the room, but they didn't look any happier to see her then the men did.

"Meet you at the bird."

She nodded and watched the others leave. Falling in behind a cocky lieutenant, she reached the door a second before it slammed in her face. Tall, dark and handsome leaned against her exit from the room. Arms crossed. The pure sexuality he oozed made her waver a second. The anger in his eyes cooled her ardour.

"You're in my way, Commander," she said without intonation.

"You ran from me while I was in the shower."

She blinked. His words shocked her, for she hadn't thought he would have mentioned it. "You're still in my way."

"Women shouldn't be flying in combat."

"This is a training facility and you need to move."

"We need to talk," he rumbled.

"No, we do not. Now get out of my way."

With a mocking smile and an exaggerated bow, he opened the door for her, only to fall in behind her. All eyes were on them as they strolled from the building, now side by side. They peeled off and she surreptitiously stole a final glance as he sauntered to his plane. He was a man who was the epitome of a fighter pilot. An unmistakable swagger and an ego the size of the sun.

Striding up to her jet, she stared at the impressive B-2. The bombers were lethal, dangerous and, to her, absolutely beautiful. She loved flying them. The excitement built, spreading throughout her as she talked to the mechanic for her new bird. His name was Tory Sedin, a Petty Officer First Class.

Chapter Two

Giovanni Cassano fought down his anger. A woman was joining them. And not just *any* woman—this one happened to be the one he'd spent nearly twenty-four hours in bed with, trying to sate his hunger for her. It hadn't worked. He wanted her even more after having seen her again. Memories were no longer going to be good enough.

It would have been damn near perfect seeing her again, if not for two things. One, her being in his command, and two, her being a pilot. Yes, he was a bit of a chauvinist. Women could fly, but combat? Not with him.

She needs to stay where it's safe.

She now had a name. Jaydee 'Dusti' Amos, a Lieutenant Commander in the United States Navy. He'd heard her first name and assumed she was a man.

"What do you think of the sweet filly, Casanova?" Jason 'Lizard' Armstrong asked him with a friendly smack on the shoulder.

Despite not wanting to, he glanced over to where she stood by her plane. Her flight suit only turned him on even more, given that he knew each and every curve and inch of skin beneath it personally.

"She shouldn't be here," he bit off.

"You'd rather them bring in an Air Force guy?"

"Yes," he snapped. "Sidewinder'd been flying these for years and look what happened. You really think putting a woman up in one is a good idea?"

"What about Tessler and Puck? They're women."

"That's different."

Lizard grunted. "Only because you gave them a chance to prove themselves. And no matter what you say, she's damn fine to look at. Been a while since a woman's stirred me like this. Wonder if she'd go out with me."

Jealousy rose swift and deadly. "Control your cock, Lizard. This ain't the dating game."

A sly look crossed his friend's face. "You thinking of trying for her yourself?"

I've had her and I'll be damned before I let you have her. "Pre-flight done," he said before he ascended the ladder and climbed into his seat.

Lizard, thankfully, became all business and climbed into the seat next to him. At take-off time, he swallowed and felt a trickle of sweat run down his back. This was his first flight since Mike's death.

"Alpha One, this is Tower. You're clear for take-off."

He glanced to his left. "Let the newbie go first," he replied arrogantly, wanting to watch Jaydee Amos take off personally.

"Roger that. Alpha Two, you're cleared for take-off."

Her voice came over the radio, smooth and unruffled. "Roger that. Alpha Two copies."

Giovanni sat there—with a hard-on, courtesy of her sultry bedroom voice—and watched her manoeuvre the one hundred and seventy-two foot wide bomber up in the air, smooth as glass.

"Nicely done, Dusti," a voice Giovanni recognised as Keel's stated.

"Thanks, Keel. Man, I've missed this."

Her voice was full of pleasure and she made that sexy little rumble in the back of her throat, the same as she'd done in his hotel room. His cock throbbed uncomfortably.

Forcing his attention to his own job, he and the rest of the squadron took to the air. The adrenaline hit him and he couldn't stop the grin that spread across his face. As his jet burst through the clouds and he was presented with the pure blue of the sky, things felt right again in his world.

Most people never get to see the world like this. Higher and higher, they pushed until they reached the stratosphere. *Here's to you, Sidewinder. Here's to you.*

Orders came into the cockpit and, with a grin at Lizard, who would assume the role of mission commander if they ever got called out, he put his game face on as the bomber streaked through the sky. He and Lizard were a unique team—normally a mission commander held a higher rank but, since this was a test facility and he and Lizard had worked together in the past, it worked for them. Not to mention that they were Navy and typically only Air Force flew the B-2 Spirit.

Once they'd made it back to base, Jason was touting how impressed he was by Dusti's ability up there. Grinding his back teeth as they climbed down, Giovanni tried to keep his comments to himself.

Fool sounds in love. The real disturbing part about that was it made him jealous to think that Jason and Jaydee could have a thing. He wanted her.

Giovanni would admit, albeit reluctantly, she had been impressive. Her voice had stayed calm throughout the exercise. Even during the tests they'd had to put the jets through. She'd completed everything asked of her with cool efficiency.

Shades on, he paused slightly when he caught sight of Jaydee slipping into a hangar. He waved goodbye to Lizard and followed her. He knew the hangar. The remains of Mike's plane were housed there.

What could she possibly want in there? Hesitation hit him before he entered the massive building. While he knew what was in there, he'd not wanted to see the wreckage. Clenching his fists, he stepped out of the sun and into the artificially lit hangar.

Twisted metal chunks lay across the floor and he closed his eyes against the memories for a brief second before pressing on. His target stood by a section of wing that concealed one of the B-2's four engines. He nodded at the guard and headed for her. She stood with her hands positioned on her hips, which only served to enhance the tininess of her waist.

He gulped as warring emotions fought within him, the powerful desire to gather her close and protect her with the wish for her to be prohibited from flying. The arrogant male side of him hated the weak-willed emotions of lust he experienced around her.

His object of focus crouched down and he groaned as his cock hardened at the way her flight suit tightened around her firm ass. Jaydee didn't have a butt, she had an *ass*, handcrafted for him to grab and squeeze as he powered deep inside her liquid heat. Ignoring both lust and hesitation at being in there, he strode up behind her. Her hair was confined in a double French braid. As he stared down at her, all that ran through his mind was how much he wanted to take it down and let it flow over his skin.

"Something I can do for you, Commander Cassano?" Her voice flowed over him, modulated and calm.

"Why are you in here?" he demanded.

She sighed and pushed smoothly to her feet before pivoting and facing him. Her eyes flickered with something akin to irritation before they became devoid of any emotion.

"I may be new to this squad of test pilots, Commander, but I don't answer to you. So, while I'm extremely sorry this incident took your friend's life and you may think I'm trying to replace him, believe me when I say I'm not. I was ordered here. If it's all the same to you, keep your damn chauvinistic and irritable attitude away from me."

She raked her eyes up and down him, unable to disguise the heat. Lord help him, he wanted to kiss her. All over.

"What's going on here?"

With a snarl close to escaping, he glanced to his left to see Lizard and a few others walking up. Crossing his arms, he focused back on Jaydee. A seductive and challenging grin lifted his lips.

"I was just telling Dusti here how we'd love to have her join us at Kerrigan's. Help us get to know one another better."

"Wonderful idea," Lizard said. "We'll see you then! Seven o'clock. Come on, guys."

Jaydee held his gaze as they were again left alone. "I'll meet you in the parking lot," he said.

She blinked and said coolly, "I don't need a ride. I'll be there." That said, she gave him her back and crouched back down by the wing.

Giovanni muttered under his breath before striding away. He made short work of a shower—a cold one at that—and was soon at his car. Peering over his shoulder, he gazed back to the hangar. *What possible reason could she have for scanning the wreckage?*

With a groan, he drove back to his apartment after stopping for some groceries. He sat around for a bit trying to forget his feelings for Jaydee.

"It's worse now that I know her name," he mumbled.

His mood was near foul when he left to hit Kerrigan's. A feeling that faded when he stepped through the door. Making his way back to where his squad hung out, he snorted when there was no sign of Jaydee Amos.

"Hey, Casanova."

He returned the greetings and caught the eye of a waitress for a beer. "Where's Keel?" he asked.

"Getting to know his pilot," Puck said. "They're over there, throwing darts."

Instantly he found her. A possessive growl rose from his chest, threatening to escape. She made his mouth water and his cock harder than steel. Tonight she wore a light blue fitted T-shirt and body-hugging jeans. No heels tonight, but plain white tennis shoes.

She laughed and chatted easily with Keel. Giovanni wanted to rip the man's head off and shove it down his throat. *What the hell is wrong with me?* He had no reason to be jealous—Keel was a devoted husband and father. But there he was, furious and hating that she was having a good time with someone other than him.

He forced himself to remain there and participate in the ongoing conversation. Unfortunately, his mind and attention continued to meander back to her. Eventually, they returned and she sat almost across from him.

"Nice to see you made it," he said.

Her full lips curled around the bottle and she took a swig. His cock pulsed. Her tongue swiped along her lower lip before she shrugged. "The place is not hard to find."

"Tell me about you," he ordered. "Do you prefer Dusti, Amos, or Commander?"

"I answer to all three, so it's up to you. Most people call me Jaydee." She blinked. "What about you?"

"Hi, Casanova!" A brunette wrapped her arms around him and kissed him straight on the mouth. "I've missed you. Call me and we'll...well, you know." Then she was gone with a flirtatious wink.

He met Jaydee's gaze and saw comprehension. "Does everyone call you Casanova?" Her question shocked him. He expected a comment on the woman and the kiss. *What was that one's name?* For the life of him, he couldn't recall.

"Some call me Cassano. Or Giovanni."

Keel touched her, taking her attention. Giovanni observed them through narrowed eyes. The blond was showing her his new tattoo.

"You seem like a tattoo woman," he said across the table, bringing her gaze back to where he wanted it. On him. "A rose? Or a heart?"

Flames flickered in the depths of her unique eyes but her expression remained composed. The others jumped in, trying to guess location and type. He let them guess a while before he spoke up again.

"I've got it." Everyone looked at him. His fingers curved about the cool bottle. "A fairy."

Her grin was more a baring of teeth. He knew exactly what her tattoo was and its precise location. It was a fairy on her lower back, left side.

"Fairies are important," she said with a warning glint in her gaze. "Men I meet tend to be...um...lacking, and, hey, a little pixie dust to help things along is always appreciated. I hate being left wanting." She got to her feet. "Thank you for inviting me, but I have a previous engagement. I'll catch you all tomorrow."

His pride smarted, for he knew damn well she'd been satisfied in his bed. "Perhaps you should meet different men."

"I'm on my way to do that now."

Anger burned in his gut. Lizard smacked him in the arm. "Casanova here has no problems with the ladies."

She nodded. "I've heard about Casanova. I'm still not convinced he was the world's greatest lover. Seems more likely he sleeps...slept...with so many because he couldn't get repeating...customers. He lacked what women wanted."

Jaydee sent him a sugary-sweet smile before walking away without a look back. The table howled with laughter as he watched her leave Kerrigan's.

"What is with you two? Hell, the way y'all are going at it makes me think there's some serious attraction there," Puck said around her laughter.

You have no idea. You just have no idea.

"Or," Lizard began, "she despises you, like you seem to do her." Another shoulder smack. "Be nice to her, man. We were new too."

He planned to be nice. Very nice, as he stripped her bare and fucked her until neither could move for hours. He shifted on his feet and tried to ignore the insistent press of his cock against his jeans.

"Sure," he muttered before draining the rest of his beer and deliberately turning his back to the door, so he couldn't see her if she and her 'previous engagement' came back in.

He went home not long after and his dreams passed full of the temptress. When morning rolled around, he was surly. In the shower, he closed his eyes and jerked himself off to the replay of him and Jaydee together.

The week was tense and he was ready for his day off. It passed all too quickly, however. Back at work, he nodded briskly to a fellow commander but didn't stop to talk. Stepping from the building, he began walking towards the building Mike's plane was in when, beyond it, he spied a B-2 partway out of its hangar.

Morning sun had barely begun to creep over the horizon. The fog seemed to hover a foot above the ground, adding to the impressive aura the Spirit gave off.

His breath caught in his throat as his mind identified who the lone person was, walking around the bomber. Jaydee. He readjusted his course and headed for her. Her flight suit was only half on, bunched at her waist to expose bare arms to the cool morning air.

"Morning, Jaydee," he said, leaning against the landing gear.

Jaydee inhaled deeply. The crisp air carried with it a raw masculine scent that belonged to Lieutenant Commander Cassano. Or, as he was more aptly called, Casanova.

It's too early to deal with this. With him. With the lust he slams into me.

"Morning, Commander," she said, flicking a glance over her shoulder. Her heart pounded hard at the man standing there. Sex. That was what he brought to mind. All-day, no-holds-barred sex. Like they'd shared already.

"Giovanni."

"Excuse me?" she asked, tearing her gaze from his impressive physique to focus back on his face.

"Call me Giovanni."

She raked hungry eyes over him one more time. "That's a mouthful."

"You'd know." A mocking lift of his lips nearly made her groan.

She coolly arched a brow. "So something shorter then. Gio?"

His eyes narrowed and he stepped closer, again making her focus on other things.

"What are you doing here so early?" he asked in a low tone that bordered on intimate.

"Working." *Which you tend to distract me from.*

"That's a very vague answer. Why are you out here so early?"

Instead of answering, she peered up at the black jet that loomed over them like a large, dark shadow. She could feel a soft smile teasing the corners of her mouth.

"Have you ever taken the time to just *look* at these birds. You can *feel* their power. The majesty."

He moved up behind her, cloaking her with his warmth. Without glancing at him, she allowed him to close in near. His breath fanned the back of her neck as his hands settled upon her waist.

Her heart skipped a few beats before returning to the breakneck pace it had around him. This contact was highly improper and yet she couldn't find it in her to pull away. Hell, she could hardly keep from sinking into his strong chest.

"Why?" he asked, the question rumbled in her ear.

Jaydee licked her lips and weighed her words. She knew he was asking about her being assigned here, to the squadron.

"I already told you, I am here on orders."

"Bullshit!"

His fingers, strong fingers, dug into the flesh of her hips and she swallowed. Those fingers had brought her such ecstasy. Her nails scored into her palms and she fought to keep her control intact.

"What reason would I have for lying?"

"I pulled your record. You've never been assigned to a squadron, so why the hell would they send *you* here to this test facility?" He spun her around to face him. In the early morning's light, his hazel eyes flashed dangerously. "Who the fuck are you?"

Her heart pounded erratically. Holding his angry gaze, she removed his hands from her waist. *I'm not even going to ask how he managed to pull my record.* "I'm not lying about who I am or why I'm here. I'm just here to do the job they tell me."

"You're lying. I don't know yet how much, but you can bet your cute little ass you're full of shit."

She ground her jaw. "My 'cute little ass' is no concern of yours," she said. "In fact, none of me is."

He moved like the wind, grabbed her arms, and spun her out of the open into the immediate inside of the empty hangar. Pressed against the cool metal wall, she had nowhere to go. He blocked her in with his hard muscled body. She could barely make out his features in the foredawn light but it didn't matter. The desire poured from him—she could have been blind and still seen it.

"The hell it doesn't," he growled by her ear. She plastered herself further back against the wall, praying the metal would keep her from reacting. "Damn you!" he swore before covering her mouth with his own.

Her resistance lasted less than a second. With a groan of surrender and submission, she sank into him, arms twining around his neck. *Oh hell!* His addictive masculine taste—which she couldn't cleanse from her memory—flooded her.

Her nipples peaked and abraded her thin T-shirt. Moisture soaked her panties and all she could envision was his thick cock pushing deep into her, filling her. She whimpered as his tongue stroked deep and with masterful control.

He cupped a breast and teased the tip with rolls and tugs. Her legs wobbled and, when she began to slide down, he wedged a thigh between hers, keeping her up. His other hand slipped around to the back where her flight suit was bunched, only to dip below it and cup her ass. Heat singed her through her thin shorts.

He flexed against her and she nipped at his invading tongue. His growl flowed over her in a possessive wave and she shuddered. She shifted against him, desperate to be closer. Remove all attire and be allowed to enjoy skin on skin once more.

As quickly as he'd pounced on her, he retreated, leaving her wet and waiting. Not to mention wanting. Chest heaving, she fought the urge to either rub her arms or—better yet—reach for him again.

"Just so we're clear," he rasped, his words low and gravelled. "I hate that you're here." He might have released her but his large body kept her penned in.

She snapped her teeth at him as she unzipped his flight suit to allow her access to his cock. He hissed when her fingers closed around it.

"Just so we're clear," she whispered. "I hate your chauvinistic attitude."

"Clear," he growled, jerking her close and devouring her.

Their movements grew frantic as her suit was shoved off and her shorts soon followed. The air filled with their harsh breaths and the sudden rip of fabric as her panties were torn from her body. Seconds later, he pushed into her with a single, smooth stroke.

"Yesss!" she expelled on a long breath.

"Two weeks I've walked around with blue balls, or else I need to jack off three fucking times a day thinking about you."

"Not my problem," she panted.

His deep strokes halted and she slashed her gaze to his. Hazel eyes burned eerily at her. She tried to draw him in more, wanting more than just the head of his dick in her.

"Oh, it very much is your problem." His sentence fell like a warning.

"Gio!" she panted, undulating her hips.

He grinned, darkly sensual. "I love that from your lips." He flicked his fingertips over her taut nipples. She whimpered and shifted with want. There was no warning before he slammed fully into her. A scream raced from her throat. He captured it with his mouth.

Talk ceased while he continued to thrust hard and fast into her. Breaking the kiss, he dropped his head and sucked her nipple into his mouth, shirt and all. His teeth bit gently, shooting pleasure spikes through her. She lost it, arching her back and coming hard, as stars exploded behind her eyes. Seconds later, he lifted his head and buried it in her neck as a low growl slid from his throat. She felt his cock jerk as he released deep within her.

His solid weight pressed her into the wall. She could feel the sweat gathered along her spine. She worried her lower lip until he drew back and glanced at her. This was how she remembered him. Eyes molten and full of passion. Lids a bit heavy, causing his thick lashes to give him an even more hooded, sensual look. She glanced past his shoulder only to tense.

The lethal and ominous beauty of the B-2—a blatant reminder of not only where she was, but also what she'd just done and with whom she'd done it.

Fuck! What the hell did I just do? A hard gulp. *Again.*

He withdrew and put himself away, still silent. His gaze continued to burn her as she shrugged back into her shorts—*sans* underwear—and grabbed the flight suit before bolting for the small bathroom. She cleaned herself up and splashed cold water on her face.

"What the hell am I doing?" She rubbed her eyes before readjusting her flight suit so it tied around her waist. "I can't get involved with him. Unprotected sex with a fellow officer. Geez." A frown crossed her face when she saw the wet spot over her nipple. "Damn," she muttered even as another tug pulled her clit at the recollection.

"No more," she told herself, zipping up the flight suit and effectively hiding the wet spot. Sure, she looked a bit rumpled, but she would be under control when anyone else showed up. *I hope.*

With one final deep breath, she nodded at her reflection before leaving the room. *He* waited for her. Arms and legs crossed, he had a blank expression on his face.

"Something you needed to say?" she asked, striding by him and heading back to her jet.

"I want to know why you're here."

"Hard of hearing, Gio?"

"Don't start, sweets. I don't fly with people I can't trust."

She didn't know what it was with this one, but her normally iron-clad hold of her control seemed to go extinct. Grinding her jaw, she whipped around to face him. The sun had crested the horizon and it bathed his body in a warm golden glow. Lust ricocheted through her and she valiantly fought it off.

"Then perhaps you should resign your commission because I'm not going *anywhere* until—" she paused, "I'm ordered to."

He stepped towards her, each pace menacing. Thunderheads rolled in his eyes but she held her ground. Yes, he was seriously intimidating and pissed off, but she trusted he wouldn't raise a hand against her.

"If you cost me the life of one of my squad..." He trailed off but she'd already received the message, loud and clear. "You'd damn well better be as good as you claim."

"I've beaten all your top scores," she snapped.

"Not a chance." Arrogance was back in full swing.

"Yes," she said, stepping closer still. "The day after it posted I'd beat it. So you may not trust me, but, like I told you before, don't try to measure your dick against mine."

Icy contempt flashed in his gaze. "We both know you don't have a problem with the size of my cock. Which is good, because, while I don't want to fly with you, I have no problems fucking you."

Her body was pleased to hear that but, before she could respond to the rest of his statement, they were interrupted.

"I knew it!" a male voice said. "You two have already slept together."

Mortified, she whirled around to find Lizard ambling up to them, a cocky and smug grin on his tanned features. He winked at her before speaking again.

"Guess that explains why you're being such a territorial ass, Casanova."

"Shut up, Lizard," Gio growled from behind her.

She didn't have it in her to face either of them, much less both, given what Lizard had overheard. With a frustrated breath, she got her head back in the game and went to her plane, determined to ignore what had just happened.

Chapter Three

Jaydee was going to ignore it all. Gio knew that without a doubt. His eyes lingered over the purposeful stride she had as she made her way back to the Spirit she flew at the facility. There was no intended seduction in her movement, just her natural walk. *Probably why it affects me so damn much.*

"When did you sleep with her?"

Reality. "Let it go, man," he warned, eyes never leaving Jaydee.

"Hey, far be it from me to keep the lover Casanova from a conquest, but you need to chill this attitude or everyone will know."

He scowled. "She's not another conquest, Lizard. I don't need your advice on women."

A derisive snort. "Of course not. Which is why you're staring at her like you can't get enough of her. Face it, Giovanni, that woman there means something to you. If you would stop being a dick to her long enough, you'd see it. Problem is you need to curb your attitude before the CO has to step in."

Those words rankled and he scowled then sighed. He knew Lizard was right, he just…had no excuse.

"I'll be civil," he ground out.

That earned him a smack on the shoulder. "Be *nice*, Casanova. Be nice." Lizard left his side and headed towards the bomber and Jaydee.

Gio crossed his arms and stared at her. She had yanked her hair back in a tight bun. He hated it, wanted to remove all the pins and let it cascade down around her shoulders. He wanted to wipe away the composed look and replace it with one of sated passion.

Jaydee barely glanced at Lizard, keeping her attention on the jet. He hid his smirk as his friend continued on out of the hangar. She wasn't interested in Lizard. But when he was around her, her eyes remained on him, not the plane. He liked that.

He strolled up behind her and watched her work. She walked under the plane, a tablet PC in one hand and a pen in the other. Glancing over her shoulder, he frowned at the numerous equations that filled the page.

"What is all that?"

"Equations for electrogravitics. I'm trying to figure out what the hell happened to the plane that crashed."

"Who are you?" he growled, spinning her to him.

Jaydee sighed and held the pad close. "I told you. Please, I'm trying to get my work done."

It was the please that stopped him. He ran a hand over his hair and grunted. "I want the truth."

Her nod was distracted as her attention had already returned to the tablet PC in her hand. *Okay, I don't like her ignoring me.* He stared at her momentarily and noticed a slight furrow between her brows as she scanned the information.

"Jaydee." He repeated it twice more to the same end. She ignored him. "Commander Amos!"

"Sir!" she said, snapping to attention.

It would have been comical—okay, so it was—if not for the scowl that leeched into her expression.

"What!" she bit off.

"Tonight, you and me. I want answers." She frowned and glanced back down. "I mean it, Jaydee. I want answers."

With a sniff, she waved him off. "Yeah, sure. Leave me alone, Gio." And, just like that, her focus wasn't on him anymore.

He allowed the smile to lift his lips. He liked her calling him Gio. A lot. Especially since she'd screamed it as he powered home into her. Hands in pockets, he left her alone in the hangar.

His day was busy with flights and manoeuvres. Again, he found himself continually impressed by her flying skills. *Perhaps she is as good as she claims.*

At the end of the day, he hung out by his vehicle, keeping an eye out for the woman he didn't know if he wanted to kill or fuck. Well, he definitely wanted to fuck her—it was the kill part he wavered on.

Jaydee was a cool cat up in the air—granted this was merely practice, but practice was as real as it could be, and her voice never showed signs of stress or strain. He'd heard her joking with Keel up there and *that* irritated him. The fact that these other men got to laugh with her brought out his jealousy.

Movement at the door grabbed his attention and he fought a scowl when he recognised his CO striding from the building. *Where the hell is she?* He lowered his gaze and fixated on his boots. *Is she avoiding me?*

"Everything okay, Cassano?"

"Fine, sir, thank you." The blue eyes that met his were sharp and assessing. Gio struggled not to shift under the scrutiny.

"Staying here overnight?"

"No, sir. Waiting on my dinner companion."

He nodded, the remaining light glinting off his salt-and-pepper hair. "Night."

"Goodnight, sir."

When the parking lot was lit solely by the lights surrounding it instead of the sun, he pushed away from the trunk of his car and strode back into the building. His frustration mounted with each step. He passed an enlisted man and stopped him.

"Have you seen Commander Amos, Petty Officer?"

The young woman nodded even while her eyes filled with appreciation. "Yes, sir."

"Where?" he demanded when nothing further was divulged.

"She was running a scenario."

"Thank you." He strode off without another word. At the door to the simulation room, he paused before opening it, then pushed in.

"Damn it! I have to be missing something."

Jaydee's voice overflowed with stress and frustration. Fully in the room, he closed the door softly behind him. On the screen to her left—his too since she had her back to him—played a flight scenario with no sound. Three whiteboards were to her right, full of equations he couldn't even begin to decipher. One more was right before her.

Her hands were fisted on her hips and in the left she held a black marker. She no longer wore a flight suit, but a pair of baggy jeans, a loose T-shirt, and...no shoes? He was captivated. Silently, he sat on the edge of a table, waiting with hooked ankles and crossed arms for her to notice him.

She moved from board to board, making notes but never turning around. Her manner seemed to have a pattern in it. She tensed at a certain moment in each scenario. It was the same one, playing on a loop. He had done enough to know.

What made her tense each time?

"Damn it!" She kicked a chair only to swear another round and hop on one foot while grabbing the other.

"Maybe it's time for a break," he said.

She whipped around, shock at seeing him prevalent on her face. He dragged his hungry gaze over her. His uptight, normally together Jaydee Amos looked a rumpled mess. He loved it. An ear bud hung from one ear.

Her tortoiseshell eyes travelled over him. "What are you doing here?"

He pushed away from the table and strolled to her. "What are *you* doing here?"

"Working. You?"

"I've been waiting for you outside." He realised how odd that was for him. Waiting on a woman wasn't in his norm. "We were going to..." he snapped his fingers before her eyes, which had drifted back to the boards, bringing them back to him, "talk tonight about who you are."

She furrowed her brow and he could see her processing what he'd said. "I'm... I'm busy."

A short burst of laughter left him. Like he was going to accept that. "Sorry, sweets, you agreed and I'm hungry. Haven't eaten a thing since lunch. Let's go."

Indecision flickered in her eyes, so he made the choice for her. He reached out and plucked the black marker from her left hand, capped it, and tossed it on the nearest table. His fingers gripped her chin.

"I'm hungry, and I know you are, too."

She blinked at him owlishly. "Why do you want to eat with me? You don't even like me."

He didn't want to hash this out now. He needed to get some food in him before he forgot himself, *again,* and took her in here.

"Come on, Jaydee, you owe me some answers."

She worried her lower lip before nodding and heading for the door. She paused and slid on some white tennis shoes then grabbed a bag, which she shouldered. As they left he noticed she locked the door behind her then strode off down the hall. After a final glance between her and the door, he sighed before striking out after her.

"Where to?" she asked when he caught up.

He wanted to put her in his car and take her home, but knew she wouldn't go for that. He gave her the name of the casual diner and she nodded then walked away. Moments later, lust broadsided him as she straddled a motorcycle and put the required helmet and reflective vest on.

Christ! She rides a crotch rocket!

He stood motionless as she started the black Ninja's powerful engine and drove away. His cock was rock hard and he was desperate to sink back inside her. She was amazing. Hot, sexy, a pilot, and she rode a motorcycle.

Adjusting himself, he groaned and vaulted into his sports car before following her. His erection had barely begun to subside when he pulled in to the lot of the diner. Jaydee leaned against her bike, bag in hand. Past her leg, he noticed another fairy. He grinned — it matched the fairy tattoo of Iridessa she had on her back.

She appeared to be entirely bored. Him...not so much. His cock stiffened all over again and he bit back a groan. This woman was giving him a serious case of blue balls.

* * * *

Jaydee licked her lips as she watched Gio walk towards her. Him. Her nemesis. The man who hated her being there, and yet fucked her as if she meant everything to him. A man she thought of as Gio, not Casanova, or Lieutenant Commander Giovanni Cassano. He was gasoline to her fire, they really didn't mix well...at work.

Not true, we were fine in the hangar this morning. Like she needed that mental reminder. She ignored how her body prepared itself for him and focused on his inherent swagger. On some men, it would have been laughable. On Gio...it just *was*.

He had a nice convertible and wore jeans with a T-shirt. His attire amplified the strength in his body. Another swipe of her tongue along her lips—she could still taste him. Desire washed over her and it took a huge effort not to show him.

Gio stopped before her and stared at her with those hazel eyes. One brow rose slightly and she manoeuvred around him, bag in one hand. She felt him behind her, close but not touching.

"Good evening. Two tonight?" the greeter asked after they entered.

"Yes." Gio's strong voice flowed from behind her as his fingers brushed briefly against the small of her back.

The woman basically ignored her, but definitely had desire in her eyes when she stared at Gio. *Date,* her brain chided.

No date. Her subconscious laughed at her.

They were led to a booth and she slid in as the greeter placed their menus and left with another blatant perusal of Gio. It bothered her—why, she wasn't sure, but it did. Their server came and took their drink order before leaving. She was quick to return and, after placing them down, she had a hungry look on her face when she smiled at Gio.

Cripes, this is going to be a long night. If she had to deal with women fawning all over him she was going to need something stronger than what she'd ordered. Too bad she didn't drink anything stronger, really. She sipped her beverage and stared at him. His eyes heated as he looked directly at her. A sexy twist of his lips made her wonder about the wisdom of coming with him.

After they'd placed their order, he watched her for a few moments. "Tell me why they brought you in."

She swivelled her straw around. "Do you question your orders?"

"You're not getting out of this, Jaydee, so just answer the question."

The way he said her name had her shifting on the seat. So low and drawn out like a sensual caress. She swallowed and took another drink in an attempt to cool off. It didn't work.

"I'm here because I know the planes."

He scowled. "So does every pilot."

She shook her head. "No, I *know* the planes. I know all about EG and how the B-2 operates beyond the normal."

"EG?"

"Yes. Electrogravitics. I told you about it in the simulation room." She could see his confusion. "What allows our bombers to go as far as they do, expending very little fuel. And why, when they land, we don't touch them for a while, or are well protected when we do."

He drank some of his beer. "How do you know all of this?"

She leant back against the booth and held her silence as their appetiser arrived. The mixture of smells hit her and she stared at the platter of fried calamari, mozzarella sticks, and loaded potato skins. Her stomach growled and she realised he'd been right, she was starving. She watched him reach for a piece of calamari and dip it in the dill sauce before eating it.

"Eat," he said gesturing at the plate.

"I'm a researcher," she said, after some internal debate.

"For what?"

"The B-2. I fly them and work on the antigravity propulsion. Or, rather, I work on material for the US antigravity squadron, as some refer to it." It wasn't entirely a lie, she'd just omitted part of the truth.

She figured, yes, she could get into trouble for telling him, not even the CO knew this, but, despite their volatile relationship, she'd found herself irrefutably drawn to him. Not just on a sexual level but also on a deeper one.

For a moment, she wondered about her decision then shrugged, deciding the hell with it. He'd find out soon enough, if he were as smart and dogged as she pegged him to be. And she bet he was.

"Antigravity squadron?"

She stifled a sigh. "The B-2s."

His gaze shuttered. "I'm beginning to think this is neither the time nor place for this discussion."

"You asked."

"I did and I'm not backing away from it. I just think it should be discussed elsewhere."

With another negligent shrug, she began to eat. She could feel his gaze upon her but he also continued to eat.

"Tell me about you."

The order fell with all the imbedded arrogance of an alpha male who expected to be obeyed. She *hated* following imperialistic commands. There were only a few who could get away with it in her mind, and he wasn't one of them.

"No." She pinned him with a calm look. His reaction was as she'd expected, those gorgeous eyes narrowed on her face. "Tell me about you," she countered.

He appeared to war with his decision momentarily but, when he opened his mouth, the waitress arrived with their meal. She immediately turned her attention to the plate of steaming food. Some days a good ol' burger and fries was what was needed. She salted her thick fries and poured the ketchup. Lifting one, she dipped it and put it in her mouth. A low groan of pleasure escaped. These were damn good steak fries.

"Is this a private party?"

Jaydee was nudged over as Jason 'Lizard' Armstrong slid in on her side, and she saw Gio had Tinman—another pilot—beside him. Both men had bottles of beer. Without asking, the two newcomers helped themselves to the remaining appetisers.

Normally, she would have been embarrassed to face Lizard after what he'd said in the hangar. But, right now, she was too damn hungry to care. That being the case, she ate.

"Why are you here, Armstrong?" Gio's question came out more of a rumble.

"We have a weekend, thought I'd find you somewhere. Just didn't know you and Dusti here had a date."

She swallowed her food. "We are not on a date. We were hungry."

Gio's hazel eyes bored into her, almost as if he was angry. With a dismissive sniff, she reached for some fries and ate them.

"What do you call it then?" Jason asked, leaning close so his breath fanned her ear.

"A meal between colleagues, Lieutenant," she said, ice coating her words. She didn't mind teasing but she refused to allow any rumours of her and Gio as a couple. Or fuck buddies.

Jason stiffened slightly beside her before shrugging and eating more calamari. A foot nudged hers before stroking up her calf. It took everything she had not to jump. Her gaze centred back on Gio, who lifted his head up and peered at her with the eyes of a predator. His foot rubbed against her while his other leg encroached on her space, giving her two options. Sit rigidly, or allow physical contact between them.

So she turned her attention back to her food and proceeded to eat, doing her best to ignore the simple yet intimate — and highly erotic — touches.

The conversation flowed around her. Lizard felt — apparently — comfortable enough to take food from her plate. She allowed it, for to her it seemed they were trying to make her feel included. And it gave her perverse pleasure to watch the fleeting scowl on Gio's face when it happened.

"So, Casanova, what do you say? Are you in?"

Jason's question caused her to look up. Gio had a blank expression on his face and she continued to stare at Tinman. The man's brown eyes twinkled as he met her gaze. *What are they talking about?*

"Come on, Cas, you know Ashley is going to be there and she would love to see you." Jason shifted on the seat when Gio pinned his eyes on him.

"Ashley?" she asked, licking some salt and ketchup off her fingers.

Either Jason didn't see the warning glint in Gio's gaze or didn't care. When he glanced at her and grinned, she realised which. Jason didn't care.

"One of Casanova's women. Our pilot here has left a trail of broken hearts behind him."

She ignored the stabbing pain that announcement gave her and lifted her glass before drinking her water. "I see, so Ashley is one of the many." She nodded as if it all made sense. It did. Giovanni Cassano was a sexual man, with an appetite she would classify as insatiable.

His gaze slashed to her face, eyes almost hidden by thick, curved lashes. Eyes that seemed to glint gold in the light. He nudged her foot with his but she glanced over to Jason, whose eyes flickered between herself and Gio.

"Watch it, Lizard," Gio said in a low growl.

"What? Dusti here is one of the squad." He shrugged and nudged her. "Do we need to censor what we say around you?"

She shook her head. "Of course not," she replied, reaching for her wallet. "I am honoured to be included. However, I must be going now. Thank you, Gio, for inviting me."

"You haven't had dessert yet," he said, reclining in the booth. She recognised the look on his face—a challenge.

One she would love to take but she couldn't. Not today. Pulling out some bills, she set them down beside her plate.

"Not a big fan of dessert. If you will excuse me."

Gio wasn't as nice. "Move, Tinman." When the man did, he got to his feet. "I'll walk you out."

"Y'all didn't come together?" Jason asked as he got up.

She grabbed her bag and stood. "Would it not be awkward if we had, and you want him to go get another woman?" At his look of discomfort, she grinned. "It was a joke."

He smiled and she could see his handsomeness even clearer. "You and I will get along just fine, Dusti."

She flashed him a grateful smile. "Glad to hear it." Reaching back across the booth, she snagged her helmet. She could use all the allies she could get.

Jason's eyes widened and he clasped his heart. "Oh hell, you even ride a motorcycle. Marry me."

She laughed and shook her head, noting how the scowl on Gio's face deepened. "I hope you gentlemen have a great time. I will see you in ninety-six."

Walking away, she inhaled sharply as the scent of Gio filled her nose. With a wave to the greeter, she reached for the door only to have Gio's arm snake around her and beat her to it. It felt like he sniffed her neck.

"Thank you," she said, striding to her bike, stowing the bag, and straddling the seat.

"Jaydee," he murmured, one hand stretching towards her face.

"I believe Ashley is waiting for you." She gathered her hair up and put on her helmet, followed by the vest. "Goodnight, Gio." Down came the visor and she drove away before she begged him to come home with her, instead of that Ashley bitch.

Probably some cute little nothing with big tits and no personality or IQ. She snarled and waited for a break in the traffic to leave the parking lot. As she got on the street, she noticed him standing in the same spot.

This is going to be a long assignment. Even with him just standing there, she craved him. *Damn you, Gio!*

Chapter Four

She'd driven away. Just like that. Slid one lean, toned leg over her sleek machine and left him so he could go to another woman. That was not how it was supposed to work. Jaydee was supposed to demand he not go, tell him to come with her. That he was hers.

A thought that froze him. He shook his head with a disgusted grunt. *What the hell am I thinking? Who cares what Lieutenant Commander Jaydee 'Dusti' Amos thinks?*

He entered the diner and made his way back to the booth. With nothing more than a look to get Tinman to move, he slid into an empty side while the other two shared.

Tinman's expression was only slightly less amused than Lizard's. The trio of men said nothing for a short while until the waitress came back over. Her hair, the colour of claret, offset her pale skin. She smiled at him and reached over to take Jaydee's empty plate.

"Is your friend coming back?" she asked. "And can I get you men anything else?"

While the question may have been directed at all of them, her bottle-green eyes never left him. They overflowed with blatant invitation. One that, in the past, he would have had no problems accepting. And his friends knew it.

Yet he couldn't force the words past his mouth. Not even the flirting decline, which seemed almost instinctive, considering how it normally flowed without a thought. Until now. Until her. Until Jaydee.

"Just the check," he informed her. Gathering up the money Jaydee had left, he pocketed it. "And hers as well."

"Leaving already?" she asked with a manufactured pout.

"Yes." He gave her a pointed look. "Check."

She smiled but it was definitely more forced. "Sure thing, handsome."

"Don't speak," he ordered Tinman and Lizard the second the waitress left.

They obeyed for all of two seconds. Tinman started.

"What's up with you, man? You're turning *that* down? And since when do women call you Gio? Hell, anyone. You damn near bit our heads off for that."

He ground his jaw. "Thought you said Ashley was waiting." He wasn't even going to address the Gio bit.

Both of them snorted at that.

"Nothing that would have stopped you before." Tinman again.

Lizard rolled the bottle in his fingers. "He's after something else. Something darker and sexier. Something which can handle a B-2 as it streaks through the sky, or a crotch rocket down here on the ground."

Gio remained impassive, despite the overwhelming urge to hurdle the table and slam a fist into Lizard's face. When the check came, he scooped it up and slapped sixty bucks down to cover it all.

"You two have fun now," he said with a grin.

"Seriously? You're not coming?" Lizard asked.

"Nope. Going home." He touched two fingers to his head and strode away.

Lizard caught up with him at his convertible. "Giovanni."

He turned and braced a hip against the door. "Jason." His reply was the same tone as his friend's.

"What are you doing, man?"

He sighed. "Going home." Alone. Damn it all, he wanted to be with Jaydee.

"That's not what I mean and you know it. You can't be in a relationship with her. Hell, you aren't supposed to even sleep with her."

"I know the rules," he ground out.

"Then why?"

"I slept with her after Mike's funeral. That's what we were talking about in the hangar." No point in telling Lizard he'd just fucked Jaydee in that very hangar moments before he'd arrived.

Lizard swore a round of curses before shoving his hand along the top of his short hair. Then he crossed his arms and stared. Gio mimicked the action and lifted a brow as well.

"What?" he demanded.

"You can't see it, can you?"

"See what, Armstrong?"

The man shook his head. "Nope. If you don't know, I ain't ruining my fun by watching the realisation hit you. Just do one thing for me."

Gio sighed and waited for his friend to continue. "What's that?" he asked when nothing else was forthcoming.

"Stop being a dick. She's a damn good pilot who doesn't deserve your derision."

Aliyah Burke

This was the second time Lizard had said this. The man was right and it annoyed him to no end to know Lizard was defending her. "Anything else?" Gio asked sarcastically.

"Yeah," he said, before spinning on his heel and walking away. "Don't get caught!"

A grin lifted his lips. He had no intention of getting caught. In his car, he headed for his apartment only to pause in the drive.

Where did she live? Was she home? Or had she gone back to base? Bigger question. Why did any of it matter?

Grumbling at himself, he parked in the garage and walked into the house. He and Mike had shared this place before he'd died. Gio strode to Mike's room and opened the door. He knew what he'd see the moment the light flicked on, and he wasn't wrong. Boxes. Sealed boxes of his best friend's things. They remained here because his family wasn't ready to get them back.

So here they sat, their very presence mocking him. With a snarl, he snapped off the light and slammed the door shut, only to stomp to the kitchen for a beer.

* * * *

It was midday on his final day of being off when Gio found himself pushing through the doors of their ops centre. The halls were quiet as he made his way to the room with the simulator in it. He opened the door then stepped into the totally dark room. Flipping the switches, he frowned as he found himself staring at the room as it normally was. No sign of the numerous whiteboards Jaydee'd had, full of that gibberish-looking crap all over them. Nothing that even said she'd been in there.

What were you thinking — that she'd be waiting for you? his brain chided.

As he exited the room, he ran into a guard. The petty officer nodded and gave a proper greeting.

"Have you seen any of the other pilots?" he asked as thunder boomed overhead.

"Sorry, sir. You're the only one I've seen since Commander Amos left."

She *had* been there. He shrugged and shoved his hands into his pockets before giving a sharp nod to the guard and walking away. He paused at the exterior door and stared out of the vertical rectangular window at the downpour.

He took out his baseball cap, snapped it open, and shoved it on his head as he bolted outside. Long strides took him to his car and he slid gratefully behind the wheel. *At least I put the top up yesterday.*

He started the engine and headed back to his place. While he was at a red light, he looked up in time to see Jaydee walk into an apartment building with bags in one hand and an umbrella in the other. He knew it was her. Something happened to him when he was around her, he could feel her beneath his skin, almost. So he didn't doubt he was seeing things.

When the light changed, he whipped into an available spot along the street and got out again. Soaked, and with water dripping off his hat and clothes, he moved into the lobby. The place was quiet and he found what he was looking for. Mailboxes.

Two B. He went to the lift and lowered the gate before pressing the button. When it stopped, he lifted the gate, slid open the door, and stepped out into the empty hall.

Thunder rumbled again and the lights flickered. The cold air made him shiver and he walked to find the right door. There was no name, just bronze numbers on black paint. Another chill hit him and he pressed the doorbell. A few moments later and he found himself once again in Jaydee's presence.

She looked soft. As she had when she'd lain in his bed. Her hair fell unconfined in soft waves around her face. She had on a tatty, long-sleeved shirt and lounge pants. No shoes, but socks.

Her tortoiseshell eyes widened. "Gio? What are you doing here?" She glanced up and down the hall before pulling him in and closing the door. "How did you find me?"

Was it his imagination or did she sound a bit panicked? He glanced around her place and smiled. It was nice. Hardwood floors, a love seat, an overstuffed chair, and a recliner. A small table and chairs to one side, and there were stools by the island. Large windows, too. The other side of her place was full of whiteboards, a table with computers, and books.

"Nice place," he said.

Her fingers tightened on his arm and he bet she didn't realise what she was doing.

"How did you find me?"

"I was driving by and saw you walk in."

She shook her head. "You shouldn't be here."

Only half teasing, he said, "You have a man who will be pissed I'm here?" She didn't answer and he peered at her. Her lower lip was caught in her teeth. "Jaydee?"

She blinked and seemed to realise he was still there. "Why are you here?"

"We have some unfinished business, you and I."

"You're soaking wet."

He arched a brow. "It's raining out."

She nodded and continued like he'd never said a word. "You should get dry."

"I have no other clothes—"

Jaydee walked off, pulling him behind. Dutifully, he followed her back to her bedroom. It wasn't girly, it was…functional. Dark, natural colours, the area was spotless and gave no insight into who she was.

She opened a drawer and pulled out a pair of men's warm-up pants. "These should fit you." A pair of socks was next. "There are towels in there." Then she walked away.

He didn't know whose clothes they were, but he was really cold. So he went to her bathroom. Again spotless but nothing feminine. He stripped down, dried off with the large, white towel then threw on what she'd given him. Rubbing his short hair briskly, he hung the towel up over the opaque squares blocking the room from anywhere else. His soaked clothes he draped in the shower.

He emerged slowly and found her sliding something in the oven. The lights dimmed a bit when another rumble of thunder rolled through. Warm again, he approached. She went to the sink.

"Thank you."

She looked up at him from where she washed some vegetables. "Why are you here? We work together so there can be no—"

"Stop." He trailed his fingers along the countertop. Hearing those words from her would only annoy him. The hell with the rules, he wasn't about to ignore the heat between them. Nor was he going to let her ignore it.

"I am merely—"

"Jaydee," he said with force.

"Then what reason could you have for coming here?"

He could taste her confusion. "Is my being here a problem?"

If he only knew. Jaydee chewed on her lower lip briefly. Gio was a distraction she truly didn't need. But she couldn't ignore him, nor could she bring herself to let him leave looking all wet and soaked.

"Jaydee?"

"No," she muttered. "It's fine."

When he stepped further into the kitchen, she retreated around the cooktop counter, trying to keep a bit of space between them. The gleam in his eyes told her he knew exactly what she was doing.

"Talk to me, Jaydee," he said, drawing back one of her stools and settling his body upon it.

She gulped and did her best to take her eyes off him. It didn't work. He sat there wearing those warm-up pants and socks. His hard, muscled chest taunted her with recollections of how it felt to be pressed against him. She itched to touch his smooth skin, lick it, and more.

"What do you want to know?"

"Tell me more about this"—he frowned and paused—"this EG."

Her heart pounded and she did a quick scan of her place. She'd got this because of its size and inconspicuous location. It was cheaper than a regular apartment and offered her more privacy. Plus the view was amazing, especially on nights like this, when the rain and lightning sliced the sky.

"Jaydee." Fingers snapped in her face.

"Huh?" Gio had moved and now stood right before her.

"EG, sweets. I think I lost you for a moment there."

She blinked a few times. "Right. EG."

With a glance back at the oven, she walked over to her corner where all her stuff was and drew a quick sketch on one of the whiteboards. She turned to face him only to discover he'd sneaked right up behind her, leaving her face to face with his gorgeous chest.

"I know most of the time when you fly, you use the jet engines, but, when you're up in the stratosphere doing those long flights, we use electrogravitics."

He backed off, grabbed the lone chair, and sat, his focus still on her. "Okay. This is why we can go for so long without fuel?"

She nodded and shoved her hands in her pockets. "Exactly. There are several relations which allow this. Gravitational mass is proportional to electric charge, is one. Gravitational mass density is proportional to electric charge density, is another." She wrote out the symbol equations for both.

"These electrogravitic relations can be expressed in terms of field potentials. That would be—gravity potential is proportional to negative electric potential." The symbol equation for this one went up on the board as well. "Consequently, an electric potential field gradient which extends between the positive and negative—"

"Oh my God, stop, please," he interrupted. "I'm so lost. You have to dumb it down for me. Can you give this to me in words I will understand?"

She capped the marker and returned her hands to her pockets. Rolling her lower lip in her teeth, she sighed. "Jet engines get the planes up in the sky. When the antigravity propulsion is turned on—the flame jet generators which are fitted on each of the four engines—several million volts are produced."

Gesturing with one hand to the tail of the plane, she said, "The engine exhaust, along with the rear of the plane, houses a negative charge which creates a 'hill' behind the jet." She moved to the front of her sketch. "All the jets have a leading edge ionizer which is positively charged. This, because of electrogravitics, produces a 'well' to fall into. With me so far?"

She paused and looked at him. His face had this slightly confused expression. But when he nodded, she continued. "So the plane—after the jet engines are off—will pretty much 'fall' towards the 'well', while the 'hill' from the back of the jet continually 'pushes'. All of this keeps the jet moving with silence, and the only reason to refuel would be to keep the voltage up."

She uncapped the marker and drew something else. "When all this is working, an ellipsoidal ion plasma sheath surrounds the B-2, which basically renders it undetectable."

"Hence stealth bomber."

Jaydee nodded with a smile. "Exactly. Even though it is not really invisible, and can be detected."

"So, what are you doing here? Why go over all of this?" He shifted then pinned her with his gaze again. "How do you know so much about this stuff?"

She hesitated. There was much more to tell him about the jets but he seemed transfixed on her for the moment. Which might work in her favour. "I'm trying to figure out what went wrong with Commander Walker's plane."

The pain in his eyes made her feel lower than a snake. Something *she* had, or hadn't, seen had been the reason for the jet going down.

"You're hedging with your answers, sweets." Gio moved in the chair and she found herself short of breath as she stared at him.

"I am not."

A sex-infused grin lifted the corners of his all too kissable mouth. "You are. How do you know all of this...stuff?"

More hesitation. "It is my area of expertise."

He stretched his long legs out in front of him and crossed his arms over his bare chest. "So how did you get your wings? I mean, I'm guessing this kind of thing took a while to learn."

Her heart thundered in her own chest. "The Navy."

Gio arched a brow. "And we're back to the hedging. What aren't you telling me, Jaydee?"

She breathed a huge sigh of relief when the timer dinged in the kitchen. Without a word, she picked up the eraser and cleaned off the whiteboard then made her way to the oven. Using the hot pads, she pulled out the enchiladas and placed the pan on a lattice bamboo trivet.

"Did you make this?" he asked as he leaned over her island and sniffed.

"I pulled it out of the box and slid it in the oven when it was at the required temperature."

"That's a long way of saying no, sweets."

She lifted a shoulder languidly. "No. I don't cook."

"Really?"

Shutting off the oven, she peered at him. He waited for her, his eyes full of laughter. She shrugged and stacked the hot pads beside the dish. Then she moved to the fridge and withdrew a pre-made salad.

"Really," she said.

"You need a home-cooked meal, sweets," he observed.

"I am home. And the meal is cooked."

"I mean one made from scratch. Didn't your mom ever cook meals like that?" Her walls began going up and, as if he sensed her retreat, his hand shot out and captured her chin. "Uh-uh, sweets. Talk to me."

"I cannot recall any of them but the last time I saw her was...years ago."

"I'm sorry. Is she dead?"

"I have no idea."

"Your parents are divorced then?"

"No. I just don't know."

It had hurt years ago and it still did now. Needing something to do, she stepped from his intoxicating touch and grabbed some plates and silverware. She grabbed two glasses and looked at him again. "All I have to offer is water, I hope that's okay."

"Fine, thank you."

She filled them from the fridge and watched him from beneath lowered lids as he dished up some of the food. He looked so comfortable there in her place. For a moment, she allowed herself to think of him as part of her life. Then, with a sharp mental shake, she shoved it from her thoughts.

Her table was small and his size dominated it. The meal was done in silence, as they both ate heartily. She didn't finish all of hers, for he'd given her more than she would normally eat.

Gio helped her clean up and, as he snooped through her kitchen, she put the remaining food into containers. The storm outside had increased in fury, the black night occasionally shattered by the brilliant flashes of lightning.

After she snapped the lid on the final container, she felt him behind her. His arms landed on either side of her, boxing her in. The heat from him warmed her and called to her to lean back and soak it all up. Take what he had to offer.

"Thank you for sharing your meal with me."

"You were here."

"One day, I'll cook for you, Jaydee." His breath fanned along her ear and she trembled.

"It's not necessary." Inside she melted. It was extremely rare for someone to cook for her. Cafeteria food notwithstanding.

"It is."

He turned her in his embrace so that they were face to face. His eyes were dark and smouldered with desire. Her heart pounded out of control—this was her weakness, this man here. Giovanni Cassano.

"We shouldn't," she murmured as his head closed the distance between them.

"Nope." He kissed her lightly, dragging his tongue along her lips.

"We could get in trouble for it."

"Big trouble," he agreed, nibbling on the side of her neck as his hands lifted her shirt.

Her breaths were ragged as he removed her shirt and bra. Bare chest to bare chest, he gathered her close and stroked his fingers down the small of her back.

"Against regulations."

"Agreed." He lifted her and carried her to her bed, laying her there and tugging down her pants.

"It's foolish."

"Absolutely," he agreed, shucking his own clothes and sliding on a condom.

"Really, *really* shouldn't be doing this."

Gio rose up over her and settled between her legs. "Career killer," he mumbled before he sank home inside her with a single powerful stroke. Jaydee closed her eyes and forgot everything else.

Chapter Five

The clap of thunder woke him. Gio opened his eyes and glanced down at the woman in his arms. The light from her flameless candles allowed him to make out her form. Jaydee still slept, their legs intertwined. She had her face buried against his chest and one arm draped around his waist. Turning his head to the left, he saw the readout on the clock. Two-thirty in the morning.

The rain continued to sluice down the large windows and he moved closer, brushing a kiss along her forehead with a smile. He stroked one hand idly up and down her exposed upper arm as he listened to the power of the unrelenting storm.

Yes, so they were violating rules in the Uniformed Code of Military Justice but, for the life of him, he didn't give a damn. He was a man who loved women but never had being with one felt so right, until he'd met Jaydee.

She mumbled and burrowed closer when the next crack and rumble rocked the building. He closed his eyes and listened to the storm. All the while, he thought about Jaydee. Two sides to the same coin.

Never had he met a woman who was so passionate and giving one minute, only to be so doggedly focused on stuff the next. He'd noticed it at the base. She tended to forget about other things when she worked on those damned equations. *Why did she look so fearful when I first arrived?*

Her curves pressed against him, pushing away all thoughts of electrogravitics and whatever the hell else she'd been trying to explain to him. A gentle chime broke the momentarily lull in the storm and she reacted immediately. She rolled away from him and lifted a phone to her ear.

"Yes?"

Gio opened his eyes and stared at the naked expanse of her back, which the flickering light of her candles added an air of sensuality to. His gaze drifted to the yellow fairy on the lower left side. Iridessa. One of Tinkerbell's friends. He'd looked it up after seeing it painted on her motorcycle, where the name was below the fairy. The fairy loved order, order, and more order. Just like the woman who wore her.

"Yes, sir," she said, her voice low. "I understand. No. I haven't figured it out yet. I will. Yes, sir." Jaydee pushed up from the bed and walked from the room, swinging a robe on as she went.

He waited all of a minute before he got to his feet, tugged on the pants she'd given him earlier and padded out after her. *Who the fuck is calling her at oh-two-thirty?* She'd clicked on a light over where the boards were and he stopped by the kitchen and just stared at her.

Her robe was tan and stopped mid-calf. It was the ugliest thing in the world and it turned him on more than he'd believed possible. Knowing she was naked beneath it made him harder than stone. She knelt on her chair as she spoke with the unknown man on the phone while her fingers flew along her computer's keyboard.

"Yes, sir. Thank you, sir." She ended the call and continued to type at a devilish speed on the keys.

"Who was that?" he demanded, moving closer.

She looked up and jumped, a small squeak escaping from her throat. He narrowed his eyes. Why did she look so surprised to see him? Didn't she know he'd been the one in bed with her?

"I thought you were still asleep," she said.

Words that only marginally made him feel better. Even that vanished with her next statement.

"You should get going."

"You're kicking me out?" He stopped when the desk was the only thing between them.

"I'm on my way to the base, so...yes, I suppose I am." She paused and looked around. "Unless you want to sleep and head in later from here." Jaydee didn't meet his gaze when she offered.

Lord help him, he wanted to stay and snoop around her place. He longed to find out what made her tick. "No, I'll get ready." More than that, though, he wanted her to tell him of her own volition about her.

"Okay." She sighed heavily and walked away from the computer.

He swept her up in his arms and carried her to the bathroom where he set her down in the middle of her large shower. Moments later, her robe lay discarded on the floor along with his pants. Tossing his drying clothes away, he drew her into the shower with him and turned on the water.

"Gio, we don't have—"

He didn't let her finish her protest. Repositioning her so she faced the wall, he pressed into her as he used a hand to guide his shaft deep inside her. Her gasp was instantaneous. He nipped along her neck and she whimpered.

"There's always time," he promised as he found a rhythm he liked.

In and out he thrust into her, alternating his speed and lifting her up on her toes with each forward, driving stroke. She clenched him tightly, her heated internal walls rippling around him as he tried to stave off his release until she found hers.

He moved her hands to reach above her head and held them there. Stretching her out. The water ran down them, plastering her hair to her skin, and he shoved it aside and continued his assault on her neck. Beneath him, she writhed and moaned as they moved as one. She came with a high cry, her slit tightening around him. He powered into her three more times before pulling out and coming on the small of her back in a rush that left him lightheaded. They remained like that as they caught their breath before he pressed a kiss to the spot behind her ear. The rest of the shower didn't take too long for them to complete.

Once they'd dried off and dressed, he sat on the foot of her platform bed and watched her swiftly braid her hair. She looked efficient, put together, and...and he hated it. Gio longed to undo what she'd just done and lay her back on the bed. To hell with this shit of leaving at three in the morning to get into work. Officially, they had to be back by oh-seven-hundred. So what had happened for her to be called in so early? His pager hadn't gone off.

He had put on the clothing he'd arrived in—it was now dry. And, as he sat there tying his boots and trying to behave himself, he realised that when he looked at Jaydee he saw something more than a fling. He saw a future with her.

Shit. He dropped his gaze, and, when he'd regained his composure and glanced back up, she was gone. Boots tied, he hurried after her and found her drinking a glass of water.

"Who was that on the phone?" he asked again.

Her gaze shuttered before she shrugged. "Someone I used to work with."

"And he calls you whenever he wants?" His tone was low and dangerous.

"Of course." She turned her glass over in the sink and met his gaze unflinchingly. "Ready?"

No. Not even close. "Sure." He led the way to the door and stopped. "Do you have a car?"

"No. I have a motorcycle."

"It's raining."

"Yes. Come on, I have to get to work."

He slapped his hand against the door, preventing her from opening it. "I don't like you riding that thing in the rain. Let me drive you."

"That would be highly improper and is entirely unnecessary. I've ridden *that thing* plenty in the rain." She opened the door and he noticed how she peered up and down the hall before she let him go.

In the elevator she appeared to be on edge. The only reason he could tell was because her fingers messed with the strap of her bag, continually. At the first floor, he stopped her before she could slide open the solid metal door.

"Jaydee," he said.

She stared up at him, those amazing tortoiseshell eyes wide and innocent. "Yes?"

"Be careful. I'll see you later at work."

He kissed her until he felt her sink into him. Ignoring the pounding insistence of his own libido, he ended it and jerked the door open. Then he walked away without a look back. He dashed through the rain to his car and slid behind the wheel. A few moments later he heard the sound of her bike's engine and watched her drive away, covered in a rain slicker and with the reflective vest visible. Didn't stop his worry, though, and he almost followed her to make sure she got there all right. In the end, he headed for his house.

After he'd changed, he sat there on the couch and stared through the darkened room, out of the windows. There was a chill in this place and he didn't like it. Gio sat like that until the beeping of his alarm clock jarred him from the semi-sleep state he was in. Oh-five-thirty.

Muttering to himself, he strode to his room and grabbed his bag. He tossed it over his shoulder then made his way back to his car and headed to work. He stopped for breakfast on the way at a small diner. The rain had only lessened itself slightly, so he ran inside.

He ate heartily, even as he realised that Jaydee hadn't eaten a thing when she'd got up. She'd drunk some water but that was it. Surely, she must be hungry by now. Shaking his head to rid himself of her, he dug into the meal before him. It didn't work, for she was back to the forefront of his mind as he drove to his parking spot and headed in to change into his flight suit.

As he entered the briefing room, his eyes immediately located Jaydee. She and Keel sat together, their heads close as they talked. He bit back his possessive snarl and nodded at those who said something to him. A few moments later, Lizard collapsed in the seat next to him.

"Have a good weekend, man?" he asked, stretching his legs out before him.

Gio fought the urge to glance over to where Jaydee sat. "Yes, I did. What about you?"

A deep chuckle emerged from the man. "Oh yeah, I had a great time. You know you should have come with me."

"I needed a bit of down time, but thanks."

"Well, Ashley asked about you and hopes you'll come see her on our next time off."

Not likely. He knew exactly where he was going to be the next time they had days off. "Perhaps," he said noncommittally.

"What's up with you, man? You still pining over her?" he asked with a jerk of his chin in Jaydee's direction.

"Why don't you just tell everyone, Lizard," he growled.

"So...that's a yes?"

"Fuck off."

"You haven't figured it out yet, have you?" The taunt fell.

Snapping his head around to glare at his friend, he ground his jaw when their CO walked in.

"Morning," Captain Fentress said. "With this weather, we're going to keep working on some of the situations from yesterday. I want everyone to hit their mark this time. Push the envelope, but make sure you nail it."

Tipping his head down, Gio slanted his gaze to the left, where Jaydee was. Her face was an unreadable mask. The CO had her attention and he wanted it on him. Another growl of possessiveness threatened to slip free when she dipped her head to listen to something Keel said. He clamped his lips together to keep it contained when a slight smile teased the corner of her lip.

"Let's get to it," Fentress barked, slamming the folder shut on the podium he stood behind. It was echoed by a thunderclap, which vibrated the building.

Gio rose with the rest of the pilots and, ignoring Lizard's mocking smirk, hung back as others streamed from the room. He intercepted Jaydee right before the door. With an easy shift, he allowed her to push by him.

"Are you okay?" he asked in a sotto tone.

She smelt fresh and clean. The vivid and clear memory of her in his embrace floated to the top of his mind. The urge to bury his nose in her hair and draw her into his chest nearly overwhelmed him. Her steps carried her away from him and he lengthened his strides to keep close.

"Why wouldn't I be?" She never slowed her movements, swift and sure.

"Because," he said, leaning around her and pushing the door open, "you left at oh-three-hundred this morning."

"No reason to be concerned," she commented. Her body brushed by his in a brief tantalising and teasing moment.

He ground his teeth but didn't say another word. They jogged in silence through the downpour towards their planes. She veered away without a word and he gave her one last look before turning his attention to his own jet.

They all took to the sky and he squinted through the rain until they punched through the storm and flew above it. In staggered formation, they all shot off towards their target, the powerful bombers responding beneath the lightest touches.

Jaydee flew at his left and he snarled silently for the numerous times he had to tell himself to fly his own damn plane and not think about her. He snapped his mask on and shared a glance with Lizard before giving his jet more speed and rocketing back towards earth to complete his dry run.

"Let's light 'em up, Casanova," his friend said before resuming countdown to the target.

On cue, he 'dropped' his payload — which for this exercise was a simulated bomb — and shot away.

"Direct hit! Direct hit!" Lizard called out to him as Gio worked his magic on the controls to avoid being lit up by the tracer lights that were being used as gunfire.

"Never gets old," he said with a smile as the large jet slipped back into the clouds and vanished from view.

"Never, man, never." Lizard kept him aware of what else was going on as he positioned them to where they would fly until the others had finished.

He listened as the others went, one by one, the storm's fury increasing with each tick of time. Finally, it was only Jaydee left and he found himself holding his breath for the words that would start her timing run.

"Alpha Two, you're up. Clock's running," Fentress stated.

"Coming in hot and fast," she retorted. "Don't want to be late."

Keel laughed then it was nothing but business. Lord help him, Gio wanted to see her exercise. Time flew by and he heard a long yell from Keel going on about the direct hit. He wouldn't know how well she had done time-wise in avoiding the tracers until they'd all got back. But he continued to listen until Keel announced their all-clear.

"Let's get back," he called out over the radio.

As one, the group headed back for their base.

"Sounds like she's truly as good as she claims," Lizard said, talking to him and only him, as opposed to everyone over the radio.

"Guess so," he replied, not taking his eyes from the fury of Mother Nature. The gale-force winds shook the bomber. He gritted his teeth as he tightened his hands on the yoke and snapped his mask back on. "Gonna be a bumpy ride home." A chill ran up his spine and he shuddered at the unpleasant sensation.

He sent the rest of his group down, glancing at the radar as well as the other instruments on the panel. A brilliant flash allowed him to see a plane drop beside him into the tumultuous clouds. Another swift glance to his screen confirmed his belief of who it was. Jaydee.

The moment the clouds swallowed her up, he angled his own jet and followed. There was no chatter across the radio as they headed home, everyone focused on returning safe. The thunder up here was louder than anyone could imagine. Lightning jagged its way through the sky and it took his skill to avoid each strike.

"Shit!" Keel's voice crackled across the radio. "We've been hit. We've been hit."

Gio's heart thundered in his chest as he searched for their position. They were still there, but much lower, and they were falling fast.

"Electrical is gone." Keel's voice was broken up over the link. "We're losing power and oil pressure. Flames on the left wing. Flames on the left wing."

Goose bumps exploded across his arms as he immediately went into a dive, needing to get visual contact. Beside him, working in perfect tandem—like usual — Lizard called off the closing distance. The eerie orange glow shone through the dark clouds like a beacon. Out of instinct, he slowed even as Lizard warned him.

There. The B-2 hurtled towards earth, spinning like a top, flames whipping around reminiscent of a fiery cyclone. His heart stopped. As did his ability to breathe. For a moment, all he could see was the jet slamming into the ground. Losing her like he did Mike.

"Shit!" Lizard muttered beside him.

Puck communicated back with the base. There was no other to do it, aside from one of those flying. Since this had been a stormy night run there was no AWACS — Airborne Warning And Control System — up there with them. And he'd be damned if he wasted time filling others in as to what was going on when he had to focus on her and seeing if there was anything he could do to assist.

It was like watching a train wreck unfold before his eyes, knowing there wasn't a damn thing he could do about it. "Eject! Dusti and Keel, damn it! Eject!" he hollered, unsure if they could hear him.

The ground rushed towards them at an alarming speed. He watched, praying to see the top pop off, and them shoot out. Then he would look for two good chutes. It didn't happen. The spinning stopped but the jet was still on a direct course for impact with the ground.

"Help...up...hold..." The intermittent radio spat out parts of the conversation on the tumbling bomber.

Gio could make out that the voice belonged to Jaydee. He shot towards the deck, aware it was dangerous, but uncaring. All the while, they were telling them to pull up and eject. When he thought there was no other option but a crash, the nose of the B-2 lifted, led the jet away from the ground, and back up into the safety of the air. He'd bet anything there was dust blowing up from the near-miss and force of air delivered from the plane.

"Fuck me," Lizard breathed out. "I don't think I've ever seen anyone pull out of a spin like that before."

He had no words, he just elevated his own jet up in the air after them. In truth, he wasn't sure he could say anything, his jaw was clenched and he shook, literally shook. His ears were full of chatter from the other jets and base. He tried to contact Jaydee to no avail. So he manoeuvred two others in front of her to lead them back to base, and he and the fourth trailed her. Four planes around the still burning and damaged one. One of her exhaust ducts still had flames streaming out. Even the heavy rains couldn't douse them.

It was another nail-biting moment for him as he watched her be led in by Puck to get lined up for her landing. At the last moment, Puck gave power and flew away, leaving Jaydee with a free and clear shot. There were flashing lights from emergency ground crews but she landed the plane with very little jarring. Hell, she probably did better than he had. After everyone had landed safely, he climbed down and they dashed through the continuing downpour to the building.

He needed to see her for himself. Needed to ensure she was truly all right. He found the rest of the group hanging out near their CO's office.

"She in there?" he asked, astonished his voice didn't tremble, like he still seemed to be doing on the inside.

"Yes. Her and Keel," Puck said, her hair dripping on her flight suit. "I...wow...I just never—"

"Me either," he said, cutting her off. His knees were a bit shaky, and, with more calm than he felt, he made his way over to a chair and sat in it. It was either that or collapse on the floor.

The door opened and Keel emerged from the office. The man looked a bit rattled but there was a smile on his face. Gio got up and joined the conversation surrounding him, all the while keeping his gaze on the door, waiting for the moment when Jaydee would join them.

When she finally exited the office, his heart caught in his throat. Lord knew all he wanted to do was gather her close and hold her. There was relief on her face and, although it appeared none of the others seemed to pick up on it, he could see the strain in her expression. However, just like everyone else, he offered his congratulations.

They made their way to the locker room and his gaze lingered on her as she, Puck and Tessler headed into the women's side. He showered quickly and kept his chatter with the others brief. Leaning against the wall in the hallway, he straightened when she walked out, bag over one shoulder, and helmet in a gloved hand. Her gaze neither moved to the left nor to the right. In fact, she strode right by him without seeming to notice he was there.

He wanted to follow her outside but his name was called by another and, with a frustrated groan, he ignored the desire to go after her. Once he'd finished talking to Tinman, he made his way back to the door and pushed outside. Her bike was gone.

Chapter Six

Jaydee sank to the floor of her shower and drew her knees up tight to her chest as the hot water fell around her. She wrapped her arms around them and rested her head against her legs. Her entire body shook — she'd managed to hold herself together through not only the incident but also the talk with Captain Fentress and her fellow pilots. All she'd wanted to do was come home and allow the cracks in her composure to splinter, then to rebuild them again.

Her hair plastered to her head as she sat there. She lost track of time as she waited for the chills to stop. The sobs arrived before the shivers stopped, but she didn't move. Only when the water began to cool did she push to her feet. Her limbs shook as she stepped free of the shower and reached for the towel. Her movements were stiff and slow as she dried off. She left the room and walked through the dark of her apartment, her old comfortable robe tied about her waist.

Touching one of her flameless luminaries to turn it on, she used the gentle and flickering light to fill her teapot. As it heated, she gathered the items needed to fix her tea. The familiar motions helped to soothe her wayward nerves. Her hands still shook as she filled the infuser with three tablespoons of her loose-leaf tea. A blend of pure Chinese white tea, jasmine pearls, and rosebuds, it never failed to help her to find calmness and serenity. One of the men she had worked with at the lab had introduced her to it. While she normally only drank water, if it was to be something else she drank tea.

Thunder boomed and she jumped, her heart pounding out of control. The whistle of the kettle snapped her from standing there with one hand over her hammering chest. She grabbed the black pot, filled her mug to the proper line, and put the top on so it could steep for about three minutes. *All I want is to drink my tea and go to bed.* While she waited, she leaned against the cool counter and tried to begin the task of repairing the cracks in her internal armour, so she would be good at work the following day.

Instinctively knowing when her drink was ready, she removed the top, flipped it over, and withdrew the infuser, placing it on the inverted lid. Slowly and with a partially distracted manner, she headed for her couch. Seated on the edge, she blew across the top of her cup and drank the tea. Once she'd had a few sips she set it beside her on the end table, lay her head back, and closed her eyes. That was all it took and she was asleep.

Bam! Bam! Bam!

The noise jerked her upright. She glanced out of the windows wondering if it had merely been thunder. When the intrusive noise came again she realised it hadn't. Her breathing was shallow and rapid as she tried to sort out what was going on. She'd been dreaming of the near crash and could feel the sweat beginning to trickle down her spine.

She got off the couch and made her way to the front door. She felt discombobulated, and like she was swimming through a mire. Wiping a damp hand down her face, she opened the door. Her breath caught in her throat for an entirely different reason this time.

Deep down, she knew she should demand her visitor leave but the words never surfaced. The lights from the hall illuminated him, creating an even more impressive view. His countenance was a mixture of stern concern and tenderness as he studied her intently, raking her up and down with hazel eyes.

She had no time to react before Gio, in a lightning-fast motion, drew her to him. His fingers dug into her flesh as he held her immobile against his body. She could hear him muttering under his breath. As fast as he'd grabbed her, he released her.

Staring up at him, she could see lines of worry in his face. His hands cupped her cheeks and the intensity of his kiss sapped the remaining energy she had. Her knees buckled but his strength held her up. In the back of her mind, she registered the door slamming yet he never stopped kissing her. There was desperation in this exchange and it gnawed at her confidence.

Jerking free, she stumbled back and touched her still tingling lips. She was torn. His kisses were wonderful, amazing, and more. The reaction she'd just had scared her. She didn't need to lose her poise or resilience, not now, and *especially* not in front of the one man who seemed determined to stop her from flying. Gripping the top of her robe closed, she turned on a lamp and stared at the wet man in her apartment.

Gio wore jeans, a T-shirt, a ball cap, and boots. His typical attire. He stared at her, his eyes burning her as he scrutinised her. She became keenly aware that she only wore her nearly threadbare robe. He prowled towards her, every step predatory. His fingers flexed and her heart sped up.

She backed away until she had the cooktop island between them. "Why are you here?" she asked, scrunching her fingers along the cool counter. She wished she had something warm to oppose the chills moving through her.

"Because I almost lost you today. I wanted to see how you were doing." His voice sounded deeper than usual but his words were spoken with quiet emphasis.

More of that doubt crept in and she fought off a shudder. "I'm not yours to lose and I'm fine."

His eyes narrowed dangerously and he leaned towards her over the only thing separating them. The countertop.

"The hell you're not," he growled. "And I doubt you're fine either."

She swallowed and ignored the trembling of her hands. "You should go."

He shook his head and her gaze was mesmerised by the droplets that trailed down the side of his chiselled features. By the time she'd pulled herself free of the allure his body held over hers, he'd manoeuvred his way to her side.

"No. Tell me what happened up there."

Her spine stiffened but she forced a deep breath. Unfortunately, that brought the intoxicating scent of Gio further into her senses. She didn't have it in her to do this right now, and she gave a negative shake of her head, not trusting her voice.

The expression on his face equalled the fury raging beyond her windows. She gulped. Stark determination etched in the lines as well.

"Talk." The order was bitten off.

"Why should I?" she demanded. "I don't owe you a damn thing."

He never took his eyes off her and she felt cornered. Did he not think she could handle herself? Her hackles rose. Frankly, she was tired of constantly having to defend her abilities. She was good, she was *damn* good. Was it so difficult for him to acknowledge the fact?

"What's your problem? That I managed to make it out, or that you realise I actually *do* know how to handle one of the B-2s?"

"Talk me through it," he said, his words calm, soothing.

The shakes started again and she gripped the edge of the counter to keep him from noticing. She didn't want nice. She couldn't *handle* nice. Not right now. And especially not from him.

"Why are you here?" she cried again, cringing at the noticeable high pitch to her voice.

He grunted and made his way to her living room. She remained where she was and just watched him. With one strong hand, he beckoned to her.

"Come here, Jaydee."

The timbre of his voice thrummed through her, making her want to run to him, curl up in his embrace, and just forget the entire thing. That knowledge pissed her off. Showing a weakened stance tended to backfire.

"What?" she snapped. "Are you here to see if I was crying in a corner?" Crossing her arms, she glared at him as something else occurred to her. "Would you be doing this if I wasn't a woman?"

He sighed and walked back over to her, tossing his cap onto a chair as he moved. This time he didn't stop until he had her backed up against the refrigerator. One hand on either side of her head, he lowered his face until it was close to hers.

"Yes." A slight grin. "Well, not the kiss but yes, I would be checking on you."

"Then why aren't you with Keel?"

"Because you need me more." She growled at that but he continued, "Keel is out with some of the guys to forget, and he's already been home to see his wife and baby. I saw it on your face, Jaydee. You need to let it go, or else it will affect you the next time you go up."

Her lower lip trembled and she tried to duck her head but he wouldn't release her gaze. There existed no mocking, no laughter, no anything but sincerity in his hazel eyes. She slipped her tongue out to dampen her lips and nodded.

"Okay."

The single word was so soft she barely heard it herself. Gio immediately backed off and paced her as she made her way to the sofa. She lowered herself to the end cushion and tucked her legs under her, aware of his appreciative gaze upon her exposed skin. Reaching out, she plucked at her robe. Worrying her lower lip, she reached out and touched her forefinger to the mug beside her. Cold. Just like she was.

Gio took a seat at the other end and adjusted his large body so he faced her. His eyes never left her face and she could feel more of the insecurity floating up from her stomach. It didn't seem to matter that he was still wet and probably uncomfortable in his attire, all of his focus remained on her.

She flexed her fingers around the mug, instinctively seeking its warmth, of which there was none. "We went in and did our drop then shot off through the tracers. After we made it clear we climbed back up and waited for you to head us home."

He shifted on the seat, laying one arm along the back. She wanted to touch him, have him help her forget. As if he could read her intentions, he shook his head.

"No distractions, Jaydee. Talk to me." The absoluteness in his tone didn't detract in the slightest from the heat in his eyes.

"It was like a wall of lightning," she muttered as goose bumps exploded up along her skin at the recollection. "I did what I could to avoid it but then one shot horizontally and hit us. I shut the burning engine on that side down but the fire had already caught. Two more strikes came and took out the stabiliser and the AI. It took us a bit to shut off the autopilot so we wouldn't be flying inverted, but by then we were already in the spin."

Her heart began to pound faster and faster and she dug her nails into her palms. The pain helped centre her and she knew she would have half-moons carved into her skin but she didn't care. It helped her focus.

"Keep going."

Her stomach knotted tight and she tried to control her breathing. "We lost oil pressure and hit a pocket of wind which first sent us into a spin. It took me a few moments to snap out of my daze and get my bearings. I went cold then hot again, hoping it would refire. It did and I had manual control. Hard and shaky but I had it."

Bile rose in her throat as she recalled staring out of the jet and seeing the rain and clouds whip around her along with the flames. She licked her lips and kept her eyes on the tattered edge of her robe, not wanting to face him.

"Keel came to and was able to help me pull it up."

She couldn't hide the tremors racking her body. Not anymore. He reached for her and she drew back as far as the sofa allowed. *Damn him, if he touches me, I'll lose it.* "We landed and, well, you know the rest."

The room spun a bit and she bit back a whimper. Her breaths were coming faster and shallower.

"Jaydee."

"I don't…can't…"

His hands closed about her upper arms, grip tight, yet gentle. He gave her no chance to pull away, just drew her close and lifted her, settling her over his legs. His pants were a bit damp and abraded the insides of her thighs slightly.

"Let me go," she snapped. "I don't need to hear you say this is why women shouldn't fly."

He shook her, not hard, but enough to garner her full attention. "Shut up, Jaydee. What you did tonight was fucking impressive."

"For a woman?" she asked in a snide tone.

His expression sobered. "No, for a pilot, Jaydee. Fucking impressive for any pilot." He sank his hands in her hair at the back of her head, his fingers massaging her scalp. "And you, Jaydee, are one hell of a pilot."

She stared in his eyes, searching for the deceit, only to find nothing but honesty. Even his statement had been straightforward. This was new for her, these feelings, and having someone do what Gio had.

"Thank you," she said.

He urged her closer to him and she willingly went. It felt so wonderful, having someone who appeared concerned about her. Someone who understood she wasn't a machine, but a person.

With a whimper, she clenched his shirt in one fist and surrendered to the tears that poured free. He never said a word, just offered her silent support. He held her tight, one hand rubbing her back in circular motions, the other remaining in her wet hair against her head.

Being held by this man made things right. She burrowed closer, accepting the comfort. Her exhausted body won and she closed her eyes in defeat.

Just a few more seconds.

Jaydee stirred before she froze. *What? Was it all a dream?* She cracked open her eyes to darkness. The sound of rain on the windows was the only noise and she stifled a yawn. All the adrenaline had left and she couldn't begin to explain how fatigued she remained.

An arm slid along her waist before resting on her hip. A hand splayed against her belly. *Gio.* She knew immediately who it was, for he was the only man she'd ever fallen asleep with.

"Go back to sleep," he said, spooning against her and pressing a kiss behind her ear.

She rotated in his embrace so they were chest to chest. His warm skin smelt like sandalwood and spice. Burrowing as close as she could, she brushed a kiss against his chest before doing just that. Going back to sleep.

When her alarm went off at oh-four-hundred, she was still wrapped up with the hard body that had held her all through the night. Wriggling free, she flopped over and floundered for her alarm. A satisfied groan left her once the offensive, blaring noise had ceased.

"Ever thought of getting an iPod docking station to wake up to music, or one of those things which have soothing nature sounds, instead of that demonic noise?" Gio's question rumbled from behind her.

She sat up and turned on her bedside lamp. The soft light permeated the room. Feet on the floor, she waited. Waited for the recollection of yesterday's incident to overtake her. Nothing happened.

A warm palm settled upon the small of her back. Gio's touch made her ready to melt. He didn't even have to speak—a simple gesture was more than enough for her.

"Jaydee?"

"Alarms are to get you out of bed, not relax you more so you fall back asleep, or sleep through it."

The mattress dipped as he shifted behind her. His lips moved up her spine and along her right shoulder. Her body craved his.

"Where's the Jaydee I met at the bar?"

"Hidden away," she said with candour. He halted her when she began to rise.

"Where are you going?"

"Workout, shower, eat, then head to work."

He tugged hard on her so she fell back. Gio loomed over her, his eyes almost golden with the faint light. He stroked the side of her face with two knuckles before he kissed her.

"Workout is just what I had in mind." His voice was low and gravelly.

After he'd made long slow love to her and they'd shared a shower, Jaydee sat on one of her bar stools, dressed and ready for work while Gio fixed them breakfast. The first strands of morning's light began to beat back the dark of night.

"Tell me about what it was like for Jaydee growing up." He cracked eggs in the pan with one hand and met her gaze.

She hooked her feet on the rungs and stared down at the glass of freshly squeezed orange juice before her. He'd actually cut up and juiced oranges to make the drink for her. She heard him at the sink washing his hands, then two fingers lifted her chin up.

"Jaydee?"

"Not much to tell. It was..." she searched for the right word, "structured."

"I know you said your mother left when you were young but was your father strict?"

She thought for a moment about a response and reached for her water. He plucked it from her hands and put the orange juice in its place.

"Drink your juice."

Astonished by the fact that he was actually fixing her food, she turned the glass.

"Drink," he reiterated.

She did. The juice slid down her throat and she damn near purred in pleasure. His grin and the sparkle in his eyes told her he understood. The next look he gave her told her he wanted his answer.

"Obviously, I never really knew my mother. You know she left when I was young. I used to have a photo of her, one picture. It was of the two of us, actually." She shrugged, disturbed by the feelings reliving this brought her. "For a while anyway. Then it was...lost, I guess."

"I'm sorry you didn't know your mother. So, then, it was just you and your father? Or do you have siblings?"

Honestly, she had no clue if she had brothers or sisters. "He raised me. No siblings."

Gio scooped eggs onto plates and placed two slices of buttered wheat toast on as well. Some cut-up melon and sausage links completed her plate.

"Eat."

The first bite had her stomach ready for more. As she ate, she realised no one had cooked for her, ever. *Well, no man I've slept with. But then I've ever only spent the night with Gio.* Even so, she couldn't imagine any of her past relationships caring enough to cook for her. But, to be fair, she wouldn't have done so for them either. There was only one she could think of who might have, but their being together had been purely about sexual release, nothing more. He'd cooked for her after their relationship had become purely platonic.

He constantly watched her and she shifted under his scrutiny. After finishing, she sipped the remainder of her juice while waiting for Gio to be done. Silent, she gathered up the dishes and placed them in her sink. She'd do them when she got home. Uncertainty settled. Now what?

With more confidence than she felt, she raised her head and met his waiting gaze. He leaned on the beige countertop and gave her a wink. Instantly, all she could think about was how nice it had been in his arms. Each time with him got better and better.

She licked her lips and his eyes followed the motion. "We need to get to work." She backed away from the increasingly predatory look in his eyes.

He glanced at his wristwatch and gave her a darkly sensual and wicked smile. "Yes, we do." Then he lunged for her.

Chapter Seven

Gio leaned against the bar and dangled the bottle from his fingertips. He was at a farewell party for Tessler, Puck, Tinman and their co-pilots. They'd been called up to join a squadron overseas. At first he'd been jealous that his name hadn't been selected. Then he realised that, by staying here, he got to remain closer to Jaydee. Everyone was here for the celebration. Correction, everyone but Keel—he was on babysitting duty, since his wife had a double shift to work—and Jaydee.

Keel he understood, but where the fuck was Jaydee? It had been two weeks since the near-death incident. Damned if Jaydee hadn't treated him like he was any other man. As if they were strictly colleagues, she did her job and left, barely speaking to him unless absolutely necessary. He hated it. How could she ignore the passion that flared between them—combustible like a spark and gasoline.

"You're looking bored, Casanova. Everything okay?"

He glanced to the waitress who stood at his right shoulder. A slender, attractive blonde. Lauren.

"Hey, Lauren. I'm just lost in thought."

Her smile was soft and inviting. And, in the past, he would have taken her up on the obvious offer. He *had* done so. However, now, the only one he could think about in that way was Jaydee. Awake or asleep, she existed in his thoughts. As if she was a part of him. Blood. Heart. Soul.

A hand settled on his back and he waited for the familiar tingle a woman's touch brought him. Nothing. *Damn it!* He'd hoped Lauren's caress would have snapped him from the desire for his hot Lieutenant Commander Amos. How wrong he'd been.

There was nothing. No spark. No tingle. No anything. For all intents and purposes, it could have been Lizard clapping him on the back.

Bottom line…he was fucked. Any way he looked at it. Royally and totally fucked.

Jaydee Amos had been in his life for two months now and it was harder each day to pretend that not a single thing existed between them other than work. His emotions were always extreme in regards to her. Horny as hell or angry as shit.

When he thought of her flying, he grew furious. It didn't matter that he knew she was good at her job, damn good, it still bothered the crap out of him. And he knew it showed. Then, when he saw her, everything changed. He saw her and thought sex. She walked by in a flight suit and his cock hardened to titanium.

A nudge to his shoulder brought his attention from lustful thoughts of Jaydee. Of wrapping her legs around his waist as he pounded into her.

"Casanova?"

Damn, I need to focus. Lauren watched him with large, jade green eyes, a mixture of understanding and craving in them. She had one elbow braced against the smooth expanse of the polished bar top. Her tray beside her with a few empty bottles and glasses on it.

He sighed. "Yes, Lauren?"

"You look like...well...you could use some sex."

His chuckle lacked humour. *You have no idea.* "Just a lot on my mind, Lauren."

She reached out and stroked idly up and down his arm. "You know all you have to do is call, right?"

Yes, he knew. Much like he knew that was all any of the other pilots had to do. Call her. He opened his mouth to respond but Lauren spoke again.

"I really don't know why she comes in here."

Tipping the bottle up, he took a drink before asking, "Who?"

"Jaydee. I mean she only drinks water." A scoff of derision. "This is a bar for crying out loud. She doesn't even drink soda. Just the same old thing. Water. Don't get a lot of tips for water."

Gio whipped his head around and fought the immediate groan that seeing Jaydee brought to his mouth. It was as if the room had narrowed down to the two of them, for all his attention zoomed in on her.

Jaydee wore a plain gold T-shirt, jeans, and black boots. Her hair was windblown as if she'd ridden without a helmet. *Shit!* His cock fought valiantly to punch free from the pants that restrained it.

She smiled gently at Puck who met her. Then her gaze landed on him and he immediately drowned in her tortoiseshell eyes. She gave him a slight nod and moved on, accompanied by Puck, back to where the others mostly hung out.

Over-familiar strokes on his arm made him almost growl. Lauren had been stroking his arm as if she'd every right to do so. Jaydee had seen it. *You have no claim over her,* his brain chided.

The fuck he didn't.

Swallowing hard, he pushed from the stool and spun on his heel. He paused at the touch Lauren placed on his arm. "Yes?"

"The offer always stands, Casanova."

He stared at her. Lauren was a beautiful woman. Her blonde hair, green eyes, and creamy skin made an extremely attractive package. But one that did nothing for him.

"Right." He strode off, beer in hand.

As he approached the table, he was met by grins and smirks. "I see Lauren tracked you down," Lizard said. "From the look on her face she's gonna get to be with Casanova tonight."

Gio sat in a chair across from Jaydee who drank...water. Holding her gaze, he took a slow drink of his nearly empty beer. He cut his gaze to Lizard and gave him a small, untelling smile. His friend roared in laughter.

"I knew it."

Gio swung his attention back to Jaydee. She paid him no attention. In fact, she no longer sat there—he was treated to the natural sway of her hips. As he watched, she, Puck, Tessler and Tinman began to play a game of pool.

Lust slammed him as Jaydee caressed her pool cue before bending over to break. He felt heat course through him and his cock pressed insistently against his jeans. *Christ! That ass of hers would make a monk sin.* Given that he wasn't even remotely close to a monk, it did way more than that to him.

Anger churned at his gut as he watched her laugh and mingle with those around her. She was so reserved when interacting with him—polite yet reserved. Hell he'd stopped by her place a few times since the incident and she'd never even answered the door. He'd been unable to get her alone. And that fact drove him crazy.

"Evening, Casanova." The deep voice preceded his CO lowering his body into a vacant seat.

"Good evening, sir." He straightened up in his chair and tore his hungry gaze from Jaydee's ass.

The man's grey eyes meandered between him and the four at the pool table. "No pool for you?" he asked.

"Not this game, sir."

Captain Fentress, aka Renegade, rose, took a drink and said, "Let's play."

He dutifully followed his CO to the table next to the one that Jaydee played at. He ensured he brushed past the woman who made him hornier than a young man while he grabbed two cues, and he grinned at her sharp intake of breath.

"Excuse me," he breathed softly.

"Not a problem." Her response was bland and hid the emotion he knew simmered beneath her composed surface.

He longed to drag his tongue along the shell of her ear, press her against him, and tell every slobbering fucking male in the establishment she was *his*. Beyond everything, he saw Lizard and Lauren talking and his gut clenched. Not with jealousy but uncertainty. The gleam in Lizard's gaze made him wonder what nefarious plan he had put into play.

Playing a game with one's CO was hard enough, but when you added outside forces to the mix it became damn near impossible. He did his best to concentrate but he continually grew hard and distracted by Jaydee. The way she touched the pool cue, how delectable her ass looked when she bent over for her shot, and even the sound of her laughter.

Pathetic? Perhaps, but he couldn't help it.

For those reasons and more, he lost. Fentress laughed as he began to rack them a second time.

"Mind's not on the game, Casanova."

"He's got a hot date with a blonde later on. I'd be distracted too." Lizard spoke up.

Fentress nodded. "Ahh, I understand. Up for another game?"

Gio shared a glance with Lizard before rolling his shoulders. "Yes, sir."

Puck came and joined them, so it was he and Lizard against Puck and Renegade. Still, his attention meandered to where Tessler and Jaydee stood talking and laughing back along a wall.

"Focus, man," Lizard hissed in his ear.

"I am."

"Bullshit. Well, perhaps not, but I need you to focus on the game, not her."

Catching a waitress' eye, he ordered another drink, using the time to ogle Jaydee. She walked with Tessler towards them.

"Are you leaving?" Puck tilted her head as she asked.

Jaydee smiled, another innocent action that slammed into him hard.

"Yes. I have things to attend to. It has been an honour serving with you."

Puck stood. "You too."

The women embraced before Jaydee moved on to the others who were leaving. With a quick glimpse at him, Lizard, and Captain Fentress, she strode off with nothing more than a goodnight. Gio watched her leave from beneath lowered lashes.

All he wanted to do was follow her. Kiss her. Fuck her. He bit back a groan and forced his attention on the game. It took a while but eventually her face settled in the back of his mind.

When he finally called it a night, said his farewells to those leaving, and headed to his car after paying his tab, he found Lauren resting against the side of his convertible.

"I've been waiting for you." She had a coy look in her eyes.

"Not tonight, Lauren. I'm exhausted." And he was. He wanted his bed. Although he had no doubts that if Jaydee called him up asking for sex he'd find some energy. A hell of a lot.

"You've never been too exhausted before," she whined.

The sound grated on his nerves. "Don't push, Lauren, it's unbecoming." He gently lifted her away from his door and opened it. "Lizard is inside if you want him."

"No, I want you, Casanova." She pressed against his back and rubbed. "I've always wanted you."

The feel of her pert breasts against his back failed to stimulate him, even remotely. "Goodnight, Lauren." He climbed in and drove away, leaving her there in the lot, probably furious and definitely alone. He knew she didn't like being ignored.

He mulled over it all while he drove. It wasn't a one-time thing anymore. He wanted no one but Jaydee. The feel of another woman had no effect on him, whereas the mere thought or glimpse of Jaydee could send him close to coming in his pants.

He took a long shower—a cold one—when he got home, to try to negate the power Jaydee had on him. Nothing worked. With a muted groan, he flopped naked onto his California king-sized bed.

Tomorrow was a day off and he knew exactly where he was going in the early morning. The thought calmed him a bit and he eventually began to relax.

* * * *

Jaydee sat on the edge of the table, her booted feet swinging back and forth as she waited. The room was silent except for the hum of the computers. She tucked some wayward hair behind one ear without stopping her feet. Palms on the desk, fingers curved about the edge, she lifted her head and stared at the person in front of her.

He was an imposing man. Tight black hair clipped close to his head. Tall and broad-shouldered, he filled out the white lab coat he wore. He had skin the hue of pumpernickel. He wore small rectangular glasses and had on a turtleneck and slacks under the coat.

She, on the other hand, wore steel-toed boots, jeans, and a T-shirt. Honestly, she felt a bit underdressed. Not that he would care—it was her problem, her hang-up. Not his.

He raised his head and pinned her with ochre eyes. A heavy sigh before he glanced back down to the tablet PC he held.

"Are you positive about this?" he questioned. His voice was as authoritative as she recalled.

"Yes, sir."

"And you filed a report with your CO?"

"Yes, sir. An exact duplicate to what you're reading now."

"You don't think this is like the *Spirit of Kansas,* where there was moisture in the aircraft's Port Transducer Unit which appeared during the air calibration?"

Jaydee shook her head and jumped off the table before approaching him. She barely reached his shoulder. But she wasn't scared, she knew her shit. And knew he knew she did, too.

"Not at all. There was no distorted information sent to the air data system like what happened with B-2 89-0127. Plus, this accident didn't happen during take-off. Had he had an extra thirty-degree pitch he could have corrected, regardless of the negative angle of attack. It's not the same thing."

He stared at her without blinking and took a deep breath. "So you've concluded it happened because of the antigravity—"

The door swung open and brought their conversation to a halt. In walked Captain Fentress and he was followed by a few other men she didn't know. Only when the last man entered and closed the door behind him did her breath catch. Gio.

He wore his flight suit and it was all she could do to keep her moan contained. He had the look of just getting out of the shower and she shifted her feet. Like a predator, his gaze snapped to her and burned her to the soles of her feet. It took more work than normal but she managed to remain composed, and to continue with her coolly professional demeanour.

Gio stood at the back of the room while the others sat down at two of the tables, facing her and the man beside her. He crossed his arms over his chest and fixated his stare on her. She barely heard Captain Fentress introduce the man beside her since she was so tuned in to the man at the back.

"Yes, like your captain said, my name is Dr Thompson."

That got her attention and she swiftly moved to a vacant chair off to the side where she could see and listen. Out of the corner of her eye, she noticed Gio move so that he lingered more in her peripheral line of vision. With a groan, she determinedly ignored him and focused on the lecture.

"Commander." A voice whispered in her ear.

She looked over her shoulder and found Fentress there on his haunches by her.

"Sir?" She glanced at him only to be met with a blank expression. "What can I do for you, sir?"

"You're going up. Keel's waiting for you so get changed and get moving."

Going up? This morning she'd been informed her day was to be spent here analysing the results with the fellow scientists. Dr Thompson had asked for her to be there. Seeing Captain Fentress and Gio had thrown her, as she'd not expected them to stop in. It wasn't unheard of having pilots come by to listen, but mostly it remained just the geeks.

"Amos, now!" The order fell firm with no room for dispute.

"Sorry, sir."

She slanted a glance up to where Dr Thompson continued to talk. He gave a nod without breaking his speech and she immediately rose and crept to the door, eyes purposefully down to avoid the penetrating and heated stare from Gio. Even so, she could feel his gaze upon her.

In a short time, she strode across the grounds to where her bomber waited for her along with Keel. Helmet tucked under her arm, she drew up at the wheel to her plane. Yes, hers.

"Hey." Keel gave her a nod.

"Do you know what's going on?"

"No clue, Dusti. Hell, we weren't even on the schedule to go up today."

They did the pre-flight checks in silence before stopping by the steps again. She held his light brown gaze and quirked her lips. "Oh well, good thing I love being up in the air. Let's do it." Keel nodded and climbed up while she faced her mechanic. "Are we all good, Sedin?"

The man smiled. "Right as rain, ma'am."

The wind blew and ruffled over her skin like a lover's caress. Immediately she envisaged Gio and his touch. Lifting her chin, she hesitated for a bit and just enjoyed the breeze. She could smell the jet fuel and a soft smile filled her expression.

"Excellent." She clapped him on the shoulder and scampered up into the waiting stealth bomber.

Once she and Keel were both ready, she contacted the tower and took them up into the endless sky.

"I never thanked you, Dusti." Keel's baritone split the quiet.

Flicking him a glance, she arched a brow. "What do you feel the need to thank me for?"

"Keeping us alive."

Her belly unconsciously clenched as the memories flashed to the surface. Maintaining a composed expression, she swallowed before responding.

"You never have to thank me. We fly together."

"I know, but I still want to thank you. So does my wife. She would love to have you over for dinner."

Shocked, she gaped at him. Sure, she'd been invited out to the bars with the other pilots but had never had any home invites prior to this.

"Please. At least think about it?"

"Alpha Two." The radio crackled.

Snapping her mask on, she nodded her consent to Keel and responded to the orders that came in. They ran repeated landings and take-offs. As if they were doing traps on a carrier. Was she curious as to why? Yes. Did she verbally question her orders? Hell no. That was not her way. She liked order. She followed orders. She didn't do waves or ripples.

Except when it came to Giovanni Cassano. With him, *all* bets were off.

They screeched down and her attention went back to the task before her. Powering back up, the black bomber rose gracefully back into the sky. The plane trembled and instinctively she corrected, all the while checking the numerous panels displayed before her.

"Keel?"

"I'm checking, Dusti. I don't know."

The wings rocked and she had to use a lot of strength to keep her steady.

"Tower. We've got something going on here."

"Bring her in, Dusti," Fentress' voice reached her.

"Roger that, sir, we're on our—"

Another shudder that rolled the bomber to about a forty-five degree angle.

"Shit!"

She corrected, muscles beginning to strain with the effort to hold them level. The plane went again and this time she had to get Keel's help to hold her.

"What the fuck?" she muttered.

"What's going on, Alpha Two?"

"Shutting off autopilot, flying manually." She did it and felt the jet lurch immediately to the left when she took one hand to flip the switch.

The response the plane gave made a grin crack her visage. Something had gone wrong with the stabiliser.

She knew that now. The plane had thought they had been flying inverted and had been trying to fix the problem. Which was why she had switched to manual control.

"Alpha Two?"

"On our final approach now." She glanced to Keel. "Did you see anything different with the AI? Did it invert?"

"No." Keel relaxed his hands and helped her line up for landing. "I thought maybe it had, but no."

Great. Another issue. No time to worry about that right now. She had to get this bird down safely.

Landing on manual had always been harder than on auto. But Jaydee was one hell of a pilot. No matter what people might have said about her, she *was* one of the best. Hell, hadn't she managed to get them out of the previous thing? Yes, she had. This was much easier — she had all engines and no flames.

Still, her breaths only came without hesitation once the large bomber had coasted to a stop. She unfurled her fingers from the control stick and glanced at Keel. His brown eyes contained a mixture of relief and excitement. She knew hers were the same. For a pilot, the rush was everything. That pumping adrenaline made the job.

"That was fun," she said, trying for a joke.

His gaze twinkled. "Never a dull moment with you, Dusti."

"Alpha Two, it's going to be a bit before you can leave. We have to wait out the lingering static."

"Roger that." She shook her head. And another problem. They'd not used the EG today, so that shouldn't have even been an issue. And yet...apparently it was. Sure, they could lower their ladders and risk it but why do that? Ending up in the hospital because of a shock would be foolish.

Slipping from the seat, she stood and made her way back to the makeshift cot they had and sat on it. The bomber even had a little kitchenette for those very long flights. Bottom line—these jets weren't your average ones.

Keel sat beside her and sighed heavily as his chin dropped to rest on his chest.

"I'm sorry," she whispered, an added precaution on the off-chance they could be overheard. She had no desire to let everyone else hear her apology.

"What for?" His question was posed in the same low tone.

"I'm beginning to feel like a jinx given what's—"

"Stop it." His interruption was harsh.

She snapped her mouth shut, just now remembering how superstitious pilots were. *How could I have forgotten?* She was analytical, not one to go on superstitions.

"Right."

"Look at me, Dusti." His words were calmer now. Licking her lips, she lifted her gaze to meet his. "Are you doubting yourself?"

She nibbled on her lower lip. "No."

"Good. I'm not, either."

Jaydee understood and she smiled her thanks. "May I ask you something?"

He flashed a grin that showed her a devil-may-care attitude. "Of course."

She knew they should be doing work, or at least keeping in contact with the tower. Instead, they sat together on the cot.

"Who did Lieutenant Walker go up with that day?"

Keel stiffened. Slightly, but she noticed.

"He didn't."

She frowned. Her report and findings had been based on the knowledge that the pilot known as Sidewinder had been with another pilot in the jet. Even though talking to that person wasn't an option. A pilot named Wicked was unable to be located.

"I thought he had someone with him." She kept her tone gentle with the hint of curiosity. Yes, the B-2s were technically two-pilot bombers, but they were so advanced one person *could* fly solo.

Keel sighed and leaned closer. Jaydee waited with bated breath for his response.

"Casanova and Lizard were scheduled for that flight."

Her palms grew damp and her heart skipped a beat at the thought of never having met Gio.

"What happened?"

"Casanova injured his shoulder two days prior and wasn't cleared to go back up. Sidewinder offered immediately to fly the mission in his plane. Fentress agreed." He shifted and his leg brushed hers. "I'm not sure why, but Lizard wasn't available the day of. Scuttlebutt said he was in the ER. Apparently, whatever happened between Sidewinder and Fentress resulted in Mike going up alone."

Unease filled her and she made her way to the kitchenette. Before long she'd found the bottled water and had handed one to Keel. All the while, she mulled over his words.

"Dusti!" a loud, angry male voice said over the radio. "What is going on in there?"

She walked back up to her seat and sat. "Nothing's going on, sir. Just getting warm in here and these seats are in the sun. We've been in the back drinking water to stay hydrated."

As she spoke, more sweat ran down the back of her neck and followed her spine. She—well, they—had removed their helmets in an effort to lower core temperatures. Hell, personally, she was all for stripping out of the flight suits and staying cooler in the tank top and shorts she wore beneath the one-piece suit. Not an option. She needed to pee, and still she forced herself to continue with drinking. She took herself out of the sun and sat back on the cot.

It grew exponentially hotter and, with a mutter of discontent, she rose and walked back to the seat she piloted from. She could see black clouds rolling in.

"Storm's coming," Keel uttered, taking his seat as well.

"Yes. Least it should cool down."

Her eyes drifted closed, grateful the sun had been concealed behind the tumultuous clouds. She couldn't let go of the information Keel had imparted to her and continued to run through it in her head while they waited.

"Come on out, Alpha Two." Their CO's voice broke the companionable silence.

Instantly alert, she did the necessary sequence to lower their steps. The outside air cooled them as it blew around, creating little dust cyclones off the runways. They each climbed down and found almost every one of the ground crew watching. Expressionless, she skimmed the crowd, then she tucked her helmet under her arm and headed for her mechanic.

"I'm so sorry, ma'am, I—"

"I don't think it was you, Sedin. But I need you to do something."

Relief spilled over the concern. "Anything, ma'am." His reply came without pause.

"Pull the AI for me. Run a calibration and note what you see. And, Sedin, I want *you* to do this. Top priority." She held his gaze.

Sedin nodded, his café-au-lait face taking on a serious expression. "Aye, Commander. Right away."

"Good man. Call me with the results as soon as you have them. Thank you, Sedin."

As she pushed into the building, she rubbed her eyes. They adjusted to the darker interior and she strode towards her locker room.

"Amos."

She froze even as she stifled a groan. All she wanted was a bathroom, shower, and food. Swiping her tongue along her lips, she spun towards the man who'd called her name. Dr Thompson.

"Yes, sir?"

"A word."

Jaydee walked to the door he stood in. She entered and felt the light touch from his hand at the base of her spine. When she turned to close the door, per the doc's order, she hesitated at the sight of Gio in the hall leaning against the wall. His gaze was harsh and angry as he glared. She sighed and shut the door, blocking out the temptation of Giovanni Cassano.

Chapter Eight

Gio stewed. He raged. He fumed.

Working out hadn't helped curb the excess energy he had. No, it had only magnified it. He rolled his shoulders and went back to attacking the heavy bag before him.

Who the fuck does that damn Dr Thompson think he is to put his hands on Jaydee? She's mine!

Arrogant? Possibly... Probably.

Determined? Yes.

Possessive? Most definitely.

Would he change? Hell no.

What existed between him and Jaydee may have once been based on a sexual attraction but it had changed, morphing into something more.

He liked being in her presence. She was wicked smart—scarily so. Took her job even more seriously than he did, which was hard to comprehend on so many levels. Hell, he was damn near fanatical. Yet, Jaydee was harder on herself than he'd even been on himself.

She made him want to protect her, for, despite how amazing a pilot she was, how brilliant she was, she—at times—seemed lost and insecure. He wanted the right to keep those fears at bay.

She was a brilliant and sexy woman on one hand and, on the other, innocent and unsure.

He couldn't get her expression from his mind when he had told her that, no, he hadn't run to the store for juice, he'd squeezed it fresh. It was as if he'd handed her the moon. A look he longed to keep on her face. Another look he liked on her as well...he gave a wry grin.

The moment his attention returned to Dr Thompson a scowl replaced the smirk from seconds before. He had no reason to be around Jaydee, in his opinion. The thought that this was a man she'd worked closely with at her other job aggravated him to no end.

His phone rang, snapping him to the here and now. "Commander Cassano."

"You do know your girl is out with that guy, right?" Lizard said by way of a greeting.

He ground his jaw and wiped a towel down his sweaty face. "Where?"

"Garrett's Place."

A flood of words not fit for polite company passed his lips. He stomped to the door, not even making an effort to quell his jealous rage.

"Be smart about this, Casanova."

He growled. "No."

"Damn it, man. Think about your career."

"Shouldn't have told me. Goodbye, Lizard." He hung up on him and slammed from his workout room.

His phone rang twice more while he got cleaned up and he ignored both calls. Shoving into his jacket, he left the house and slid behind the wheel of his car. He tried to calm down but nothing worked. All he could envision was that professor-geek-doctor man placing his hands on Jaydee. Peeling off her clothing and…

His fingers clenched tight around the wheel and he forced them to loosen. Revving the engine, he drove to Garrett's Place. He found a parking spot, locked his car, and headed for the front door.

Garrett's was a mid-scale restaurant. They had a bar on one side and a sit-down eatery on the other. He strode straight for the bar. After glaring a man out of the seat he wanted, he sat and stared into the sit-down part.

Jaydee and her 'date' were seated at a table off to the side. A cosy one, for two people who probably wanted something intimate. The man wore the same as he had at the base but Jaydee had changed. In the light, he could see the pale blue of her outfit and a red haze settled back over his eyes again.

As they ate, he drank. His gaze remained fixated upon the couple. When they had finished—again no dessert for Jaydee—he settled his tab and escaped out first. A veritable feat, considering how tipsy he'd become.

He leaned against the wall and waited. Sure enough, they soon walked out, talking quietly between themselves. He almost managed to not say a word. Almost. Then that man put his hand on Jaydee's lower back in a highly familiar way.

"Hey!" he shouted and pushed away from the wall.

Jaydee and her date paused and faced him. He recognised the surprise on her face. When he watched the man reach across her body and touch her hip, the rest of his control snapped.

"Don't you fuckin' touch her!" he hollered in warning.

The doctor narrowed his gaze, one hand lifted, and Gio reacted. There was no thinking it through, he just struck out. A sickening grin lifted his lips as the crunch of a busted nose could be felt. He countered a return punch but got hit under the eye regardless. The sting from the ring cutting into his skin made his eyes water.

"Gio!" Jaydee cried. "Stop this!" She immediately inserted herself between them. He halted his next strike—he'd never hurt her.

The world shifted and spun around him. He was slow to react when two others jumped in and restrained him. He struggled but was too damn drunk to fend them off with any favourable outcome for him. Eyes locked on Jaydee, he tried to get to her. She glared at him in the parking lot light, before she turned her back on him to tend to the man with the bloody nose.

He wanted to get to her side. Tell her that she meant more to him than any woman he'd ever met before. He couldn't get the words out. He tried, but no one seemed to be listening.

Time blurred and, when he blinked away another round of the spins, he was in the back of a squad car. *What the fuck?* He shifted and winced at the feel of the flex cuffs tight against his wrists. His right eye stung like hell and his head still swam. Nausea rode him hard and he swallowed to keep it down. After the car stopped, he found himself being led into the station by a burly officer with a scowl on his face.

He didn't put up any resistance when they booked him and put him in holding. Scowling at the numerous men in with him, he stumbled to the back and secured himself a seat in the darkest corner.

Christ, what did I do to get put here? He recalled... "Ahh, shit." A crystalline recollection of his fist connecting with Dr Thompson's nose flashed. He dropped his head into his hands with a groan. *I am so screwed.*

How was he going to explain to Captain Fentress that he'd got drunk and punched a man who was a visitor to their test facility? And as to *why* he did it? Well, that was easy. The man had touched Jaydee in an overly familiar manner. Yes, the same Jaydee who was actually Lieutenant Commander Amos whom he worked with, and yes, he was well aware of the impropriety of having any personal relationship with her.

Yep, should go over real well. Maybe they'd keep him locked up in here for a while. Just until his CO calmed down a bit.

"Hey, man!"

He lifted his head slowly. A trio of men stood there and he cocked a brow. "What?" he snapped. Apparently, he wasn't sober enough to remain quiet and stay out of trouble, not even in jail.

"You're in our seat."

He leaned back against the wall and stretched his legs out before him. "All three of you in this one seat? Must be so cosy. Fuck off! I'm sitting here." He didn't rise, not even when they growled and stepped closer.

"Who do you think you are?" the middle man demanded.

"The one sitting here who wishes you'd shut up."

"We're gonna bust you up," the skinny man growled.

This time he got to his feet, the alcohol still powerful enough to goad him into another confrontation. "Really? You wanna do this? Let's." He stepped flush to the man in the middle who looked like the leader and grabbed his shirt. "You go around challenging people, jackass, you'd better be prepared to fight. Well, I am."

"Knock it off!" a deep voice barked.

Gio released him with a growl and a shove. He watched them slink away. Then he focused on where the other voice had come from. He was still spoiling for a fight. A cop stood there and beside him...Jaydee.

She no longer wore the blue dress that had moulded to her like a lover. Now she wore white hip-hugger jeans, a blue T-shirt, and blue shoes. Sobriety slammed into him and he moved towards her as if on a thread. She tossed him a quick glance but it was enough to share the rage she felt for him.

"He's the one," she said in an inflectionless tone.

"I'll be the one," a guy hollered from the other side of her and he bit back his possessive growl.

Jaydee never even cracked a smile. As he was released from the cell, she ran another disapproving gaze over him. He gave her a sheepish grin that had no effect on the ice surrounding her.

Without a word, she walked off, leaving him to follow. Shortly after, they were treading down the precinct's steps. At her bike, he reached out and touched her arm. Her stare slashed to him and froze him it was so cold. Arctic would be a better word.

"Jaydee—"

"Shut up, Gio."

He tightened his grip on her and tried again.

"No," she interrupted. "You zip it and get on the bike or I call you a taxi."

He released her and swung a leg over her bike. The muscles in her jaw flexed a few times before she climbed on in front of him. His gut clenched as her evocative scent filled him and, true to form, his body responded.

When she frowned at him over her shoulder, he got the message and gratefully wrapped his arms around her waist. His cock got even harder than when he'd first seen her there at the jail. The rumble of the engine prompted him to slide even closer. They wore no helmets and he sniffed her hair while struggling against the urge to nuzzle it along with the back of her neck.

She rolled them towards the exit only to pause. "Where do you live?"

"My car's at Garrett's."

"I figured that, considering you got arrested. You're still too drunk to drive. What's your address?"

He murmured it in her ear, revelling in the way her breath seemed to catch. She didn't ask him anything else, nor did she say another word as she drove to his house.

Jaydee handled the bike like a pro and he had no problem with the fact that he rode on the back. She was in his arms again, that was all that mattered to him. They slowed before she turned into his driveway. He climbed off and moved to the front.

"Come inside," he said over the engine.

He honestly expected an argument but she didn't give one. She glanced pointedly at his garage and she backed her bike in once he'd opened it. A light illuminated the way as he led her to the kitchen. With the press of a button, he lowered the garage door then gestured her inside his house.

She stood in the middle of his nickel-blue kitchen, hands shoved in her back pockets. When he looked at her face he realised she was no less angry.

"Thank you," he said.

"How dare you!" she seethed. "How fucking dare you! What were you doing?" She paced in his kitchen and raked her hands through her windblown hair. "What were you *thinking?*"

He hadn't been. After receiving Lizard's call, all rational thought had vanished like water in a desert. All he'd been able to see and focus on was that *man*—if he could be called that—touching her.

A fresh wave of raw jealousy overtook him. He stalked her until the clean countertop stopped her retreat. Her amazing eyes met his and were filled with anger and challenge. He crossed his arms so he wouldn't break down and touch her.

"Who is he?"

She narrowed her gaze. "None of your business."

"You're wrong, Jaydee. Now tell me who the fuck that professor-doctor dick is to you."

"Fuck off, Giovanni Cassano. You don't own me and you have no say over who I spend time with. I can't believe you punched him."

"He was lucky I only hit him once for putting his hands on you. Isn't he a bit old for you or is that what you—"

Crack!

The stinging pain from her palm made him blink rapidly. Lightning flashed in her eyes and he realised just how furious she was.

"You're drunk and I shouldn't have even wasted my time getting your ass out of jail."

"And yet you did." Realisation set in and began to soothe his out-of-control anger. He stepped closer, eyes boring into hers. "You left him after I punched him and came to me. Me, Jaydee."

His voice deepened as he ran a knuckle down the side of her face. Her skin was so soft, he had no idea how she managed to keep it that way. She didn't smell like any scented lotions, no, not his Jaydee. She smelt fresh and clean. And tasted like mint.

She trailed her tongue over her full lips and his cock thrust against his zipper. Jaydee exhaled noisily and shook her head. He watched in absolute silence as she struggled to regain her composure. She was rattled, he knew that. Jaydee didn't curse like that.

"Do anything like that again and I'll leave your ass in jail. And encourage him to press charges."

He grinned as he brushed against her. One thigh settled between her slightly spread legs. "You convinced him to let it go." A pause. "And you left him to come to me." He positioned his hands on either side of her. "I happen to find that very telling."

"I don't care how you see it," she snapped. "Why?"

Her refusal to accept—much less acknowledge—what existed between them tipped him right back to the pissed-off side of the scale.

"Why?" She nodded. "Because he dared…" he raked his gaze over her in a proprietary way, "touch you."

Lightning returned this time, accompanied by thunderous clouds that swirled with ominous conditions. Her nose flared and he knew she was losing the battle of control.

"You. Do. Not. Own. Me." She bit each word out and they were coated in ice. "What I do is my business."

"Not when it comes to another male touching you, Jaydee. Now tell me who he is."

She squeezed her hands into fists before relaxing them.

"Dr Thompson. Surely, you remember. He was introduced this morning."

He ground his jaw. "Who is he to *you*?" he demanded, his face directly in front of hers. Her gaze shifted and he knew she was about to lie. "Don't lie to me, sweets."

"Get out of my way," she said, her voice cold and professional.

He pressed closer, ensuring to rub his hard length against her. Her eyes shifted again, this time going molten. In that second, his anger slid away. All that mattered was that she was here, with him and no one else.

Lowering one hand, he cupped and manoeuvred her leg so it rested along his hips. Content being back between her legs, he flexed his hips, rubbing against her core. Her soft whimper shot fire through his veins.

"Jaydee," he whispered.

Her desire overflowed from her alluring eyes but she shook her head.

"No." The word sounded tortured.

He licked his lips and backed off. Disappointed as he was, he'd never forced a woman. He palmed her leg and slowly pushed it down so her feet were both on the ground. Then he stepped back and tried to ignore the steel rod in his pants.

"Come on," she said, slipping by him and heading further into his home.

Hell yeah! His eagerness faded when she led him to the bathroom.

"Sit."

He sat on the edge of the counter. "Wanna shower together?"

Her growl only made him smile. The next second it got wiped from his face as she slammed the bottle of peroxide down beside him.

"Clean it yourself," she snarled before vanishing from view.

He rose too fast and stumbled. By the time he had righted himself he heard her Ninja as it left his driveway. Once he made his way to the connecting door between the garage and the kitchen, he stared out of the raised garage door.

"Way to go, Giovanni," he muttered before slapping a hand over the button to shut out the night.

He made it to his couch before he crashed. When he woke the next morning, he got ready for work, only to swear up a storm at the realisation that his vehicle resided in the Garrett's Place parking lot.

With a glance at his watch, he strode to his front door with the intention of getting a ride from his neighbour to Lizard's. He jerked open the door and halted in his step. In his driveway sat his vehicle, just as pristine as she'd been last night.

"I'm such an ass," he commented as he grabbed his keys and hurried down to his car.

He hadn't a clue how but he knew who had done this. For him.

Jaydee sat on her motorcycle in the lot at work. She didn't want to go in. Unfortunately, she had no choice. With a self-deprecating sigh, she climbed off and headed inside, her bag over one shoulder.

Having changed into her flight suit, she made her way over to the individual shelter her plane was housed in. Both front and rear doors were open. The hangars were built this way to allow the engines to be run up inside. Other necessary items—fuel, electrical, air services, and other fluids—ran in tunnels beneath the floor.

Upon her entrance, she found her plane's mechanic waiting for her as he'd said he would. Sedin had called her at home and said she should come see what he'd found. Given last night's fiasco, she'd arranged to meet him here, this morning. After all, she needed some sleep and last night had taken it all out of her.

"Morning, ma'am."

"Morning, Sedin. Thanks for meeting me here."

He flashed a smile before heading to a workstation he had set up his computer on.

"What'd you find?" she asked moving up behind him.

"You were right to check it, ma'am. It had inverted."

She massaged her temples and sighed. "Nothing showed on our end to even indicate such a thing."

Sedin reached to the laptop and pressed a button that started a sequence on the seventeen-inch screen. She watched, frowned, then watched it run again.

"It's the numerous landings and take-offs. Like we'd do on a carrier." She still didn't understand why they needed to test that way—these bombers didn't belong on carriers.

"Yes, ma'am." He rubbed his hands along his thighs. "I ran it twice just to be sure and…well…"

She grabbed a stool and sat beside him. Petty Officer Sedin had never been at a loss for words before. So she waited. It took him a few minutes to find a way to say what he needed to.

"There was also this." His fingers danced along the keys and she stared in disbelief at what she witnessed.

"Store this on a zip for me," she ordered.

His entire body tensed. "We're—"

"Do it, Petty Officer. I'll handle any repercussions if they come."

"I can transfer it to your tablet if you prefer."

She retrieved her tablet PC in moments and watched as he did as he'd said.

"Commander Amos."

She snapped her head up and saw a guard approaching. "Yes?"

"Your presence is requested in the ready room."

"On my way, Staff Sergeant. Thank you." A glance down assured her Sedin had finished the transfer, so she scooped it up and stepped away. "Thank you, Sedin. We'll talk more later."

"Yes, ma'am."

She followed the staff sergeant and smiled at the sight of the two men of the maintenance squadron crew on top of her bomber performing a fingertip inspection of the fuselage, checking for any damage to the stealth skin. As she left, more ground crew entered but her mind was already focused on who could have sent for her. Not to mention the information she had on her tablet.

At the door to the room, she paused briefly before pushing through. Captain Fentress waited in there along with Dr Thompson.

"You wished to see me," she said, unsure of which of the two had actually called for her.

"Dr Thompson asked if you could be his guide today. No one's flying so I said okay."

"Of course, sir."

He gave a slight smile then left.

The moment they were alone, she glanced at the man in there with her. She could see the swelling on his nose but otherwise he looked as put together as always.

"Come." He walked by her to the door.

Jaydee followed him to a room that was set up for the professors. The room was crammed with whiteboards and a full coffeepot despite the lack of people. She closed the door behind her, the click amplifying the fact that they were alone.

Dr Thompson merely arched a brow and asked in his smooth, unhurried way, "Who is he?"

The question made her stomach clench a bit, even though she'd been expecting it.

"A fellow pilot."

No expression change. "Come sit, Jaydee." He gestured to a chair near him.

She didn't want to but she couldn't refuse him. So she sat where he indicated.

"I've never been told not to touch you only to get hit after. Is he someone special to you?"

Was she imagining things or did amusement exist in his tone? Picking up a pencil, she began working on the equations on the pad before her. "Nope," she lied without remorse or inflection.

"You ask me not to press charges for someone who's not anything to you?"

Composing her facial features into a bored look, she lifted her gaze and met his head-on. "I'm a scientist and a pilot. You taught me to take apart and analyse things. Make smart, informed decisions. Not ones based on emotions. That man is an ace pilot and is the top test pilot for this facility. It would be nonsensical to have him removed from duty because of his one night of bad decisions."

"I also told you the smallest thing can change outcomes."

She yawned and shrugged. "Like I said, he's an ace pilot. Our overall goal is these planes. He's the best they have."

"What about you? Is he better than you?"

She blinked. "No. However, I'm not permanent here."

"Still doesn't explain why he felt the primitive urge to hit me." Dr Thompson narrowed his gaze and stared at her with shrewd eyes.

"The men here are a bit on the protective side."

A noncommittal sound left him. "Have you flown with him?"

"Not in the same plane but yes, I have."

"He's the one whose scores you beat?"

"Yes, sir."

He smiled at her. "That's my girl."

She barely hid her shock at his comment. He wasn't a man given to compliments. All she could do was focus back on the stuff before her.

They worked in silence for a while, Jaydee on some boards in the back, wishing she didn't have her flight suit on. And wishing she had her music in her ear. Even so, she fell into the same easy and consistent work as she'd done in the lab numerous times.

"Jaydee."

She popped her head around a board at the call from Dr Thompson and promptly lost her breath. Gio stood there, looking all kinds of delicious in his flight suit. She clenched her hand into a fist then spoke in a calm tone.

"Yes, sir?" She forced herself to keep her gaze upon Dr Thompson as she spoke to him.

"Take a break."

"Yes, sir." She vanished from their view and replaced her marker. With a deep breath, she walked around the board, past the men, and out of the door. It took so much for her to avoid staring at Gio. The cut below his eye added to the air of danger he seemed to be enveloped by.

Jaydee found herself in the cafeteria. She got a bottle of water and strolled outside into the late morning. Seated at a picnic table she took a long drink before sighing heavily. What if Gio attacked him again? Shaking the thought from her mind, she looked around. From her position, she could see people from both bombers' ground crews working.

This facility had seven hangars but only two were in use for the moment, aside from the one that housed the wreckage. She loved it here—the smell of jet fuel never failed to bring a smile to her face, and the noise and the undercurrent of energy she always felt around the Spirits made everything worthwhile.

The long hours, intense training. All of it was worth it to be able to take one of these babies up in the sky. To be able to watch the sunset as a backdrop for one of these amazing planes. To see one coasting down right before take-off in the pre-dawn where they seemed spectral.

She'd miss it when the time came to leave. *I wonder how it would be to have* my *name on one of the bombers.* She knew. Deep down she knew it would be such an honour. Another sigh. Such a thing wasn't her future. She was first and foremost a scientist. A geek. Someone others used for their own benefit.

Shaking away her somewhat depressing thoughts, she powered up her tablet and got back to work, grateful to be outside. While she wanted to look at what Sedin had transferred to her, she had other things to finish up first.

* * * *

Hours later, she stood between Keel and Lizard before Fentress. Gio stood on Keel's other side.

"The way you all have been flying is wonderful. Take your ninety-six and be prepared for another battery of tests upon your return. Have a great weekend and try to stay out of trouble. I don't want any calls from the LEOs about anyone. Dismissed."

She studiously avoided Gio's gaze as everyone left. At the room Dr Thompson had taken over, she slipped in. He was the only one in there and glanced up at her entry. Silence stretched between them for a bit.

"Why are you here?" he eventually questioned.

"We are on our ninety-six."

He nodded. "Go. Enjoy your free time." He saw her hesitation. "You deserve some rest. Meet me for dinner tomorrow at seventeen-hundred. The place called Carlotta's. Do you know it?"

"Yes, sir."

"Great. I will call if I need you." A pointed look. "Get some rest."

"Yes, sir." She turned the handle and stepped out. "Tomorrow night then," she called out over her shoulder.

Quick steps took her out into the afternoon sun. She slid on her sunglasses and strode to her bike. Once she left the base a wide grin filled her face. She was free for her entire time. Shifting, she asked for more speed and raced for home.

At her apartment, she showered and dressed in purple shorts and a grey T-shirt. She cut herself up an apple and settled in comfortably in her chair as she opened her book—a mystery she'd wanted to read for some time now. She felt herself relaxing as each page passed.

Ding-dong.

Jaydee blinked and looked around. She'd fallen asleep in her chair. A peek out of her large windows informed her night had fallen.

Ding-dong.

Pushing up from her seat, she padded to the door, turning on a light as she went. She stifled a yawn and opened the door. Her traitorous heart stopped then pounded hard and fast. And it wasn't the only body part with an extreme reaction.

Gio stood there, one hand braced against the doorframe. His baseball cap concealed his eyes from her. She saw his straight nose, those bow-shaped lips, and wanted to touch him. There was no feeling of panic, like she'd had at his first appearance at her apartment.

Silent, she stepped back and allowed him entrance. The scents that made up Giovanni Cassano—masculine and fresh—filled her as he passed. Dampening her lips, she took a deep breath, closed the door, and turned to face him.

Damn! Gio had this thing about him—a magnetism—that made her forget her surroundings.

"What are you doing here, Gio?"

He strode towards her and her breath hitched even as her body responded in a more sexual way. He pushed back the brim of his cap, allowing her to see his hazel eyes. They smouldered and seared her with their heat. She shivered at the darkly sensual promise lingering in them.

"Spend the weekend with me."

Okay, not what she'd expected to hear.

"What?"

He reached out and stroked a knuckle along her face. "We have ninety-six hours before we have to be back at work."

She shook her head until his fingers gripped her chin. "Our having a...a sexual relationship is highly unprofessional."

His hold gentled before he trailed his fingers down her neck and along her shirt's neckline. "What we have is more than purely sexual, Jaydee." His words were seductive and she fell under his spell again.

"Unprofessional," she reiterated.

"Say yes."

"I can't have you here all weekend."

He never hesitated. "Then come to my place. You can keep your bike in the garage. I have plenty of food. We won't have to leave the house."

She swallowed. Could she? Was she brave enough? Gio must have sensed her indecision for he cupped her face in his hands.

"Think about it, Jaydee. You know where I live. I want you with me. Let me take care of you for a weekend. Let me get to know *you*. The real you."

His kiss was tender and brief. She dug her fingers into her palms so she wouldn't grab him. He backed to the door, his eyes never moving from her face. Hand on the knob he winked and said, "Clothes are optional. Don't be long."

He was gone. And she was alone, *again.*

Lip between her teeth, Jaydee went and sat on her couch with a loud sigh. How'd he do it? How did he manage to blow past every wall she'd erected?

The thought of spending their time off together appealed to her, more than anything. To sleep and wake in his arms...an experience she'd never get enough of.

But attachments were risky. And she had already become more attached to him than was advisable.

She rose and roamed to her phone. After she'd located the desired number, she pressed 'Call' and waited.

"Yeah?" an out-of-breath woman answered in a sharp tone.

"I have a problem," Jaydee said without preamble.

"Hang on a sec, hon." Shuffling sounded and a masculine grumble. "I have to take this, babe, I'll be back soon." The voice got louder. "What's up, Jaydee?"

"I'm sorry for interrupting, Lexy." She knew what she'd disturbed. "I forgot the time difference."

"Who cares? He'll be there after we're done. And, if not, there are always others. You know you can call me any time. Now, stop stallin'. What's going on?"

Jaydee curled up on her couch, grateful for whatever had allowed her to meet Lexy. Honestly, how many women would stop fucking a guy because a friend called?

"Can't help you if you've decided to go mute, Jaydee. Come on, talk to me." Lexy's voice was warm and welcoming. So she did as Lexy had bidden.

Chapter Nine

Gio did his best to ignore the clock on the far wall but he couldn't quite seem to manage that simple feat. Three hours had passed since he'd got home from Jaydee's apartment. He'd truly thought she'd come right after him. Even if just for some more sex because, to be honest here, what happened between them was explosive to say the least. Off the charts and out of this world, if you wanted to get more specific.

He'd been called many things. A player. A Lothario. A Romeo. Women had rarely held his interest more than once. Sometimes they did, but he was, as his call sign stated…a Casanova. Lover of women.

Until he'd met Jaydee. He had been shoved head first into uncharted waters. Now, no one else could do it for him. He was fine with that, for he wanted only Jaydee Amos. Pilot extraordinaire. Genius. His lover. What he wasn't okay with was the way she continually seemed able to shut out the passion between them. He longed to be able to claim her in front of everyone. She was amazing. She was…here.

The roar of her motorcycle brought him to his feet in a single, smooth motion. At the front window, he stared out into the dark. A single headlight swung into his drive and he hurried to open the garage door. He waited at the top of the two steps and watched her back her bike in. The door closed behind her and, once it hit the floor, she shut off her yellow-trimmed black Ninja and removed her helmet.

His breath caught as she tossed her hair then glanced at him over her shoulder. He growled low in his throat when she swung her leg over and hung the helmet on a handgrip. While she removed the reflective vest and unfastened her bag from the back, he stared at her. She wore a white T-shirt that had some symbol on the front he couldn't decipher. Some baggy, holey jeans and white canvas slip-on shoes.

Fucking hot.

She strode towards him and stopped at the bottom of the steps. Her gaze met his. "I have a dinner tomorrow night at seventeen-hundred I can't miss."

He stepped down, forcing her to move back. "We'll worry about that later. This all your stuff?"

Guileless eyes blinked at him. "You did say clothing was optional."

She was in his arms before her words had faded from the air. It took him very little time and he had her naked in his bed as he slid his hard length deep inside her.

"Oh, Gio!" she cried as she bowed her back almost immediately.

Fuck, she is so tight. He rolled them over so she was on top. Hands on her hips, he watched her eyes change colour in the light. "Ride me."

She placed her hands on his shoulders and lifted herself up and down. She found a speed she seemed to like and he was biting the inside of his cheek to keep from tearing control from her. This was some of the most exquisite torture he'd ever experienced.

Fast and slow. Up and down. Back and forth. She rolled her hips, took him all the way in, and barely moved, aside from her snug internal muscles. She was killing him and doing it with a smile on her face. Her passionate cries and moans were such an aphrodisiac.

He reached for her breasts once but she beat him to it, so he watched her, head back in ecstasy, riding his cock and tugging on her own nipples. He had been so close to bursting and her mewls hadn't been helping, so he reached for her clit and flicked it. Her response had been explosive, as had his. They'd barely got their breath back before he flipped her to the bottom and started again. It was almost midnight before their need had been sated.

The following morning they were in the kitchen, Jaydee dressed in one of his shirts. It hung to the middle of her thighs, and he wore a pair of shorts. As she put ice in her glass all he could think of was how his shirt was the *only* thing she wore.

"You're staring again."

He blinked and watched her approach. "Yes, I am. You tend to do that to me."

She cocked her head to the side. "How is it my fault you're staring?"

"You're beautiful."

Jaydee rolled her eyes and took a drink of her water.

"You don't think you're beautiful?"

"Am I supposed to?"

He sensed genuine bafflement in her question. "Well, no, but come on, Jaydee, you have to know people find you attractive." She blinked at him. "The night we met, that short skirt, skimpy top, and fuck-me heels?"

She nodded. "Ahh. Those weren't my clothes. My friend Lexy convinced me to wear them. She said I needed something other than my dweeby lab attire to wear."

"And the second night?"

"Lexy again."

He remembered her friend. Very sexy, yes, but she'd not done anything for him. No one had done to him what Jaydee had.

"And the men?"

"Lexy's brothers."

"Are you..." He trailed off.

Jaydee stared in his eyes. "Am I what?"

"Involved with either of them?" Honestly, did he want to know?

"Why would I be involved with either of them?"

Again, nothing but pure curiosity in her tone. He swallowed. "You were out with them."

She frowned. "Why would I have kissed you if I were involved with another man?" She glanced to her water before back to him. "I am not in the habit of doing that." Her tone was affronted.

"And the man...from last night?" He spoke hesitatingly, unsure whether he wanted to know this either.

"Did I not just spend one hundred eighty minutes in your bed? Am I not sitting here wearing nothing aside from your shirt? And did I *not* just get finished saying I don't behave with such proclivities?"

Gio hid his smile. Only Jaydee would say things like that. He'd noticed it when she was frustrated or stressed. She would tend to sound geekier.

"Actually, sweets, you used smaller words but I get the gist of it."

She ducked her head but he still saw the flush. He didn't mention it, merely waited for her to look up. She didn't and so he spoke again.

"Tell me about him, Jaydee."

"Who?"

"The man from last night and the one I'm assuming you're leaving me tomorrow to go out with."

She stared at him then sighed. "Does it really matter to you, my relationship with Dr Thompson?"

"Yes." He reached out for her hand. "You saw me last night, Jaydee. The thought of you in another's arms makes me...well, you saw."

"Your actions had little to do with me and everything to do with the amount of alcohol you'd consumed."

Perhaps, but the knowledge of her out with him had started it. "Who is he to you?" he asked, a command more than a question.

She didn't want to say, that was obvious.

"What did you two talk about today?"

He shook his head. "You first, sweets."

"I've worked with Dr Thompson for a number of years." She pursed her lips briefly. "Since I began working in a lab on the technology for the B-2s, actually."

He knew she was holding back.

"So, he's like a mentor?"

Watching her, he knew she would love to be discussing anything else. But, *damn it,* he had to know. She finished her water and placed the glass by the sink. He could see the tension radiating from her. Downing the rest of his own drink, he moved up behind her, set his glass down, and tugged her back to settle against his bare chest.

"Jaydee?" She muttered something under her breath he didn't catch. "What did you say?" he asked.

"He's my father."

Not what he'd expected to hear. He turned her so he could see her face. Her eyes—those amazing tortoiseshell eyes—sparkled in the low lighting from behind him.

"Dr Thompson is your father? I slugged your *father*?"

"Yes." Her response was as straightforward as her gaze.

His stomach churned. Christ, he'd sucker-punched the father of the woman he wanted more than his next breath. He closed his eyes and sighed. Not good. Not good at all.

"Explain."

Although she seemed reluctant, Jaydee nodded. She shuffled by him and he observed her head back to his bedroom. Following, he stopped in the doorway and watched her sit at the foot of his platform bed, his green shirt offsetting his tan bedspread—mussed bedspread—and her brown skin.

"I carry my mother's last name. They never married and, when she realised I was...different, she tracked him down and left me in his possession."

The dispassionate way she spoke disturbed him. He crawled on the bed beside her, rested against the wall, and drew her back to settle against him. She stiffened slightly but didn't struggle.

"I thought you didn't know where your mother was."

"I don't. I just said she dropped me off."

"When?"

"I was seven."

His heart dropped like a rock. "You're different how?"

This time she did stiffen. He should back off, he knew he should. But he couldn't. He wanted to know everything about her. Wanted to be there for her, the shoulder she could, or would, cry on.

Crap. He was in way over his head. Instead of running, Gio moved his hands up and down her arms.

"Jaydee?"

She didn't want to tell him. Didn't want to relive powerful memories she'd taken great pains to bury. "I was smart. And it bothered her. A lot."

"Why would she be embarrassed you were smart?"

Jaydee shrugged, grateful for his warmth behind her. "I tended to blurt things out in public which...she found reprehensible. So when her *gentlemen* callers began to get upset by my comments they gave her an ultimatum. Them or me. She chose them. Packed up a bag for me and drove me to California and left me with Dr Thompson in the Mojave Desert at his lab."

A deep breath. "I was seven, like I said before. He was less than pleased to have me, and employed a woman to care for me and a tutor. Not much later, he took me to the lab and began testing me. I was eight when I corrected some of his equations for an application of antigravity propulsion."

She rubbed her hands on his bedspread. "I have not just a photographic, but an eidetic memory. So I began working in the lab. By age eleven I had mastered flying a B-2."

"Wait. Eleven?"

"Yes." Her voice was low. "I'd read the manuals and had worked in the simulator. When I did go up, I went up with two test pilots just in case. They weren't needed." She brushed her hair away from her eyes. "Anyway… I began pulling double duty with both lab and bombers. They sent me to OCS and I graduated then headed back to the lab."

"Christ."

She sighed. He was like her mother in thinking she was a freak. She'd hoped he would be different. Drawing away, she began to inch off the bed. His grip on her arm had her examining him over her shoulder. There was no odd look in his eyes, nothing like the others who'd called her a freak had. She paused.

"Where are you going?" His question was direct, much like the man himself.

She blinked a few times and glanced to her bag, which currently sat on his black bergère in the corner near the window. "Home."

His eyes crinkled at the corners when he gave her a grin. Not a patronising one, no, quite the opposite. Sexuality in its rawest eidolon. His eyes smouldered with heat and passion.

Half expecting him to tug her back to him, she tensed. He released her and let his body relax against his bedroom wall. She wasn't fooled, for she knew he had incredible reflexes.

"I never pegged you for running away, Jaydee." He drew a leg up and rested his arm upon it.

She couldn't keep from staring at him. Professionals had a term for what she'd become around him. A nymphomaniac. Even his powerful legs and feet could distract her.

Tearing her gaze from the leg, which seemed to be fascinating her unconditionally, she met his eyes. "I am not running."

"Yes, you are."

She wanted to deny it. "Yes, I am."

He beckoned to her. "Come here, sweets."

Her body listened immediately. Up on her knees, she shuffled back to his side. His gorgeous eyes burned hotter. He licked her lips and stroked down her side, pressing the cotton tighter to her skin. Her breath hitched when his callused palm continued on over her thigh. His fingers spread and, with gentle pressure, he encouraged her to settle across his lap.

"I'm not like your mother. I don't think you're odd. I happen to think you, Jaydee Amos, are an amazing woman."

A groan threatened to slip free. There he was, hard beneath her. The feel of him settled so intimately against her core made her long to shift her hips, to rub against him.

Their eyes were locked. Her entire world shrank to Giovanni Cassano. It smacked her. At some point, during her many weeks at the test facility, this man had come to mean a lot to her.

"I want to know everything, Jaydee. Your past. Why you almost always drink water. And not only why you ride a crotch rocket, but how long you've been riding."

"Why?"

He slid his hands up under the bottom of the large shirt she wore. She'd never worn another man's clothing before. She liked it. The T-shirt carried a faint smell of Gio that she would never grow tired of.

"Because this is more than sex—great sex—but it's still more."

She didn't want to analyse what they had. Analysing was what she always did. With Gio, she wanted to experience. To shut off the part of her that normally ruled her decisions. To take more than a few hours to be a *woman*.

Lexy's loud whoop of encouraging approval reverberated in her mind and she smiled slightly. Her friend had always been after her to have fun.

She shifted and watched the spike of heat in his hazel eyes darkening them. With slow and careful movements, she leaned in and kissed the skin over his clavicle and deltoid. He stiffened, flexing his fingers along her hip, but otherwise remaining immobile. She took her time, exploring his pectorals, loving how his nipples hardened beneath her touch, before kissing a path down his sternum. Tiny tremors moved through him.

"Jaydee." Her name sounded tortured as it left his mouth.

She gazed at him from beneath lowered lids. His jaw was clenched and she watched a bead of sweat roll down from his temple. "Gio?" He looked at her, barely restrained desire emblazed in his gaze.

"Yes?"

"Tell me what you and Dr Thompson spoke about yesterday."

"Yesterday?"

"It's after midnight, so it means you spoke to him yesterday." She rocked again and he groaned.

"He...he...oh God, Jaydee."

She ran her short nails down his chest. His fingers flexed again. She tossed her hair and slid her hands back up his chest before looping her arms around his neck. She leaned in to brush their lips together.

"Tell me."

"Inside," he ground out.

"Tell me."

"You're killing me here, Jaydee."

With a short nod of her head, she lifted up and he quickly removed his shorts. His cock rose up towards her. Large, thick, and all hers. He reached to his drawer and withdrew a foil packet. She took it from him and ripped it open.

She carefully covered him and gripped the base of his shaft, holding him at her entrance. Back and forth, she rubbed him along her and all the while she stared at him.

"Jesus, Jaydee. Stop torturing me."

This power she had made her smile, but she couldn't wait any longer. With agonising slowness, she lowered herself upon him. Lord knew she wanted to slam down on him, but the part of her that won wanted to drag it out. As he filled her, she released a pleasured gasp. A deep moan escaped him and his fingers settled back upon her hips.

"God, you feel so good," he uttered.

So did he, but her ability to speak appeared to have abandoned her. All she could do was close her eyes and begin to move. Up and down his length, she lifted and lowered until they both panted with desire.

"Open your eyes, Jaydee. Open them and watch me."

She did. His black, thick lashes were lowered halfway, which only added to his darkly sensual appearance. She couldn't help but shiver from their intensity. So much existed in that stare, she dropped her gaze.

"No," he said, sliding his hands up her ribs, "watch me, sweets. Watch me as we make love."

Her entire body flushed even as she forced herself to keep her eyes open. She curled her arms around his neck as they continued to move in slow, harmonious synchronicity.

She could feel the sweat trailing down her spine, her body hovered on the cusp, and yet he refused to take it to the next level. His strength allowed her to move but ensured she kept the pace nice and slow.

Something was changing between them, right here, right now. Before it had been mostly fast, with an almost fierce edge to what they'd shared. Hot, fast, and explosive. This was just the opposite. Even their calmer times had been less intense, in that he'd never insisted on the eye contact. Bottom line—before they'd fucked, sometimes gently, but it wasn't like this. Not even close. Now he was making love to her. No-holds-barred love.

No words passed between them but she could *feel* him. He was making his way into her, in more than just the physical way.

"Please," she murmured, craving the release he brought her. What only he could give her.

He didn't make her ask again, nor did he make her beg. Which at this point she wasn't averse to. Gio dropped his hands to her thighs. "Take it, Jaydee."

She dug her nails into the skin along the back of his shoulders and increased her speed. Yes! This was what she needed. Her lids fluttered.

"Uh-uh, sweets. Eyes open. Look at me."

Nothing had ever been so difficult but she managed to do as he said. Strain etched on his expression and she knew he was close as well. She captured her lower lip in her teeth and moved faster.

He muttered something too low for her to decipher but the gravelled rasp was like his touch and elicited a passionate reaction from her. She could taste her release—it hovered so close, swarming her.

"Watch me, sweets," he rumbled.

His fingertips grazed across her overly sensitive clit. That was all it took and she exploded. Her body tightened around him and she felt him come within her, a low roar erupting from him.

Boneless, she collapsed against his sweaty chest. Gio rolled them to the side, still buried to the hilt inside her. His lips brushed her head. Eventually he withdrew and left the bed. She watched him return, unashamed of his nudity. Hell, she couldn't blame him. His body was to die for. Back on the bed, he gathered her close.

She closed her eyes and allowed the moment. Beneath her ear, his heart beat out a tattoo. With one hand, she stroked his chest.

"Why?"

His arms curved around her, holding her tighter. "Why, what?" A pause. "Why did I want to watch your eyes?"

"Yes."

"I've never seen your eyes when you come. I wanted to. They go gold, it's amazing. You are truly beautiful, Jaydee."

For once, she felt it.

Chapter Ten

Morning's light streamed in through his blinds, filling the room with golden rays. Gio moved his head slowly and gazed down at the woman lying in his bed. In his arms. Jaydee lay pressed against him, her head on his chest, over his heart.

Her lashes were long, thick and curved. When she looked at him…man, the things he thought and wished for. Right now, her lips were slightly parted as she slept. He wanted her. The tent in the sheet gave that away, but he held off and refrained from sliding his cock deep inside her to wake her.

Jaydee had looked as if she was so tired and he wanted her to get enough rest. Besides, he was rather fond of having her naked body in his arms. So while she slept he spent the time just staring at her. How her skin was all soft and smooth. She had a cluster of freckles on the back of her left shoulder.

Her body was strong, with lean muscles that helped make her look so delicious in anything she wore. Right now, he could imagine her having fun with friends at a pool or the beach. All that would change the moment she woke.

Fun wasn't something she seemed to understand. He grinned. Luckily for her, he did.

She stirred. One leg rubbed along his, heating his blood as the neatly clipped hair between her legs caressed his upper thigh. Sweat gathered on his brow and he tried valiantly to remember he wanted to let her get all the sleep she needed. She moved again and he barely kept his moan contained.

Moving slowly, he untangled himself from her luscious form. She made a small moue before deep sleep claimed her. He left her there bathed in the sun's soft glow. He grabbed a shower and headed to his kitchen where he emptied his dishwasher.

The doorbell rang and he glanced towards his bedroom door as he made his way to the front. Opening it, he arched a brow at the familiar face that watched him in return. Jason.

"Morning, man."

Rubbing his hand along his jaw, he sighed. "What's up, Lizard?"

"You seem shocked to see me. Don't I usually stop by for breakfast on a ninety-six?"

Lizard was right, he normally did. "Right." He still didn't move.

"What, man? I don't care if you have a woman in here. I've seen them here before."

Again, all truth but none of them had been Jaydee. And since their being together was a violation...he didn't want to risk her career.

One brow rose. "Unless it's—"

"Yes, I have a woman here, so just keep your voice down. She's still sleeping." Shit, now he had to feed him.

Lizard had a smirk on his face. "Well, I guess this woman was good."

He frowned, not appreciating the attempt at a joke. Lizard shook his head.

"You okay, man? You seem relaxed and yet like you're ready to bite my head off at the least bit of provocation."

"Sorry, man. Just cancel the jokes about women, okay?"

He stepped back and his fellow pilot stepped through into the house. *Please stay asleep, Jaydee.*

They went to the kitchen and he began fixing a meal for himself and Lizard. It had been a thing they'd been doing since he and Mike had moved in to the house. They'd always had a meal, just them, and shot the breeze. It was different with Mike gone, but this was kind of their own way of keeping him around. His memory alive.

Not much later, they were eating omelettes and drinking coffee.

"Have you ever met someone who made you willing to do anything to keep them happy, Lizard?"

Jason's blue eyes widened before he rested his elbows on the table.

"This have anything to do with the woman sleeping in your bed?" His tone was completely serious. "Or are you talking about the hottie who's joined our squad, no matter how temporary?"

He'd got his proof that Lizard didn't think Jaydee was sleeping in his bed, since he'd posed it the way he had. Or so he hoped.

"I guess just in general. Have you met someone like that?"

"No." He ate his final bite of breakfast and quietly laid his fork down. "You *are* talking about Jaydee, aren't you?"

He ran his finger under his nose. "Why do you think that?"

"Because I see how you watch her, especially when you think no one is any the wiser. I've seen the rage when another man talks to her, even Keel—who we both know is a blissfully married man. And I've seen the fear for her when we fly." A light shrug. "But perhaps I'm all wrong and it's just some hot-assed babe with big tits."

Gio nodded, because his assessment was just too damn close to the God-awful truth. Unfortunately for him, his friend knew him better than that.

"Don't bother trying to lie, Giovanni. We both know the truth, just like we both know if I were to go down to your room I would find Jaydee there." Jason held up one hand. "I don't care, Casanova. I don't. I'm happy for you. Jealous too, but mostly happy. She's done something to you which I never thought I'd see."

"Which is?" he asked. No point in trying to hide it from him, he'd given his word. Besides, if he couldn't trust Lizard, who could he trust?

"Made you unsure of yourself with a woman. She doesn't fall prey to your considerable charms. She makes you question all the smooth lines and swagger you've used before. Basically, she's put Casanova in training."

He narrowed his gaze at his soon-to-be-murdered best friend. "Excuse me?" he growled.

"Calm down, Superman. I just mean this woman has you having to relearn your skills with women. Jaydee is...well, let's face it...smokin' hot."

A dangerous rumble rose up from his chest. Lizard just continued, undaunted.

"I don't blame you for your actions. I'd be breaking all kinds of regs for her if I thought I had—"

"You don't," he bit off.

Lizard shook his head and smiled. "I said if, man. If." He laughed. "She's an amazing woman, Casanova. Brilliant and sexy as hell. And, from what I've seen, she's not a fan of your caveman attitude. And, with a woman like her, sex—no matter how great—won't keep her around."

Those words sobered him and created a knot of worry in the pit of his stomach. Was Lizard right? Yes, the sex between them was phenomenal. He knew there was more to be explored between them, but would she not only acknowledge it, but accept it as well?

"I won't give her up, Jason."

"She's only here temporarily. Surely you remember that bit of information?"

Yeah, he recalled that. "I don't care. There's just something about her…" He trailed off, unsure of how to put it in words.

"I'm happy for you, Giovanni. Truly I am, but you need to be careful. Fentress has been asking about your cut and the doc's black eye. Not to mention, with it only being us four in the ready room, he's able to watch you a hell of a lot closer." He leaned nearer. "Do you get what I'm saying?"

He nodded. Bottom line, he had to watch his behaviour towards her. Jason stood and carried his dish to the sink then he turned his body to face him.

"Good. Now I'll make myself scarce. You"—he winked—"have a wonderful weekend."

"We will."

"Lucky bastard," Lizard said with good humour.

Gio rose and walked him to the door. They shook hands and he stated with complete honesty, "Thank you, Lizard. For everything."

"We're best buds, man. You know I've always got your back. But, on the off-chance you find another like her, remember my number, would ya?"

He laughed. "Sorry, man. Jaydee's one of a kind."

"I know. Damn, do I know." He jogged down the steps and headed to his truck. Lizard waved and drove away.

With a sigh, Gio entered his house and closed the door. It was oh-eight-hundred and he went back to his kitchen where he cleaned up. Once the room was spotless, he ambled down the hall to his room. He cracked the door and peeked in.

She lay on her belly, arms akimbo. Her head was pretty much buried under one of the pillows on his bed. The cream sheet bunched up at her ass and Iridessa played peek-a-boo with him.

Her whipped-chocolate skin reminded him of satin or silk. *Damn, she's beautiful.*

He approached slowly and sat on the mattress edge. One hand reached out and trailed down her spine. The ridges were present and he took a deep breath. Here and now, she seemed so delicate, fragile even. Not the woman who was his equal in the air. No, correction, his superior. Yes, he might have combat experience, but her skills were unbeatable. And on the ground, she was brilliant to his average.

He could make out her ribs and he just longed to pull her into his arms and protect her. He traced his fingers over the circle of freckles. She moaned and shifted. The sheet slid off her ass and he muttered his approval.

"Gio." His name left her lips on a barely audible breath.

Lightning sparked through him. Lowering his head, he pressed kisses up along her spine. Jaydee groaned and arched more into his touch.

"Right here, sweets," he whispered in her ear.

"Mmm. You never answered my question of what you and Dr Thompson talked about."

He stroked her spine and wondered about how odd it was for her to call her father Dr Thompson. "I haven't?"

She grunted and rolled on to her back, the sheet somehow covering her enticing body. "No. Now tell me."

He sighed and stood up. "Okay. Over breakfast?"

Jaydee lay there and watched him, her hair around her like a cloud of black silk. A whole slew of things hit him as he stared at her. Like how much he wanted to…

"Why are you attempting the removal of the sheet?" she questioned.

He grinned. "Why do you think?"

"Classic avoidance technique."

With a groan, he positioned himself over her. His hands rested on either side of her hips.

"Do you know," he said brushing his lips along hers, "you taste like fresh, pure mint."

She coolly arched a brow. "Dropping chaff."

He laughed at her use of the phrase. Dropping chaff was a way to try to get missiles off your ass by giving them other targets to focus on. "Only you, sweets. Only you can make that sound sexy."

"Tell me."

He could hear the need in her voice.

"Dr Thompson wanted to know about my history as a pilot. We talked about you and my position on your flying with us."

She stiffened but her expression remained impassive. He leaned close and sniffed her hair. Peace flowed through him.

"I told him I hated it when you first arrived because you were yet another reminder of how Michael wouldn't be coming back. Ever." Her breath hitched and he kissed her jaw. "I don't blame you, sweets. Not now."

When she wriggled free and left the bed, he knew the words weren't believed. She tugged on a shirt, hiding her amazing body from his lustful gaze. The sorrow in her eyes prompted him into action.

"Jaydee."

She paused in the act of gathering her hair into a ponytail. "What?"

He prowled towards her, grabbed her hand, and led her to the bed. "Sit," he ordered.

He noticed her hesitation but she followed his directive. Once she had, he joined her. Her entire body was rigid and he stretched a hand out to cup her cheek. The eyes that met his were tormented.

"Jaydee, believe me, please. If not about anything else, believe I don't blame you for his death. Do you believe me?"

Her nod was slight and he expected her agreement to lift a weight from him. It didn't happen. And when he looked—really looked—into her eyes, he realised why. She might believe he didn't blame her, but it didn't matter because *she* blamed herself. And that bothered him, more than he could even begin to fathom.

"This wasn't your fault, Jaydee."

"It was." Her voice sounded so tired and lost. So unlike the confident one he was used to—a bit haughty and almost, not quite, but almost condescending.

"No, sweets, it wasn't."

She stared at him, her large tortoiseshell eyes shimmering with unshed tears. They tore a hole in his gut. *Christ! She truly believes it was her fault.* It explained so much. Why she'd been busting her ass going over everything.

"Yes, it was. Something went wrong with the EG." She ground her jaw. "That's my area, *mine!* So, since the system malfunctioned, the blame falls upon me."

Rage filled him. "Is that what your *father* told you? Is it? Because, if so, he's full of shit, Jaydee." He longed to slug the man again.

"I know where the fault lies, Gio. I'm the expert and I failed." She shifted and sighed. "I have attempted to discern what went wrong."

Something else was going on here. He slid closer so that their thighs touched. "What is it, Jaydee?" He witnessed her hesitation. "Trust me."

"I based my report findings on the information I'd been given. But, after I'd finished, I found out what I had been told wasn't accurate."

"How so?" He frowned.

"Everything I did, all the tests I ran were based on the belief Commander Walker and Wicked had flown that day."

Silence reigned and he scowled as anger grew in the pit of his belly. Anger that the death of his best friend possibly hadn't been an accident and was being covered up. But for whom? He'd been the one scheduled to take the test flight and would have been there if not for his shoulder. Was it Lizard? Could he have set Sidewinder up? Surely not. Then who?

He shoved to his feet and swore a blue streak as he paced the hardwood floor of his bedroom in a meagre attempt to work off his excess energy.

"So…someone is lying about what happened." He didn't make it a question.

Gio went to his window and stared out into his backyard. He squeezed his eyes shut and Mike's face flashed before him. His friend had always been upbeat and positive. And now…all that easy-going attitude and smooth charm was gone. Forever. Possibly snuffed out on purpose.

"God damn it!"

He punched the wall to his right, fist sinking into the drywall. The pain was welcomed. He struggled with the need to do it again. And again. Until all that remained was his own pain. Gio rested his head on the wall and took a deep breath. Eyes open, he stared out into the sunny morning. In the window's reflection, he made out the woman sitting on the foot of his bed. Jaydee.

She made no noise and he couldn't read her expression. He wiped the drywall dust off his hand and rotated towards her. Unsure of what he'd read in her eyes when he faced her, he was a bit hesitant. This was his second display of violence in front of her and he hated it. However, her gaze was guileless and straightforward.

"Do you realise what—" he broke off and shoved a hand over his short hair.

"I'm well aware of the implications."

"Who've you told?" he demanded.

"About what?"

"Damn it! Don't play games with me."

"Playing games isn't something I participate in." Her chest rose and fell enticingly as she breathed. "I asked for clarification to ensure I didn't give you the wrong information."

"About your report." He tried to calm himself, but it was an uphill battle all the way.

"Dr Thompson and Captain Fentress. I, however, finished that report based on the belief there'd been two pilots up there. I only acquired this new bit of news recently."

"How?"

She did a quick scan of his room. "I asked Keel about where the other pilot was. He said Commander Walker had gone up alone."

"Sidewinder," he said without thought.

"I'm sorry?"

"Mike or Sidewinder. He wouldn't want you calling him Commander."

Dawning filled her eyes. "He was your friend."

Pain lanced through him. "He was my best friend. We rented this place together. Christ, what if he died in my place? What if whatever happened was meant for me?" He made his way to his black chair and sank in it. Eyes closed, he fought for some composure.

Hands on his thighs brought his eyes open. Jaydee crouched before him. "I didn't say this to make you feel worse, and I am sorry. This is on me."

He could feel her personal devastation and taste her absolute belief in what she spoke.

"Come here, sweets."

She pushed to her feet then settled across his lap, her head tucked beneath his chin. He held her tight against his chest.

"This isn't your fault."

"Nor is it yours."

Since Mike's death, Gio knew he'd blamed himself. If only he'd not injured his shoulder. If only... He sighed and closed his eyes, brushing his lips along the top of her head.

"Help me. Help me to discover the truth, Jaydee."

"I will do what I can. I won't be around much longer."

He didn't want to hear such things from her. Her presence had become so familiar to him, he loathed the thought of losing it.

"I have to know the truth."

"Okay."

Face to face, he gave her a sad yet grateful smile. When their lips met he realised, yet again, how lost he truly was. And how this woman seemed to turn his 'lost' status into 'found'.

Chapter Eleven

Jaydee smoothed her hands down the yellow knee-length skirt and ensured her cobalt-blue shirt hadn't got messed up on the ride over. With one final deep breath, she walked across the parking lot towards the entrance to the restaurant.

She glanced at her watch as she nodded to the man who held the door for her. One minute before the hour. She was on time. Amazing, really, considering Gio had not wanted to let her out of bed. Not that she'd minded all that much.

All day they'd spent in bed, reminiscent of the twenty-four hours she'd spent with him when they'd first met. He'd cooked for her and held her tight when she'd slept. However, when she'd told him she had to leave he'd not been exactly happy.

"You can't possibly be jealous," she said.

"Why not?"

"Because he is my father."

Gio put his face close to hers and replied, "He can be seen in public with you. I can't. You're damn right I'm jealous."

Unsure of how to respond, she'd showered, dressed, and left him. After promising to return.

So, now, she was meeting a man, who might technically be her flesh and blood, but with whom she'd never felt that familial bond. He sat at the bar and rose when he spied her. Apparently, he'd been watching the door.

"Good evening, Dr Thompson." He wore loafers, slacks, and a nice dress shirt. His coat hung over his arm—as always, he was impeccable.

He placed a hand at the small of her back and guided her to a table, after the hostess had walked off. Once they were seated, she stared at him, waiting for why he had wanted to see her.

"I read your report." She waited. "Very thorough."

"Thank you."

"Don't thank me yet. Why no conclusion aside from the one you gave? Which we both know is a long-winded and fancy way of saying you don't truly know."

"I regret that that is true."

The waitress arrived to take their order and talk ceased until she'd left them alone.

Dr Thompson placed his elbows on the table—a shock all on its own—and set his chin atop laced fingers. She watched him cautiously, but she truly 'looked' at him, assessing him. It had never been a secret he was her father, yet he'd always kept her at a bit of a distance. He treated her like anyone else who worked in his lab, demanding results. Perfection.

They weren't a family who had meals together or shared holidays. In fact, her first celebrated Christmas, when she'd actually got a gift, had been the one she'd spent with Lexy and her family. Still, she'd had a roof over her head and food to eat, so she harboured no grudges against Dr Thompson.

Sitting here now, though, she was a bit suspicious. He'd never wanted to do two dinners with her before when she'd been on loan to Uncle Sam. His eyes appeared older. One side of his mouth twitched and he shook his head.

"You need to stop blaming yourself."

She blinked. "It—"

"No. It was not your fault." His tone was absolute and she nodded. "You need to remember how to separate personal feelings from fact. You can, you just need to."

"Yes, sir."

"Now, tell me about *your* two incidents."

That knot in her belly formed again as she relived her fear of almost certain death. None of it showed on her face and she began with the most recent.

By the time the meal had finished, she felt emotionally overwhelmed. Lethargy seeped into her and her breathing became uneven. She took a deep inhalation in an attempt to calm herself.

Yes, she was thrilled to still be alive but she would be lying if she said she wasn't worried. If…*if* there was someone out to kill or maim Gio she wanted to do whatever to save him. If it was just purely circumstantial about Mike's plane, she needed to do her best to guarantee it never happened again. Not only for the lives of the pilots and their loved ones but also for the money. Each aircraft cost over two billion dollars to procure. Wouldn't do for them to fall out of the sky like raindrops.

"What aren't you telling me?" he asked as he finished his final bit of pecan pie.

"Nothing," she lied without remorse or inflection. "I was thinking about something Lexy said."

Black brows converged as he scowled. "Humph." He'd never liked Lexy. Considered her to be a waste of his time. But he'd never forbidden them from seeing each other. He just didn't approve.

She and Lexy were like night and day. Lexy was exuberant and sexy, a consummate joker. A woman who rarely took anything seriously outside of her job. She loved life and it showed in everything she did. While, personally, Jaydee was far on the other end of the spectrum.

"Still associating with her." It wasn't a question. No, it was a statement, one laced with disappointment.

"She's my friend."

Her only female one. Even though she got along with Lexy's brothers and she called them friends — brothers — they weren't in the same vein as Lexy. There was no one else who didn't seem to mind her odd behaviours, or the fact that she asked what others might perceive as rude questions. Lexy didn't care.

What about Gio?

That thought made her heart go pitter-patter.

Dr Thompson grunted and gave his card to the waitress. Truth of the matter, Jaydee figured he didn't actually mind so much. There had been some things he'd disapproved of and she no longer did them, or associated with those people. So the fact that all he did was grumble about Lexy, she took it as his approval. Or as much as she'd receive from him.

After returning his card to his wallet, he gave her a look that said, without actually saying a word, the time for them to leave had arrived. Without hesitation, she got to her feet while he did the same. Coat in his hand, he waited for her before ushering her to the door. As they trekked into the parking lot, he whispered a question to her.

"I'm not going to be assaulted again, am I?"

Startled, she jerked her head towards him. Did he jest? There was no way for her to know. "Assaulted?"

"By your Commander Cassano."

She heard his wording. "He is not my commander, and I cannot believe he would strike at you again, even should he happen to show up."

"Perhaps you're right." He walked her to her bike. "Then again, perhaps I am. And he is yours. Goodnight, Jaydee." A simple nod and he went on his way.

The breath she took helped calm her wayward nerves. She felt a bit uneasy after his comment. If he suspected something between her and Gio, then perhaps so did Captain Fentress. That would not be good.

Helmet and vest on, she sat on her motorcycle for a short time before leaving the parking lot. She rode around for a while, unsure of what she should do. Getting Gio in trouble was the last thing she wished to do. She slowed down at the corner and realised where she'd gone. Gio's. Turning on to his street, she drove slowly to his drive.

He sat out on the porch, feet propped up on the railing. The garage door sat open and she saw him rise and walk down the steps to meet her.

With familiar actions, she backed in carefully to park beside his car. Gio stepped in and strode towards her. His face was an unreadable mask. Uncertainty grew within her. He hit the light and pressed the button to lower the door. As it closed, she removed her helmet. She watched him, rolling her shoulders a bit to loosen them.

The sound of the door hitting the cement spurred him into action. In a second, she'd been drawn tight against him. His strong arms embraced her. Then he pulled back and covered her mouth with his in a passionate and possessive kiss.

She moaned and pressed closer. Her body aflame for him. There were no more thoughts of anything other than him. She twined her arms about his neck, arching into him. His large hands drifted down and cupped her cotton-covered ass, fingers lifting the skirt until he had skin on skin.

He thrust against her, his hard length rubbing teasingly against her needy core. Slickness coated her and she whimpered, sucking hard on his invading tongue.

She cursed mentally when he set her away from him. His eyes were liquid fire.

"How was dinner?" he asked in a gravelled tone.

She cocked her head to the side and bit back her instinctive retaliatory question. Surely, he hadn't just kissed her like that only to talk. What would Lexy do? Strip and jump him. She, on the other hand, wasn't that brave or forward.

"Fine, thank you." She watched him from beneath lowered lids. "Did you eat?"

"Yes."

Good. That was out of the way. She swayed towards him, noting how his nostrils flared and fists clenched. "Wonderful."

Halting before him, she reached out and placed a hand on his chest. He backed away, only she pursued until the wall prevented him from further movement.

"We...we should talk," he said, closing his eyes as her second hand joined the first.

"Can't you multi-task?" She untucked his shirt and stared at his Adam's apple as it bobbed. "I was positive you could."

"Sweets," he groaned.

She moved on to the button for his jeans. He grabbed her hand when she began lowering the zipper. Dragging her tongue along her lower lip, she met his gaze. Time to channel her inner Lexy.

"I'm horny, wearing a thong under this skirt, and I really want your cock buried fully in me." A slight, disappointed sigh. "But you want to talk. Fine, let's talk." She stepped away from him, tugged her skirt back down so it covered her completely, and turned to the door leading to the kitchen.

She never made it. Gio had her back against the cool wall, panties ripped off, and his mouth hungrily devouring hers while he pounded fast and deep inside her. They barely left the bed for the remainder of their weekend.

* * * *

On the evening of the final full day, they lay together in his large bed. She lay draped partially over him while he indolently stroked a hand up and down her bare back.

"Jaydee."

She halted in her idyllic drawing of abstract designs. "Yes?"

"Stay tonight as well."

"I cannot. We are due back on base come morning."

"Leave from here," he coaxed.

If only. "No, that isn't advisable."

"Making me feel like a dirty little secret here, sweets." There was thick displeasure in his tone.

"You are." He stiffened and she pushed up on his chest so she could meet his gaze. "We're not supposed to be together like this, Gio. You know that. It *is* a secret. It's had to be one. And can't continue after this."

"What!"

Her heart felt like it was being ripped from her chest. "You need to be the man you were before I arrived. Giovanni Cassano…Casanova. If we're going to be figuring out about Mike and his accident there can be zero reason for Fentress to think there's something between us other than a work relationship."

One black eyebrow rose. "Are you telling me to date other women aside from you? You want me to fuck another woman? Take her in this bed, where you're lying now? Where we've made love? All for appearances' sake?" He sounded incredulous.

Hell no! She swallowed. "I have no claim on you."

His eyes darkened dangerously. "So this is it, then."

He was mad. Furious even. She could see it but didn't understand. Surely he'd known they'd not had a chance of being a real couple. Not with the rules they were breaking.

"This thing is just sex between us. You know that, right?" Better question would be, did she know that? And could she live with it?

"Right." His voice was flat. Cold. Unemotional. After a deep breath he asked, "So how do we discover about Mike?"

She edged off the bed, expecting—no, hoping—he'd stop her. He did no such thing, just stared at her with dispassionate eyes. Swallowing, she made her way to her clothes. She could feel his eyes on her but he never moved or said a word.

"I'll let you know what I find. After all, we'll still see each other at work," she told him after drawing her shirt on over her head, movements slow and stiff, for her body was sore after the weekend spent in his bed. His arms.

Gio sat up but never left the bed, his white sheet pooled around his waist. She ignored her own pain at the way this had unfolded. Not how she'd anticipated it would happen.

Should have backed off before the attachment was formed. Like that would have been possible. Even she couldn't deny there was something between them. But, whatever it was, it had no future. *They* didn't have one.

Reaching for her bag, she grabbed her jeans and drew them on. It didn't take long for her to gather the few items she'd brought with her. Forgoing socks, she shoved into her shoes and tossed her bag over one shoulder. She didn't want to leave but she had to. Gio remained in his bed, bare chest taunting her. The man appeared to be cast from marble, for all the warmth he exuded.

In silence, she made her way to his bedroom door. She stepped through and paused. One hand on the doorjamb, she glanced at him over her shoulder. His hard body in the exact place, his expression the same—angry. She allowed herself a final indulgent look before she walked away. On her bike, she put on her helmet and opened the garage door.

She didn't want to leave. She wanted him to come after her. Sweep her up in his embrace and carry her back to his bed. Revving the engine, she shook her head. This wasn't on him. She had made the decision.

Goodbye.

And so she left, ignored the pain, and made her way home. Along her way, she drove slow and took the time to build up her walls. Had she really just told him to find, date, and yes, even sleep with other women? A heavy sigh. Apparently, she had.

She parked her motorcycle and walked inside the old building. Unable to think any further on Gio with another woman, she shoved it into the back of her mind, in a box, and ran through the information on her tablet. Work. That would fix it.

Before long, she straddled a chair, dressed in shorts and tank top while eating a carrot stick as she studied what she'd written on the board. A sigh of relief slid from her lips as she realised something. It couldn't have been an attack geared to hurt or kill Gio. Lieutenant Walker…Mike had flown his own plane.

Of course, someone could have fixed whatever they did to Gio's plane only to turn around and sabotage it on Mike's. But that didn't seem likely. Then there was the fact that nothing else had happened to Gio's plane.

Still, I'm basically nowhere.

Gaining her feet, she ambled to the kitchen where she put together a light plate of finger foods. Bringing that along with her ice water, she returned to her seat and began looking over the file Sedin had transferred. Yes, she knew it all, but she felt a bit out of focus and therefore went to the hard copy.

She munched on her array of fresh veggies and read through the information. Every so often, she'd jot something down on the notepad beside her. When the plate sat empty, she stopped and readied for bed. Lying down, she tossed and turned, unable to capture the sleep she needed. It dodged her, elusive, until the wee hours when she finally acknowledged she'd had no problems falling asleep in Gio's arms.

When morning arrived, exhaustion lingered but, like usual, she ensured none of it showed as she walked into the facility. She sat in the room with a bottle of water and waited for the other pilots to arrive.

"Morning, Dusti."

She glanced up in time to witness Keel grab himself a cup of joe and two pastries. Then he made his way to her side and sat next to her. A genuine grin lifted her lips. She truly liked him.

"Morning, Keel. Coffee and pastries, did you not eat this morning?"

He dropped his head and sighed. "Not this morning. Baby wasn't very happy and my wife needed the sleep."

"You're such a considerate husband."

He winked at her while he bit into the fruit-filled treat. She smiled and took another drink.

"You free tonight?" he asked.

"I'm sorry?"

He met her gaze. "Free. Unencumbered by previously made plans. Free. Dinner. My house. Meet the wife and kid?"

"Are you sure?"

An affronted look spread across his face. "Of course I am."

Keel continued talking but, honestly, the words ceased making any sort of sense to her. It wasn't his fault, it truly wasn't. She was distracted by Gio in his green flight suit as he walked through the door. He turned his head and stared at her, eyes devoid of anything other than a cool dismissal.

"Dusti?"

He walked in their direction and she forced herself to pay attention to Keel who was in the process of finishing off his last doughnut. She could feel Gio closing on her, she didn't have to see him. He had this presence that she couldn't ignore even if she wished.

"Yes," she said. "Dinner would be wonderful."

"Great."

Chapter Twelve

Gio advanced further into the room. It hurt seeing her. He hurt. Hell, he knew he had it bad for her. But he was also angry. Her words last night had been like a knife to his heart.

When their eyes met today, he had maintained his icy demeanour. Still, he wanted to be closer to her and had strolled in their direction, telling himself he wanted some coffee. He stared at her as he moved. Her flight suit showed off her form in ways that should be illegal. But, then, she could wear anything and he'd want to strip it off her and sink his hardness completely in her.

He got his coffee and overheard her accepting dinner with Keel. *Oh, so it's just me she has a problem being with.* Jealousy rose up swift and deadly inside him.

"Breathe, man."

He blinked and Lizard's face came into view. "What?" His question rang sharp.

"What's with the scowl? Didn't you have a good weekend?"

A quick glance told him they wouldn't be overheard. "Yeah, it was. Right up to the part where she told me it was over and I should spend time with other women."

The expression on Lizard's face was priceless and any other time would have made him laugh. However, right here, right now, it pained him. Had he been a fool thinking it was more than just really amazing sex with Jaydee? Lizard stared at him and he knew what his friend waited for.

"There's no punchline, Jason, don't expect one."

He turned to walk off only to freeze when his friend grabbed him. Eyebrows arched, he waited for him to speak.

"Are you kidding me? I thought..." Lizard lowered his voice, "you two had a thing."

That damn pain made itself known again. Gritting his teeth, Gio found a small measure of restraint. A sarcastic smirk filled his features. "She said it was best to end it." He almost told Jason about their still working together dealing with Mike's accident but at the last minute kept that nugget of information to himself.

"I'm sorry, man."

He didn't want sympathy, damn it! He wanted...Jaydee. With a nonchalant shrug, he drank some coffee, relishing the burn as it slid down his throat. "She was a fuck. A good one, but still just a fuck."

Lizard's snort told of his disbelief but he didn't say anything, merely grabbed his own mug of java. Gio observed the room and, consequently, Jaydee again. This time her gaze waited for his. A punch to his gut almost took his breath. Those large tortoiseshell eyes shimmered with emotion briefly, before they cooled to how he remembered them from when they'd butted heads.

He could do this. He *would* do this. If it killed him. Which it very well might do. Clapping a hand on Lizard's shoulder, he drifted towards the shared table of Keel and Jaydee. He held her gaze the entire way, daring her. Stay or go. If she stayed, she had to deal with him. If she ran, she looked like a coward. *He* wasn't about to run.

At the last minute, he grabbed a chair, spun it around, and straddled it as he set his cup down on the tabletop.

"Morning," he said.

Keel smiled. "Hey, Casanova. How are you? Have a good ninety-six?"

Flashing the man a quick check he went back to study Jaydee. He raked his gaze over her and said, "Oh yeah, I sure did. You know how it is when you're single."

"Man, I'm a married man now. I've not been single in a long time."

Jaydee's expression was bland and so he purposefully moved his gaze from her to Keel. Out of the corner of his eye, he watched her chat with someone who'd stopped by the table on their way past. That jealousy began growing again from deep in his gut and spreading throughout his body.

She lifted her bottle to her lips and drank. His gaze was drawn to the graceful way her throat moved. The light sheen of sweat on her skin made him recall how she looked above him, riding his cock. Hell, even beneath him. He wanted to lean close and lick it from the column of her neck before biting it.

He knew what reaction that would give her and he jumped slightly when a foot connected with his shin.

Slashing his gaze to Lizard, he scowled at him but stopped when he realised what he'd been doing. Losing his mind as he daydreamed about Jaydee.

The CO entered and strode over to their table. "Morning."

A chorus of "Good morning, sir," filled the air.

He grabbed a chair and drew it close before leaning his lanky body against it. "We will be briefing in the air today. Be ready to take to the air in thirty." Then he left.

Gio watched the man stride away. Was he behind the incident? He hated the indecisiveness that filled him over this entire situation. Keel and Lizard rose and he took his time. He returned his empty mug in the rack and pivoted on his heel. His pulse skyrocketed.

Jaydee stood a way back from him, waiting with what he knew to be endless patience. A sudden icy contempt burst through him and he narrowed his eyes while stiffening his posture. He knew that they were alone but couldn't make himself move.

"Thought this was not to be advised," he forced through clenched teeth.

A brief spark of hurt lit her gaze before it vanished, leaving him once again facing the unflappable, ever calm Jaydee Amos.

"I had a thought about Mike," she said. Her voice dragged over him like crushed velvet, setting nerve endings on fire.

Ignoring his physical reaction, he strode towards her, all attention on Mike. "What?" he demanded.

She twisted around and headed for the door. He fell into step beside her. It barely took any time and his mind was drifting back to them.

"I don't think it was an attack on you. Mike took up his own plane and while I don't know what purposefully caused the accident—if anything—it would take a lot to fix your plane and sabotage Mike's without anyone noticing."

He mulled that over for a bit. Made sense. "Okay, so it would be hard, but would it be impossible?"

They pushed through and made their way to where their bombers waited.

"No, not impossible. I haven't figured it all out yet but wanted to let you know, taking into account I said I would keep you apprised."

"Jaydee." Her name sounded tortured as it rolled from his lips.

She met his seeking gaze, her own brimming with sorrow and passion. "Don't make this harder than it already is." Her tone was soft yet insistent.

He watched her walk away with part of his heart. It had been hard as hell to lie in bed and let her leave. How the hell would he get through this? In his periphery, he saw her meet Keel and begin their pre-flight.

"What the hell, man?" Lizard asked.

"Let it go."

"Fuck that. What's going on?"

Moving his gaze from the underside of the wing to Lizard's questioning face, Gio sighed. "I told you."

"So, what, that bitch can just—"

One step put him directly into Jason's space. "Do *not* call her that!" He shook with the extent of his anger. The urge to throw Lizard against the landing gear and beat the shit out of him swam over him.

"Okay, sorry." Lizard stepped back. "You really love her, don't you?"

Gio stared at his friend for a moment. "Get the pre-flight done," he barked and got back to it himself. Love. Damn him for mentioning that four-letter word.

She'd made her choice, there wasn't anything he could do about that particular shitty situation. Not anything that would be legal, anyway. Kidnapping was still a crime as far as he knew.

Outside pre-flight done, he climbed in, ignored Lizard, and sat in his seat. His actions were automatic. He shouldn't be here, his mind was anywhere but where it should be.

Smack!

He blinked and snarled. "What?"

"Get your head out of your ass," Lizard snapped back. "I have plans tonight."

"I'm fine."

Lizard snorted and looked away. *Damn it!* She wanted him out with other women, did she? Wanted him to act like he had before she'd arrived on the scene? Fine. He would. He forced everything but flying the B-2 to the back of his mind and waited for the go to take to the sky.

He nodded to Lizard as they headed from the plane back to the building. The day had been a good one. Lot of tests, pushing the envelope, and whatnot. He'd loved it.

After his shower, he left the building to see Keel and Jaydee standing together, laughing. Her relaxed attitude tore through him like a jagged knife. Why couldn't she be like that around him? In public?

More pain speared him as he watched her follow Keel's car from the lot on her motorcycle. Logically, he knew there was nothing between her and Keel. Logically. None of that mattered to the primitive male in him who was beating his chest and demanding he kill another for touching what was his.

He shook his head in disgust as he walked to his car. Jaydee wasn't an object.

Mine! his brain demanded.

Keel was happily married. With a kid to boot. Or was he?

Shit! I have to get over this.

He climbed in his car and headed towards Kerrigan's for a much-needed drink.

The rest of the week passed in a similar fashion. He was coolly polite to Jaydee. She looked tired but it seemed he was the only one who noticed. The lab geeks were still around and he knew, he *knew* she put in time with them as well.

* * * *

He glanced across the open area and spied her and Lizard at the same picnic table. He grabbed a drink for himself and Lizard then paused, went back and picked up one more.

"What's going on here?" he asked, lowering himself to a vacant seat. He used one hand to slide a drink to Jaydee then to Lizard. Although one of the hardest things he'd ever done, he kept his eyes off Jaydee's sweaty body. Everyone had gone running together and damn if she didn't look amazing.

"Thanks." She spoke softly before uncapping the bottle and taking a healthy swallow.

"Yeah, man. Thanks." Lizard also drank.

Keel ambled up with his own drink in hand and sat down beside Jaydee with a grunt. "Crap, is it just me or did that feel like torture?"

Gio agreed with him. PT this time of day seemed ludicrous. But they only had certain times to get their workouts in. So, when Keel had asked if they wanted to accompany him on his run, he'd accepted. Then he'd learned Jaydee would be running too.

She'd shown up in a black top and tight shorts, the colour of which showcased the lean muscles in her legs, along with her amazing ass. She'd barely glanced at him and he'd made sure to run abreast of her, not behind.

Once they'd begun running the weather had changed and grown hot. So, now, here they all sat, grateful for the shade from the tree and the refreshing water and sports drinks.

"You suggested it," he said with a wry grin.

"There was a breeze then."

Gio finished his drink and used the opportunity to steal another peek at Jaydee. She was lost in thought. He knew the look.

"So," he said, cracking his neck, "who's up for going out?"

Lizard chimed in immediately and surprisingly Keel did as well. That was two. Spinning his empty bottle, he stared directly at her.

"What about you, Amos?" She didn't say anything and he knocked on the table to snap her from her thoughts. "Amos!"

"Sorry, what?"

Like always, those eyes made him melt. Professional relationship. He'd said it over and over until he sort of believed it. Yeah, right.

"We're going out tonight. You joining us or are you too good to hang with your fellow pilots?"

"Won't it cramp your style having me along?"

If she only knew. "Nope. The women there know you're one of us, so you're not a threat." He waited for any flash of pain in her eyes or expression. There was nothing.

"Sure, why not."

He stood. "See you all tonight."

With a wave he headed off. He had to leave or there'd be no way for him to control himself. How could he? She wore next to nothing, her firm body aglow with sweat. Christ, his cock was so hard in his shorts, it hurt.

Inside he took a shower. A *cold* shower. Captain Fentress waited for him when he made his way to his locker. Standing up tall, he ignored the fact that he wore only a towel.

"We're getting another pilot." Fentress leaned against the other row of lockers.

"Sir?"

"Next week. Another is coming in."

A bad feeling grew in his gut. "To replace Amos?"

"Yes." Green eyes held his. "That a problem for you?"

Yes. It meant she would be leaving soon, and no matter what crap she'd spouted he knew she had feelings for him that went beyond bed partner.

A blank expression on his face, he arched one brow. "No, sir, any reason it should?"

"Just curious. I've seen the way you look at her."

He shrugged with way more nonchalance than he felt. This screamed dangerous waters to him. "The same as pretty much every other red-blooded male. She's hot. I'm not blind."

"But?"

"But what, sir?"

"Nothing." Fentress pushed away from the lockers. "I merely wanted to give you a heads-up on the new pilot."

"Thank you, sir." He frowned. "Permission to speak freely, sir?"

"Go ahead."

"If he's not flying with me, how is his arrival relevant to me?"

Fentress gave him a stare that would have quelled another man. Fortunately, he wasn't just another man. "It's relevant, Lieutenant Commander, because you two will be going head to head to secure the final spot in a combat squad." He strode off.

Combat squad. Just the thought got his pulse thrumming. It had been a while since he'd actually been assigned to one. He'd been taken from one and sent to the test facility because he'd forever been pushing the envelope. Had he been pleased? Hell no. But the man who had sent him had known exactly how to push his buttons.

"They are saying there's no way a Navy pilot could be better than one of theirs. Guess, by your attitude, they were right," Admiral Griffin had said.

Better than him? Not likely. So he'd turned his attention to learning to fly the B-2. And he was the best now. Sure, it had been like flying a tank at the beginning, but now he loved it. Jaydee's face came to him and he sighed. Second best, perhaps.

Glancing at his Blue Angels Citizen Eco-Drive watch, he put on clean clothes in a hurry. As he tied his shoes, he felt his skin prickle at the knowledge that he would be seeing her soon.

She was the last to arrive at the bar. He, Keel and Lizard were already at their table when he lifted his head in time to see her walk through the door. She wore jeans and a T-shirt that happened to cover considerably more than other women in the establishment, but she was one hundred per cent sexier, in his opinion. Jaydee rocked a pair of heavy black boots and her hair was drawn back into a serviceable ponytail. She sliced through the crowd with ease and she stood at their table in short time.

"Hey, Jaydee," Lizard said.

"Hey." She sat in the lone vacant chair. Across from him. He'd planned it that way.

"Here's your drinks," Carly, the waitress, said. "I brought you water, Jaydee, since that's what you normally have, but if you want something else..." She trailed off with the offer.

"No, thank you, water is perfect." She took the bottle with a smile.

Carly gave her a grin. He noticed how Lizard continued to watch Jaydee and wondered. But Gio didn't remain focused on Jaydee and Lizard too much longer for a brunette walked up, trailed her fingers along his shoulders, and the back of his neck. Then she sat her scantily clad ass in his lap.

"What'd I miss?" she asked while picking up her 57 Chevy and taking a sip. "Hey, who are you?" Everyone there knew she meant Jaydee. "And why would you only drink water at a bar?"

For her part, Jaydee barely blinked as she slowly lowered her bottle. Despite the trim and stacked woman seated on his lap, it was the slow swipe of Jaydee's tongue to capture the single lingering droplet of water from her lip that did him in. It was an act that made blood rush to his cock.

"I'm a pilot with these men and I drink water because I prefer not to dull my senses and possibly engage in something foolish."

"Shelly, that's Jaydee," Gio informed his date.

"Hi," she chirped, obviously dismissing Jaydee. Her heavily perfumed body settled closer to him. "Can we play pool?"

"Sure." Anything to get her off him. "Go grab a table."

She slid from his lap, plastered a big wet kiss on his mouth and sauntered off, drink in hand. *Damn her!* Although he wasn't sure which her he meant. But Jaydee was supposed to be jealous, not lost in thought. And he knew she was, for he knew her expressions.

"Anyone else want to play?"

Keel stood up. "I'm in." He nudged Jaydee and said, "Come on, partner."

She blinked up at him. "I'm playing?"

"Yes. You n' me against Casanova and his date."

He waited and, sure enough, she lifted her head and met his gaze. "All right."

She walked with Keel to the pool table. He stared at her ass before putting his attention on Lizard.

"You're playing a dangerous game, Casanova."

"This is on her, man. I'd much rather be with her. She's the one who told me to go back to my old ways." His words were bitter.

"There has to be a better way."

"What's with the change of heart? You were almost as pissed as I was when I first told you."

"I know." He clapped him on the shoulder. "I was wrong. Go on, they're waiting on you."

He sighed and headed to the table with his drink. Keel and Shelly watched him while Jaydee never spared him a glance. In fact, she currently spoke to a man at the next table. The growl had to be forced back.

"Ready?" he asked, forcing his tone to remain calm.

They played two games and each pair took one. Racking the balls he said, "Best two out of three?"

"Sorry, no. I must get going." Jaydee's smooth voice slipped tantalisingly along his skin.

"Hot date, Dusti?" he asked as if talking to any other pilot.

As if he wasn't on eggshells awaiting the answer. And as if he'd actually be able to curb his raging jealousy should her answer be in the affirmative. Those multi-hued eyes slid to him.

"No. Thank you for the invite. Have a good night."

She said her farewells to Keel and Lizard, who'd found a blonde to adore him, then made her way to the door and left after stopping at the bar. He assumed she had paid for her water.

Lord help him, all he wanted to do was follow her and...

"Casanova," Shelly whined, dragging her long, painted nails down his chest.

"What?"

"I want another drink."

"Go get one then." She pursed bright red lips. "Tell them to put it on my tab." The smile returned and she sashayed off, tugging at the hem of her very short, tight dress. *What the hell was I thinking?*

He hadn't been. All he'd wanted to do was make Jaydee jealous, so he'd gone back to his usual. Gorgeous, fake, and not at all what he wanted. These women were merely a distraction because, *yes*, he loved women. And it wasn't to say Jaydee wasn't gorgeous, because she was. Hers was a real beauty, not one bought and paid for.

His gaze landed on Shelly as she sauntered back through the increased crowd. He leaned against the wall and observed her. She flirted heavily and he continued to wait for some bite of jealousy and got none. Just like before.

With a groan, he gave his empty bottle to a passing waitress. She winked at him and blew him a kiss before continuing on her way. "I'm out," he told Lizard who was playing tonsil hockey with the blonde. Keel had left moments after Jaydee had.

"Catch ya later, man. Have fun." Lizard's face disappeared again.

Shaking his head, he scanned for Shelly. She stood with another man, his hand possessively upon her ass. He chuckled and moseyed up behind her.

"Night, Shelly." He ignored her squeal of surprise. "You be safe," he added with a pointed look at the man whose hand had never left her ass.

She stared at him before giving him a tentative smile. He knew she was after having an itch scratched and didn't begrudge her. And, since he wouldn't have been going home with her, he figured she might as well get it somewhere. He'd known after finding Jaydee again, she was the only one for him.

He turned and headed for his car. The weather had become stormy and he sighed. Time to go home.

Jaydee yawned and worked out the kinks in her back. She was leaving in three weeks. Part of the time she'd be up with Keel, and when he was up with his new pilot she would be working with three of the doctors who were staying behind. Her secret was out now—everyone knew she had the title 'Doctor' in front of her name, along with Lieutenant Commander.

It bothered her, but Dr Thompson had told her she would be remaining for a while to help straighten out some things. Okay. It was bullshit. She had one week back in the air and then she would watch *another* pilot fly *her* plane.

She always knew she would be back in the lab and had accepted that. Just, typically, she didn't have to see the jets, smell the fuel, or watch the pilots talk and joke about how amazing it had been.

"Damn it," she muttered, kicking an imaginary object.

"Hmm. Now here's a sight, the great, unflappable Jaydee Amos swearing."

Gio's voice made her close her eyes briefly before she summoned up the courage to face him. Her breath caught as she stared at him. He wore jeans that hung from lean hips—they had worn spots on them. A tan shirt hugged along powerful shoulders and arms before falling around his rock-hard abs. She lowered her gaze and moved it down to where his black shoes were on the carpet.

"Gio."

His name was dragged from her on a sigh. A sigh of longing. The past week had been hell on her. Each day, the looks he'd given her had grown less and less personal. She continued to tell herself it was for the best, but it wasn't easy. Not at all. Until finally she ignored it and went on with her work.

"Dusti." He strode in and gestured with his chin at the boards behind her. "Find anything?"

Hurt speared her before she understood why. Liar, she knew exactly from the first second. He'd come for information, not her.

You're the one who told him to end it, her subconscious took much pleasure in reminding her.

Info. Right. She nodded and presented him with her back. With a slight dig of short nails into her palm, she composed herself. Time to forget emotion and do her job. It didn't matter—despite her resolve, her body reacted sexually when he appeared next to her.

"What'd you find?" he asked on a thread of urgency.

"It wasn't personally against you or Mike." She rubbed her eyes before picking up the eraser and cleaning off the board.

"How can you be certain?"

Sitting on the edge of the nearest table, she swung her legs. "I went back and pulled some records. The struts between the leading edge sections..." She trailed off.

"What? What about the struts?"

"Do you have time to accompany me to the shelter?" She paused. "Or do you have someone waiting?" Hopefully he didn't pick up on any bitterness in her voice with the final query.

"Mike's more important than anything. Let's go."

She ignored that he never denied having someone waiting for him and finished straightening up before heading to the door. Gio fell into step beside her as they strode from the building. She knew he'd automatically adjusted his stride for her shorter one. Silence stretched between them and she could feel his gaze assessing her.

Bypassing the hangar where the pieces of Mike's plane were housed, she froze at the strong grip of Gio's hand around her upper arm. Heat flushed her and it took incredible calm to merely glance at him over her shoulder with an eyebrow raised.

"His plane is here."

"I know. And there are people in there. Do you want to answer their questions?"

He couldn't release her fast enough it seemed, before he continued on his way. She followed and soon they were inside the hangar where her bomber was kept.

The front and back large doors were closed so they entered through a small side door. She flicked on the lights and felt the familiar buzz in her blood as the Spirit was highlighted. The black shape never failed to take her breath away.

Gio moved up behind her, nearly overwhelming her with his presence. There was no actual contact, but she could feel his heat.

"The struts segment the leading edge into sections. The ten-centimetre-wide pieces are there to allow each section to be electrified individually." Her belly tightened.

"Okay." He stepped beside her, arms crossed, and gave her his full attention.

"This setup allows us to actually steer the craft gravitically."

"More of that EG stuff."

His wry tone brought a smile to her face. "Precisely." She sighed. "Anyway, for it to work, everything else has to align as well, you know this. I had not taken as big a look at this before but going back through I did. I double-checked his maintenance logs."

"What'd you find?" He reached out to touch the landing gear before he sank to the floor beside the large wheel.

She hesitated, taking a moment to look at him. Right here, right now she faced the true Giovanni Cassano. His pilot arrogance still remained, but it was not as prevalent. His thick, gorgeous lashes weren't partially shielding a sexually infused gaze, with just enough to get the woman he wanted. No, right now they rested on his cheeks as he sat there. She knew he still paid attention even though his eyes were shut, so she answered him.

"There were some discrepancies in the logs so I'm digging deeper. But one of his struts was wrong. From the wrong batch or something. Whatever it is, it didn't belong."

She squeezed her eyes shut and pinched the bridge of her nose. This job had become draining and she needed some rest. A gasp escaped her when she opened her eyes. Gio stood right before her. The look in his incredible hazel eyes could be summed up in one word. Hunger. Pure, undiluted, raw, and ravenous hunger.

She stepped back, trying to focus on something other than how he made her feel. "Th...that's all I know for the moment."

He stalked her until a wall at her back prevented any further retreat. One hand on either side of her head, he boxed her in, his gaze travelling from her eyes to mouth and back. His desire clear.

"I thought we were doing this together."

She swallowed. "We are. I'm doing my job. If you start nosing around someone may become suspicious. You keep doing what you are. I will keep you in the loop on what—if anything—I find."

A dangerous growl rumbled from him. Her own desires flared up but she quickly and efficiently put them in a compartment. It was her way of doing things. Compartmentalisation. So no matter how much she lusted after the hot Italian-American pilot before her, her focus could, and would, remain on her job.

Confident in her ability, she stared at him. "What's wrong?"

"We're alone in here and you're standing there like there is nothing between us."

"We're alone to ensure people don't overhear us. And there isn't. Were you not with that brunette, Shelly, recently? Perhaps you should return to her for some relief." She ducked by him. "When you're up next keep an extra eye on the AI and let me know if it even flickers."

Her cell phone rang, cutting off whatever he was about to say. "Amos."

Captain Fentress.

"Yes, sir. Right away. Oh, I know where Casanova is, sir. I'll pass along the message. Right away, yes, sir."

Gio stared at her, a scowl on his face and his arms crossed. "What's that about?"

She chewed on the inside of her cheek. "My replacement is here and Fentress wants us to meet him."

A myriad of emotions passed over his face. "He said it was a man, did he say who it was?"

"No. We should go. Look at the bright side, Casanova, you won't have to fly with me anymore." She headed for the door.

Gio's arm reached around her, stopping her from opening it. "This isn't over between us, Jaydee, not by a long shot. And, for your information, I'd fly with you any day."

His words made her feel mushy. "There is no us," she stated.

His chuckle wasn't the least bit humorous and was definitely menacing. "Whatever you have to tell yourself, sweets."

The door opened and she walked through. He kept pace beside her as they approached the main building. The doors opened before they arrived and a man in shorts, flip-flops and a tank top stepped out.

"You must be Casanova," the man said, stepping forward with a smile.

Gio reached out a hand when the man pulled back and tilted his head forward. He stared at her over the top of his aviator glasses and his lips curved up into a wide grin.

"Lieutenant Amos? As I live and breathe. It's good to see you again."

Beside her Gio stiffened. Recognition hit her. Thomas Hirsch. "Colonel Hirsch, how nice to see you."

He smiled, transforming his handsome face to downright mouth-watering. She took his offered hand, somewhat mollified this was the man taking her place.

"You know Lieutenant Commander Amos?" Gio butted in.

"Lieutenant Commander now, is it? Congrats, Dusti, that is well deserved."

She reclaimed her hand. "Thank you. This is Lieutenant Commander Cassano, aka Casanova. This"—she indicated the newcomer—"is Colonel Hirsch."

The men shook hands. "Got time for dinner, Jaydee?" Tommy asked.

Gio growled again but she refused to acknowledge him. "That would be great." A slight hesitation. "Would you like to join us?" She addressed Gio.

"No, thanks, I've got a date. Nice to meet you, Colonel."

"Call me Beast. Or Tommy." He put his attention back on her. "Let me get changed and I'll give you a call around…nineteen-hundred? I hope you still prefer to eat then."

"Sounds perfect."

Thomas walked off before turning so he moved backwards and calling out, "Number still the same?"

"Absolutely."

Another knee-knocking smile before he pivoted and jogged off to the parking lot.

"He knows when you like to eat and has your number?"

The question came on a low rumble of fury. She slanted her gaze to Gio's face. He reminded her of a warrior, a tic in his clenched jaw.

"Everyone has my number. I should get going."

"Who is he to you?" A dangerous undercurrent surged between them.

"No more your business than your date is mine. Goodnight, Cassano." She veered away from him and headed for her bike. As she geared up for the ride home, she glanced back to where she'd left him. Gio had vanished. Stifling her sigh, she went home.

A short time before seven she climbed off her bike and this time made her way into a restaurant. Thomas waited right outside the door for her.

"Hi, Jaydee," he said with a smile.

"Tommy."

She couldn't help but notice his looks. Military cut on his medium brown hair, tanned skin, a perfect smile along with a magnificent body. Enough to make women swoon. Probably some men, too.

He held her chair for her and waited until they'd placed their drink order before saying anything. The unpleasant churning in her gut returned and she shifted in her seat. Tommy's clear blue eyes sparkled and he grinned at her.

"So, tell me about this place and the one I'll be flying with. Follow that up with all the information on this Commander Cassano."

Chapter Thirteen

Gio scowled. He sat outside eating his lunch. Two days had passed since Air Force pilot Thomas Hirsch had arrived, which meant that in less than a week Jaydee wouldn't even be flying. Then he and this newcomer would be competing to see which of them would be seeing combat. And Jaydee would still be leaving.

His scowl deepened. A feminine squeal split the air and he jerked his head up and around. Jaydee ran towards another woman and they embraced. Squinting against the sun, he stared at the one with Jaydee.

She wore heels, a short skirt, and a tight skimpy top. It hit him. Her friend Lexy from the first night. He watched Tommy as the man went over and also said hello to Lexy. Another mark against the man in his opinion. He knew her friend, which begged the question *how* well did Jaydee and Thomas know one another? He breathed a bit easier when Tommy left.

All he could glean about their past was they'd flown together before. And respected one another greatly.

His gaze drifted back to where Jaydee stood talking to her very animated friend. This woman brought out an entirely different side to Jaydee.

Dr Thompson approached the duo and Gio watched avidly, ignoring Lizard when he sat at the table. Jaydee quieted down a bit and it didn't take a genius to understand Dr Thompson wasn't a huge Lexy fan.

"Who's the babe?"

"Jaydee's friend, Lexy."

Jason gave a low whistle. "Is she single?"

"Lizard!"

"What, man? She's smokin' hot."

Gio rolled his eyes. Sometimes there was no stopping Lizard.

"We should welcome her as well." Lizard stood and tugged on his shirt. "It'd be the gentlemanly thing to do."

This time he snorted. "What the hell do you know about being a gentleman?"

Lizard's grin was shameless. "For a piece of that ass, I'll learn. Come on."

He groaned even as he followed his friend. By the time they reached the women, Dr Thompson had left. Which was fine. Personally he still felt a bit uncomfortable in the knowledge that he'd socked her father in the face.

"Good afternoon, Dusti. Ma'am." Lizard broke the ice.

They fell silent and faced them both. Lexy's grey gaze snagged his and it hardened briefly, yet enough so he knew that she recalled exactly who he was. Then her stare drifted over Lizard in a long, drawn-out perusal before a foxy grin turned up the corners of her full mouth.

"Aren't y'all just gorgeous." The thick, syrupy Southern drawl made him smile. Although he'd been verbally included, he couldn't help but feel left out. "N' don't call me ma'am, handsome. I'm Lexy."

"Lieutenant Jason Armstrong, at your service." Lizard jerked a thumb over his shoulder. "That's Casanova." The way his friend said it made him feel like an afterthought.

Lexy smiled and he could practically see the heat between those two. Over their heads, he met Jaydee's gaze. Hers was a bit unfocused and he knew she no longer paid attention to the conversation around her. He was amused—it was like her mind never took a break.

Unless she is exhausted after a long session of hard, sweaty sex. Then she tends to sleep like a baby.

He realised something. She was logical. He was Italian and went on emotions. Not that it was an excuse, it was just how he was. Part of his DNA.

"What do you say, Casanova?" Lizard nudged him in the side.

He had no idea what had been said. "Sure."

"Wonderful. So, we'll get the food and see you two around eight."

"Awesome!" Lexy said before dismissing them and putting all her attention back on Jaydee. The women linked arms and strolled away. Only Lexy peered back.

"So tell me, Romeo, what I just agreed to."

"A cookout. You, me, Tommy, and Keel with his family. And of course those two ladies. Tonight. At your place."

Shit. He wanted to go home and crash, not entertain. On the other hand, Jaydee would be there.

"If all you wanted was to get in her pants why did you bring me into your schemes?"

"Who else would I bring along?"

"Bastard," he muttered good-naturedly. "Now, come on. I don't have enough food for everyone. We're shopping and you're paying."

"What?"

"Your idea, your dime."

Jason grumbled a bit but paid. That night, with his backyard full of friends and some neighbours, Gio waited on pins and needles for Jaydee and Lexy to arrive. He perked up at the familiar sound of her motorcycle's engine and he moved to the gate to witness their approach.

His breath caught as her Ninja came into view, Lexy riding on the back. They parked along the street and he ignored the desire to go to her and claim her before everyone.

They headed towards him. Lexy wore a bit more than earlier, but what she did wear was skin-tight, while Jaydee wore baggier attire. And, like usual, it was his sexy scientist-pilot who made him lose control.

"Thanks for the invite, handsome," Lexy purred, brushing by with a pat on one pectoral.

"You're...welcome," he said to air. Lexy had progressed, leaving him alone with Jaydee.

"Hi." Her voice was hushed.

"Come on, Lizard's about ready to feed us."

She nodded and walked beside him. He couldn't help reaching out and trailing two fingers through her hair. Jaydee stiffened briefly before she continued on as if he'd never even touched her. His fingers dug into his palms so he didn't grab her to him and kiss her with all the pent-up sexual tension that had been building for the past few weeks.

This fucking sucked!

The evening passed with a blink. Keel's wife, Felicia, had brought some desserts and they were well received. He stood on his porch and watched his visitors play volleyball in the waning light. Except for Jaydee. She sat on a lounge chair beside the sleeping baby.

"So you're him," Lexy said. She leaned beside him on the railing. "I remember you from the bar."

He sliced his eyes down to her before staring back out at the loud game. "And you're the friend who encouraged her to wear what she did."

She gave a low laugh. "That's me. So, I'm guessing by the way you've tried so damn hard to not stare at her all night, it's over between you two. Her decision, of course."

"Of course?"

"I hardly think you'd be acting like this had you been the one who ended it, handsome." Her tone was light yet matter-of-fact.

True. When he dumped a girl that was it. There was no pining after her, or wanting more. None of what he was going through at this moment with Jaydee.

"She tell you that?"

"Didn't have to. Jaydee is my best friend. I can read her like a book."

"She's infuriating."

More laughter. "Jaydee isn't like most women you'll meet."

"I know that." Man, did he ever.

"No, I don't think you do. It takes a lot for her to do this," she waved a hand to the yard, "and come across as 'normal' to everyone."

He observed Jaydee. She didn't look lonely over where she sat—she seemed more relaxed than she'd been all night.

Lexy shifted to sit on the rail. "She was tired of being labelled a freak. Wanted to try to fit in with others. It's hard, she is a private person. And an inquisitive one."

"She said she was sent to live with her father because—"

"Because that bitch of a mother wanted to please the men she brought over to fuck, and having a child ask them questions and not appear embarrassed by anything tended to ruin that." Thick venom dripped from her statement.

He thought about that for a bit and nodded. "She is smart."

"Yeah, she sure is. Do you even know how smart?"

"Nope. She just said she was considered smarter than some."

Lexy coughed. "Wow. Well, she was tested above genius level when she was nine, which was when we met. Let me break it down for you. My girl is fucking brilliant. Off the goddamn charts brilliant. Despite all that, she lacks a lot of social graces, because they weren't important for her to learn. That's where I come in. I am safe and she can have fun and know it's okay."

He frowned. "So, it's all an act?"

"Yes. And no. Not with you, but this, here, tonight, yes. She is trying desperately to behave normally."

"Surely her father—"

"His focus was her smarts. She's a commodity to him. Always has been. And, right now, she's one who works for the United States government."

"But she graduated from Annapolis. How did she do that if she has such an issue with social interactions?"

"Daily emails."

He shook his head. "Plebes aren't allowed outside contact except for the parent day."

Her smirk made him arch a brow. "I told you, fuckin' brilliant. We emailed daily and no one was the wiser." She shrugged. "Look, my point is, she's not the same. No matter how she tries, you can't lump her into the category you would me. She likes you. I know this. She knows this."

"I don't. She told me it wouldn't work."

"Jaydee likes rules. She follows them for the most part. And she compartmentalises. It is her coping mechanism. And I'll tell you right now, if you don't force her to face whatever is between y'all, she never will. By the end of her time here, she'll look in that box that contains her feelings for you, sigh, and delete it. Then she'll move on."

He watched her slide off the rail. "Delete it. Like it was a file on a computer?"

Lexy's expression was serious. Disturbingly so. "Exactly like that. It's how she's survived, she's had to. Only problem, now she can't stop doing it. It's an ingrained habit."

"Why are you telling me this?"

She stepped closer. "Because you get through her barriers. You brought her into the land of the living and I want her here with me." Another step and their chests almost brushed. "Don't think, though, that if you hurt her I won't come after you, because trust me, handsome, I'll be on your ass. Sure as shittin', I will. And I'll bury my five-inch stilettos right through your balls and heart without any hesitation."

He flinched at the deadpan statement. He couldn't help it. Lexy walked away and joined Jaydee on the loungers. He mulled over the stuff she'd told him about Jaydee. Yes, she was different, but he loved that about her.

Huh, would you look at that. He didn't panic at the word love. He strolled down the steps and to the makeshift volleyball court.

"You playing, Casanova?"

"You got it." He whipped off his shirt and shoes then joined them.

* * * *

Jaydee strode through the hallway, a particular destination in mind.

"Amos!"

Twisting around, she found Fentress bearing down on her. She waited. "Sir?" she asked when he halted.

He seemed drawn and tired. "I wanted a chance to speak to you privately."

"What can I do for you?"

"I'm sending Beast up with Keel today. I know it's not time for the switch yet and it's not on the board but that's what it is. The replacement for Dr Thompson arrived today and, since you two will be working together overseeing the final training of our guys, I wanted you to work with him today."

"Very good, sir." She isolated the pain and disappointment and locked it away.

"Speak freely, Dusti, if there is something you want to say."

"No, sir. I understand. He's your permanent pilot, he should be logging the hours. If there is nothing else, I will head over to the lab."

"That's all. You will be in the air tomorrow."

"Yes, sir." She stood straight then walked away. There was no point in going to change into her flight suit so she made her way with her comfortable clothes and music to the lab. She entered the large room and glanced around. There were a few people there but not many.

"Good morning, Dr Amos," one woman said as she went by, a steaming cup of coffee in her hand.

"Kelly," she replied smoothly.

"You're here, why?" Dr Thompson's voice came from behind her.

"Orders. Captain Fentress wants me working with the one replacing you when you leave."

He grunted. "Good idea. He's in the cafeteria at the present. Come look at these equations on the board."

She followed him without question to a whiteboard. Ignoring her belly's demands for substance, she got directly to work. In the process of correcting the third equation, she halted when her name was called and a hand touched her shoulder.

Lifting her head, she rotated to see who needed her attention. As she realised who it was, a large smile crossed her lips. Tall and leanly muscular, with blond hair and startling blue eyes, Dr Ivan Vinokourov stood before her. Iceberg blue, she called his eye colour, for it reminded her of the pale tinting the icebergs picked up from the reflection of both sky and sea.

"Ivan!"

"Jaydee." He wrapped his arms around her and held tight.

She closed her eyes and welcomed it. Ivan was her second truest friend after Lexy. After a moment, they drew apart. She stared into his eyes.

"You're replacing Dr Thompson?"

"On his recommendation."

Ivan sounded as surprised as she was by his announcement, although she knew she shouldn't be. Ivan was at the top of his game. He'd been Dr Thompson's protégé for a while.

"He picked well." She sneaked a glance at her father to find him watching them with a calculated gleam in his eyes. Ignoring that puzzle for the moment, she focused back on Ivan. "I was told this morning to come here and meet you. So, have you had a tour or did you want to get right to work?"

"Let's work, then we can chat after lunch."

She agreed and went to her boards and got back to work. Time flew and, before she knew it, Ivan made his presence known. She capped her marker and gave her work on KVA a final perusal. KVA stood for kilovolt-amperes. In their field, the term had exclusive use in referring to power consumption by an AC power source. Part of their investigative use of time-varying electric fields for EG propulsion.

Rolling her shoulders, she set the marker down and walked beside Ivan. She pointed out things as they slowly made their way to the cafeteria.

"Where are you staying?" she asked, grabbing a tray.

"Same place as you. Dr T recommended it to me."

"It is a very comfortable place." She put down a cheeseburger and a fruit cup on the tray.

"I like it. Probably even more so once I unpack all of my things and make the place my own."

She didn't respond, she wasn't required to. Ivan did that quite a bit, making lots of rhetorical statements. Questions, too, if she wanted to think about it. He reached around her and grabbed two waters, placing them on her tray. Then he grabbed himself a Coke and a water.

"You still drink two with lunch, I would assume," he whispered in her ear.

The side of her mouth curved up. "I do."

He always made her smile. Ivan was a man she felt comfortable with. That was how everything was between them. Nice and comfortable. Even the sex. It had sated an urge, but never would she say it had affected her like…

Don't go there, she reprimanded herself.

They paid and made their way to a table. Thankfully, Ivan was a man who ate during lunch. He didn't do chitchat when the time came to feed oneself. She didn't mind—most of her meals were eaten alone.

She had just finished her fruit cup when a loud masculine laugh reached her ears. The fork wobbled a bit in her hand before she managed to pull herself back together. In her peripheral, she watched Gio and Lizard swagger in followed by Keel and Beast.

Ivan glanced up and scoffed. "Pilots."

"Yes, the four who fly here."

"Only two are staying. I heard they're going to be competing for a final position in a combat squad."

She blinked. "You know more than me." A slight shrug and a subject change. "It's a nice area, Ivan. We just got out of the rainy season. Some parks and a place to base jump."

His burst of laughter made her chuckle. She'd been forever trying to get him to go with her. To feel how it was to fly.

"Not in this lifetime."

She sighed dramatically. "I keep telling you, it's science."

"No way. You got me in a helicopter with you for 'science' — no more of that for me."

"Why are you complaining? We survived. In fact, I did very well, considering."

His blue eyes narrowed. "I was fifteen and you...you were thirteen."

She grinned. "It was an experiment on aerodynamics. I'm an awesome pilot now, Ivan. Not to mention base jumping. You'd be in charge of yourself."

"No way," he uttered in Russian. She knew he spoke it when he was being very adamant about something.

"If you change your mind..." Her offer was also given in Russian.

"I won't."

Something caused her to look up and, when she did, she was met by hazel eyes. Gio watched her from his table, his expression an unreadable mask. His gaze flickered from her to Ivan and back to her. Suspicion narrowed her eyes but he merely broke the connection.

"Who's he?"

"That's Commander Cassano, the ace around here."

"And the look he gave you?"

"He's not wanted me here from the beginning. The one lost in the incident was his best friend. So I'm sure he's just reminding me I don't belong with the pilots." She tucked a stray lock of hair behind her ear.

"A dick, then."

She loved his immediate support of her. "Crudely put, perhaps, but yes, at times he has been." Her phone rang. "Amos."

"Sorry to bother you, ma'am, but I have something you should see. I'm sending it to your email. I wanted to let you know to expect it beforehand."

"Thank you, Sedin."

"My pleasure, ma'am." He hung up.

She finished her second water and rose. "I have to go."

Ivan stood as well. "Everything okay?"

"I think so. Just got some information I've been waiting on."

"Let's go."

They cleared their table and left. Although she never looked directly at him, she could feel Gio's gaze upon her until they were out of view. She reached the lab and made a beeline towards her area where she had left her tablet. Perhaps in some places people wouldn't leave their things, but this group had worked for Dr Thompson. Stealing got you booted, no questions asked. So there'd never been a reason to lock things.

She sat and opened her email to scan what Sedin had sent to her. The news didn't make her any happier. Concealing her reaction, she merely put her music in and got back to work after closing down the email.

The rest of the day she dealt with KVA, and double-checking another's report on electrohydrodynamics. When they'd finished up, she gathered her stuff and trooped to the door. Ivan fell into step with her.

"How'd you like it?" she asked.

"This certainly is an impressive facility. I was shown my permanent lab and all things will be moved there by morning."

"Terrific."

"Dinner tonight?"

"Can't. Lexy's visiting."

"No problem. I'll swing by and say hi to her."

"Bye, Ivan."

She broke away and headed for her bike, more than ready to be home. A sigh of relief escaped her as she parked at her own building.

The music could be heard as she stepped from the elevator, the loud sound escaping from an open door. Her open door. She pushed it wide and saw Lexy speaking to a guy she didn't know.

"Hey, Jaydee! This is Steven. He delivered some groceries for me."

"Steven," she said.

The young man replied but, even as he made his way to the door, Jaydee could tell he was doing everything in his power to remember Lexy. When the door had closed behind his exit, she tossed her bag down and sank onto the couch.

"Everything okay, hon?" Lexy turned the music down and sat next to her.

"I was grounded today. Ivan Vinokourov showed up as Dr Thompson's replacement and he's moved into this building."

Lexy chuckled, tried to stop but couldn't and soon it was a full laugh. Jaydee stared at her friend who was still laughing.

"How is this amusing?"

"It will make things interesting, don't you think?"

"How so?"

"Your ex living in the same building as you, not to mention working with you and your current flame." Her eyes twinkled. "Yeah, I'mma go with interestin', hon."

She shook her head. "Gio is not my current anything."

Lexy punched her in the shoulder. "Good luck with that."

"Luck with what? There is nothing needing luck."

More laughter. Lexy stretched out one long brown leg adorned with a blue stiletto. "Babe, if you think that, you're in for a big shock."

"You're not being logical."

"Neither are you, Jay. Gio doesn't strike me as a man who will let this go, let *you* go, without a fight."

"We aren't allowed to be together."

"Didn't stop y'all before," she replied without missing a beat.

Jaydee stood. "Which was also a mistake." She turned. "I'm showering."

Lexy stared at her foot while she rotated it. "Letting yourself live life isn't a mistake, Jaydee. You deserve to be happy as well."

Lexy's words stayed with her throughout her shower.

They shared a light dinner and spent the rest of the night competing against one another using the Kinect. When she rolled from bed, she tiptoed around so she didn't wake Lexy. She swiped her keys and opened the door to find herself face to face with Ivan.

Chapter Fourteen

Gio stared out of the cockpit as they streaked through the sky. The rush that being up here usually gave him had abandoned him today. All he felt was sorrow. Today was the second to last day Jaydee had to be a part of the squad. Then, two weeks later, she'd be gone.

Lexy's words echoed through him. He would force her to face it. Just as soon as they had a moment. But, hell, the way the clock was currently ticking down before her departure, if it had to be done in the women's locker room, then that was where it would occur.

"You okay over there?"

He glanced at Lizard and gave him a small nod. He wasn't really, but he didn't want to hash it out with Lizard in the B-2. Besides, he didn't need therapy, he needed Jaydee. He needed her in his life.

The memory of her walking around his place wearing one of his shirts made him smile. Made him hard too, but it didn't set up anxiety in his gut. Other women he'd wanted gone, especially if they'd actually fallen asleep at his house, in his bed. Part of why he'd tended to go to them, so he would leave and not have them curved all over him come morning. Something else he didn't mind with Jaydee, the feel of her pressed against him…one of the best experiences ever.

Somehow, he *had* to get her alone. It wasn't as if she avoided him, they were just that busy.

"You're sighing again, man. What gives?"

He ground his jaw and shook his head.

"It's just us, Giovanni. You look like hell, what's going on?" A brief pause. "God damn it, man. If you're not on your A-game here, there's a chance we don't go home at the end of the day. And I for one have a lot more women to sleep with before I call it quits. So spill."

"Just mulling over the upcoming completion for the combat unit."

"Uh-huh. And I'm flying in my skivvies just looking for the chance to eject out of this perfectly sound bomber."

Oh Geez, a bit of sarcasm.

He took a deep breath. "Fifteen days."

"You lost me, Casanova. What's happening in fifteen days?"

"She leaves." More specifically, she would be leaving him.

"This is about Jaydee."

He glanced briefly at his friend. "I can't let her go."

"Why? Because you feel pained she ended it with you lying naked in your bed?"

"No. Because somewhere along the line of her being here I fell in love with her. Totally. Head over fucking heels in love. And I can't begin to imagine my life without her."

Lizard didn't laugh at him. He merely nodded.

"About damn time you admitted it. I know how you operate. I told you before, I knew this woman meant more to you than all those others. From the first day, I knew."

"Whatever. Point is, I don't know how to proceed."

"You're emotional and not thinking straight."

He banked left and checked the position of Jaydee's plane. Exactly where she should be. She always flew precisely where she should.

Her voice flowed from the speaker and he ground his jaw as she chatted with the air traffic control officer. The woman was calm personified. Even during the troubles she'd had, her tone had been remarkably composed.

Sharing a look with Lizard, he followed the orders that came across the airwaves. As they shut off the flame-jet engines and ran on the electrogravitics, he thought again about Jaydee and how she'd tried to explain this to him.

"How stealthy are we really when flying like this?" he asked.

The question was meant for Jaydee—he wanted her to talk to him. Lizard just gave him a weird look.

Silence met his question and he knew she wouldn't answer. Still a smile lifted his lips as he envisioned her eyes sparkling while she taught him something with her very descriptive explanations. He knew she'd heard him and would have responded in her head. She couldn't help herself.

Lizard gave him yet another odd look and he merely lifted his shoulders in a brusque motion. He had no explanation for his comment. None at all.

"Fifty seconds to the line," Lizard informed him.

Gio snapped to. All attention on the mission. This was the time to be professional. They were going in on a mock bombing run. He was actually flying second in this, so if Jaydee missed her target then it would be on him to complete the task.

Like that would happen. He was content to be backup for her. And only her.

"Alpha Two, you have a green light. The mission's a go." The voice crackled over the radio.

"Roger that, going in hot."

"On your six, Dusti."

"Always good to know, Casanova."

The words were delivered in a professional way, yet it was like she stroked him. Damn, he wanted her. He watched her shoot forward towards the target.

Clouds rolled in but they didn't slow. In fact, if anything, they went faster. Beside him, Lizard did a countdown until they hit the target. He flew a bit above and behind her to keep an eye out for any incoming bogies. Fentress always liked to throw something in, and on this mission they had no AWACS to watch out for them.

"We've got two MiGs approaching from the South." Lizard spoke calmly.

"Keep on target, Dusti, we've got this." He banked starboard.

"Roger that, Alpha One."

"One-sixty degrees heading in fast. Contact in one hundred miles." Lizard kept him apprised.

Checking the array of gauges on his instrument panel, he adjusted. "We'll come in high."

It would be a challenge. These were bombers, not the smaller, easier to manoeuvre fighter jets. Didn't change the fact that he was first and foremost a fighter pilot. So he responded accordingly.

It didn't take them to long to take out the MiGs with their AGM-69A SRAMs. Over the radio came Keel's victory cry of "Target destroyed." He and Lizard joined in.

Levelling off beside Jaydee's Spirit, he glanced over. He was proud of her.

"Nice job, Dusti."

"Right back at you, Casanova. Thanks for keeping us alive."

"My pleasure." And he meant it one hundred per cent.

The rest of the trip went by in silence. He didn't mind, for he took the time to appreciate how much went into these planes. The massive bomber cut through the air flawlessly and to be nigh invisible...well, even more impressive.

What topped it all, though, was the fact that Jaydee—his woman—was instrumental in making it all work. His crazy, super-genius, incredible woman.

After landing, he and Lizard climbed down, grateful there had been no incidents. Spying Keel and Jaydee striding away from their bomber, he released a loud whistle. Both of them spun around and stared at him. He jogged over, unable to maintain distance from her.

"You up for a celebratory dinner?" His words may have been for both of them but his eyes were only on Jaydee.

"Sure," Keel said.

"I'm sorry, I still have company."

Evasion tactic. "Come on, Dusti, think of it as a farewell dinner. Bring Lexy." Seconds ticked by until she nodded. "Great, Kerrigan's? Nineteen-hundred?" He waited for another nod. "See you then."

He loped off and vanished before he did something like pull her close and nibble on her plump lower lip, then slide his tongue...

Shit! Looked like *another* cold shower was in his immediate future.

He arrived at Kerrigan's about thirty minutes early. After he got seated at a table by an overly attentive waitress he nursed his drink and waited for everyone else to show. He purposefully positioned himself so he could view those entering, a habit of his when waiting to see Jaydee. That was the reason he noticed her the moment she strode through the door.

In a millisecond, his life became slow motion. The bounce of her hair, the sway of her hips, everything. It all magnified, rocketing him to a new level of his own personal hell. She was coming closer. Close enough to touch and yet he couldn't.

Jaydee wore slightly baggy khaki cargo pants and a white oversized T-shirt. Despite her attempt to disguise her femininity, he knew what lay beneath her attire and it made him harder than titanium. Beside her, turning every red-blooded male's—and some women's—head was Lexy. Tight leather pants and a skimpy cornflower-blue halter top that exposed her flat midsection and belly-button piercing.

Lexy had this presence about her that drew men like flies to honey. And she deserved it, she was a gorgeous woman. Thick black hair, dark brown skin, and a killer figure.

None of it mattered—those guys could stare at her all they wanted, so long as they left Jaydee alone.

He knew the moment she spotted him. She stilled briefly before touching Lexy and continuing towards him. He ran his gaze appreciatively over her figure. God damn it! How long would he be able to keep this up?

Two weeks before she leaves.

The mental reminder sobered him in an instant. The women approached and he smiled. "Evening."

"Gio." Jaydee barely looked at him and he wanted to force an eye connection. A longer one.

"Hey, handsome. Thanks for the invite. Jay, order my usual, I've got to hit the ladies n' make sure I still look okay." Lexy was gone in a flash, leaving behind a trace of floral perfume.

It was the two of them and he stared at her. Remembered how it had been in her arms and let it leech into his gaze. The responding heat in her eyes when she finally glanced at him educated him that she knew his train of thought.

"Jaydee—"

"Don't. We can't."

Devastation filled him. "Why not? I should have argued this before with you when you first spouted the shit. Why do we have to ignore this between us? We're good...damn good. Hell, we're fucking amazing together, Jaydee. And you damn well know it."

Her eyes closed, those sinfully thick lashes resting upon satiny skin. He bit the inside of his cheek and willed his body to—for once—to behave.

She exposed those incredible eyes to him and he was witness to the stark frankness of her own desire. Unfortunately, as fast as he saw it, it faded, leaving him to stare into cool and impersonal tortoiseshell eyes.

"What we had was a mistake."

Lexy reappeared and halted his response. A mistake? Like fucking hell it was.

"So," Lexy said. "How did y'all do today?"

He ripped his gaze from the ever-tantalising view of Jaydee and focused on something safer. Lexy.

"Fine, thanks." The waitress came with their drinks and left after dragging her hand up his arm, blood-red nails vivid against his black shirt.

"Well now, she was right friendly." Lexy arched a brow at him. "She's a hot little number."

He truly didn't know how to respond. She wasn't a guy, but Jaydee's best friend. Not to mention she'd threatened a vital part of his anatomy.

"You've fucked her. Are y'all still an item?"

His mouth moved but nothing came out. Lexy's grey eyes stared at him over the rim of her Martini glass. Was that humour in there? Or a warning?

"Leave him alone, Lexy." Jaydee's statement shocked him. "It's no one's business but his own who he does what with."

No emotion in her words. Hell, she could have been commenting on the weather for all the sentiment her tone contained.

He stared at Jaydee, only to be met again by that coolly impersonal regard. There were so many things to say, but Lizard and Keel picked that time to show up. Lizard had a hot little redhead on his arm.

At least Lexy laid off him and soon everyone had drinks and appetisers while they waited on their food. Because of Lizard's date, they'd had to shift down, which had put Jaydee right nice and close to him. Close enough to touch.

He'd held out as long as he could but had given in by the time their food arrived. Shifting slightly, he'd moved his left leg until it pressed against her right one. She'd stiffened and pulled away. Lowering his hand, he'd settled it along the upper part of her thigh and determinedly repositioned her leg so that the physical contact was back between them. Lifting his hand, he'd waited. Sure enough, she'd gone to move it again and he'd halted it. It took four times before she'd allowed the contact between their thighs to remain. So, reluctantly, he'd set his hand back on the table.

Lord help him, all he wanted to do was caress her and slip his hand up...

"What about you, Casanova?"

Damn. He'd lost track of the conversation. Shaking his head to bring himself back in the moment, he sighed. "Sorry, what, Lizard?"

"Man, I was asking how long it had been since you went to a movie. Veronica here asked if we went a lot."

"Been a long time," he replied, moving his leg along Jaydee's while he watched surreptitiously for her reaction. Nothing.

Instead, Jaydee fished her phone from a pocket and answered. The others continued talking but he focused partially on the one side of her conversation he could hear. When she said "Ivan," he ground his back teeth but continued to talk as if he didn't pay her any mind.

But he did. And he cared. Too much. Which was why it made him green with jealousy to hear that man's name on her lips. Especially with such affection and familiarity.

Just how well *did* she know Ivan Vinokourov?

* * * *

Jaydee finished putting her hair back in the bun she would wear today. There was the unpleasant nagging feeling inside her. All her logical reasoning didn't do a damn thing about it.

The bed dipped when Lexy threw herself down beside her. "You're glum, hon. Why? You've been pulled from flying before."

"I know. It makes no sense."

"Sure it does. These guys were your family. You almost died with one, met his wife and kid, and they treated you like family. Then there's your hunky man, Giovanni Cassano. You shared a lot with him both physically and mentally. Cut yourself some slack, Jay. Better yet, admit the truth to yourself that you've fallen in love with him."

She readjusted a bit so she lay beside her friend and chewed on her lower lip as she mulled over her words. Admit she loved him. She shook her head, nope.

"Stop thinking so hard, Jay, and feel. Just let yourself feel. You'll know when the time is right. Just don't force your feelings for him into a box and throw it away."

Ankles hooked and knees bent, she rested her head against Lexy's shoulder. "I don't know if I can do that. Besides, I don't have time for a relationship, Lexy. I've got too much left to do before I leave."

"Bullshit. You can and we both know it."

"What? You know I'm leaving."

"You can come up with any excuse you want, hon. I can't force you to face this. But I happen to think he's perfect for you. There's always time if you make it. Your job doesn't *have* to be twenty-four-seven and you damn well know it. You give them everything, and for what?" Her tone was sharp.

"A man died, Lexy!"

They stilled, legs settling against the mattress. "I know, hon. And, as cold as this sounds, people die all the time. It doesn't mean you kill yourself next. You work for them, but don't think for one second they own you."

"I'm good, Lexy."

She snorted. "You're fuckin' awesome, hon. But listen to me. You keep going like this and you'll not be any use to anyone. You *can't* keep going like this. I heard you last night out there working on things when your ass should have been sleeping."

Jaydee frowned. She'd tried not to wake her friend. "It's just there's something going on at work and—"

"Not gonna change, Jaydee. There will *always* be something. And you need to take care. I'm fuckin' selfish, I'll admit it. I want…no, *need* you around."

"Things will get back to normal once I return to the lab." She heard Lexy mutter something under her breath. "What?"

"I said bullshit. It is inevitable that something else will come up, be an 'emergency' and they'll send for you again. What about Gio?"

Just the mention of his name made a flutter rise up in her belly. "He drives me crazy."

"But in a good way."

She wasn't so sure. "I don't know, Lexy."

Lexy brushed her lips along her forehead before rolling off the bed. "Well, you have fourteen days to figure it all out." She waved a hand. "Now, go on, get to work. You said you needed to be in early today. We're having dinner with Ivan tonight. I'll have a bagel for you to eat on your way."

Jaydee got to her feet. There just wasn't any motivation here. She was going in for her last flight. As Lexy had said, it wasn't the first time she'd been pulled from flying but, damn it, this hurt. It didn't take her long to leave the bedroom and she found Lexy waiting with, as promised, a bagel. She sent a grateful smile to her friend, hurried to the door, and headed in to work.

Much to her surprise, Sedin was waiting for her when she left the locker room. She gave him a brief nod.

"Sorry to bother you, ma'am."

"You're never a bother, Sedin. What can I do for you?"

His eyes shifted around before he met her gaze again. "Can you come with me for a moment?"

"Of course." A quick glance at her watch. "I'm here early today."

He began walking to the door and she followed him out into the pre-dawn. She watched him. Agitated, he constantly glanced around as he led her to the picnic tables.

"Something on your mind, Petty Officer?"

He reached into the side pocket of his utilities and withdrew a PDA. She waited while he pulled something up and then turned it so she could read it.

A sinking feeling rushed over her. This…was not good news at all. With a groan, she glanced back over to the mechanic who stood there waiting, that same uneasy look on his face as well. After all the stuff they'd been sifting through, this final bit connected all the pieces.

"I need this sent to my tablet, Sedin, and I need you to not breathe a word about this to anyone. And I mean *anyone*." She looked at his expression, it was as if he had recently finished chewing on a lemon. Too bad, she needed his affirmation. "Petty Officer!"

"Yes, ma'am. Not a word to anyone."

"I will handle this today, Sedin. I promise you that. But I have to make sure he doesn't run. And, for that, I have to set a few other things up."

"Yes, ma'am," he responded immediately.

"Very good. And, Sedin, thank you so much for all your help on this. I will make sure they know."

He shook his head. "If it's all the same to you, ma'am, I'd really rather not be known as a rat."

"I understand. In that case, I'll do everything in my power to keep your name out of it."

"I would greatly appreciate that, ma'am."

"Carry on." She returned his PDA to him and he nodded.

"Yes, ma'am. It's sent to yours now."

"Good man." With a tilt of her head, she sent him on his way, then sank to the table and dropped her head in her hands. "This is a clusterfuck," she uttered.

Worrying her lower lip, she pushed to her feet and began to head for the main facility building. She went and changed into her flight suit then grabbed her tablet PC and made her way down to where Ivan would be working.

Sure enough, he was in there working with Kelly. He looked up at her entrance and gave her a smile that warmed her.

"Morning, Dr Amos," he said.

"Doctors," she replied.

He whispered something to Kelly then approached her, a furrow between his brows. "What's going on?" he asked in Russian.

"I need you to do something for me." She spoke to him in the same language.

"Anything, you know this."

She handed him her tablet. When his fingers curled around the edges she said, "Tell no one you have it. Give it to no one."

"This is your property. I'll keep it safe."

"Thank you. I'll be back for it this afternoon."

"Are you okay?"

"Last day flying."

"You know I'm here for you if you need me, Jaydee."

"I know. I have to get going. Thank you." She gave him a brief smile and left with a wave to Kelly. Before she got to the room, she placed a phone call.

She was the last one into the ready room and she felt their gazes upon her. "Sorry, sir."

Fentress scowled at her. "Something more important to do than come here, Amos?"

"No, sir."

He grunted and she took a seat in the back. Gio glanced at her before he focused again on their CO. She didn't look at him again. She listened to the briefing and headed out immediately to her bomber, wanting to spend as much time as she could with the large, deadly object.

She was pensive as she flew, cataloguing all she could for her memory banks. There was no doubt she would miss this, but, like with all things, she would move on. Surely, some day she would have the opportunity to fly one again, for, no matter what anyone said, the simulator just couldn't compare.

"It's been an honour, Dusti," Keel said to her, "a real honour." His voice conveyed his sincerity.

Blinking back tears, she smiled at him as they readied for landing. "Likewise, Keel." Her heart stuttered a bit when the wheels touched the runway and she throttled back, bringing the massive bomber to a crawl and manoeuvring it into the open shelter so that the crews could go over it with precision care, and make sure nothing was wrong before the next flight. The flight she wouldn't be piloting.

Chapter Fifteen

Gio finished talking to his mechanic and waved at the group who had entered to begin going over the bomber as he strode to the door. Lizard had left immediately but Gio had wanted to put in a request for a new seat—the one he was in felt like a spring was digging into him and he was a bit concerned that there might have been something up with the ejection seat. Not something to find out when he needed it to work.

The area was mostly quiet—their flight had been long today and non-essential personnel had already gone home. The sun had begun to set, and bathed the land in a gentle golden glow. He passed the next shelter and gave it a passing glance as he walked.

What he saw halted him. Jaydee was in there. He knew it was her and he adjusted his angle and slipped in unnoticed, stepping into a shadow where he could observe her. Her slender shoulders were slumped and she looked like she was carrying the weight of the world on them.

He watched her climb up the steps to the plane's interior and, after a minute, he followed. She lay on the cot in the back and he made his way to her side, crouching down.

"Jaydee," he whispered, reaching out and stroking his hand down the side of her face.

Her eyes opened, yet he could see it took a bit of time before they became focused. He saw the remnants of tears lingering on her face and in her eyes. Then they opened wide and she drew back from him. "Wha...what are you doing here?"

He frowned and slid his hand around the back of her neck and applied pressure so they were closer. The silken strands of her hair teased his skin and he felt the lust he had for her slam into him with the force of a hurricane.

Not just lust.

Jaydee sat up and he moved with her, refusing to let her go. She tried unsuccessfully to get him to release her. When her hand gripped his wrist, he arched a brow.

"Let go," she said.

"No. You and I need to have a chat." His thumb stroked along her pulse and he felt it beat harder.

"No, we don't." She glanced at her watch before chewing on her lower lip. That plump lower lip that he just wanted to...

He gave in. He couldn't help it. These past few weeks — having to see her daily, and the frustration of not being able to touch her — the urge to haul her close and just let her scent flow over him had reached its breaking point.

The kiss was fierce and he took not only what his body needed. He also took what his heart and soul needed from her. Everything she was. Beneath his assault, Jaydee stiffened. For maybe two-hundredths of a second. Then she softened and released a moan that went from her mouth directly to his cock. Nothing else mattered. Not where they were, not the fact they needed to talk. Nothing.

"Sweets," he rumbled against her mouth as her hands tore at his flight suit. "Boots."

She nipped at his tongue before pulling away. They attacked their clothes in frantic motions and soon he rose above her on the cot and slid home in one smooth stroke.

"Gio," she groaned as he filled her.

"Yes, sweets. Jesus, you feel so good. I've missed you. I've missed this."

Her arms curled up around his shoulders, holding him tight to her, and she began to move with him. So many feelings ripped through him—he thought he was dying. Flames licked along his skin and he thrust deeper, harder, faster, needing more. Craving to be so deep inside her he could feel her heartbeat.

Jaydee moaned into his shoulder, her teeth scraping his skin as she undulated beneath him. He sank his hands into her hair, pleased when the bun gave way and allowed him to wrap his fingers in the strands. The pins holding it in place scattered to the floor and he didn't give a damn.

"Legs around my waist, sweets," he ordered, licking along her neck, revelling in the familiar taste and scents that were associated with her.

She obeyed instantly and he sank deeper.

"Ohhh," she gasped.

They moved as one and he could feel his balls tightening up. Tugging on her hair, he said, "Jaydee."

Her nails dug into his flesh and her eyes, which looked more golden at this moment, met his. He brushed his lips along the tip of her nose. Their gazes locked and he refused to let her go.

She crested first, her body clenching around his cock, and she dragged him over. Staring deep into her eyes, he came within her, her body continuing to ripple around him until he had nothing left to give. Or so he thought, until she gave him a siren's smile, soft, inviting, and sultry.

"I've missed you, sweets," he murmured right before his mouth captured hers again. Everything else faded away and he was swept off into a world composed of two people. Him and her. Gio and Jaydee. All he ever needed.

"Commander Amos! Are you in here?"

The voice woke him. It took him all of two seconds to evaluate the situation. He and Jaydee were naked, limbs intertwined on the small bed in her bomber. And people were coming closer. She lay sprawled on top of him, their bodies pressed as close as possible.

"Commander Amos!"

Her eyes snapped wide, full of panic. Her lips were still rosy from his kisses, her skin a bit flushed, and damn if she didn't have this look of a woman who'd just been pleasured. And well. An arrogant smirk lifted the sides of his mouth.

"Shit!" she hissed and scrambled for her clothing.

He followed suit, not really wanting to be caught naked when whomever was yelling for her showed up. He knew they were busted, but he didn't give a damn.

A head popped up as she was swiftly braiding her hair. One of the MPs stood there, a sergeant who, with one look, took in the entire situation. Gio saw the nearly indiscernible smirk before he composed himself.

"Excuse me, ma'am, but Admiral Fitzroy is looking for you."

He slashed his gaze back to Jaydee who glanced at her watch and paled a bit. "On my way, Sergeant."

"Correction," a loud voice boomed from down below, "the Admiral is here."

The sergeant's face morphed into an apologetic one. Gio suddenly didn't feel as confident as he had before. He glanced to Jaydee but she refused to look at him. There was nothing while she made her way towards the man who'd interrupted their secluded rendezvous and not even when she climbed down and out of sight.

He debated up there for maybe a minute before he scrambled for the way down. There wasn't anything to think about. He was in this as much as she was and he'd be damned if he would let her take it all.

"Jaydee, wait," he hollered as he hit the floor of the hangar and spun around.

Jaydee stood with three men. Two he knew and one he didn't. Admiral Fitzroy he assumed to be the one he didn't know. Crap, make that Vice Admiral Fitzroy. The other two were Captain Fentress and Rear Admiral Griffin.

He'd just been caught with a woman he worked with in a highly compromising situation by a captain, a one-star admiral, and a three-star one who wore the Budweiser. He was so fucked.

"We'll be discussing *this* later," Fitzroy said, his voice sounding like a bass drum. Direct blue eyes pinned them both before he homed in on Jaydee. "We have something to discuss preceding this, I believe."

She stood straight, as if her spine had been infused with steel. "Yes, sir, we do."

The man was huge and certainly had the intimidation factor down when he crossed his arms over that barrel chest. Nope, he didn't feel any better when he couldn't see the pin that marked the man as a member of the Teams, a Navy SEAL. One of the country's most elite military groups—*the* top, some would say. Uh-uh. Not at all.

"Get on with it, then."

"Here, sir?"

One brown eyebrow rose. "Well, I was waiting where you asked me to be, Amos. You were the one who wasn't there."

"Yes, sir, it was regrettable and I thank you for taking the time to come out here at my request."

Her words were like a punch to his gut. But he didn't move. Griffin gave him a shake of the head and he held still. How? He had no clue, but he did.

"Don't try to placate me, Amos. You never call, you don't write, and when you finally do you say something about a traitor to *my* country working here at this facility. Did you really think I wouldn't show up here?"

Gio narrowed his eyes at the casualness that rang in his tone. These two had a history with one another. Then the words he spoke sank in. A traitor? What the fuck was going on?

"I have proof of who it is, but I don't have it on me."

"Is this dealing with Mike's death?" he butted in the conversation.

Three sets of eyes bored into him but his gaze remained riveted on Jaydee. She barely afforded him a nod but it was enough for him. He lifted his gaze and tracked hers to land on Fentress. The man seemed a bit green around the gills but his expression was set in stone.

Could it be?

"I need a word with my two pilots," Fentress said.

"I don't think so, Fentress. We're all going in to talk about this." Fitzroy's tone left no room for argument.

He positioned himself beside Jaydee as they headed back to the main facility. With each step they took he could see the walls erecting back up around her. He hated it and longed to tear them all down but, at this moment, he wanted to know more about the situation with Mike.

At the door, he allowed his hand to graze along the small of her back as he held it open for her. There was no reaction. And he didn't know if that was a good thing or not. He figured not so much but a guard stepped between them and he had to force himself not to thrust him away.

"Don't make this any worse," Griffin hissed in his ear as they entered an empty room and he brushed by him to head to the front.

"Speak," Fitzroy barked as the door closed behind them all.

Jaydee stepped forward and faced all three officers. She lifted her chin and spoke.

"You wanted to know why I called you here and I'll tell you." She whispered something to a guard standing beside her and he nodded before stepping away to the phone on the wall. "We know why I was sent here and I did my job. I came and inspected the systems in the planes, including the one which went down, and found the electrogravitics to be fine. However, upon further and a much more in-depth review, I began to notice some disturbing discrepancies in the maintenance logs. You, gentlemen, have a traitor among you."

His blood ran colder than it had the first time the word was mentioned. The door opened and he turned to see Lizard and Keel come in escorted by armed men. His heart sank. Please don't let it be one of his friends. It hit him when they looked at him and raised their eyebrows in question. Did they suspect him?

Head whipping to Jaydee, he frowned. Did *she*?

"And who is it, then?" Fentress demanded, his scowl matching those on the two admirals.

Jaydee looked at Lizard and Keel before her eyes found him. In them, he could read her sorrow. Then she turned and shocked the hell out of him with the words that came out of her mouth.

"You should know, Captain. You're the traitor."

Gio knew that his mouth had dropped open and chaos erupted throughout the room.

Jaydee stood there as voices, raised in anger, circled around her. She was aware, highly aware, of where everyone stood, especially Gio. She couldn't even begin to describe the depth of her embarrassment. Not only did the sergeant searching for her know what they'd been up to, but also Captain Fentress, Admiral Griffin, and Vice Admiral Vincent Fitzroy.

Her inexcusable behaviour would filter back to her father. Not that that was what bothered her. She hated that she'd been late and they'd had to come find her.

Gio. He stood to her left and she could feel his intense stare upon her. She'd done it, given in again to allow herself the pleasure of his touch. And, Lord have mercy, it had been amazing, like usual.

"Amos!"

"Sir." She snapped out of her thoughts of Gio and his touch to focus on Fitzroy.

"Explain yourself. You'd better have some iron-clad proof to be slinging accusations like this."

She glanced to Fentress, whose face was mottled red, then skimmed over the two admirals. Griffin, tall and lean, his gold wings reminding everyone he had been a pilot. Fitzroy, salt and pepper hair, fit and impressive with his gold trident.

Regardless of the severity of the situation, she still bristled slightly at Fitzroy's suggestion that she not be able to back up her claim.

"I can, sir."

She peeked towards Lizard and held out her hand, pleased Ivan had delivered it as she'd asked. He stepped close and handed over her tablet. She gave him a nod of thanks and met Fentress' glare. She knew full well he'd been looking for that.

"I have it all right here."

Bringing up the files, she handed the item to the Vice Admiral. He skimmed and scowled ferociously.

"Get this piece of shit out of my sight," he snarled at the guards waiting in the room. "Put his ass in holding until I get there."

"Yes, sir!"

They dragged Fentress away, everyone ignoring his cries of innocence and his threats against her.

"Get out!" Fitzroy barked. "Except Amos." A few seconds passed before he bellowed, "Now!"

The click of the door sounded so final. Blue eyes met hers and he gestured at the table. She claimed a seat without hesitation. The two men sat across from her.

"How did you come across this?"

She laced her fingers and placed them on the smooth surface before her. "While I was finishing up my report, I learned some disturbing facts."

"Such as?" He looked at her briefly before returning his attention to her tablet.

"I had been misinformed about the parameters of the incident. The second pilot was made up, so Lieutenant Walker had been flying alone."

Both men frowned. "What?" Griffin this time.

"I was informed at the beginning that it had been Sidewinder and a man named Wicked up there. That wasn't—"

"Damn it! There are supposed to be two at least." Griffin slammed his hand on the table.

She didn't bother to respond to that specific statement, just continued on. "I wondered if it wasn't a deliberate act then and went back to Commander Cassano who'd originally been scheduled to take the flight along with Lieutenant Armstrong."

"But Casanova hurt himself and Sidewinder volunteered." Griffin filled in.

"Yes, sir. However, Sidewinder could have had someone with him. Keel offered to go but Fentress told him it was covered. So Sidewinder went alone." She waved a hand. "I went back to the wreckage once I'd determined it wasn't a deliberate act and ran maintenance logs. That's when I started noticing the inconsistencies. The planes are high maintenance and require a lot of upkeep. Not to mention, everything has specific batch numbers for tracking purposes."

"Wait...why were you doing this?"

"It could have been my fault, Admiral." The disgust she felt was obvious in her tone. "When the lies began I checked deeper." She shrugged. "Some of the items in his wreckage were from newer batches. So I knew they'd been switched. I had someone look deeper in that venue and the information is all there. It was only this morning that the final connecting piece came in. Then, and only then, did I allow myself to call."

"You're not a detective." She stared straight ahead. "Well?" Fitzroy demanded.

"Waiting for a question, sir."

He grumbled low. "Christ, I forgot that about you, always so—"

The door burst open and she spun in her chair to see Gio charge past the armed guard. "This is bullshit, you can't put the blame fully on her!"

His eyes overflowed with steely determination and her heart skipped several beats as their gazes met. Why was he doing this? She could take care of herself. The look in his gaze changed and, while only for an instant, she understood what he and Lexy had been trying to get her to realise. Emotions weren't a horrible thing.

"Stand down, Commander," Fitzroy advised, tone hard.

Gio continued on until he stood beside her chair. Something prompted her to stand as well. His scent flowed over her and some of her tension loosened.

"I won't let you face this alone," he remarked in a sotto voice.

Well aware of the scrutiny both admirals gave, she still turned an eye to the handsome pilot at her side.

"This isn't about our misconduct. It's about Fentress."

Something foreign flashed in his eyes turning the hazel more green for a second. "I'm staying. They'll have to shoot me first." His announcement was loud enough for all to hear.

"If you two are done," Griffin's voice dripped with sarcasm, "perhaps, now, Amos can finish telling us what happened."

"How did you figure this out?" Fitzroy again.

"I'm nosy and I ask questions. There were missing pieces and wrong trails."

"And you did this on your own?" Fitzroy leant back and held her gaze.

"No, sir. I had help."

"By his presence here I'm assuming he 'helped' as well?"

"Yes, sir."

"Who else?"

She hesitated not wanting to say.

"I suggest you tell me, Dr Amos."

"Sorry, sir. That person wished to remain anonymous and not receive the title of a rat. I have to respect their wishes."

Fitzroy's blue eyes narrowed. "It wasn't a request."

"I'm sorry, sir. I will not betray a confidence."

The man's hands fisted before he apparently relaxed. "Okay. I'm sure more will come out once the bastard's been charged. I need this sent to my office."

"Already done, sir."

"Good." He cracked his neck, leant forward, and rested large arms on the table. "Now, about you two. We will meet in forty-eight hours, this room, and at that time I want to know what the hell is going on here. I have to call General Nelson and get him informed on all this. Until then, you two stay away from one another here. I mean it. Stay away."

"Yes, sir." They both responded together.

"Dismissed. Get out of here."

She stepped up for her tablet PC then walked to the door, face composed, insides a tempest. Lieutenant General Nelson. Not good. Not good at all. He was the second in command overseeing this test facility.

"Cassano, stay."

She ground her jaw and left. By the time she reached her home, she wanted a drink. An alcoholic one. Once out of the lift she trudged to her door and entered. The scent of her tea wrapped around her and she nearly wept with relief as Lexy pushed a mug of it in her hands while divesting her of the bag she carried.

"Sit down, hon," Lexy ordered.

Unable, or was it unwilling, to argue, she listened. She curled up on her favourite end of the couch and just inhaled the fragrant brew. Her apartment was bathed in the sunset's glow, which helped her unwind as well.

She closed her eyes, drifting off, and opened them when the smell of freshly cooked food filled her nostrils. Ivan stood with Lexy in the kitchen. They spoke softly while dishing up food onto plates.

"Go change, hon. We'll be ready to eat soon." Lexy didn't even look at her.

Crap. She'd forgotten about the dinner plans. After placing her tea on the end table, she made her way to her room, grabbed some clean clothing, and headed for a shower. After she had dressed and put her clothes in the hamper, she felt somewhat better.

The table was set, her flameless candles offering more ambiance, and her two friends sat there waiting. Ivan, gentleman that he was, rose and held her chair. She looked over the food and smiled.

"Thank you," she said.

Ivan had cooked. Before her sat some solyanka, a rich stew. She could smell the mushrooms in it and her stomach growled in anticipation. Pelmini, meat dumplings, and a red beet salad.

"You doing okay?" Lexy asked after they'd said grace.

"I guess so. Just tired."

"Eat," Ivan stated, gesturing with his spoon.

So she did. It was delicious, each bite better than the last. Afterwards, they all sat on her couch and started a movie. Snuggled against Ivan, she barely stirred when a knock came at her door.

"Hon?" Lexy said.

She dangled between sleep and consciousness. "Hmm?"

"Are you hiding tonight or should I get the door?"

"Whichever," she slurred. Ivan draped his arm around her and she burrowed closer. The knocking halted and she figured whomever it was had left. However, it was the voice that pulled her exhausted eyes open.

"Where is she, Lexy? I'm not leaving until I see her." A pause and she was faced with the lower half of a body instead of the television. "If you can tear yourself away, Jaydee, I need a word with you." Gio's voice was clipped and cold.

Ivan squeezed her shoulder before releasing her and she stood. An eerie fire burned in Gio's hazel eyes and it gave her a moment's pause.

"You shouldn't have come here. Admiral Fitzroy said —"

"Said for me to stay away from you *at work*. We're not at work."

He grabbed her wrist and dragged her to the bedroom area. Although not totally, it did offer a mediocre amount of privacy. The moment they were behind the divider squares, he had her close, his mouth feasting on hers.

Fire erupted along her skin, banishing all her exhaustion, and she wanted more. Craved more. With no hesitation, she wrapped around him and returned the kiss. Arching against him, she nearly cried with relief at his touch again.

"Jaydee," he rasped, tearing away from her.

A cold reality settled over her, dissipating the raw haze of desire. "You have to go."

"So you can be with Ivan?"

The words were so sharp they could have cut her. He was jealous.

"Ivan is a friend, nothing else."

Gio stared intently at her before he nodded and cupped her face. "I'm tryin', sweets. Really I am. I want to kill him for touching you. I hate he can and does. And I hate how comfortable you are with him." A light brush on her mouth. "Are you okay after today?"

She gripped his wrists and pulled them from her face before stepping close to rest her cheek against his chest. Her hands smoothed along his back and she breathed deep when his arms wound around her to hold tight.

"Jaydee."

One more minute was all she wanted. In his arms, she felt invisible to the trials of the real world. But, more than that, she felt safe and protected. Cared for. Steeling herself, she sighed.

"I'm fine. You shouldn't have barged in."

"I wasn't about to let them blame only you, sweets. And I'm sorry." She stepped back but he lifted her chin to ensure eye contact. "Not for what we did, but because of who caught us."

"I'm sorry, too."

"For?"

"Everything. This cannot happen again." She walked out to where Ivan and Lexy sat with eyes and ears glued in their direction. "Thank you for —"

"What do you mean?" he snarled, positioning himself before her, halting her progression.

"Goodbye, Commander." She went around him to the door and opened it, giving him a pointed look.

His expression as furious as she'd ever seen, Gio stalked towards her. He stared at her before his hand snaked out to land possessively and dominatingly on the back of her neck. He jerked her forward, and kissed her. He never relented until she sagged into him. When he finally backed off, her fingers gripped his shirt and her body swayed in his direction, wanting more.

"You're not getting rid of me that easily. See ya around, sweets," he murmured. With a tug on his cap brim, he left her apartment and strode away.

Touching her swollen lips, she pivoted to lean against the door. Both Lexy and Ivan had raised eyebrows and shocked expressions on their faces.

"Oh my," she uttered and slid down the door to sit on the floor. Suddenly, she felt extremely and totally out of her league.

Chapter Sixteen

Gio operated on a hair-trigger. The date for dealing with the inappropriate behaviour between him and Jaydee had been pushed back even further. He didn't know why and frankly didn't care. All he knew was that Jaydee had damn near vanished. She never answered her door, or her phone either.

He hadn't seen her since that night in her apartment and, if not for cornering Ivan Vinokourov and asking about her, he would have assumed she'd been transferred early. As it was, he'd learned Ivan had been her lover. News that nudged him closer to the edge of his control. Rumours were circulating all over about how he'd fucked Jaydee. Although, to be fair, they weren't rumours but still it irritated him. It was nobody's business.

Finished with his food, he made his way to the door. Admiral Griffin halted him as he began to leave the cafeteria.

"A word, Commander."

"Yes, sir?"

They stepped to the side and Griffin ran a hand over his grey hair. "You've really stepped in it this time, son."

"Why the delay?" he asked, figuring this man would answer him honestly.

"Brigadier General Thomas is arriving to oversee the charges against you. Nelson reported the information on to him and he figured it was time to get involved." He grimaced. "I'm sorry, son, but, with all the heat coming on Fentress, they don't want to go light on you two, either."

Could his career be over? "I understand, sir."

"For what it's worth, Giovanni, I'm proud of you, son. I knew you'd prove me wrong and out-fly these Air Force boys."

Hell, even Griffin sounded like his career had just crashed and burned. "Thank you for the opportunity to prove myself, sir." Christ! What would he do? Flying was his life. The urge to strike out nearly overwhelmed him and he drew deep breaths in an attempt to calm down.

"The general wants to see you tomorrow at eleven-hundred."

"Yes, sir."

"Go home and get some rest, son."

Gio walked away, a deadened cathexis within him. Retire because of age, sure. Or even loss of ability. It had always been a probability. But this?

"You okay, man?" Lizard asked, pacing him to his car.

"Sure. Have a brigadier general coming in to decide what my fate is. Tomorrow at eleven-hundred. I'm fuckin' great."

Jason gave a low whistle. "Where are you going?"

"Firing range."

"Want some company?"

"Nawh, man, but thanks." Gio left before Lizard could pry any more.

That night he sat on the floor of the room containing all Mike's belongings. A glass of Scotch dangled in the fingers of his left hand. Untouched. In his right, he held the shadow box he'd got to display Mike's flag, picture, and awards.

"I miss you, man," he uttered, ignoring of the tears that rolled down his cheeks.

He woke in that room, back against the wall, drink still full and beside him, with the memorial to Mike on his lap. Gio readied for his day, and, with a heavy and unsure heart, made his way towards his face-to-face with the general.

* * * *

Brigadier General Hardy Thomas was an imposing man. He oversaw the test facility and didn't seem happy in the least to be here. His blue uniform had creases so sharp Gio wondered if he'd cut himself with just a touch. The general's chest was covered by rows of ribbons, attesting to the fact that he was no paper pusher. His silver wings gleamed against the blue of his uniform. Beside him were the admirals, one on each side, also resplendent in their uniforms.

Gio stood before them after they'd called him in. The room was deathly silent and he wondered what they waited for. He watched the second hand on the clock behind the three men who held his life in their hands. He observed it near the top when the time would be eleven-hundred exactly.

Behind him, the door opened at the same time the second hand hit the twelve. A tingle up his spine told him all he needed to know. In his periphery, Jaydee appeared.

She wore an outfit of charcoal grey. A skirt suit that made him forget the seriousness of the situation. Holy hell! It halted above her knees, the short-sleeved top conforming to her curves like a dream. His *wet* dream. Her long legs were covered in sheer black stockings with—holy shit—the dark line down the back. And damned if she didn't have on another pair of those fuck-me stilettos she'd worn the first night they'd met. Grey in colour, matching her suit.

He bit the inside of his cheek to stop his cock from rising in admiration and lust. He focused straight ahead but couldn't stop himself from taking in the chignon her hair was confined in. Still, it was the blankness on her face that worried him.

"Let's begin," Thomas said, sitting forward.

The beginning of the end.

"You both know why we're all here. This is an informal hearing, more of a meeting, for us to decide on how to proceed with charges."

Gio wanted to move closer to Jaydee and offer her some support. But he held still and stared just past Thomas as he blabbed on about the UCMJ—the Uniformed Code of Military Justice.

"I knew it was only a matter of time with you, Cassano, before you messed up," Thomas uttered.

That got his attention. What had he done to this man?

"Excuse me, General, but personal opinions hold no place here. We're here to decide a course of action." Fitzroy made the observation.

"Bullshit. This is my programme. I run it. No one else." Arrogance dripped from every syllable. "I make the final decisions."

Yep. He was really fucked. Up the ass and not even a nice dinner beforehand. As he stood there, Gio could basically see his career exiting stage left.

"Wait now," Griffin began, only to be cut off.

"No. I am glad that the traitor has been discovered. However, if I want to use this unprofessional incident as grounds to get him and the brainiac gone, I can. And there isn't a damn thing you can do about it." Thomas' smugness grated on his nerves and Gio wished he could wring his neck, if not for anything more than the derision with which he'd spoken about Jaydee.

The three senior officers got into a shouting match. Stunned, he faced Jaydee. None of her thoughts showed on her face. In fact, she looked bored.

"Enough!" Hardy shouted. "I'm through discussing this. My decision is made. I am going to throw the book at him and when I'm through" — the general glared at him — "you'll be lucky to pilot a biplane."

"No! I won't let you do this," Griffin protested.

"My programme, Admiral. You can't stop me."

What had he done to this man? He had no clue. The others didn't either and Fitzroy asked.

"I have a daughter, Melisande Ramos. She lives with her mother and told me of a man she fell for and," he paused, "you used her and tossed her away like she was trash. You took my pure baby and ruined her!" His face was red with fury.

Shit. Shit. Shit.

Gio remembered Melisande, and that hadn't been how it had happened at all. She had been a freak in bed, good fun, but she hadn't got the message of no strings, so he'd ignored her calls. He'd never known she was the brigadier general's daughter.

"Say goodbye to your wings, *Casanova*." The loathing his call sign was uttered with chilled the room to absolute zero. Or zero degrees Kelvin.

"This...this is outrageous," Griffin hollered.

"Too bad." He waved it off. "Your fraternisation is costing you your job."

The bastard sounded so gleeful. Gio had no clue what to say. None. Nothing would help. Telling him his precious daughter had lied to him because she was mad he'd ended it...nope, he wouldn't buy that. From the sounds of things, this man had been looking for a way to get rid of him and now he'd finally succeeded.

Jaydee faced him and he saw compassion in her eyes. That made him angry—he didn't want pity. Then it vanished and he couldn't read her at all.

"I don't think so." Jaydee's voice was soft and yet somehow the other three, who were still embroiled in a nasty argument, fell quiet.

"What? Did *you* have something to say to me, Amos?"

Gio growled low in his throat—the hell he'd let this fucker talk to her like that. "You can't—"

Jaydee cut him off. She stepped beyond him so he had a clear view of her body-hugging skirt and those damn stockings and heels.

"I am sure you heard me just fine. You can't punish Commander Cassano for the fraternisation."

Everyone looked at her. Thomas scowled, his face twisting into an ugly mask.

"And why not?"

Gio was a bit curious himself.

"I'm senior to him. I became lieutenant commander three days prior to his promotion. So this is on me. Not him."

Wait, she was protecting him?

"You conniving... Fine, but it's still my call about kicking him out of the programme so I—"

"Will not be doing it," Jaydee interrupted.

"You have no say!"

"Let me put it to you like this. This man stays, his record remains as it is now. No letter of reprimand and he is up for promotions when the time comes."

"Jaydee, you can't do this," he said, stepping up beside her and gripping one arm.

"What gives you the right to think you have any power here?" Hardy sneered.

"I don't think it, I know it. And this will happen, because, despite your desire to have him gone, you don't want to tell *my* superiors you lost me."

Silence descended like an ominous cloud. Tension ran high as if just waiting for the first break.

"What?" Thomas said, a sentiment echoed by him and the other two in the room.

"This is how it is going to work, or I walk now and I will never work for anything government-related again."

Gio didn't believe what was unfolding before him. His by-the-book, sexy-as-hell woman was actually threatening a brigadier general.

"You wouldn't dare." Thomas didn't look very confident, however.

He repositioned so he could see Jaydee's face. As he stared at her, one elegant brow rose. Her face a cool mask of disdain. The same look she'd levelled at him when she'd told him not to measure his cock to hers, for he'd come up short. Now that icy contempt was all for Brigadier General Hardy Thomas.

"I don't lie. And I don't make idle threats." A careless lift of one shoulder. "I don't make threats, period."

"You're defending a man who's slept with so many women? Why would you protect him when you're nothing but another notch on his belt?"

"A fact which has no bearing on this. He is the best pilot, and for the benefit of the programme — or combat unit — he stays." She shrugged. "It's the logical decision."

"I just brought in Colonel Hirsch."

"A good pilot, but not up to the same calibre as Commander Cassano."

Gio smiled at her praise.

"You will not get away with this, you little—"

"Funny thing about my memory, Brigadier General Thomas, is I remember. *Everything.* Including our very first meeting."

Thomas' face paled a bit at her statement. "Fine. Get out of my sight."

Jaydee nodded. "Sirs." She glanced at him ever so briefly as she pivoted around, but never spoke. He tracked her progress to the door where she paused and peered over one shoulder. "I'll be keeping track of his career, General."

"Why do you care?" Thomas snapped.

Her gaze flickered over him with zero interest in it. "I don't. He shouldn't, however, be forced to pay for my mistake."

With those enunciated words, Jaydee left and crushed her stiletto heel into his heart. He stood there staring at the door she'd vanished through when a hand on his arm startled him. Admiral Griffin.

"Come on, son."

They left Admiral Fitzroy with Thomas, still shouting at one another. Not going far, Griffin speared him with a stare.

"I don't know what happened there but you had better thank that woman for saving your ass. She just pulled your six out from in front of the firing squad."

He had every intention of doing so. Right after he yelled at her for doing it.

"So what happens now?"

"You get ready for tomorrow. I hear the competition between you and Hirsch starts bright and early."

"That's it?"

"Dr Amos made sure of that. She's an amazing woman."

Gio stared at the man who had been both mentor and father figure to him. "I know."

Griffin's gaze was sombre. "Does she know you love her?"

Love. "She's about to," he avowed. "She's about to."

* * * *

Jaydee sat in the window seat, her cheek pressed to the glass, watching the rain slide down in rivulets. For the first time in her life she was torn. She didn't have a problem with what she'd done to save Gio's career. That wasn't it.

She found herself conflicted about her own future. The familiar aroma of her tea dragged her eyes from the window and she saw Lexy standing there.

"Drink up, hon." Jaydee's friend sat down by her feet. Lexy placed a hand on her knee. "Do you need me to stay?"

She sipped her tea before compiling an answer. "No, I'm okay. Besides, you have that conference to attend."

"There are always conferences happening, I can go to the next one. Not to mention, Eugene and Hector will be there."

Lexy and her two older brothers co-owned a veterinary practice. She handled small animals, Eugene handled exotics, while Hector took care of the large animal portion of the clinic.

"If you say so."

"I'll stay for just a bit longer."

She smiled her gratitude. Lexy wore sweats, no shoes, and a T-shirt, showing Jaydee the softer side of her personality. After navigating some boxes, Lexy returned with another cup of tea.

"It'll feel odd to be back home," Jaydee blurted out. Lexy's look encouraged her to continue. "It's never been an issue for me before. There's no logical explanation why it's happening now."

"Sure there is." Lexy crossed her legs and leaned against the wall. "Commander Cassano."

Her traitorous pulse kicked up a few notches at the mere mention of his name. With a determined shake of her head, she said, "I did what I did for the good of the programme."

An amused grin flitted across Lexy's dark features. "Right. You defended him only to turn around and work nights when he wasn't there. Followed that by preparing plans of leaving without a word."

"So you're telling me my feelings are because of him."

"I'm not telling you anything, hon. I'm merely questioning your endless choices, which seem to increase the gap between you and this man—whom, according to you, you have no feelings for." A sardonic smirk. "Or so you claim."

"I'm going to see him tomorrow, Lexy. After they're done for the day."

Lexy nodded her approval.

Since her staunch defence of him six days ago, she'd not allowed herself to be near him. He'd come by her apartment a few times, pounding on the door, but she'd never answered. It hurt her but she was leaving and, as she'd shown, she had little to no restraint when it came to Gio. But he'd left a few things and she would return them. Tomorrow. Tonight she'd watch the rain and read before she headed in for her last night of work.

Ivan met her at the entrance to their building and said, "Come on, let me give you a ride."

They dashed through the rain to climb into his older Toyota 4Runner. "Thanks."

"My pleasure."

On the ride in, they chatted amicably about work. Out of habit, she scanned the lot for Gio's car.

"He's already gone," Ivan supplied.

She couldn't quite determine if her sigh was one of relief or regret. Either way, she would ignore it.

The night passed quickly with the final handing over of the reins to Ivan. At least her father had left before the news of her scandalous behaviour had come to light. Many people still gave her odd looks. Some envious, some jealous, and some downright confused.

After work, Ivan took her out for breakfast. As she nibbled on her toast, he put his fork down and stared at her.

"What?" she asked after a few moments had passed with his gaze unwavering.

"Marry me."

She slowly set her toast down on the edge of her plate. Perhaps she'd misheard. As she stared into those pale blue eyes of Ivan's, she realised she'd not. She didn't laugh or attempt to make a joke of his statement. What she did do was consider his offer.

It could work, she discerned. Ivan was a good man. Smart, handsome, and he had genuine affection for her. They were compatible, for lack of a better word. Sex would always be pleasant and he already had been acquainted with most of her quirks—as others referred to them.

Yet, as she sat there and stared into his blue eyes, she couldn't help but notice there existed no heat. No passion that seemed all-consuming. As it had in a pair of hazel eyes when Gio had watched her.

The tip of her tongue slipped out and skimmed her lips. "Ivan, I don't know what to say."

"Don't have to say anything right now. We'd make a good couple, Jaydee. Our children would be brilliant."

Children. She resisted the urge to press her hand along her abdomen. The last time she had been with Gio, in the B-2, there'd been no use of protection. Could there be a possible child from that union? An unsettled flip in her stomach disturbed her. She wasn't ready to be a mother. In the realm of maternal instincts, she had none.

"Just think on it, Jaydee. Really, think about it and let me know. It doesn't matter where we end up." He reached across the table and captured her hand in his, giving it a gentle squeeze. "Think about it, okay?"

She released his hand and nodded. "I will."

After they'd finished eating and had gone back to their apartment building, she gave him a hug.

"I'll miss you, Ivan," she murmured.

"And I you, Jaydee. Let me know what you decide."

She nodded and headed inside. The place bustled with activity as the other residents prepared to head out for their day. She called out her farewells and made her way finally to the elevator and to the second floor.

Mrs Atag, her landlady, stood there, hands on her ample hips. She smiled when their eyes met.

"Good morning, Mrs Atag."

"Morning, dearie."

"I could have come by."

"Nonsense. I was down here anyway. Shall we?"

With a nod, she opened the door and they stepped inside.

* * * *

That afternoon, when Jaydee left, she headed down to where her motorcycle sat. She would meet Lexy later on but, for right now, she had something to deliver.

On her bike, she gathered up her hair and slid the helmet on. Assured that her bag would sit right on her back, she started the engine and drove away. She took her time, not pushing hard.

The late afternoon was nice and relatively cool. Still, heat seemed to singe her body the closer she drew to her destination. Before the turn to his street, she paused and almost ran.

Almost. Girding herself, she gave it some gas and slowly went around the corner of his street and drove until his house appeared. His car sat in the drive and she pulled in before parking at an angle behind it.

She removed her helmet and raked her fingers through her unbound hair. Another sigh and she swung off, set her helmet on the seat, and walked up towards his front door. Once there, she knocked.

The door opened and she lost her breath. Gio stood there, his eyes a bit red, and she knew she'd just woken him. He had on a pair of jeans that hung low around his hips. They were zipped but not buttoned. That was all he wore. His hair had been recently cut— it was shorter than it had been the last time she'd seen him. And his jaw sat covered in shadowed growth, adding to his sexual allure.

He blinked a few times, almost as if unsure he saw her. "Jaydee?"

"I'm sorry to wake you, Gio." She removed her pack and opened it. "I have some things to return to you."

He reached for her but she stepped back, well aware of what would happen if she allowed him to touch her. All her clothing would be gone in barely any time and he would be deep inside her. Her skin burned at the temptation, her pulse quickened, and her body prepared.

Anger flashed in his hazel gaze, darkening it, but he didn't pursue her. "Come inside."

After a quick glance at her watch, she offered him a small nod. He retreated and she followed him into his home, doing her best to ignore the masculine scent that surrounded him. They'd had a long day—she knew the pilots had come in around two and had been running drills. "I won't take up much of your time, I just wanted to give these back to you."

He didn't speak, just stared at her with raw hunger in his eyes. She couldn't deny wanting him. Especially not standing here staring at his near-naked state. He crossed strong arms over that cut chest and waited for her to say something.

Ducking her head, she dug through the bag and withdrew the items he'd left over at her place. She held them out for him and he just stared at her. She worried her lower lip before placing the things on the straight-backed chair by the door.

There were so many things she wanted to say but she couldn't bring any of them up past her lips. She tried for a smile and failed. "I...I should get going."

He caught her before she could reach the door handle. His callused fingertips sent shock waves through her system and her knees trembled in remembrance. Remembrance of what he did to her and with her.

"Jaydee," he said. The word, gravelled and rough, dragged along her skin, setting up goose bumps in its wake.

Ding-dong.

She glanced back at him, licking her lips. His gaze narrowed on the door as he shoved his free hand through his short, buzzed hair. She read his command in the look he gave her before releasing her and stepping around her to open the door.

"Giovanni!" the feminine cry reached her as he swung the door wide.

"Michelle." There was definite recognition in his tone. As well as affection.

From where she stood, she could see the thin pale arms of this Michelle person wrap around his tanned body. Jaydee closed her eyes and reined in that unpleasant feeling of jealousy which that threatened to run roughshod over her. She'd had her chance with him. And she'd made her decision.

Gio carried her back and set her down once they were fully in the room. The woman drew away and glanced over to where she stood. A flash of warning lit her green eyes as they stared at one another.

"I didn't know you had company, Giovanni," Michelle said in a low voice. Her fingers stroked familiarly along his arm.

"Don't mind me," Jaydee said. "I was just on my way out."

She stepped to the door and over the threshold only to pause and look back. Nothing in her life could have prepared her for the spear of hurt that jabbed her at what she saw. Gio stood there, one arm around Michelle, who had her hand resting familiarly against his chest, and a proprietary glint in her eyes.

"Jaydee, wait," he said.

"No, I have to get going. Again, I'm sorry to have disturbed you. Good luck on your quals."

Before the first traitorous tear could escape, she shut the door, blocking out his image. She walked calmly to her bike, past the convertible Mustang parked beside Gio's car, and left. When she reached her destination, the sun had begun to set in the sky. She waited for the gate to open then drove through to where a man waited. After talking to him, she signed some papers and climbed into the back of a waiting taxi. Two hours later, she walked with Lexy through the airport, one black leather bag in hand.

Chapter Seventeen

Gio stared at the door after it shut. A small sniffle yanked his attention from the sound of Jaydee's motorcycle engine. Michelle's eyes had large, dark circles underneath them.

"Michelle, what are you doing here?" he asked, brushing some of her hair behind one ear.

"I missed you," she said softly. She rested her head against his bare chest.

"I've missed you too, but what are you doing here? Did you come for Mike's memorial?"

Her arms gripped him and he sighed when she burst into tears. With care, he held her close while she cried. Even as he stood there staring out of the window he realised he had to go after Jaydee. Had he known she was coming over he wouldn't have slept, for he was just too tired to have kept her from leaving.

"Let me get you something to eat, Michelle."

Gently he prised her away from him and led the way to the kitchen. He gave her a Coke from the fridge and detoured to his room to grab a shirt and button the fly on his jeans. He paused and stared at his reflection.

Damn, I look rough.

Remaining barefoot, he made his way back to where his guest waited. As much as he loved Michelle, right now he really just wanted her to vanish so that he could go after Jaydee.

He pulled out some chicken salad and set some crackers down before her, then grabbed some flatware and joined her. "Help yourself."

They ate in silence for a bit then he leant back in his chair and sighed. "What's going on, Michelle?"

"Do I need an invitation to come see you? I never did before, when Mike was alive."

Guilt ate at him. "No, of course you don't. You're always welcome here. You know that. But it doesn't tell me why you've come."

"Who was she?" Michelle asked instead of answering his question.

It didn't escape his notice that there was a slight bite to her tone. He cocked an eyebrow and stared at her. She met his gaze head-on, defiance blazing in her eyes. A sinking feeling grew in his gut. She couldn't...

"A pilot. Now answer me."

Her lower lip quivered and he steeled himself against his instinctive reaction towards her. "Daddy is just so angry. I couldn't take it and had to get away."

"So you came here."

"Yes, just until they finish painting my new place. I want you to come see it."

"Of course," he replied automatically. "And Mike's stuff?"

"I've rented a storage locker and once my things are out of it I'll have his moved in. That way I can go through them at my own pace and they won't be here as a constant reminder." She took a drink. "I'm sorry it has taken me so long to get my shit together, Giovanni. It's just that I still feel so empty without him. I mean, he was my twin."

"I know, and he was my best friend. It will take some time to get past this tragedy."

"And the girl?"

He shook his head. "Let it go, Michelle."

"She's something special to you then, isn't she." It wasn't a question, not that he'd have answered anyway. "I know Mike and Daddy always wanted us to get together. And so did I." She lifted her head and pierced him with her green eyes. "I admit I was even a bit jealous when I got here and saw that woman in your house, especially with you only wearing your jeans. Unbuttoned, at that."

He opened his mouth but she shook her head. "Let me finish before I lose my nerve. I'm sure I gave off some vibe that told her you were mine and I'm sorry but all I could see was myself losing you like I lost Mike. I wasn't ready to face that. Still not ready. But I saw the way you stared after her once she'd left. In all the years I've known you, I've never seen that look in your eyes. So despite what *I* want—hoped for—I know you will only ever see me as a younger sister."

Her expression appeared pained and hurt. However, she met his gaze square on.

"I never meant to lead you on, Michelle. Ever."

She gave him a small smile. "I know. It was my own fanciful thinking. I just don't want to lose you."

"You never will, honey. We're family." He reached across the table and squeezed her hand.

She released a heavy sigh and gave him a grin. One with a bit of sorrow in it, but a grin nonetheless. "Now, tell me about the woman who was here."

He had to admire Michelle. She wasn't a person who whined or threw tantrums. She had told him up front how she felt and accepted he didn't feel the same. Well, not in the same vein as she would have liked.

"That was Jaydee Amos, a fellow pilot."

"Uh-huh."

He lifted his gaze to find her giving him a look identical to the one Mike used to level at him when he disagreed with whatever Gio was saying. Her green eyes twinkled as she laced her fingers upon the tabletop and asked him another question.

"What would you have told Mike about her?"

* * * *

Gio drove towards Jaydee's apartment building, his mind full of the stuff he'd told Michelle before she cried off to crash. There were no more excuses, or anything like that. He loved Jaydee — that was the bottom line.

He parked his car and dashed inside the brick building, heading for the stairs, unwilling to wait for the elevator to return to the ground floor. As he stepped on to the second floor, he breathed a bit easier.

She would hear him out. He wouldn't leave until she did. On the way over, he'd tried reaching her by phone only to be sent immediately to her voicemail. Her floor was silent.

Night had fallen and he didn't expect to see her other neighbours. At her door, he knocked. No answer. He knocked again. Still nothing.

Biting back a frustrated groan, he reached for the knob and turned. He breathed a sigh of relief as it spun easily under his touch.

"Jaydee," he called out, not wanting to scare her. "I'm coming in, sweets. We need to talk."

He stepped through into the dark and a tingle went up his spine. Something felt wrong. He didn't like it. Sidestepping to the left, he flipped on the light switch. A warm soft glow enveloped the room but did nothing to stop the chills from converging on him.

The apartment was empty.

He blinked a few times, hoping, *praying,* it was nothing but his mind playing a dirty and devious trick on him. Unfortunately, it wasn't to be so. The reality of the situation smacked him head on.

Jaydee was gone.

And not in the 'I'll catch her at work tomorrow' gone sense. There was no trace of her. No items lingering around that indicated she would be back. Ever. Nothing remained aside from bare floors and walls. No furniture, either.

He hurried back behind the opaque blocks to where her bed had been. Also gone. The place was so sterile it looked like it had been scrubbed.

"Shit!"

Back in her open kitchen, he leaned against the countertop and tried to find his lost breath. Lexy's words streamed like a mantra in his mind.

By the end of her time here, she'll look in that box that contains her feelings for you, sigh, and delete it. Then she'll move on.

"The hell she will."

He stormed to the exit, shut off the lights, and closed the door behind him. Trying hard not to think of the click as being something so final, he paused before the elevator. Ivan lived here.

Back on the first floor, he checked mailboxes and got the number to Dr Vinokourov's apartment. Three A.

Gio paced in the elevator as the machine took him up to the third floor. He tried her number one more time. Same result, her voicemail.

"Jaydee, call me when you get this message. We need to talk." He hesitated. "Please."

Shoving his phone back into his pocket, he rapped sharply on Ivan's door. No sound could be heard so he pounded again, louder this time.

"Yes?" Ivan asked as he swung the door open.

Gio stared at the man and anger churned in his gut. Ivan wasn't your typical geeky lab rat. No, his luck wasn't that good. He couldn't be faced with a skinny, pale guy who barely looked strong enough to carry his books. Of course not. Ivan stood before him in nothing but a pair of sweats, and it wasn't hard to tell that the man was in very good shape.

"Where is she?" he bit off.

Pale blue eyes narrowed at him and Ivan crossed his arms over his bare chest. "Well, well, well. If it isn't the pilot. What do you want?"

"You know damn well what I want. Don't fuck with me, Doc. I can guarantee you won't like the end result." He clenched his hands into fists so he wouldn't touch the man. "Now answer my goddamn question!"

Ivan barely blinked at the blatant threat. "Where's who?" he asked, leaning indolently against the doorframe.

His control slipped another few notches. "Jaydee. Her apartment is empty."

"I know that. I supervised the moving of her things while she was at work. I'm not in a place to tell you where she is or is not."

He narrowed his eyes. "Tell me," he growled.

"No. I do hope that, wherever she is, she's considering my marriage proposal."

Ivan's sentence was issued with that lingering Russian accent and the condescending manner of a person who hated spending any of his time around those he felt were inferior to him. And Gio knew that Ivan considered him to be in that pool of substandard people.

His restraint snapped and he lunged at the man, grabbing him and throwing him against the wall just inside the apartment.

"You stay the fuck away from her!" he rumbled in a low voice. They were damn near nose to nose, but Gio was a bit taller and he used it to his advantage.

"Going to hit me like you did her father?"

The taunt was palpable, and Gio didn't know how he felt that Jaydee had shared that incident with Ivan. He snarled and shoved away from the man. Damn it all—Ivan didn't even look remotely rattled.

"I was thinking of beating you into a pile of pulp. How about that?"

"I think it's amusing how you turn to violence at the least bit of provocation. Is that *all* you know how to do?"

"I'm not in the mood, man. Putting my fist into your face is really seeming like a wonderful idea and each second you waste of my fucking time it becomes a better and better one. So why don't you cut the shit, and tell me where the *fuck* Jaydee is!"

"I thought she came to see you today. Didn't she tell you?"

"Obviously not or I wouldn't be here indulging you in this stupid-ass game you want to play."

"Hmm. Why should I tell you?"

"Aside from the fact I'll kick your ass if you don't?"

Ivan smirked. "You wouldn't. Because I still wouldn't tell you where she was and then you'd not only be out of luck but you'd also have to tell her why you did that, if you ever got to see or talk to her again. I'm cooking so I don't have time to waste. I'll ask you again, why should I tell you?"

Gio stared at this man who had, at one time, slept with Jaydee. Who still had a relationship with her, granted a professional one. However, the uncertainty was there. Especially given how Lexy had said she would just move on. He knew what he had to do. With a sigh, he raked a hand over his hair and stared directly into those pale blue eyes.

"Because I love her. And she loves me."

* * * *

Jaydee sat on her rattan sofa combination on the chaise, a glass of iced water beside her and a book on physics turned over beside her. The backyard of her property aglow with a mixture of the setting sun and the solar lights that were starting to come on.

The wind had picked up a decided chill but she was glad—she loved the differences in temperatures here. She wriggled her toes and sighed heavily as she leant back and closed her eyes.

She'd been home for two weeks now and, despite everything, it hadn't been as easy to just pick up and go on as it had been in the past. It hadn't been as smooth a transition as she'd expected to forget about the enigmatic Giovanni Cassano.

As was her wont, she'd put her memories of him in a compartment and basically tossed it. However, he hadn't stayed gone. He'd taken to popping up at night and disturbing her dreams.

Night wasn't the only time he reappeared. There had been plenty of instances at the lab when she'd just spaced out and stared off as she relived some of their moments together. And it wasn't just the sex she experienced again, but all the occasions she'd spent in his company — at the base, talking at a picnic table about the flight. Working out with him. Hanging out at Kerrigan's. How amazing it had been to be in the room with him as he'd cooked breakfast for her.

Damn it! She missed him. A hell of a lot. She dropped a hand to cover her belly and sighed. What were the chances? What was the probability that at this very moment she carried his child?

She worried her lower lip as she ran over percentages in her head. The time in the bomber would have been perfect for her to get pregnant, since they'd not used protection. In the medicine cabinet of her bathroom, she had a pregnancy test. In fact, it had been there for a week and still sat unopened.

A cold wind whipped up around her, making her shiver. She reached for the folded quilt and covered her lower body. As the sun lowered in the sky, she dozed.

She could see him clear as day. Those intense hazel eyes burning into her as he held her, kissed her, stripped her and…

Jaydee whimpered and shifted against the cushion. Her body felt aflame and she needed relief. She bit down on her bottom lip to snap herself from the haze of desire which hovered around her, waiting, tempting, and drawing her in.

With a frustrated groan, she got to her feet, folded up the Galveston star quilt, and headed back inside, water in hand. She was hungry. While the microwave heated up her supper, she opened a small salad. She was eating a salmon fillet with lemon pepper seasoning, topped with a mixture of capers, sautéed in olive oil and butter, and miniature pear tomatoes. Served on a bed of rice pilaf.

She sat at her table and ate a quiet and solitary meal. She cleaned up and had been reading for about an hour when she got up to put on the kettle for tea. The doorbell made her pause before she sighed and made her way there.

"Yes?" she said, opening the door on the night that had grown considerably windier and colder.

Her father stood there, his expression completely neutral. She immediately stepped back and allowed him to enter. Closing the door behind him, she watched him shrug out of his light jacket and hang it up before facing her.

"Is everything okay?" she asked, unsure as to why he'd stopped by.

He stared at her in surprise. "Yes, why?"

"Because you came here."

"Is it a bad time?"

She moved by him and walked back to her kitchen. "No. I was reading and about to make a cup of tea. May I fix you one as well?"

"Please."

Jaydee didn't look over her shoulder, knowing he would follow her. So she busied herself with getting another mug down and scooping the proper amount of loose tea into the infuser.

"I was asked by NASA if you were available to come help them with their electrogravitics."

"Of course." Her response came automatically.

"They'd like to see you as soon as possible."

"A lander?" she asked, referring to a moon or planet lander.

"That's what I was led to believe."

She nodded absently. As she poured the steaming water from the whistling teapot, her mind reviewed the first time she had watched the videos of the Apollo moon lander taking off from the surface of the Earth's moon. Even to her young mind — and despite all she'd read about the 1969 Apollo 11 mission and the denial of the use, and/or application, of EG — she'd taken special notice and spotted indications of the truth. The lander had never had to slowly gain speed similar to a rocket — no, it had *popped* up at full speed instantly.

A vehicle utilising EG could accelerate from twenty to two hundred miles per hour in a mere two seconds. Even more impressive, since EG not only made its own gravity, cancelling the Earth's, it also cancelled inertia. So that same vehicle wouldn't even cause the pilot to spill his coffee during the short yet extreme acceleration.

She loved EG and trying to find more everyday applications. Hard to do that with a concept that had belonged to black ops for more than half a century and was just becoming more prominent in the public eye.

Covering the mugs, she stared at her father. "Texas?"

"No. You'd be going to Virginia."

NASA Langley Research Center, LaRC. Hampton, Virginia. It wouldn't be all bad, she'd be close to Lexy. Well, closer than she was now, and she could really use her friend near. And she was curious as to why they wanted her there — it was well known that the LaRC focused primarily on aeronautical research, although the Apollo lunar lander had been flight-tested there along with a number of high-profile space missions being planned and designed on-site.

"When do I need to leave?"

"They'd like you there by the end of the week."

"And how long will this be for?"

"Plan for a few months."

She sighed. Another few months away from home. She loved her house and the peace it brought her. Unfortunately, as of late, she had not been spending much time there.

"Okay."

"They have housing ready for you so there's no need to locate and secure an apartment."

One less thing for her to deal with. "Very well. I'll make flight arrangements tomorrow."

She removed the lids and slid his cup of tea over to him. He took it with a nod of gratitude and they drank in silence. After he'd finished, Dr Thompson left and she cleaned up and went back to reading her book. She climbed into bed early after sending a short email to Lexy announcing her impending arrival in Hampton.

Late the next morning, she packed her clothes for her few months of being in Virginia. Her flight had been set for tonight and she even had a taxi lined up to get her and take her to the airport. She'd called Langley and they had given her the address of her temporary housing. The house phone rang and she picked it up without sparing a glance at the caller ID.

"Hello?"

"When do you arrive? I'll be there to pick you up." Lexy's familiar voice responded to her greeting.

"I leave here around six and don't get in until two-thirty in the morning. You don't have to pick me up. I'll take a taxi."

"Pshaw. I'll drive down and meet you. I'm used to all hours anyway. Just as long as you let me crash with you at your new place."

"Of course. I mean, I have no idea what kind of accommodation they're giving me but you are welcome to stay."

"I don't care. I have to go, have a surgery to prep for. I will see you tonight."

"Thanks, Lexy."

"No reason to thank me, hon, you're my best friend. Besides, I miss you and will take any opp I can to see you." A short pause. "I'll see you soon. I have to get this man out of my house and get to work. Love you, hon."

"Bye, Lex. Love you too." She hung up and shook her head. It would be good to see her even though Lexy had just been out to visit her a short while ago.

Not much later, she had three boxes packed, sealed and addressed. They would be sent to her so she'd not have to worry about hauling it all on the plane, only her carry-on.

Two men from the lab swung by and picked up the boxes and she then began to pack her final bag. She ate a late lunch and waited outside for her ride to arrive. Once on the plane, she stowed her bag, sat in her window seat, and rested her head while waiting for the spiel from the flight attendants.

She didn't sleep well and disembarked feeling more than a bit cranky. All that vanished when she left the restricted area to find both Lexy and Eugene waiting for her. It was a sight that made her smile.

Arm in arm, the trio headed out to the parking garage where she saw Eugene's bike beside his sister's car. She tossed her bag in the back seat of the Spyder and tried to work out the kinks in her back.

"Why didn't you all ride in together?" she asked Lexy as they headed for the gate, Eugene behind them on his Dark Custom Blackline.

"He was up here and decided to come meet you as well. Me? I think he kinda likes you."

She glanced in the side mirror at the large man behind them. Eugene was handsome enough but not the one her body ached for night after night.

"He's like a brother to me."

"I know. I've tried to tell him but he does his own thing. Always has. Even told him about Ivan asking you to marry him. Waiting to hear all about that too, little missy. And also I want to know what Gio wanted with all those calls."

"I've not told Ivan anything and I haven't talked to Gio." She shifted on the seat. "I'm scared to talk to him."

"Why?" Lexy slowed down as they entered Hampton and headed for the apartment. "He wouldn't have called so many times if he didn't want to talk to you."

"Right here on the left." She pointed and Lexy turned in the drive to a brick duplex. "It's not that simple anymore, Lex."

Lexy parked and shut off the engine. With the door open and the overhead light illuminating her, she sighed as she unbuckled her belt. "And why not? Damn it, Jay, I've told you so many times you deserve a life and I *know* you like him. So what makes it so damn difficult for you to talk to the man?"

Jaydee chewed on her lower lip for a few ticks of time. Removing her own belt, she swallowed and met Lexy's disapproving gaze head on. "I think...well, I mean, there is a chance I could be pregnant." Jaydee climbed out of the car, shutting the door on Lexy's sputtering.

Chapter Eighteen

Gio sat in the uncomfortable, cracked plastic chair as he waited in the sterile reception room for the person he'd had paged. There were no magazines, no newspapers, hell, no anything for a person to pass the time. He'd asked for Jaydee, only to be informed she wasn't here. The woman wouldn't share anything other than that, so he'd asked for Dr Thompson instead.

Guess they don't get many visitors here. The accommodations surely weren't recommending coming back for another visit. Still, the woman behind the glass was nice and she'd even offered him some coffee. He'd declined but at least he'd been asked.

He'd shown his identification more than once and still waited. All the people he saw wore sombre expressions along with their lab coats. Perhaps it was a prerequisite to work here.

A large white door with a red sign reading 'Authorised personnel only past this point' swung open and Dr Thompson stepped through. The man was impeccably dressed, as he'd been at the test facility. Hell, he wondered if the man ironed his lab coat.

Brisk steps echoed as Dr Thompson walked with authority towards him. At the last moment, Gio rose. He held out a hand and said, "Dr Thompson, thank you for seeing me."

"What is the meaning of this?" Dr Thompson demanded, ignoring Gio's outstretched hand.

Licking his lower lip, Gio wiped his hand off on his pants, not liking how this had already begun to play out.

"I'm sorry, sir. I came to see Jaydee but she isn't here, or so I'm told. I need to talk to her."

"This is a working lab. We don't have time for idle chitchat."

Gio ground his jaw and strove for patience. He'd put in for time off and had finally figured out where this lab was located. Now that he'd arrived, he had found more walls and hurdles before him. Damn it! He wanted Jaydee. And no one, not even her father, was going to stop him from accomplishing his goal.

"I'm not looking for idle chitchat. I'm looking for your daughter."

Beyond the glass partition he watched as the woman's head popped up, eyes wide, at his statement. Hmm, perhaps no one else knew. Dr Thompson's brown eyes narrowed slightly and his nose flared.

A deep, dark part of Gio longed to needle the man who had seen fit to raise his child as a co-worker as opposed to his daughter. However, he wasn't a fool. He knew Dr Thompson's assistance was necessary if he were to find Jaydee. So he tried again.

"Just tell me where she is and I'll go."

"I could have you removed."

"And I'll keep coming back." He meant it.

"Ordered you shot on sight is another option."

Gio didn't even blink. "If that's what you have to do. I'm not giving up."

A few moments of charged silence passed between them before Dr Thompson pivoted around. "Come."

Jaydee's father strode towards the door he'd recently come through. On his heels immediately, Gio followed him through and sucked in a breath at the numerous wall-mounted guns that were trained on them. The weapons rotated in time with their progress down the corridor.

Shit. They aren't playing here.

The good doctor didn't seem to even notice them but, then, this was his lab. A few doors, a short elevator ride and some stairs later, Gio stuck with Dr Thompson as he entered another room. One Gio presumed to be his office. There had been no nameplate for identification purposes, no anything to indicate what — or who — resided behind the door.

It was a nice room. Small prototypes were scattered all around. A large desk sat in the middle, some bookcases lined the windowless walls, and there were a few chairs. Gio sat in one after Dr Thompson lowered himself into the one behind his desk.

Arms resting on the smooth dark top of the desk, Jaydee's father asked, "Why are you looking for Jaydee?"

"Can I just talk to her?"

He shrugged. "She's not here, as I know you were informed."

Gio forced himself to remain relaxed. "Can you tell me where I can find her?"

"I could."

He sensed a 'but' coming and didn't say anything.

"However, I think you should tell me what you want with her."

Yep. It was official. He was going to kill the man who would be his father-in-law. Gio itched to reach across the wood and beat him until he told him what he longed to know. *Probably wouldn't work very well in my favour.* So he stayed put in his seat, the look on his face one of calm.

"With all due respect, sir, that's between me and Jaydee."

"Well, then call her."

"I have." Numerous times without anything.

"And? Did she tell you where she was?"

There was this smugness in his gaze that told him he knew damn well Jaydee hadn't even talked to him. "We both know she hasn't talked to me. If she would speak to me, I wouldn't be here letting you get your rocks off by trying to make me squirm."

"And, yet, here you are."

"Here I am." He shifted on the seat. "You said you were busy. Tell me what I came for and I'll leave."

The man lowered his head for a second before lifting it and pinning him with serious brown eyes. "Tell me *why* I should help you."

Because I love your daughter. "As I said, that's between me and Jaydee."

"The first day we met you ploughed your fist into my face. Why?"

He blinked, a bit taken aback by the shift in conversation. "I was drunk and made a mistake."

One eyebrow rose. "Is that so? Jaydee said something similar and I believe you as much as I did her." Thompson laced his fingers. "What's going on between you and her?"

"What do you care?" Gio snapped, at the end of his rope. "You're the one who raised her like she was a fuckin' commodity. Only good for one thing and that was making you look good. Do you even know the meaning of family? She's your daughter, man, would it kill you to show her that you're proud of her? Or that you love her?"

"Have you told her you love her?" Dr Thompson asked after a brief pause.

"No, but then how can I? You won't tell me where the fuck she is!" He shoved to his feet and began to pace.

"Such rash behaviour. This is what brought around you getting caught in the bomber."

He whirled around and stared at the doctor, who had leant back in his chair, fingers beneath his chin. There was a definite sparkle in those eyes but Gio didn't let down his guard. This was one man who exemplified the word cagey.

"What about the bomber?"

The man flashed a cynical grin. "Don't even try it. There isn't anything that goes on surrounding Jaydee that I'm not aware of. I knew about the bomber the day Vice Admiral Fitzroy discovered the two of you."

Gio released a breath and made his way back to his vacated chair. Standing behind it, he gripped the back and waited for whatever was coming next.

"Don't look so shocked. After you punched me in the face and Jaydee defended you and asked me to let it go, I knew. I knew then you were something special to her. That told me all I needed to know."

"But you won't tell me where she is?"

"No." Dr Thompson held up a hand. "Let me finish. I'll do you one better. I'm taking a flight out to where she is tomorrow and I have room for you if you want to accompany me."

"Yes."

"Very well. Go get whatever you need and come back here. We'll be sleeping here and leaving in the morning." Dr Thompson got to his feet and walked to the door only to pause and turn back. "And while you're right, I've not been much of a father to her, trust me when I tell you this—you hurt her and I will have you killed." He opened the door and was gone.

Gio swallowed and made his way out of the room where he found a guard waiting for him, armed with an automatic machine gun as well as two sidearms.

"This way, Commander." The man strode off leaving him to follow.

He spent the night in a remarkably comfortable room. This lab seemed to have it all. He ate breakfast in a cafeteria where people gave him odd looks but never said a word to him. A different guard came and took him out of another door to see the morning sun. There was a landing strip and he found a Cessna Citation X waiting.

Dr Thompson stuck his head out from the jet and hollered, "Here he is. Let's get going."

Shouldering his bag, he jogged up the steps and into the eight-passenger double-club seating arrangement. Noting where the doctor had sat, Gio claimed the seat across the aisle from him, not wanting to be directly opposite from the man for however long the flight would be. The pilot came, grabbed his bag from him, and stowed it. Moments later, he could hear the engines powering up and soon they had taken to the sky.

"Where are we going?" he asked after they'd levelled off.

"Do you always ask so many questions?"

"Only when I'm not getting any answers."

"Virginia. She's working with NASA."

"NASA in Virginia?" He glanced out of the window at the robin's-egg blue sky.

"Yes." The man powered up his laptop and got to work.

Gio sighed. He wanted answers. Seemed all he got from this man was more questions. *At least I'm getting closer to her.* A fact that calmed him a bit more. He reclined in his seat and put in his music before allowing his eyes to drift closed.

It was afternoon when they landed in Virginia and he stifled a groan when he stepped off the jet. Hefting his bag, he trailed behind Dr Thompson and climbed into the waiting SUV. No one spoke. The second their doors closed the vehicle was off and moving.

They halted on a street of houses right before a duplex. Dr Thompson looked askance at him and said, "This is her house. Two-seven-three-one. You'll have to wait here. She should be home in a bit."

"So you're not taking me to her?"

"This is taking you to her. You can't talk to her at work, she'll find something to ignore you with. You can have zero audience here and get all your issues worked out. Go on. Like I said, she should be home soon."

Gio opened the door and stepped back out into the humid and stifling afternoon. Hand on the door, he looked into the interior. "Thank you."

"Don't thank me, son. Because, like I said, you hurt her, I'll have you killed." The doctor stared him dead in the eyes. "Good luck."

"Right," Gio muttered.

The vehicle left immediately after he'd shut the door. So there he stood, early evening, in the street before a building he hoped Jaydee would be back to soon. He glanced up and down the deserted street then meandered up the sidewalk to the porch. Not much later he sat on the bench seat by her front door, feet propped up on the railing before him and bag at his side.

Almost an hour passed before he heard the loud rumble of a motorcycle. He didn't think anything of it since it didn't sound like her Ninja. But when he watched it come into view, his breath caught in his throat. It *was* Jaydee. Just on a Harley. Damn, she looked good on it, too.

She pulled into the drive and shut it down. When she swung one leg over the black machine, he got to his feet. Even from the distance between them, he could see her eyes widen. Seeing her again gave his system a jolt. Electricity powered through him and he felt more alive than he had since she'd left.

She wore medium blue jeans that were slightly baggy, tennis shoes, and a zipped-up leather jacket. Helmet in hand, she strode up the walk, one hand lowering the zipper on her jacket, which allowed him to see the bright yellow shirt she wore beneath it. Her hair fell in a dark silken cloud around her face and shoulders.

He longed to sink his hands in it, angle her head and kiss her like there was no tomorrow. Leaning against the porch pillar, he crossed his arms and waited for her to reach him. He could read her, and knew the minute she began to put up some walls, for her eyes shuttered, the heat he'd seen vanishing behind a cool and composed mask.

Damn but she looked beautiful. He wanted to rush to her side, hold her. Kiss her. Love her.

"What are you doing here, Gio?" she asked, pausing at the bottom of the four steps.

"Well, sweets, you've been ignoring my calls and, like I said, we have to talk." He dug his nails into his palms so he wouldn't grab her. Talk first.

But after...oh God, after they talked...all bets were off.

Jaydee stared up at the man waiting for her on her porch. Giovanni Cassano. A man she'd done her best to forget about, only to fail miserably. He stood there, a black bag behind him on the cement, looking mad enough to fight through hell and good enough for her to want nothing more than to run into his arms.

He wore pale stonewashed jeans held up around lean hips by a black leather belt. A black shirt was tucked in at the waist. He had black boots on his feet and aviator glasses on his face. Hotness personified.

"Talk," she mimicked him.

In an unhurried motion, he removed the shades and she got to see his eyes. Those damnably gorgeous hazel eyes zeroed in on her face, the browns and greens swirling into an exotic blend of perfection.

"Unless there's something else you'd rather do first."

Shit! And she'd thought the day couldn't possibly get any hotter. How wrong she'd been. She felt like she was melting beneath the heat in his stare. His comment had been laden with sexual promise and suggestion.

Her belly clenched with the suggestion of having his touch on her again. Nipples tightened and pressed insistently against the fabric of her tank top.

Thankfully she still had her jacket on so he couldn't see that. And, if that wasn't enough, her clit decided to make its presence known as well and she shifted on her feet so she didn't squeeze her thighs together in what she knew would be a futile attempt to stem the flow of moisture.

"It's been a long day, Commander. I'd just as soon eat and go to bed."

"Bed works just fine for me, sweets, but I promise you I'm not going anywhere until we talk."

Bed. Him. Her. Lots and lots of sweaty passion. Oh Lord, that sounded divine. She cut off the moan that threatened to escape and bit the inside of her lip as she moved up the steps and past him to unlock her front door.

"Talking is all I'm offering."

"I'll take it," he murmured in her ear as his larger body pressed intimately against hers before the door opened, allowing her some respite from the heat of his physique.

Her knees trembled. Like she needed more reminders of what they had done together, or how often. She shrugged out of the heavy leather jacket and hung it on the coat rack by the door. Her helmet went on another one, then she walked to the kitchen to grab a glass of water. She seemed more than a bit parched.

This place was not as open as her other apartment and so she didn't see him coming up behind her. One minute she was alone and, the next, his hard body had melded itself to her back, strong arms pinning her in between him and the fridge.

Closing her eyes, she prayed for strength. Somehow, she didn't think there was enough in the world. Not for her and definitely not when it came to this man.

"You ran from me," he rumbled in her ear. "Why did you run?"

"I didn't run. I came to see you but you seemed busy with your guest. So I left."

Her skin burned as he nuzzled his way along behind her ear and down the side of her neck to her shoulder. A puddle. That was what he turned her into.

"That was Michelle."

"I know." She hated that her voice sounded so sharp. "You introduced us"—a slight pause—"in a manner of speaking. I mean, I gathered that's who she was when you said her name. You remember, seconds before she jumped into your arms."

"If I didn't know any better, sweets, I'd say you were jealous."

She was, damn it. More than she'd ever been in her entire life but the hell she'd let him know that. Many nights she'd lain there cursing over the image of that green-eyed woman jumping familiarly into his arms. Pushing back against him so she could reach into the fridge, she withdrew two bottles of water.

"Well, then, you apparently don't know any better, do you?"

His rumble vibrated into her back and she shivered at the darkly menacing sound. Before she knew what had happened, he spun her around and slammed one hand against the refrigerator beside her head. She jumped and tried immediately to calm her heart. Fury radiated from every pore of his body.

"So it wouldn't bother you to know she stayed at my house for a few days, then?"

She shrugged. "Why should it? There's nothing between us. Can you move back, please?"

"No."

"I'm sorry?"

"I'm not moving back. In fact, I'm thinking it's time for me to move even closer. Eliminate what little space there is between us and see what happens." The gleam in his gaze nearly unsettled her. He seemed on the edge and yet all too controlled.

She gulped. She was confident of what would happen. Damn if she didn't want it to again. But she couldn't…could she?

One hand stroked up along her side, over her hip, and up her ribs. Two long fingers worked their way beneath the hem of her shirt and lifted it. The simplicity of his touch took her breath away. The calluses she felt sent her for a ride.

Shit. Much more of this and she'd be orgasming without him even removing their clothing. As it was, she felt like panting.

"Nothing would happen." The words were forced out from her lips.

"I beg to differ, sweets." He nuzzled her temple and she jumped when his teeth grazed her outer ear. "Yeah, I beg to differ."

Her thoughts were so jumbled she knew that there was no way to straighten them out. She couldn't seem to focus. Well, not true. She had an intense single-mindedness about each feathery stroke of his fingers along her skin, the whisper of his warm breath through her hair, and the heady and masculine scent of him.

He moved, just a bit, and she whimpered at the feel of his erection pressing into her. So close and yet so damn far.

"Tell me the truth," he said.

"This…this can't happen."

He shifted again and she felt her heart speed up even more as his left hand settled upon her side and began lifting that side of her shirt. Higher and higher his touch skimmed, his thumbs slipping along the underside of her breasts.

She gave in and gripped his upper arms, unable to stand on her own any longer. Jaydee wanted him with everything in her. One more time. Tilting her face up to his, she groaned in relief when his mouth covered hers.

It wasn't gentle—he demanded. And she gave all he asked for. His tongue stroked deep and hitting everything it could reach. The passionate fires that only this man inflamed pushed to an out-of-control raging blaze, kicking into high gear, racing over her and incinerating the last shred of restraint she had. She slumped against his solid physique with a moan of surrender.

Gio broke the kiss long enough to rip her tank top off. She tugged on his shirt, too, and it followed hers to the floor. His hands settled along her waist and, with a deft spin, he moved them from the front of the refrigerator and settled her upon the countertop before wedging himself between her thighs.

God! She could feel the long hard length of him pressing into the apex of her thighs. His fingers dug into the flesh of her ass as he held her to him, grinding slowly, allowing her no chance to escape.

Tilting her head to the side, she gave him more access to her neck. Goose bumps broke out as he nibbled along her skin, nipping and laving. She ran her hands up over his back, hooking her legs around his waist and kicking off her tennis shoes.

"Jaydee," he mumbled into her ear as he sucked on the lobe.

She felt the flick on her bra, which undid the clasp in the back, and whimpered as his teeth grazed along her shoulder, dragging the satin strap down. First one side then the other.

Her movements grew frantic as she slid her hands around to the front of his jeans and unbuttoned them. His mouth feasted upon hers again as she slowly lowered the zipper, his tongue thrusting deep and licking everywhere it could. A purr of contentment slipped from her mouth to his as she curved her hand around his stiffness.

So hot. So hard. Hers.

He bucked against her touch and she began stroking him. It didn't take long before he was getting her out of her own jeans. He removed her underwear, which was soaked with her desire for him, and he flicked two fingers over her sensitive clit.

She reached for him again and guided him to where she needed him to be. He didn't make her wait. He powered deep into her with no hesitation. Her eyes rolled back in her head as he stretched her.

"Mine!" he growled as he began to move.

She bit her lip, not responding to his possessiveness. Hell, they hadn't been apart that long but damn if it didn't feel like it had been a lifetime since he'd been inside her.

He gripped her hips and began driving hard into her. She hooked her ankles behind him and held him tight. Held him close. Held him hard. She buried her face into his neck and shoulder as her nails dug into his skin. He didn't seem to mind in the slightest.

"Mine!" he reiterated, his single-word statement punctuated by a powerful stroke that made her gasp and bite him as the pleasure ricocheted through her.

Her slit clenched around him and his rumble of satisfaction would have made her smile had she been able to catch her breath. As it was, everything within her was attuned to the man buried deep inside her wetness. She wanted to climb into him and never leave, for fear of losing the feelings he created in her.

Gio stimulated her clit and she disintegrated around him. "Fuck, you're so damn tight," he growled before he pounded into her with unrelenting strokes. A low roar escaped him as she felt him release inside her.

Before her heart even had a chance to slow, he lifted her off the counter, still buried deep, and carried her to her bedroom where he proceeded to start all over again.

Chapter Nineteen

Gio slowly opened his eyes. The room was not familiar but it didn't matter, for the woman in his arms was. He'd know her scent anywhere. Jaydee slept soundly against him, her body pressed tightly to his, just how they'd fallen asleep. She lay partially on her stomach and part on him. One leg draped over him, her face buried into his shoulder, and one arm rested along his chest.

Jaydee. What was he going to do with her? He couldn't explain the possessiveness he experienced when he thought of her. Was it wrong to want to lock someone up and keep them from everyone else? Well, yes, and he knew that, yet it didn't seem to stop him from wanting to do that very thing.

Tilting his head, he stared down at the woman he held. There were two times when he'd been allowed to see the real Jaydee. Not the one who could blow his mind with her memory, flying ability, or the way she seemed uninterested in anything but her job. One was now, when she was sleeping, and the other was when they were having sex. Correction—making love.

Now she looked soft, tender—a woman he wanted to protect more than anything in the world. When she was awake there was this cold wall around her which made her seem almost untouchable, even unapproachable. Not that it had stopped him but…he could see it with others.

She was a loner. And, for all intents and purposes, she didn't seem to mind or even acknowledge that she came across that way. She just had other, more important things to focus on.

All that aside, he knew he would have to force her to talk to him about the two of them. He wasn't about to let her delete the memory she had of their time together. Nor was he going to let her marry that Ivan guy. Oh, hell no!

He stroked a hand down the side of her face and brushed his thumb along her lips. They were still slightly swollen from the kisses they'd shared earlier. His heart lurched when she burrowed closer to him and spoke his name on a whisper of a sigh. He loved her. So much it scared him.

He carefully disengaged himself from her and slid from the double bed. Normally he preferred a larger one but he had to admit, smaller made them sleep even closer together, and *that* was something he liked immensely.

Tugging on his jeans, he ran a hand through his short hair then walked out of the bedroom. This place was nice and, like her place before, there was zero in the way of personal touches. He made his way through the quaint two-bedroom place and, peering in the second bedroom, he noticed it was set up like an office.

The living room boasted a sofa and a single recliner. There were a few tiny tables along the wall but he saw no sign of a television. Once in the kitchen, he picked up the scattered articles of clothing and carried them back to the bedroom where Jaydee still lay, dead to the world. She'd rolled over and he stared hungrily at her naked body.

Christ, he wanted her again. And again. He didn't think he'd ever get enough of her. The sun had begun to set and sent golden rays through the windows and onto her exposed skin. Her tattoo teased him and he longed to lean over and press his lips to it, maybe give her a slight bite.

He left her there—reluctantly, but he did. He walked into her bathroom then took care of business. A box on the corner of the sink's counter caught his eye and he frowned while he dried his hands.

Sneaking a peek back into the bedroom, he assured himself she was still out then he approached the box, slowly, as if it may jump up and bite him. *What the fuck is she doing with this?* Why would she need a pregnancy test unless…

He spun around and strode back into the bedroom. His blood pumped and he tried to calm down. Surely there was a logical explanation as to why she had this. Wasn't there? Unfortunately, all that flashed in his head was Ivan telling him he'd asked Jaydee to marry him.

"What the fuck is this?" he demanded.

Jaydee stirred and rolled over. Her tortoiseshell gaze was sleepy but in a second it sharpened as it focused on the box he held in his hand. She sat up and jerked the sheet up around her breasts.

"What are you doing with that?" she snapped.

"What are you doing with it?" he countered.

"Nothing. Which is why it was in the bathroom, *unopened*."

He tossed the rectangular box on the bed and followed it down. Hands on either side of her legs, he leaned closer to her. "Are you pregnant?"

For the first time since he had met her, she looked completely petrified. It didn't last more than a few hundredths of a second, but damn if he didn't spot it. Then came the icy demeanour he was used to seeing when she wasn't about to let anyone in. The woman she was at work.

"Get out of my way."

"Not a chance."

She grumbled something he didn't understand and scooted around his arms before getting off the bed. He kept his eye on her, ensuring she didn't bolt for the door but otherwise remained sitting as she covered up her body with clothing. More's the pity, he'd rather enjoyed looking at her nakedness.

Once she'd pulled on a shirt and shoved into a pair of shorts, she ran her hand through her hair and crossed her arms. Even so, he noticed how her gaze continued to drift towards the box by his left hand.

"Talk."

She shook her head and put her hair up in a ponytail. "No. There's nothing to talk about."

"The fuck there isn't."

He shoved to his feet and prowled towards her. Damn it all, he'd never had to pursue a woman like this before. But here he was, refusing to give up and let her go.

"We had a fling," she said, her voice higher than usual. After a deep breath, she continued her tone, calmer now. "That's all it was. A fling."

He clenched his jaw and crowded her against the wall of her bedroom. "Are. You. Pregnant?"

There was another flash of fear. "How would I know? The box is closed."

"Don't push me, Jaydee."

"Then leave."

"No."

She tried to duck by him but he restricted her movements, capturing her wrists in one hand and pinning them against the wall over her head. This time the flare in her eyes was lust, but, like the fear, it was swiftly masked.

"What we had was more than a fling, Jaydee Amos, and you know it."

Hell, like this her breasts pushed up against the thin material of her shirt and his mouth watered. He wanted to dip his head and suck one breast into his mouth, roll the tight nipple, and hear her moans of pleasure. *Focus!*

"Are you pregnant with my child?"

"How would I know? I just told you the box isn't opened yet."

"Possibly?"

He forced himself to calm down as she seemed to be getting more agitated. Hell, even he knew it was possible. Even this most recent time they'd not used protection, but damn if he'd wanted to feel a barrier between them. He loved how she gripped him, the heat, the snugness, the slickness. And, to be honest, he didn't even think about being unprotected until after, something that only happened with her.

"Of course. You know full well there was no condom on the B-2, or just now." Her tone had a slight edge to it.

It had been almost four weeks since the bomber. A child. And not just any child but a child with Jaydee.

"Take the test."

"I beg your pardon?"

"Now. Take the test." She shook her head and he used his other hand to hold her chin still. "I have a right to know if I'm going to be a father, Jaydee."

"Why? Worried it will get in the way of the *great Casanova* and all his conquests?"

He wanted to crow. The door had been opened, now it was time to get her to admit there were feelings there. "Is that what you're telling yourself?" he asked, even as his body rebelled at the mere thought of being with another. "That it will be easier to forget all about what we've shared by thinking I'll be mad if you're pregnant because it will mess up my time with women? Other women?"

"I don't care if you fuck every woman you meet."

"Liar," he murmured, leaning in close to swipe a kiss. "It's burning you up inside. Just like you were jealous of Michelle." Another kiss. "Know this, Jaydee. There is no other woman for me but you." He pulled back and stared in her eyes. "I love you."

She shook her head. "Don't say that."

He frowned. "Why not?" It bothered him greatly that she didn't immediately say it back to him.

"You can't...can't love me."

"So now you're telling me how I can feel?"

She struggled and he released her hands but refused to let her go. "It's just...just that, well, look at you."

He was not at all pleased with that statement. "What about me?"

"I'm not your type."

"Sweets, you are exactly my type. Passionate, brilliant, and all-around amazing. More beautiful to me than anything."

"Don't say things like that." She pushed against his chest and he pushed back, repudiating her silent command. "What happens when you want your old life back and you decide you were wrong and don't love me?"

"You don't believe I love you."

"I think you're reacting to the slight probability I may be pregnant." She licked her lips. "If, and I mean if, it turns out that I am, I don't want anything from you. I won't ask for anything from you. Nevertheless, if you want to be a part of your child's life, I won't deny you, either. But, please, don't assume I'm going to fall into your arms because you say 'I love you'."

He just stared at her, unbelieving what he'd just heard. Then the rage pushed through. "So what, you planning on marrying Ivan Vinokourov instead?" Her eyes widened. "Yes," he snarled. "I know all about him asking you and you won't be marrying him."

"You can't—"

"The hell I can't, Jaydee. I'm not going to stand here and let you marry a man I know you don't love."

"You don't know that."

"Yes, I do," he said assuredly. "You love someone else, Jaydee. And you need to recognise that."

The tip of her tongue sneaked out and swiped along her lower lip, sending him right back into another, lower level of his own private hell.

"Maybe I don't love him, but…but we are compatible."

He scoffed, less than thrilled that she was trying to pull this shit. "Is that what you want? Someone who is 'compatible' only? Because I don't think you do want that. You need passion, raw and explosive passion. Not compatible. You want that and you go get a pet."

Her jaw clenched. "It would work."

"Sure. Maybe." He tucked some hair behind her ear. "But what about passion?"

"An emotion."

"Yes. A very important one. Are you truly willing to give it all up? Heated touches? Intimate caresses? Sex so intense you see stars?" He gave a negative shake of his head. "You can try to deny it all you want, sweets, but you know you want those things. Crave them."

Her breathing increased in speed and grew shallower as she stood there. He pressed his advantage, shoving his hand down the front of her nylon shorts to find her panties soaked.

"Does he make you this hot? Burn this much?" He slid his fingers under the edge of her panties and over the damp curls. "You are mine, Jaydee. From the very beginning, you've been mine."

Her hips gyrated and he knew she sought the fingers tantalising her pussy but he refused to enter her, keeping up his teasing strokes. She stared at him with desire-darkened orbs and he could read her want.

She began to make small, erotic moans as she melted back into the wall. He slipped two fingers into her molten heat and had to swallow a groan of his own. She gripped his fingers like a warm glove. His cock throbbed painfully in his jeans. He pumped his fingers in her, revelling in how responsive she was to his every touch.

He watched her face and held still right when the familiar expression of her impending orgasm lit her features. Her frustration at his denying her overflowed from narrowed eyes and he bit back a smile. No matter how adamantly she tried to refuse to accept what existed between them, her body continually responded to him.

"Gio," she panted. "Please."

"So close aren't you, sweets. So close. Look at me."

Glazed eyes met his. He moved his fingers and used his thumb on her clit, aware it would give her what she so desperately sought. Her eyelids fluttered as her body trembled. Lips pursed as her moans grew louder. One hand snagged his wrist, encouraging his fingers deeper. He complied and watched as she came by his touch.

"I love you, Jaydee," he whispered before capturing her cry of pleasure with his mouth.

She sagged into him and he made short work of her clothes. And his. He sank deep inside her — heat and slick cream covered his cock as he carried her back to the bed. After another mind-blowing release followed by a nap, he woke to her trying to slide from the bed.

He rolled towards her, pressing her to him. "Where are you going?"

"I need to get up."

"Why?"

"Because I'm hungry. I haven't eaten since my early lunch."

He brushed a kiss along her lips. The clock read eight, so he knew she must really be hungry. "Let's go to dinner."

She stared at him. He could see her assessing him. He held her gaze, allowing her to find whatever she sought.

After a bit, she blinked. "I don't need to go out, I have food here."

"Let me take you out."

"I don't have a car."

"I saw the bike. Is it yours? Did you sell your Ninja?"

He stroked her bare skin, unable to refrain from touching her. She didn't pull back. In fact, she placed a hand on his chest and caressed him. He'd learned

Jaydee was very tactile with him. Something he didn't mind at all.

"It belongs to Eugene."

"Who's Eugene?" he asked as politely as he could.

"One of Lexy's brothers."

He recalled the two large men who'd been with the women that night at the bar. A grunt left him—he didn't trust himself to speak just yet. Jaydee wasn't even looking at him—her focus was on the abstract pattern she was drawing on his chest.

"A good friend?" He winced after the question had slipped free. Could he sound any more pathetic? Whining about people she knew?

She shrugged. "I suppose. I've known him as long as I have Lexy. They've always been nice to me."

"But you don't consider him and his brother good friends?"

Jaydee tipped her head so their gazes could meet. "I consider Lexy and Ivan good friends. Eugene is Lexy's brother. He's sort of like mine as well."

It gnawed at his gut to hear her say such a thing about Ivan but he nodded. There were times he forgot that Jaydee saw things differently from most people. But there was one thing he couldn't ignore.

"You need to take the test, Jaydee."

Reality. Jaydee stiffened slightly in Gio's arms as he reiterated what she'd been trying to get up the courage to do. Hell, she'd taken the first step in actually purchasing the item. But that was as far as she'd got. Part of her wanted to fight with him about this, yet she kept her argument to herself. She wasn't a fool and knew if it turned out that she *was* pregnant, then she needed to be seeing a doctor to ensure the best for the baby.

His callused fingers gripped her chin and held her there. "Don't ignore me, Jaydee."

"I'm not."

"Then you'll take the test." She didn't think he'd made it a question.

Dread welled up inside her all over again. A baby? Was she ready? The logical part of her brain told her there was no point in freaking out until all the facts were in evidence. That was what she latched on to and held close.

"Fine."

Gio nodded and released her. She watched him roll away and vacate the bed. His expression was serious and, if she dared think on it a lot, possibly a bit nervous. There was nothing left to keep her from peeing on the stick and finding out what her future held. She reached for the robe she kept at the foot of her bed and slipped it on before she stood.

Her hands shook slightly as she tied the knot and picked up her scattered clothing from earlier. On silent feet, she made her way to the bedroom door only to pause when he called her name.

"What?"

She faced him and noticed he held the rectangular box out towards her. Another clench of her stomach muscles and she reached for it. She could read his need to say something in his expression, but she didn't think she could handle it, so she pivoted and left.

She closed the bathroom door and almost locked it behind her. Shaking, she rested her hands on the counter supporting the sink. She stood up tall after several deep breaths later and stared at her reflection.

"Just do it," she told herself.

She took an expedited shower and dressed in her clothing, ignoring her bladder. She put her hair up in a ponytail, picked up the box, and stared at it. This was it. All she had to do was pee on the stick and wait three minutes for the results to show in the little window. Easy. Right?

Apparently not, since she continued to stand there and stare at it. Hell, she hadn't even opened the box yet. Setting it back down, she whirled for the door and opened it to find Gio leaning in the doorway to her bedroom, watching the bathroom.

"Well?" he asked, one brow lifted towards the top of his head.

She swallowed. "It says it's best to do it in the morning." One hand waved. "You know, first thing and all that."

"Is that so?"

"Yes."

"Okay. Then let's go to dinner."

That was it? He wasn't going to argue with her? He raked his gaze up and down her before pushing away and striding towards her. Her breath caught as she watched him move. Predatory. Powerful. He'd dressed in his jeans and T-shirt, no socks or shoes on but it in no way detracted from the image he presented.

"You thought I was going to argue." Another statement.

"Yes."

"If they say morning is the best, then morning it will be. Come on, we need to get some food in you."

Not much later, they were out by the bike, fully dressed, and she took the helmet he handed her and buckled it on under her chin. Eugene had the turtleshell-style head protection. She sat on the seat and looked up at the man standing beside her, fastening his own helmet.

Without a word, she slid back so he could drive. He straddled the sleek black machine and she wrapped her arms around him, balancing her feet on the bike. Eyes closed, she allowed the masculine scent of Gio to flow over her. The motorcycle started with an easy rumble and she opened her eyes as he got them on the road.

Soon, they were out on the interstate, the warm wind blowing over her as they wove in and out of the traffic. Gio handled the bike like a pro and she found herself enjoying the ride. The throb of the powerful machine beneath her, Gio's hard body before her, heck, what else could a woman want?

He drove for a while until he eventually pulled off on an exit and took them to a restaurant. After he parked, she released him and removed the helmet before swinging a leg over as she dismounted.

Gio didn't say anything, just held his helmet in one hand as his other splayed along the small of her back while he guided her to the door. They were seated at a cosy booth in the back of the establishment. The sounds of classic rock filtered around them. She'd never been here before but, if the smells, which made her tummy rumble, were any indication of how the food was, she would be in good hands.

A chipper waitress came over to take their drink orders. After she'd left, Gio reached over the table and captured her hand in his. Instinctively, she began to pull back only to have him tighten his hold and shake his head slightly.

"Let me hold your hand, Jaydee."

She felt a bit out of her element here. Public displays of affection were uncommon to her, aside from a Lexy hug. But she couldn't deny it was extremely nice touching him. She'd spent numerous hours just allowing her fingers to explore his body — granted all of that was in private...but still. So, she relaxed and was rewarded with a warm smile.

They kept the chatter light and neutral as they ate their meals. She was right, the food was excellent. Gio waved off her refusal of dessert and ordered a piece of seven-layer chocolate cake for the two of them. It came with a coffee for him and hot water with lemon for her.

"Here." Gio offered her a bite as she stirred the lemon into the steaming mug of water.

She shook her head in polite refusal. Gio sighed and scooted around the table to settle beside her on the brown vinyl booth seat.

"Open for me, Jaydee," he whispered seductively.

He held a forkful of the cake before her mouth. Staring into his hazel eyes, she did as he'd ordered. A deep-throated groan slid from her as the cake melted against her tongue. Oh dear Lord that was good.

"Oh my," she murmured after swallowing the bite. The cake had felt like silk in her mouth, smooth, satiny, and oh so moist.

Gio's eyes darkened before he slanted his mouth over hers and kissed her until her toes curled. "You said it," he stated. "That is some damn good cake. Chocolate tastes good from your lips, sweets."

He offered her another piece and she shook her head, this time holding up the mug of tea in an attempt to dissuade him from feeding it to her. She watched him eat it and smile in contentment.

"Why don't you eat dessert?" he asked, reaching across the table for his coffee and indulging in some.

"It wasn't anything I had growing up. And I don't eat a lot of sugar anyway. I prefer fresh fruit." She gave a wry smile. "But that...that is some damn good cake."

"And that's why you drink water all the time as well?"

"I drink tea, too," she mumbled a bit defensively.

His smile was accompanied by another forkful of cake poised at her lips. Automatically she opened and he slid in the bite.

"I know you do. Loose tea."

She ducked her head and swallowed. That was how dessert went. He alternated forkfuls between them both. His large body remained on her side and one powerful thigh pressed intimately along hers. He asked her questions in between his forkfuls. They ate slowly, not in any rush to leave.

He slipped his credit card in the bill before she could say anything and, while they waited for the waitress to return for his signature, he laid an arm along the back of the seat and stared down at her. With his free hand, he caressed the side of her face.

"I love you, Jaydee," he said.

That familiar bout of panic erupted in her and she shook her head. His gaze narrowed and she picked up on the tic in his jaw.

"Why does it bother you so much to hear me say that?"

"Can we talk about this later?"

He glanced around and shook his head. "No one is paying us any attention."

Just then, the waitress reappeared and set down the black folder. "Have a nice night, y'all."

"Thank you, ma'am," he replied. The moment she'd walked off, he put his attention totally back upon her. "Now, answer me."

She worried her lower lip as he opened the folder, signed, and returned his focus to her. "I don't want you to feel obligated to say such a thing to me. And...it scares me to hear." The admission took a lot from her but she refused to back down.

"One," he said in a low timbre, "you should never think I'm obligated. And two, why does it scare you to hear me say I love you?"

His deep voice gave her goose bumps. He created such immense feelings within her. "I could grow used to hearing it and when you leave..." She trailed off, unable to actually finish the statement.

He swiped his thumb along her lower lip. "Come on, let's get you home."

Gio slid from the booth and held out his hand to her. She hesitated before she accepted his assistance, feeling this somehow was an offer for more than just help getting out of the booth. Like it symbolised something about their future. Could she take his help? Better question, would she?

With a deep breath, she placed her hand in his. He drew her smoothly to her feet and helped her on with the leather jacket she wore. Then they headed for the exit holding hands.

She held him tight around the waist on the ride back to her place. Gio made love to her and they eventually fell asleep, naked bodies entangled. When she woke, she was alone. The heavy curtains had been opened and the sunlight streamed in through the sheers, bathing the room in morning's light. The bedroom door sat partially propped open and she could hear him singing off-key.

Aliyah Burke

She swung her feet to the floor, then grabbed her robe, tied it, and padded up the hallway to the main part of her apartment. Gio stood in the kitchen dicing up fruit, clad in loose dark blue jeans and a grey sleeveless T-shirt. She could see his hair was a bit damp and she knew he'd showered.

"Mornin', sweets." He lifted his head and pinned her with that hazel gaze that never failed to make her belly clench with desire and need. "Breakfast will be ready in a few minutes. Did you take the test?"

Test. Test. Test. Cripes, did he sleep only to wake and immediately think about the test? It wasn't as if a positive reading would change his life any. *Don't be like that,* she reprimanded herself. His would change as well. Just not to the same extent as hers would.

Again with the downer attitude. Hell, she didn't even know if she was or not. She didn't feel any different. Perhaps she was just a bit late. He cleared his throat and she silently shook her head, pivoted around, and made her way back to the bedroom where she grabbed some clothes for the day.

She showered quickly, lotioned her body, and dressed in lounge pants and an old, comfy T-shirt. Then she brushed her teeth and put her hair up so it would be off her neck. Today was working at home day, no need to get overly dressed up. At the very last moment, she did what she had to and left the test to sit on the toilet tank before escaping to the front after washing her hands.

Gio never asked and she figured her expression gave enough away that he knew she'd gone through with it and actually peed on the stick. All he did was glance at his watch, briefly, and wave her towards the table.

She sat and he brought her a bowl of fruit and yogurt. "Eat."

After picking up the spoon, she stared down at the grape, apple, and banana mixture that was covered by plain yogurt. "Thank you." She continued counting down the one hundred-eighty seconds until she could go discover how altered her life would be.

Gio occupied a chair across from her. He had a bowl as well and two plates, each with half a bagel covered in cream cheese on it. He had just slid one plate over to her side when the doorbell rang.

She frowned. There shouldn't be anyone coming to visit her. Lexy would just walk right on in, so it couldn't be her. Setting her spoon down in the bowl, she got to her feet.

"Excuse me." At the door, she drew it open. "Yes?" she asked only to freeze. Time seemed to slow to a crawl. Everything moved in über-slow motion.

Words wouldn't come. Some things didn't matter in situations like this. Yes, it had been some time, but, in recognising the woman who'd been oh so eager to get rid of her, time didn't matter. She'd not seen her in person since she was seven, and only a photograph until the age of ten. It didn't matter, none of it did. Jaydee knew the woman standing before her just as sure as she knew her own name.

"Hello, darling," a syrupy-sweet voice said. "It's been a while. Don't you have a hug for your dear, loving mother?"

Dear, loving mother? The impression would be laughable if she didn't feel so damn sick to her stomach. She blinked, slowly, giving herself time to recuperate. The woman looked just about the same. Thin and wearing tight clothing to show off her body.

"Vivian."

"Vivian? Dear, please. Call me Mother."

She would do no such thing. "What are you doing here?"

Vivian Amos brushed back some of her short black bob. "I came to see you, sweetie. I mean, we haven't seen each other in a while."

About twenty-five years. Nine thousand and ninety days. But, hell, who was counting. The urge to vomit filled her and she swallowed, trying to keep it all back.

"You showed no interest in me when I was seven, I hardly believe you've stopped by now to attempt to play the nice mother. So I'll ask again, what do you want?"

A flash of anger appeared in Vivian's brown eyes but vanished so quickly that Jaydee wondered if she'd just imagined such a thing. The hand slipping around her waist told her nope, she was just preening for a handsome man. Like she'd always done.

"Can't a mother just visit her baby? And who are you, handsome?" Vivian swayed closer, her hips doing things most people's didn't unless they were in bed or swinging around a pole. She held out her hand. "I'm Jaydee's mo—"

"This is Vivian," Jaydee interrupted, noticing the tell-tale signs of her having already been drinking this early.

Gio took the offered hand and gave it a polite shake, ignoring the way she held it for a kiss upon the back. "Giovanni Cassano, ma'am."

"Ohh, are you Italian? You look absolutely divine. Are you dating my daughter?"

Jaydee stiffened, only to relax a bit under the gentle caresses of Gio's fingers along her side.

"Yes, ma'am."

"Ma'am," she cooed. "Aren't you just so polite." She waved a finger between them. "Now, how'd you two meet?"

"None of your business," Jaydee interrupted before Gio could respond.

Brown eyes slashed back to her and Jaydee received a perfect flashback of the woman who'd never wanted her to open her mouth at all. Disapproval simmered there. However, she wasn't the child who'd wanted a mother's approval. She hadn't been for a long time now.

"No need to be disagreeable, Jaydee. I was just wondering about the man in your life."

"My life is of no concern to you. You would do better to worry about why you are drunk at this early hour." Condemnation dripped from her tone, her nausea had receded but anger had come forth full bore.

"Mind your tone, you ungrateful little—"

"Vivian!"

Jaydee started and stared past the woman at her porch who'd also turned around. So intent had she been on the unexpected and unpleasant visitor that the arrival of a dark SUV had totally escaped her notice. She blinked, only to do it rapidly three more times until she realised that this, too, wasn't a cruel trick her mind played but reality.

Her father strode up the walk. In a light grey suit and impeccable as was his norm, he moved as if he had every right to be there. She snorted lightly—a family reunion. One she could definitely have done without.

"Reginald." Vivian's tone was laden with scorn.

"I thought I saw you trying to be granted access at the lab this morning. Why are you here?" His own voice was colder than Jaydee had ever heard it.

"I've come to see my daughter, Reggie. Is there a law against that?"

Her father stood beside her mother, both of them glaring at one another. "There could be. Don't think I don't know about your association with Captain Fentress."

Jaydee could have been knocked over with a feather by that news. Fentress...really? She'd had dinner with his wife before—to know now that her own mother was sleeping with him. Would she ever not feel dirty?

She glared at the woman who had given birth to her. "Is that why you're here? To try to plead for your lover?"

"You... You know, you always made snap judgements about men. You're wrong. He is an honourable man and you...with your accusations—"

"*He* was a married man with three children. And you..." She trailed off, unable to credibly voice her disgust without losing the final bit of her composure.

"Leave, Vivian. You have no reason to be here." Dr Thompson spoke in his typical authoritative manner.

Vivian's face morphed into an ugly mask. "Neither do you. I remember you didn't want her either."

Gio's arms tightened protectively around her as he stood behind her. For the life of her, she just wanted to run inside and curl up into a ball, allowing the hot tears to fall. But she didn't. She stood there, like the topic of which parent didn't want her more had no bearing on her whatsoever. It was all a big lie and it hurt more than she'd ever dreamed.

"Shut up, Vivian. If you are going to talk, please do try to keep your drunken facts straight. I wasn't sure she was my daughter. You'd been so promiscuous I wanted to be certain she was mine before I agreed. You were a drunken whore then, and you're one still."

Her father looked at her. "While it's true I didn't want a child at that time, my feelings are not like that anymore. She is my pride and joy. I've never been more proud of anyone than I am of her." He looked back at the woman who'd carried her for nine months and apparently had zero maternal love. "And I'll be damned before I let you come in here and try to ruin her life, like you've ruined your own."

"Oh, go stuff it, Reggie," she sneered. "This is between my daughter and myself."

"She's not yours any longer, Vivian Amos. Jaydee is my daughter, not yours. She's not been yours since six months after you left her with me. I took care of that."

"I don't remember that."

"Of course not. You were wasted like usual, in bed with one of your men." He shook his head at her. "I've always kept tabs on you, Vivian. I will not let you interfere in *my* daughter's life. So turn your intoxicated ass around and get lost. You approach her again and I'll have you arrested."

"You can't do that!" she sputtered. "She's my child, too."

"We just went through that and no, she's not. But let's be honest here, Vivian. Why are you here? How much money do you need?"

Jaydee's heart twisted in agony inside her chest. After all these years, this woman sought her out for money? Surely her father was overreacting. *Not something he does often, though.*

Vivian turned beseeching eyes to her. "Jaydee, you see how he is. This is why I had to leave him. Let me come in and we can talk. I've missed you."

She narrowed her eyes. "You're lying."

"What? No, sweetie. I'm not. He was impossible to live with. You wouldn't remember that, you were so young."

She snorted and shook her head. Stepping away from Gio's touch, she moved to the edge of the top step. "You're lying. I remember everything. Your drinking, the men, all of it." She began to tremble and her father grabbed Vivian by the arm and propelled her down the drive.

"Let go of me, Reggie!" Vivian screeched.

Whatever he said to her, they couldn't hear from the porch, but Vivian stiffened and stomped to the SUV before she was unceremoniously shoved into the back. Dr Thompson slammed the door and the vehicle left with him still at the edge of her drive.

He turned and strode slowly up the walk. For the first time he looked a bit older. Lines drawn tight around his mouth. He paused at the bottom and glanced up at them both.

"They'll be back to pick me up. I know I'm not who you want to see right now, but do you think I could come in until they return?"

She nodded. "Of course."

They went inside and she shut the door behind her, staring at the two men in her small rental. Her nerves felt shot and she just wanted to hide from everyone.

Gio broke the silence. "We were just about to eat, would you care to join us?"

"That would be lovely, thank you." He wiped his hands down the sides of his pants as she moved through to the kitchen to begin preparing a bowl for him.

She glanced up when Gio walked in and brushed his lips along her cheek. "Are you okay, sweets?"

"Where's Dr Thompson?" she asked instead of answering him.

"Bathroom. Answer me. Are you okay?"

Her lower lip quivered a bit but, before she could answer, her father stuck his head in the doorway to the kitchen. "You're pregnant?" he asked. His facial expression conveyed his shock.

The floor fell out from under her and it was just too much. She tore away from Gio and shoved past her father before bolting to the bedroom. She slammed the door behind her then stumbled to the bed and gave in to the furious and scared tears which streamed from her eyes.

Pregnant. She was pregnant.

Chapter Twenty

Gio was so stunned by her father's blurted comment, he didn't—or perhaps it was couldn't—move quick enough to halt Jaydee's rapid escape. Pregnant. She was pregnant. Correction—they were pregnant and he was going to be a daddy.

His knees trembled a bit and he wanted to sit down. He wanted to hold Jaydee and tell her over and over how much he loved her and how excited he was about the baby. *Their* baby.

Dr Thompson moved towards the hallway and that spurred him into action. He manoeuvred to block him. "Let her be. Don't you think you've done enough for the day?"

"That's my daughter!"

Gio crossed his arms, refusing to budge. "One you've never showed any emotion to previously. She's overloaded right now, can't you see that?"

"Is she not happy about being pregnant?"

Gio shrugged. "She didn't know. Neither of us did, before your announcement."

Her father seemed genuinely distressed by that. He sighed and ran a hand over the short hair on his head. "I...I just...wanted..." He trailed off.

"Go home. Give her some time. Just...let her work through this at her own speed."

Dr Thompson sighed and turned around. He headed to the front door and said, "I'll wait on the porch for my ride."

Gio didn't speak, just waited for him to leave so he could shut the door and make his way back to Jaydee. But the man stayed there, one hand on the doorframe. Dr Thompson's brown eyes had a lot of concern in them, but Gio wasn't budging.

"I should go back and talk to her before I go."

Gio shook his head. Like hell he was going to subject her to more of this drama. They had their own things to work through and out. "No. She needs to relax and work through all of this." He paused. "At her own speed."

The concern segued into a warning. "I know all about you, Giovanni Cassano. The trail of broken hearts you've left in your wake. Everything. This is my daughter here."

"Perhaps," he said, losing his remaining bit of patience. "But you seem to be forgetting two very important things."

"What's that?" Dr Thompson asked.

"She's the woman *I* love and she's carrying *my* baby. So I will protect her the best I can and that means keeping the stress you bring away from her. When she's ready, she will contact you. Not before and I don't want to see you back here, bothering her." He stepped close. "You say you're her father. Act like it and do what's best for her. Give her some space."

"And I suppose you do know what's best?"

"That's it. Get out. I have more important things to do than stand here and argue who is more knowledgeable about what's best for her. I just found out I'm going to be a father. I need to spend some time with the mother of my unborn baby. Shut the door on your way out." He spun around and headed down the hall.

When he heard the door click he knew Dr Thompson had left. At the closed door to Jaydee's bedroom, he paused. Closing his eyes, he rested his head and one hand against the wood. No noises filtered through the door but he knew she was in there crying. She didn't make sounds when she cried, almost like she was ashamed to be doing so and not wanting to risk anyone finding out.

His belly was in knots and his palms were sweaty. With a deep breath, he turned the knob, and pushed his way into the room. Jaydee sat in the corner of her bed, back against the walls, and her knees drawn up so her chin could rest upon them.

She never even looked at him, merely stared out at something only she could see. The tears streaming down her face tore a hole straight through his heart to his soul. It killed him to see her this distraught. He quietly shut the door behind him and made his way over to the bed, steps slow and measured.

He made it to the edge of the bed before she rotated her head and looked at him. Such devastation filled her expression and he struggled to say and do something to make her feel better. "Are you okay?" he asked, carefully lowering himself to the bed.

"Go away," she whispered before turning her head and leaving him to face the back of her skull.

He bit back his immediate retort and ensured his voice remained calm and cool. "Not gonna happen, sweets. And we'll get to us in a minute. I need to know if you're okay from dealing with..." he hesitated, unsure how to phrase his inquiry.

"The psychotic mess that is my family?"

Gio scooted along the bed until his back touched the wall as well. He made sure he didn't touch her, for he truly didn't know how much more she could take before she broke. And, Lord help him, he already wanted to punch out both of her parents for the incident this morning.

"Go away," she reiterated. Her voice sounded so defeated.

"I already told you, that isn't going to happen. I am staying right here."

"Why? Do you get some perverse pleasure in seeing me at my worst, Giovanni?"

To hell with his no touching rule. A low grumble slipped up from his throat as he drew her into his arms. She struggled a bit but he refused to give and, before long, she sank into him, burying her head in his chest.

He closed his eyes and lowered his face to the top of her head. His nose in her hair, he inhaled slowly and allowed her subtle scent to wash over him. He ignored the wetness of her tears soaking through his sleeveless T-shirt and just held her. Held her in his arms and offered all he could through touch alone.

Eventually he fell asleep, her body tight against his.

* * * *

However, it wasn't that way when he woke. He was alone, sprawled diagonally across the bed. He sat up and looked around, the place was silent.

On his feet, he padded out to the main part of her apartment. Nothing. No sign of her at all. She wasn't in the bathroom or the office, either. He went to his bag and withdrew his cell phone before pressing the numbers to call her. It rang three times before she picked up.

"Leave me alone," she muttered.

"Where are you?" he asked.

"I need some time to think about things."

"Don't you think we should talk about the fact you're carrying my baby, Jaydee?" Damn it, he knew he shouldn't have gone to sleep. She didn't respond and he repeated his question.

"I told you I didn't want anything from you, Gio, if it turned out the way it did. You don't need to feel obligated to—"

"Don't you fuckin' dare finish that sentence, Jaydee," he growled, suddenly furious.

"I need to think," she said. Her voice still seemed so subdued.

"And I want to talk to you about this." He squeezed his eyes shut and took several deep breaths. "Will you please come back here so we can discuss this?" His heart and breathing felt suspended while he waited for her response.

"Okay. I'll be back in a bit."

"I'll see you then."

She hung up before he could say any more and he swore a round of curses as he tossed his phone down onto the bed. Swiping it up again, he shoved it into his pocket and headed back to the kitchen where he found she'd cleaned up the breakfast he'd prepared for them.

With a glance at the clock, he began to dig through her cupboards to figure something out for lunch. He didn't know how she did it but Jaydee had to be one of the easiest eaters he'd ever met. She liked salads and hamburgers with fries.

He opened her refrigerator only to shake his head again at the lack of items in there. He'd used up the rest of the yogurt this morning and most of the fruit. So he moved on to the freezer. She had a small enchilada casserole up there so he pulled it down. He had to make do—he had no vehicle to even go shopping, not to mention he wanted to be here when she returned.

So he turned the oven on to preheat and went back to the sparsely furnished fridge to gather salad items. As he worked, he tried his best to calm down but, to be honest, he was still furious with her attitude. He knew he had to cut her some slack but why was it so damn hard for her to believe him?

He rolled his eyes and shook his head at himself. Christ, it had been right there in front of him. Hell, he'd been privy to it this morning. If this was how she'd been raised it was no wonder she had doubts about the honesty of his own words. Her own parents had never shown her love or affection. He wondered if Lexy knew how lucky she was to have Jaydee's complete trust.

Jaydee didn't return for another hour or so and he was pacing when she finally made it back. There was no television in her house so he couldn't watch that. And her books, well, truthfully he didn't understand them. That kind of stuff was way over his head. But when he heard the powerful rumble of her on-loan bike, he made his way to the couch and lowered himself into it.

Moments later the front door opened and in she walked. He watched her shrug out of her leather jacket and hang it up before continuing on into the living room where he sat. His heart froze at the expression on her face. It was blank.

Shit. She had already begun to pull away and into herself.

Dropping the magazine he'd pretended to leaf through, he got to his feet and met her before she could vanish from this room as well. Her tortoiseshell eyes lifted to his and he licked his lips before deciding the hell with it and kissing her.

She moaned into his mouth and he bit back one of his own as his taste buds were swamped with her flavour, pure, fresh mint. He closed his arms around her and held her tight. She pressed against him, her arms twined around his neck while her fingers scraped along the shorn hair on the back of his head.

He couldn't get enough of her and kept surging his tongue throughout her mouth. Her nails dug in and the brief pain drew him back from the edge. Lord help him, but he could kiss her for hours and never grow bored. She tasted divine and was so responsive to him.

Ending the powerful kiss, he stared down at her. Those big eyes of hers hazy with desire and restrained passion. He knew what lay beneath the iron control she preferred to have over every aspect of her life. Volcanic in nature and hotter than the sun.

"Jaydee."

"This isn't a good idea," she said.

"Bullshit."

She opened her mouth to say more but his phone rang. He glanced at the caller ID and ignored it. Lizard. He could call him later. Right here and now was where his attention needed to remain focused.

"I don't want to ruin your career or your...lifestyle." Her words were barely above a whisper.

"Forget that for a minute and answer something, honestly, for me." He held her gaze until she gave him a slight nod. Dear God, what if she said she wanted nothing to do with him? "Putting all that aside, is there something wrong with me? Is this why you are considering Ivan's proposal?"

She blinked a few times and he knew she'd not been expecting his question. "There is nothing wrong with you, Gio. You're a dream catch for any woman. Sexy. Protective. Caring. And an amazing lover."

There was a 'but' in there somewhere and he waited for it. Jaydee stepped out of his embrace and put some distance between them. He didn't approve of that move but he didn't force her to stay closer to him.

"I still believe you said what you did because you thought—"

"Thought that you might be pregnant? Which you are, I might add." He swore and raked a hand over his head. "Come on, Jaydee. I've told you I love you. Do you really think I want to go back to being the guy I was before you came into my life?"

She shrugged. "It seems to have served you well so far."

More curses dangled from the tip of his tongue. Somehow he managed to keep them to himself. Lizard had been right. His past had come back to haunt him. The woman he loved more than anything stood before him, pregnant with *his* baby, doubting how he felt about her. All because of his past reputation.

He stepped towards her and captured her upper arms in his hands, holding her securely, but not painfully. "Listen to me and listen well, sweets. We both know how I was, yes. But that all changed the day you walked into my life. I don't want any other woman. I only want you. I look at you and I smile. I look at you and I want you, naked, with me. I don't know how else to say it. You...*you* are the one I want to be with. I want to be there with you, for you." He cupped her cheek with one hand. "And our baby. Ours, Jaydee."

His phone rang again. Lizard. He jerked it off his belt and answered. "This had better be good, Lizard!"

"Hello to you too, Casanova." He growled and Lizard sighed. "Yes, it's good."

The man fell silent and Gio prompted. "Well?"

"We made it."

"Made what?"

"Damn, man, I thought you'd be waiting on pins and needles to hear. We made it to the combat group. We beat out Keel and Beast." A slight pause. "Honestly, I think Keel's okay with it. Considering his wife just had the baby not too long ago, he'd really rather be nearby."

The combat squadron. Overseas. He'd wanted it so bad but had totally forgotten it given his need to find Jaydee. He should be jumping for joy and ecstatic but, honestly, all he could do was stare at the woman standing right before him, watching him with those incredible eyes. Eyes he'd dreamed about when they were apart, the way she would stare up at him with them so full of desire it nearly took him to his knees. The way she would gaze at him as he made love to her.

"Dude. You there?" Lizard's question snapped his attention from Jaydee.

"Yes. I'm here."

"What's up with you, man? I thought you'd be happy."

"I am," he said, forcing a smile. "Congrats, man. I just need to digest it a bit."

"Okay. I'll call you later. You know they want us ready to ship out in forty-eight hours."

His heart plummeted to his feet. "I'll be there. Later." He hung up and slipped the phone back into his pocket.

"Congratulations," she said.

"For?" he asked, tugging her closer. He needed to feel her alongside him.

"The squadron."

"How'd you know?"

"It wasn't hard to figure out." A slight smile. "And there's the fact that Lizard isn't exactly a soft-spoken man."

Very true.

"So where does that leave us?" He stroked a hand down the back of her hair, tugging it free of the ponytail it had been in.

"It leaves us with you heading back to the west and then on to your next designation, wherever that may be."

He ground his jaw. His phone rang again and it was the new CO telling him what Lizard had already shared. Hearing it again only seemed to further pound the nails into the coffin on his future with Jaydee. At least she didn't move while he spoke to the commanding officer.

"Jaydee, this isn't...I didn't want this to happen like this." He brushed his lips over her forehead and stepped back in order to see her face.

Her smile was bittersweet. "How was it supposed to happen, Gio?"

Ring. Proposal. Marriage. Kids. House. Mortgage.

He ignored the next ringing of his phone and took her hand in his. "Marry me." Her eyes widened and she shook her head.

"No...don't ask that."

"Why not?" he said, refusing to release her hand when she pulled. "I love you, Jaydee. We're having a baby together. Marry me."

"You don't really want to marry me, Gio. Think of your future."

Her words hurt him and he tightened his fingers around her. "I am. Christ, I'm damn near begging you, Jaydee. Marry me. Let me be a part of your life and that of our child."

Jaydee stared at the man holding her. Marry me. Two words she'd never believed Gio would ever utter — but he had, more than once. And he loved her. Heaven help her, she wanted to say yes but she was scared to.

"Look," she said trying to ignore the furious pounding of her heart at something so simple as touch. "The test may be a false positive. It happens, they're not foolproof. Let me make an appointment with my doctor and have them run a test as well."

The pain in his eyes was quickly masked. "So if you're not..."

"Then there is no reason for us to entertain the notion of marriage."

His lips pursed. "Entertain the notion. Is that what you think I'm doing?"

"I just—" She broke off when he whirled around and left the room.

Alone, she made her way to the kitchen and set the table for two, realising just how hungry she truly was.

Her mother and father had arrived before she could eat this morning and they'd napped before she'd left.

Once all had been set for the meal, she made her way back to the bedroom and entered. Gio sat on the bed talking on the phone. His expression was serious and he spoke in Italian. He looked at her and arched a brow.

"Lunch is ready, whenever you are," she said softly before leaving.

She sat at the table and worried her lower lip. Man, she wished Lexy were here to talk to. She knew calling her wouldn't do her any good. Lexy had sent her a message informing her they had some emergencies today and she would have to miss their normal chat.

Gio walked into the room, setting every nerve she had on high alert. He gave her a small grin. "Sorry."

Wait, he wasn't mad? She remained silent as he made his way to the chair and sat. He beckoned for her plate and served her before himself. Gio never said a word as they ate. He did, however, watch her unblinkingly and she began to feel herself wanting to shift beneath his scrutiny.

"What are you doing?" she asked, placing her fork down.

"Eating."

"Why do you continue to stare at me?"

"I love looking at you, sweets. Surely you've realised that by now."

She had, but still...

After taking a drink of her iced water, she sighed and placed her arms on the table. "I'm sorry if I hurt your feelings, Gio."

"You did. But you can't think I'm going to give up that easily." She blinked and he gave a rather humourless laugh. "You did think I would." He sighed. "I wasn't lying, Jaydee."

"You're leaving."

"Yes. Many people have relationships that work in the military. I want to be a part of this, Jaydee. Why can't you let *us* be something?" He scowled. "Are you seriously still considering marrying Ivan?"

Ivan. With everything going on today, she'd totally put him out of her mind. Gio took her silence to mean yes, for his face hardened to stone.

"I will not let another man's name be the surname for my child, Jaydee." His tone was absolute.

"I'm not marrying him," she said softly, not wanting to fight. Why did she feel bad he hadn't said she couldn't marry Ivan?

You're the one who's telling him marrying is not a good idea, her subconscious chimed in.

He seemed to relax after that bit of news. Then he didn't say anything else, just continued to eat. She'd just finished when the doorbell rang and her heart clenched as she flinched involuntarily. Gio waved her back into the seat and wiped his mouth before he went to get the door.

She'd just put the dishes in the sink when he returned with her father in tow. She wasn't sure what shocked her more. That he'd returned here or that he wore jeans and a T-shirt instead of his usual attire.

"Have you got a moment, Jaydee?" he asked.

Gio moved to her side, slid an arm around her waist, and whispered in her ear, "You don't have to talk to him if you don't want. Say the word and I'll get rid of him."

As tempting as it was to take him up on his offer, she patted his hand. "I have to talk to him eventually." She looked at her father. "We can talk on the back porch." It was the only place outdoors she had furniture to sit on.

"Thank you."

Once out there, she sat in the corner rocker and waited for him to choose and take his seat. Silence lingered for a while but she wasn't about to break it. He'd sought her out—it was on him to make the first overture.

He looked more nervous than she'd ever seen. He rubbed his hands along his thighs and leant forward.

"I'm sorry about today."

She rested her hands over her stomach—almost like that simple touch would protect her unborn child. Assuming the test had provided the correct result. There still remained a chance—a small percentage— that it wasn't true.

"Sorry for what? That you were put on the spot? Or that it came out at all about you not even wanting me?"

Her voice sounded foreign to her. Rasped and tired. She knew this man should be treated with respect, like she'd always done, but at this particular junction in time forgiveness and kindness weren't her top priorities.

Pain leached into his expression but he didn't apologise again. "I did what I did, Jaydee. I'll win no Father of the Year awards but I've always done my best by you."

His best. Was this the future for her own child? Her career taking so much precedence the child would suffer?

"Really? Is that how you justify your actions? You were doing your best?"

He leant back and crossed his arms. She knew the expression.

"You were different from Vivian in that you didn't try to keep my smarts contained." A sneer crossed her face. "But then...you had ulterior motives for the freakishly smart child who'd been dropped in your lap. Didn't you? Otherwise, there is no difference in you two. Not to me."

To her immense surprise, he nodded. "I did. I admit it. I had plans for your intelligence. But that is the past. I want things to change between us, Jaydee. I want to be a father to you—learn how to be a father—and a grandfather to your baby."

He stood and moved before her where he reached out and took her hand. "I know it's a lot to digest and for me to ask, but please think about it. And, while you're doing that, I want you to go home. You need to be in your place. Had I known about your pregnancy I never would have had you come out here. I'll arrange a flight for you. Go home. Rest. And think about what you want to do next."

He crouched before her, still holding her hand. "I wish I had been better. For what it's worth, Jaydee, I always have been extremely proud of you and I've always loved you. Despite my inability to show you that very thing."

Her father walked away after squeezing her hand. Never looking back, he vanished from sight. She heard a door slam and assumed he'd just driven away. Less than thirty seconds later, Gio stepped from the duplex and joined her on the back porch.

"What's next?" he asked after a while.

She closed her eyes. "I'm going home." This was one time she wouldn't even try to insist that Dr Thompson let her finish out the work here. He had been right—she did need to go home.

"Damn it, Jaydee!" His outburst brought her eyes open. He leaned against the railing and shook his head. "When exactly are *we* supposed to talk? I have to report to base in forty-eight hours. You're not making this easy on me and, honestly, I'm losing patience. You've already scheduled your doc appointment to after I leave, so I won't know. Can we not just *talk* about this?"

He was absolutely right. "Come with me." The words had slipped free before she could call them back.

Gio faced her. "Come with you? Okay. You'll have to tell me the nearest airport so I can arrange a flight."

"We'll make sure you get back. That's not a problem." She got to her feet. "I should get some packing done."

He stared at her. Assessing. "Can I help?" he questioned.

"Please." She led him to the second room closet. Stuffed in there were boxes and she sighed and waved a hand. "Never mind. They'll do it. I just need..."

He followed her into her bedroom and joined her once she sat. When he draped an arm around her she didn't argue, just silently accepted his strength. She had nothing left at that point.

Gio spent the night and she, in turn, spent it in his embrace. Her dreams were tumultuous but, every time she woke, his voice and touch were what calmed her. The plane ride in the wee hours of the morning was quiet as well. When they landed at oh-eight-hundred, a dark SUV with tinted windows waited for them.

"Welcome home, Dr Amos."

"Thank you, Travis." She gave him a smile even as Gio slid his arm around her.

Travis stowed their bags as they climbed in the back. She sighed and rested her head against the seat. Home. So close, she could taste it. Gio reached across the leather seat and took her hand. They hadn't talked on the flight—she'd felt nauseous and slept.

"You live here?" Gio asked when they turned in her drive.

"Yes."

Travis left them and their bags before driving off. She stared at her three-storey A-frame log cabin. A lake was down to the left behind the house and the large windows in the front offered a majestic view of the Cascade Range.

"Jesus, sweets. This is amazing." There was awe in his voice.

She smiled, glad he found her sanctuary as appealing as she did. "Thank you." The cool crisp air flowed over her and helped to energise her.

Side by side, they walked up the steps to the wraparound porch to the front door. She entered a code and a series of clicks echoed before the door swung open.

Hardwood floors were covered here and there by area rugs. She made her way to the staircase, Gio following behind her. On the second floor, she stopped and made her way past the five extra rooms until she reached the master suite at the end of the hall.

Her spacious bedroom was accented with daffodil yellow, whites, and a deep violet. French doors on one side opened out to her balcony and had yellow and white sheers with the darker purple, heavy curtains tied back to allow in the light. Bag down, she walked by the large picture window on the other side towards the doors and opened them before standing out on her balcony to stare out at the crystalline lake below.

She was home. The feeling of peace flowed through her.

A few moments later, strong arms settled around her waist and she leant back against Gio's rock-hard chest. His fingers splayed over her belly and she settled her hands over his.

"You have a beautiful place, Jaydee."

"Thank you." The breeze blew around them and she shivered. It was decidedly cooler here than it had been in Virginia, yet she wasn't cold. Not with the man behind her who held her like she was his everything.

"We're having a baby together, sweets. I want to be a part of his or her life. And yours."

She mulled over her thoughts and said, "If I am pregnant, I'm not having an abortion, nor will I give the child up for adoption."

"But you don't want to marry me."

Trouble was, she did. So bad, she could taste it. But she didn't believe she had what it took to make their marriage work in the long run, and didn't want him to ever regret marrying her.

"I don't think you really want to marry me."

His body tensed. "I'm getting tired of you telling me what I want, Jaydee. I know my own mind." He turned her in his arms, so the balcony was at her back, and braced her in with his body. "Answer yes or no."

She waited and he stared. "Okay, what's your question?" she asked, a bit disconcerted by the intense way he watched her.

"Do you love me?"

Her heart pounded so loudly she was sure he could hear it. "I...I...I—"

"Yes or no, Jaydee."

"Yes." Her response was so soft she could barely hear it.

"And I love you. That's all that matters," he whispered before his mouth slanted over hers.

With a sigh of surrender, she sank into him. He lifted her in his arms and carried her back to her bed where he laid her back. Gio drew away and stared at her, his eyes molten.

"I love you, Jaydee. Never forget that. Never."

Chapter Twenty-One

Gio stood looking out of his barracks window. He could see the hustle and flow of the base and sighed. He'd missed being in a combat squadron, or so he'd thought, right up until it had taken him from Jaydee. And their unborn child.

He'd been here for going on two months now and she'd sent him an email message confirming her pregnancy. He still looked at the email and wished he had been there to accompany her to the doctor.

"You okay, man?" Lizard asked from behind him.

He rested his head on the glass pane. "Not really." He sighed. "Man, I thought I wanted to be back here. Flying high in the skies, being in combat but…"

Lizard clapped him on the shoulder and leaned against the window as well. "You're about to be a father for the first time. It's understandable."

"I want to be her husband."

"Really?" He laughed. "I'd not noticed."

"I don't know how else to convince her she's the one I want."

"Look at her examples of family, Gio. She's not even known you for a year and she had that type of conditioning since day one. I think it will take a bit more than just you saying the words for her to see what a real family is like."

Lizard's words made sense and he gave himself a mental smack. No longer could he ignore what he knew. Yes, he'd seen it, he'd known for a while now that he loved her, but how could he have not registered her need to see how a family should act?

"That's it. She needs to see what a family is like. A real family." A wry grin and he winked at Jason. "Thanks, Lizard." He hurried to his cell phone and flipped it open to place a call. His friend left the room.

"Hello?" a deep voice said.

He frowned and said, "I need to talk to Tiziana."

"Oh sure, hang on." Muffled voices then a gentle, feminine one.

"Hello?"

"Who's he?" he growled.

A deep sigh. "Giovanni. What a surprise. I don't hear from you in months and, when you do call, you feel the need to ask who answered my phone. How are you, big brother?"

"I'm... I've been better. I need your help, sis."

"I'm intrigued. What do you need?"

"I need you to go to Oregon and check on someone for me."

"Giovanni, really? What makes you think I can just drop everything and fly out to check on one of your...um...whatevers. And who the hell do you know in Oregon?"

He bit back his growl of frustration. "It's not just anyone, Zia."

She laughed. "Wait, let me guess, you love her." Maybe this had been a mistake. He strove for patience. His silence must have been understood for she said, "Oh my God. You do love her. Or think you do."

"She's pregnant with my child, Zia. And yes, I love her. I just need you to go see if she's okay. I can give you the address. I won't be going anywhere for a few more months." No sound came from the other end of the phone. "You there, Zia?"

"Ye...yes I'm here. Did you say she was pregnant with your child?"

"You know damn well that's what I said. Now, can you help me out?"

"I can go in a while, after I take care of what's on my plate. Unless you need me there immediately. Who is she?"

He leant back against the wall before sliding down to settle on the floor. With a deep breath, he began to fill his sister in on who this woman was to him.

* * * *

Two days later, he and Lizard ran across the tarmac to where their bomber waited for them. The fuelling truck passed them heading the other way. They'd just completed some training exercises and had finished for the day when the call came in. They had a mission. Shrugging back into the flight suit he'd taken off moments before he'd showered, Gio met Lizard on the way out of the door. The air was cold on his damp hair as they hurried along.

The other members were scurrying along as well to their respective planes. Once settled they took to the sky like a flock of black birds, armed to the nines, and struck out for their bombing target. The sun had set and so they blended in perfectly with the dark sky. Three B-2s and three F-22s for support streaked along, maintaining radio silence.

Tension ran high the nearer they got. He continually glanced to his screens as they flew. The target tonight was an ammo dump and a flight facility headquarters. Yes, he should be fine—this should be a surgical strike and they were high enough up to escape detection but still…he worried. No pilot worth his salt didn't. It was part of the job. There was always a possibility of being shot down.

They never deviated from their course and he could hear Lizard softly counting down until the time came to release their payload. He took a moment and peered to his right to where Lizard sat. The man offered up his fist and they fist-bumped before getting back to the task at hand.

"Eagle One, we've got bogies coming in fast and hot. Seven o' clock."

He didn't even take time to swear. Shit happened. "Roger that, Red One," he told the pilot of the F-22.

"Steady on to target, we'll handle them. Red Three will continue to escort."

"Roger that. Good huntin', boys."

"Likewise, Eagle One, likewise."

He noticed two of the Raptors peeling off to deal with the credible threat. Gio breathed slow and easy as they continued on their approach to the target. Lizard beside him counting it down. He allowed the familiarity of it all to finalise him being in 'the zone' for the remainder of their mission.

On the radio, he heard the dogfight between the Raptors and the enemy. MiGs, if memory served him.

"Contact in five minutes," Lizard said.

"Copy that, five minutes," he repeated.

He flipped the necessary switches and readied to press the release button. They counted down and dropped simultaneously. On their screen, they could see the flare from the huge explosion, but their joy was cut short by another announcement.

"We've got company, boys. It's like they knew we were coming. Shit...six bogies. Three at eleven o'clock and three at one o'clock."

Fuck. Those first ones must have been a decoy. "What's your ETA, Red One?" he asked as they did one-eighties and headed back towards home.

"We're still engaged, Eagle One. Can you lead them back this way?"

"We're coming fast and they're on our six."

"Eagle One, this is Big Pappi. We've launched other birds and they're on the way."

He shared a look with Lizard in the interior — it was mostly dark but the panel lights offered them a bit of illumination. Enough that their gazes met and, when he got Lizard's nod, he replied in kind. He knew what they needed to do.

"Eagle Two and Three, head up high and get out of here," he ordered, well aware that the incoming fighter jets couldn't keep up with them at their full speed.

"What about you, Eagle One? You're a bomber, not a fighter jet."

"Eagle One, you need to return to base as well," their CO commanded.

"Negative, sir," he replied.

"That wasn't a suggestion, son, it was an order."

"No, sir. I will not leave him here to fight alone." He was pleased that the other two had done as he'd ordered and shot off out of danger.

"Damn it! That's an order, Commander."

"Sorry...sir...breaking up." He switched off the comm for a moment and said, "You in this with me, Lizard?"

"To hell and back, my man. To hell and back. Let's help this Air Force jock out of this mess. He kept us safe, the fuck we're leaving him behind to fend for himself."

Switching back on the comm, Gio said, "Eagle One to Red Three. Eagle One to Red Three."

"You should head home, Eagle One."

"Like hell, Red. Like hell. Before I flew these, I was a fighter pilot. We'll get out of this. We can do enough to keep them at bay until the reinforcements arrive."

"Well, glad you're here then."

"Damn it, disengage, Eagle One. Disengage!" The orders were hollered into the mic and their ears. He ignored each one of them and stayed with the Raptor.

So they flew and fought. Fought and flew. It was kind of like driving a double-decker bus when one had been used to a Maserati—that was how he would equate the experience of flying the Spirit to that of the Super Hornet he'd flown for the Navy. But they made do. Even so, when the cavalry made their presence known he was glad.

Back at the base, the cheers were loud as they disembarked and walked to the building. Handshakes and back slaps all around.

Their CO waited for them and with a scowl on his face barked out, "My office, now!"

At the door he paused and sighed, his mind flashing back to the last time he'd been ordered before his commanding officer. It had been after he had been caught in the B-2 with Jaydee. That one had turned out well but he wasn't so sure this one would have the same outcome.

"No worries, man," Lizard whispered beside him. "No matter what, we were in the right."

He gave him a slight smile before knocking and pushing through at the bellowed command to enter.

* * * *

Jaydee rubbed her expanded belly and stared at her reflection. *Should I be this big?* She was barely hitting five months and she looked much larger. Well, in her opinion. She rolled her eyes and left the bedroom, heading down the stairs to get a snack.

Gio had been gone a little over four months. She missed him, more than she'd believed she would ever miss someone. He called occasionally but mostly they emailed back and forth. She realised, as she read his emails and answered them, she was learning more about him than she'd ever known.

He would write stories about his childhood and growing up in the family he did. At first, she thought he'd been trying to make her feel bad she hadn't had the same experience. Then he explained he wanted her to know about him. When he would call, he would ask about her and the baby.

She'd asked him one time why he didn't confine those questions to emails as well. His response had been simple. "You and our unborn baby are worth the phone call while stories of my youth are just fine for emails."

He had the ultrasound picture — she'd emailed it to him. He'd called her the next day, wanting to talk to her while he looked at it. She sighed and rubbed her tummy again.

Have I said I miss him?

Despite them growing closer, he'd never asked her to marry him again. It was like he'd got past that and was doing what he could just to show his support for her decision. That was what saddened her. She didn't want to have a shared custody with him. She *wanted* to try to make it work between them. However, it wasn't anything she would mention over the phone.

Her doorbell chimed and she hurried down the remainder of the stairs and to the front door. She pulled it open and paused. Five people stood on her front porch. Two women and three men. It took her about ten seconds for her to realise who she had on her property. His family.

The older woman reached for her hand. "Oh, aren't you just beautiful." She kissed her cheeks. "I'm Antonina and this is my husband, Giuseppe." She gestured behind her to the remaining three.

"My daughter, Tiziana. Our youngest, Enzo, and the eldest, Valentino."

Jaydee wanted to run, slam the door, and hide in her bedroom. What were they doing here? And why in God's name were there bags beside them?

"Hello," she managed to mutter. "Can I help you with something?"

She looked at them all again, focusing on the children this time. The daughter had an apologetic expression on her face as she stood there dressed in a power suit. The youngest, Enzo, had a grin that made her realise just how good-looking he was. It was the eldest who made her wonder, his face an unreadable mask as he stared at her.

"We're here to help you. Gio was worried about you, so we've arrived to help you out."

She shook her head. "He's not here."

Antonina gave her a smile. One that, to her, meant 'poor child can't fend for herself'. Jaydee instinctively stepped back when they moved towards her, and damn if they didn't all take it as an invitation and swarm the place.

The two sons carried in the bags and set them down. Valentino still without a smile.

"Now," Antonina said, "don't worry about us. We can crash anywhere."

She felt like screaming. Her sanctuary was being violated. But manners were manners and she shook her head, biting back her cry.

"Nonsense. I have rooms upstairs. Second floor. There are five rooms so take the ones you want. I'll...I'll get some sheets and pillowcases for each of you."

They headed up the stairs, chattering easily in Italian, and she followed slowly behind, feeling almost run over. At the hall closet, she gathered what she needed and went to the first room.

Enzo had claimed it and he gave her a disarming grin when she knocked. "You have a lovely home, Jaydee," he said, stepping forward to take the linens.

"Thank you."

She moved on to the next. The interaction was the same. Tiziana was in the next room. Then their parents and in the closest one to her was Valentino. She knocked on the frame of the open door and waited for him to acknowledge her.

He looked at her and nodded with his head, not saying a word. She stepped in and made her way to the bed. "Here you go. There are blankets in the closet if you need more at night."

Valentino grunted. She couldn't believe it. He didn't think her worthy enough of an actual word? She bit back her discontent and left to find the parents in the hall.

"I'm afraid I don't have much in the way of food right now. I was planning on going into town later, but help yourselves. Just, please, my office is on the third floor, so don't go up there."

"Not a problem, baby. You shouldn't be doing much, anyway. We brought food, so let's go downstairs and we can get to know one another while I cook us a big meal."

Antonina headed back down and she sighed, releasing a heavy breath. Giuseppe gave her a gentle smile and waited for her to reach his side.

"You'll fit right in with us, sweetheart. We can be a bit overwhelming at times but all families can." He took her arm and escorted her down the stairs to a waiting Antonina in the kitchen.

"Enzo, Valentino! You two get out to the car and bring in those groceries so I can start cooking." She smiled and gave an exaggerated sigh. "Boys, sometimes they just need to be prodded along."

"Yes, ma'am," Jaydee said, unsure of proper protocol for this.

The boys thundered down the stairs and outside. Soon the bags had been brought in and unloaded. Questions were being fired at her from all directions and, honestly, she was beginning to come unhinged.

Her phone rang and she excused herself before hurrying to pick it up. "Hello?"

"Hey, hon," Lexy said on the other end.

She sighed and sat down on the couch, aware of Valentino's scrutiny. "Hey."

"I know that tone, what's going on? Everything okay with the baby?"

Jaydee instinctively smoothed her hand over her belly. "Yes. Baby is fine." She should really decide what to call this child growing within her instead of 'Baby' so it was time to come up with some names.

Lexy muttered her thanks. "So, then, what's going on?"

Even though they were now all in the kitchen since Valentino had returned there, she still lowered her voice a few notches. "His family is here."

"Really? He brought his family to meet you? Damn, I'm telling you he's —"

"No, Lexy. *He's* not here." A deep breath and a prayer for control. "His family is."

"Ohhh, shit. They just showed up? Unannounced?"

"Yes. And they brought bags."

Lexy started to laugh and she scowled. This was nowhere near anything humorous.

"I fail to see the amusement," she bit off.

"Come on, hon. You have to see it. It is funny if you think about it. You don't like people in your house or around your things and here come your in-laws and they make themselves right at home."

"They're *not* my in-laws."

"Not yet. But they will be."

"Five people, Lex. Five. In my house."

Damn her but Lexy only laughed harder. "How long are they staying?"

"I don't know. But then...I didn't even know they were coming."

"Hon, you'll be fine. And you know I'll come up there if you need me, too."

"Can you get away?"

"For you? Of course. I'll tell Eugene he needs to cover for me. I'll be on the next flight I can swing. A few days tops, just let me set things up here."

She felt better already. "I'll tell Travis to pick you up. Just call him with the time."

"I'll be there soon, hon. It'll be okay."

"Thank you, Lex." Sure, she might have been a baby but, damn it all, she needed the one person she could count on with her.

"Love you." Lex was gone.

Hanging up the phone, she made her way back to the kitchen where the conversation still flowed and food cooked.

"Here, honey, drink this," Antonina said. "It helped me when I was pregnant with these ones."

She wanted to refuse, so badly. But she swallowed that desire back and curled her hands around the mug of something. It smelt like tea but she wasn't sure. She ate only a little bit for lunch, which prompted Antonina to tell her she needed to eat more for the baby's sake.

The boys went outside after the meal while Tiziana cleaned up. Every time she turned around, Gio's mother was telling her how to feel, what to eat, anything and everything baby-wise, since she'd had four. She excused herself to go to her office and was sent off with smiles and waves. Once up on the third floor she spent more time staring out of the window and wondering what the hell had become of her life until she snapped herself out of it. That was how it went for the next few days. Her life had been overtaken by the Cassano family. She spent a lot of time in her office, just not okay with dealing. They didn't seem to mind, for they found many things to keep them occupied.

A knock at the door brought her head up in surprise. Valentino stood there, those hazel eyes, so much like Gio's, watching her with intense focus.

"Can I help you?" she asked, rolling her chair back from her desk.

"Mama said to come get you. You need to eat something and supper will be ready in ten minutes." He turned and walked away without waiting for a response.

She glanced out of the window and found the sun had gone down. A peek at the time told her it was after seven. She pushed to her feet and headed downstairs. The table was set and the aroma made her stomach growl.

Tiziana gave her a smile, even as she walked around with a Bluetooth stuck to her ear. Enzo played chess with his father and Valentino sat on the couch and just stared at her. Shoving back her nerves, she made her way to Antonina and said, "Can I help?"

"Aren't you a dear? No, baby. You go sit down. I have this all under control."

"Yes, ma'am."

"What? No, none of that. You're carrying my first grandbaby, there is no ma'am from you to me."

Jaydee's head felt light and she walked away, heading back to the living area when headlights coming up the drive grabbed her attention. Lexy. Immediately she felt calmer. She moved to the door, barely noticing that Valentino had got up as well. Outside, she made her way down the steps.

Lexy got out as Travis did, too, and he unloaded her luggage.

"Look at you, hon," she called as she jogged closer for a hug. "You look incredible."

Jaydee wrapped her arms around her friend and didn't want to let go. Tears threatened and she didn't know how she would handle this.

"Hon, let go. There's something you have to see."

Reluctantly she pulled back and stared at her friend. Beyond her, coming around the back of the SUV, was none other than Giovanni Cassano. He stopped when he spied her and dropped the bag in his hand.

She flew from Lexy's arms to his open ones. His familiar scent imbued her soul as he held her. There was comfort in his embrace and she wanted to crawl inside him and never leave. He manoeuvred her chin up and claimed her lips in a kiss that made her legs weak.

"Hello, sweets," he whispered against her mouth. "I've missed you."

"Giovanni."

His head snapped up. "Valentino? What are you doing here?" He glanced back to her. "What's he doing here?"

"He came with his family," she said. "Your *entire* family."

She looked over her shoulder to see the rest of them step out on to the porch as well.

"Oh, shit," Gio muttered, his hold on her tightening.

Chapter Twenty-Two

Gio blinked a few times, wondering if what he happened to be looking at would vanish. But no. It didn't matter how many times he did it, the result was still the same. His brother stood at the top of the steps at Jaydee's house.

"How long have they been here?" he whispered to her, loath to release her.

"A few days now. Why don't you go say hi to them while I get Lexy settled."

She removed his arm from around her and he rotated his head to follow her and Lexy as they made their way up the steps, past his descending family, to vanish inside.

His family swarmed him. After hugs and kisses were done, he rounded on his sister.

"What in the hell did you think you were doing?"

She arched a plucked eyebrow. "What the hell did you think I would do when you call me and tell me you want me to check on a woman you love, who we've never met, and who just happens to be carrying your baby? Keep my mouth shut?"

"Yes. I just wanted you to check on her, not bring the entire Cassano clan down here and invade." He was livid.

"What's wrong with us meeting her?" his mother demanded.

"Nothing, Mama. But you don't understand Jaydee. She is very private and doesn't like people encroaching on her space." He shoved a hand through his hair, wincing at the thought of what she'd had to go through.

"Really? Doesn't she have family who visit?" Valentino's question was more than a bit on the snide side.

He whirled around and glared at his eldest brother. "No. In fact, she is barely on speaking terms with her father and her mother is no longer in her life." He blew out a sharp breath. "Damn it!"

"Mind your tongue, boy." His father finally spoke up.

Enzo talked next. "She didn't seem put out. She offered us all rooms and has been a wonderful, albeit a bit absent, hostess."

"Of course she wouldn't kick you out. She's spent her entire life pleasing people. I have to go talk to her."

"Well, do it after supper," his mom said. "Everything is hot and ready to eat now."

Christ. He wanted to argue with her but he couldn't. It wouldn't matter how old he got, he would never be able to refuse his mother. And she knew it. "Yes, Mama."

Everyone headed back in and he watched his mother and sister quickly set two more places at the table. It would be close and tight for the meal, just like he remembered them being. This was family and they were his.

"I'll go get them," he announced to no one in particular. He took the stairs two at a time and headed down the hall towards her room, his boots making noise as he moved.

"Where are you staying?" a voice behind him asked.

He veered around and sighed when he saw Valentino standing there, his bags in hand.

"I don't know," he said. With Jaydee would be preferable but who knew what mood she was in. *Or how much shit I'm in for this particular crapfest.*

The bedroom door sat closed and he knocked before swinging it open. The space was empty. Which left one option. The third floor in her office.

"Seems like she's avoiding you."

He turned and drew the door closed behind him. He flicked his gaze over his brother from head to foot. He wore jeans and a sweatshirt with hiking boots. His black hair hung around his shoulders and around his neck hung the gold chain with the ring his first wife had been given. Ever since that fiasco, Valentino had become a bear of a man, losing himself in work and forgetting anything about pleasure.

"Yes. Well, I told you, she doesn't like people."

"What does she do?"

He frowned but was kept from answering by a sharp female voice. "She's a doctor, not that it's any of your business."

Past his brother, Gio spotted Lexy and Jaydee standing there. Lexy had her arms crossed and she glared at his brother, fire flickering in the depths of her eyes. Odd really, he'd mostly seen her happy and flirty. He was pleased her ferocity wasn't focused on him this time. Then all his attention zeroed in on

Jaydee and he walked past the other two, gripped her hand and tugged her back to her bedroom where he shut them in.

"Sweets, I'm so sorry."

"When are they leaving, Gio?"

He cupped her face in his hands. "I'll tell them tonight." Stress lingered in her gaze and he brushed a few kisses along her lips. More for him than her. "I never meant for that to happen. I'm so sorry."

Stepping back, he stared at her and looked. Really looked at her. He could see the swell of her stomach and her breasts appeared fuller. Dropping to his knees, he slid his hands over her belly, under the shirt she wore and along her skin.

His fingers moved to the buttons on her shirt and unbuttoned the bottom three, exposing her belly. He placed his hand back over her and tried to imagine his child growing inside her. Gio smiled and brushed a kiss near her belly button before pushing back to his feet and gathering her close.

"You're so beautiful, Jaydee."

She ducked her head and he refused to allow her to keep it down, nudging it back up so their eyes could meet.

"I've missed you," he whispered, lowering his mouth to hers. Scant millimetres from connection a knock sounded at the door.

"Come on, Giovanni. Supper's on the table. You two can play kissy face later."

Mothers. He sighed and pressed their foreheads together. "Have I apologised for them all showing up here?"

"I believe you have."

"I only wanted my sister to come make sure you were okay, Jaydee. I swear I had no intentions of sending my entire family to your doorstep."

Her smile was a bit sad. "We should get going or your mother will come in. She's done that to my office before."

He had a lot to make up for. "Okay, sweets. Let's get you fed. Are you sleeping okay?"

"No," she replied immediately.

He gathered her close and scowled when the knocking began again. "Give us a minute, damn it!" he hollered. "Five minutes."

"Is that all you need? Hmm, well, that explains so much," Enzo said in a teasing voice.

"I am going to break you," he growled, moving towards the door.

Jaydee touched him on the arm and he froze. "Gio."

Her voice was a mere whisper and his heart clenched. Immediately his attention reverted back to her.

"God, I love you," he said. Before he took his next breath, he gathered her close and kissed the hell out of her.

"I love you too, Gio," she murmured.

He pressed his hand to the back of her head and sent a prayer of thanks up to the Lord above. Her strong hands slipped around the back of his head and she tugged him down for another kiss. This one was different. Heated. Passionate. Needy.

And he wasn't about to ignore her silent plea, for he wanted it as much as she did. No words were exchanged as he lowered her lounge pants and panties. Lifting her, he pressed her back against a wall and freed himself before sliding inside her wet, velvet heat.

"Shit!" he barked in a harsh whisper.

Christ, it felt so good to be back within her. It had been more than four months and she held him tight. Shuddering she moaned and tightened around him.

"Gio...please...I...oh, please..."

"Yes," he breathed against her neck.

He began to move. Deep, thorough strokes which rocked him to the core as he relearned her body. There wasn't enough time. He had to hurry but all he wanted to do was slow down and take his time with her. Kiss every inch of skin, become reacquainted with the body that belonged to the woman he loved more than anything in this world.

There was no way he would last long. Already his balls had drawn tight. "I can't wait, sweets. Come with me."

She did. She exploded around him and muffled her cry against his shoulder. He came moments after that and kissed her as they sailed over the edge together. Her body trembled as he stayed inside her, waiting for her to stop coming. So responsive. So electric.

Reluctantly he withdrew from her heat and placed her back on her feet. Gathering up her clothes, she slipped into the bathroom while he put himself away and sat on the edge of the bed.

As he predicted, a furious knock came on the door before his mother opened it. "I told you supper was...where's Jaydee?"

He looked calmly at his mother. "She felt a bit nauseous. We'll be down as soon as she is feeling better. Go ahead and start eating without us."

She watched him with brown eyes and immediately she made to move towards the bathroom door. "I should see if I can help her."

"Mama. I think she'd just prefer not to have this public knowledge."

She nodded. "I understand. I feel bad—I thought you were up here having sex."

Something about his mother talking about his sex life was all kinds of wrong but he managed not to wince. "Well, you see me sitting right here with all my clothes on. Trust me, I'd much rather be on the bed with her."

His mother arched an eyebrow at him and shook her head. "As soon as she's ready, Giovanni." She spun around and left.

Once the door shut, he almost got up then paused, remaining there. As he'd suspected the door once again opened. His mother pointed at him. "You need to talk to Valentino." Then she vanished again.

He flopped back with a groan and draped an arm over his eyes. When the bed dipped, he removed it and turned his head to meet Jaydee's tortoiseshell eyes. He could see her face was slightly fuller, too. Some people believed pregnant women glowed and he had to agree. She looked positively gorgeous.

"Are you okay?" she questioned.

"No. I want to strip you naked and make love to you until we're both too tired to move. But I can't. Not right now. I have to take you downstairs for dinner."

A small smile curved up her lips and she leant forward to kiss him. "There's always tonight." Then she got up and headed for the door. "Let's go. Don't want to keep everyone waiting."

He popped up and twirled her back to him for another kiss. It was an intense, spine-tingling kiss and he was hard-pressed not to say to hell with supper and lock them both in the room. With a groan, he escorted her to the stairs and down to the first floor.

The entire family paused in their meal and glanced at the two of them when they walked in. Lexy gave them a smile which erased the almost-scowl she'd been sporting.

"Sorry we're late." He held a chair for Jaydee, which put her beside Lexy, then made his own way around the table to sit between Valentino and Tiziana.

The meal was loud and familiar to him, yet he knew it had to be almost overwhelming to Jaydee. She could handle groups, she'd done so with the other pilots, but this…this was her sanctuary and it had been invaded.

After the supper dishes had been cleaned away, people settled down and Jaydee and Lexy left to take a walk. His sister was on her phone, again, so he went over to his brothers and jerked his head towards the door. They got up and came with him.

"What's up?" Enzo asked as they headed down the front steps.

"As much as I love seeing you, you need to leave."

Enzo laughed. "Need some alone time with your girl?" he punched him in the shoulder. "I told you five minutes wouldn't be enough."

He chuckled and slugged his brother back. "It never will be enough. But that's not the point. She's beginning to stress again and it's not good for the baby."

"You really think her pit bull is going to let you have any time with her?" Valentino asked.

"Her pit bull?" He frowned. "Do you mean Lexy?"

"Yes."

Their mother hollered for Enzo and with a grin he jogged back up inside. Gio focused on his eldest brother. "Why do you call her that?"

"She read me the riot act on the way downstairs. Telling me how lucky you were to even have a shot at a woman like Jaydee."

He bit back his smile at the disbelief in his brother's tone. "She's right. I am." They headed around the house towards the dock. "Valentino, she is amazing. This woman can fly a B-2 bomber better than I can. She's qualified to pilot the shuttle into outer space should the need ever arise and more. Not to mention she's scary smart. And I mean *scary* fuckin' brilliant."

"She's a pilot? I thought you said she was a doctor."

"She's both. Not only that, but she saved my career by going toe to toe with a pissed off brigadier general. Every moment I spend in her presence, I'm more than just happy. I don't know how to explain it but she's the one for me."

"So why don't you ask her to marry you?"

"I have, twice. She was under the impression I asked her because there was a chance she was pregnant."

Valentino snorted. "And now?"

"I love her. I was coming here to ask her again. Lizard is arriving tomorrow along with a minister. I wasn't going to leave until she agreed to marry me."

"You know Mama won't leave if she knows there is a wedding."

He sighed. "I know. I just…man, I really wish…" He trailed off for he saw her and Lexy on the dock. A few solar lights illuminated them.

As if she knew he was there, she turned and glanced in their direction. Smacking his brother on the shoulder, he hastened down to her side. Touching her, he immediately felt better and, with a smile for Lexy, brushed his lips along Jaydee's.

"Oh, it's you." Lexy crossed her arms and stared at his brother. "Don't you have some small child to scare with your scowling?"

His brother mimicked her stance and glared right back at her. "Am I scaring you?"

A sharp, derisive snort. "I ain't been a little child in a long time and it would take a lot more than that scowl to scare me."

Arm around Jaydee, Gio escorted her away from the bickering duo. He led her to the backyard where he sat her in a swing then joined her. Her place was amazing. The back was lit with soft amber lighting and he tucked her close.

"Marry me, Jaydee," he said. "Marry me."

She turned her face up towards his. "What about work? I'm not anywhere near where you would be."

"That's not going to be an issue much longer."

"What happened?" Her question was sharp.

"I refused a direct order to return to base on an op."

"Why would you do such a thing?"

He tensed. "Because I wasn't about to leave the plane with us flying support alone against six other bogies. Tower wanted me to come back and I refused. We stayed together and alive until the others arrived."

"Everyone was okay?"

"Yes. The plane got a bit shot up but everyone made it back safely. Higgins, the new CO, was less than pleased with my...mine and Lizard's decision. I don't care. I was a fighter pilot and we don't leave men alone to face those odds. Not if there is a chance we can help."

He wasn't sure what he expected her to do or say, but he was surprised when she kissed him on the mouth. "I'm proud of you for doing what was right."

"I am going to resign my commission, Jaydee. Just, please, let me be here for the pregnancy and birth."

Resign his commission? Jaydee stared at him in the muted light. She didn't see any signs of distress when he spoke of that. He must mean it. Her heart swelled with the amount of love she had for this man.

"Yes."

He pinned her with his intoxicating hazel eyes. "Yes, what?"

"Yes, you can stay for the pregnancy and birth, and yes, I'll marry you."

How could she not? Every moment they'd been apart, she'd wanted to be his wife. Was she scared? Yes. But she had talked to Ivan about it after she'd turned him down, and again with Lexy. Both of them had convinced her to give it a shot.

He lowered his head and covered her mouth with his. She sank into him and returned the kiss with fervour. Only when a whistle broke into their own little world did she find some way to drag herself away.

"I hear there's going to be a wedding?" Antonina said from where she stood with the rest of her family and Lexy. "I can't wait to get started on the planning. Giovanni, we have to make sure Father Crispin is available to do the service."

She tensed at those words. Antonina continued on but all she could do was stare at Lexy, who gave her a smile and a wink.

"No, Mama." Gio's arm tightened around her.

"No? What do you mean no?"

"Just what I said, mama. Nothing big. We're getting married tomorrow. Here."

Jaydee looked at him. "We are?"

"We are. Lizard is coming and is bringing a preacher with him."

"How did you know I would say yes?" she asked him.

"I didn't. I just didn't plan on leaving until you did. You know how much I love you, Jaydee. I want to be your husband."

Uncaring of those watching, she cradled her hand along his face. "I love you too, Gio."

"Giovanni, if you do this, how am I supposed to plan for it? What about our family and friends?"

"So plan a reception, Mama. But the wedding is tomorrow. And then you all need to leave."

Jaydee's heart pounded and she looked from Gio to Lexy. "Will you stand up with me?"

"Hon, you never have to worry about that. Of course I will. Now…we have work to do, so kiss your man goodnight. You aren't sleeping with him and we have a dress to ready for the morning." Without further ado, Lexy pulled her up and away from Gio.

Tiziana gave her a hug and a kiss. "Congratulations and welcome to the family. Come on, Mama, let's go bake a wedding cake."

The men gave her their congratulations as well, then Lexy led her inside and up to the bedroom. Behind the privacy of the closed doors, she drew her in for a huge hug.

"I'm so proud of you, hon. Look at you, getting married."

Both of them had tears in their eyes before wiping them away. "I'm scared, Lexy."

"Of course you are. This isn't something you can read a manual on and memorise. I've said it before and I'll say it again. That man loves you. So much."

"And I love him."

"I know, hon. I knew a long time ago. Was just waiting on you to realise it yourself." She squeezed her shoulder. "Now, let's see what we can do for a dress." Lexy disappeared into her closet and hemmed and hawed for a bit. Popping back out, she said, "You go downstairs and mingle with your in-laws. I'll work on this."

"I don't want you to—"

"Get out of here, Jay. Go be with Gio. I have this."

She nodded and with a kiss to Lexy's cheek headed to the stairs. Valentino was on his way up and he gave her a nod.

"Thank you," he said in a low tone.

"For what?"

He ran the ring around his neck along the chain a few times before he answered. "For showing my brother how to love someone."

"Your brother is an amazing man."

"I can see you love him."

She nodded. "I have loved him for a long time."

"We can tell. No one has ever been allowed to call him Gio. He hated the nickname. But, tonight, his eyes lit up when you said it."

Her cheeks heated at his words. But it was his next words that brought tears to her eyes.

"You are my sister now. If you ever need anything, *anything*, you come to me." He leaned in quick and pressed a kiss to her cheek before disappearing down the hall.

A bit amazed, she touched where he'd kissed her and made her way to the first floor. Tiziana and Antonina were in the kitchen, busy baking her wedding cake. Enzo, Giuseppe and Gio sat in the living area, drinking beer and chatting easily with one another in Italian.

The minute Gio spotted her, he put down his beer and walked to her side. "Hello, gorgeous," he said before kissing her.

She melted into him, tasting him and beer. "Hi," she said.

"Where's Lexy?"

"She is working on my dress. Told me to come down here."

"Wonderful," Giuseppe said. "Come play Go with me. I want to learn a little more about my daughter-in-law."

She smiled at the sight of her board waiting there before Giuseppe. The grid of black painted lines had the stones ready for play.

"Yes, sir," she said, sitting down in the chair across from him.

"None of that 'sir' stuff. You can call me Pops, like the others do."

She glanced at Gio, who gave her a wink and a smile of encouragement. They began to play and, a bit later, Gio handed her a mug of tea and brushed a kiss along her cheek.

"Thank you," she said.

While they played, they chatted about her work and what everyone else in the family did. Lexy and Valentino showed up and joined in the conversation. Every now and then, she would sneak a peek over at Lexy and the women would share a grin.

Lexy stayed in her room that night, and Gio got the final remaining available room. When the morning came, she woke to loud male conversation outside. Lexy had told her to sleep in and it had felt amazing. Rising from bed, she padded to the window and peered out. Nothing there, so she went to the side with the balcony and stepped out. She smiled at the sight of the men lining the path to the dock with flowers.

"Get away from the window," Lexy said from behind her.

She turned and her breath caught in her throat. "Lexy, you look beautiful." Her friend wore a pale pink dress that hugged her body.

"Thank you, hon. Now come on, let's get you dressed."

Jaydee took a shower and came out in her robe before sitting down on the foot of her bed. Lexy did her hair then walked to the closet and withdrew something before gesturing for her to get on the undergarments then to come back, so Jaydee did.

She stared at the dress Lexy handed to her and her eyes pricked with tears. In her hand, she held a long, silky white gown, sweetheart neckline, and a slight tuck at the waist.

"Lexy," she said. "This...this is stunning."

"Try it on."

She stepped into it and drew it up. It was a satiny material which smoothed over her skin. She zipped up the side and twirled around. It flowed around her and settled about her ankles. Lexy brought her a pair of shoes and helped her into them.

They weren't stilettos but there was some heel to them. Lexy applied a light touch of makeup to Jaydee's face then pressed a kiss to her cheek.

"You are going to knock his socks off, hon."

Together they walked out of the bedroom and down the stairs. Lizard stood at the bottom and gave her a kind smile.

"Hell, just look at you, Dusti. You...you look amazing. It's good to see you." He leaned in and gave her a kiss. Then looked at Lexy. "You too, Lexy. Damnation."

Lexy gave a sultry chuckle. "Good to see you, handsome. Good to see you."

Lizard blushed and brushed a kiss along her cheek before slipping away, saying he needed to check on the groom.

"What a surprise, to see you fawning over a man who wears a uniform."

Jaydee turned to see Valentino walking in. His attention was on Lexy, whose entire demeanour stiffened for a moment. Then she gave another one of those sexy laughs. "Don't be jealous just because I don't call you handsome. Maybe if you learned how to smile you'd…well, you'd be passably good-looking, I reckon." With a wave of her hand, she tugged Jaydee along. "See you at the ceremony."

They made their way down the steps and she heard talking and laughing. Her belly clenched a bit but she ignored it. She wasn't going to let anything get in her way of acquiring her happily ever after.

Everyone stood before the dock except for the minister, Gio and Lizard. Her breath caught as she spied Gio standing there in his dress blues. He looked so handsome, he took her breath away.

On his chest were his wings, glowing in the sunlight, and she just wanted to run to his arms and be held. His eyes focused on her and he gave her a small grin. Right before she walked out on to the dock, Lexy handed her a bouquet of flowers. Then she made her way to stand beside Gio before the minister.

She stared into hazel eyes as the minister did his thing. The ceremony passed in a blur and only when she felt him take her hand and slide on a ring did she realise she'd lost a bit of time.

"With this ring, I thee wed," Gio said in a confident, assured voice.

Jaydee gazed down at the ring on her hand. Nothing elaborate, a diamond centred on a band of gold. It wasn't until she looked closer at it that she could see the band looked like their wings.

It was her turn and Lexy handed her a ring for Gio. Then came the kiss and the pronouncement that they were man and wife.

Gio drew her close and when their lips brushed along one another's he murmured, "I love you, Jaydee Cassano. From now until forever."

Her eyes overflowed with tears and she kissed him. "I love you too, Gio."

His kiss, like all his kisses, never failed to make her knees weak. And she dug her fingers into the material of his uniform. The hollers and catcalls eventually brought her back to the realisation that they weren't alone.

His family swarmed them, offering up all congratulations. Lexy, too, and Lizard. The party moved to the backyard where his mother and sister brought out the food and someone brought out music. There was dancing and laughing.

When she began to feel a bit overwhelmed, it was Gio who found her off by herself. Skimming her face with his knuckles, he cocked his head and looked down at her.

"Are you okay, Mrs Cassano?"

Mrs Cassano. Never had a name meant so much to her.

She offered him a small smile. "I've never been better, Mr Cassano."

"I love you, Jaydee. You and our baby. You know that, right?"

Slipping her arms around his neck, she nodded. "I know. *We* know that."

That night, she spent her first night in Gio's arms as his wife. There were no nightmares when she finally fell asleep. His arms held her tight and close until they woke together for their first full day of wedded life. Still a bit tired, she snuggled back in close to him. Gio draped his arm around her and his hand settled over her belly.

Things might not always be perfect but she couldn't complain. This was what she wanted. He was who she wanted. Giovanni 'Casanova' Cassano.

About the Author

Aliyah Burke lives on the East Coast with her husband. They have two dogs and a cat. A Navy wife, she enjoys hearing from her readers. If you visit her website, please don't forget to sign the guestbook. Her debut novel, A Knight's Vow, is available through online retailers or Author House. She has one book published with Red Rose titled 'A Little White Lie', and another one titled, 'An Unlikely Encounter', to be released with them 06 Sep 07.

Aliyah Burke loves to hear from readers. You can find her contact information, website details and author profile page at http://www.total-e-bound.com.

Total-E-Bound Publishing

www.total-e-bound.com

Take a look at our exciting range of literagasmic™
erotic romance titles and discover pure quality
at Total-E-Bound.